SHIFTER MOON

A WYRDOS UNIVERSE NOVEL

GWENDOLYN DRUYOR

SHIFTER SCHOOL BOOK FOUR

Get your Bonus Wyrdos Books!

Want to know more about the Wyrdos world? Visit my website below and join my newsletter to get your complimentary copy of *Doug vs. The Boogeyman*!

Wyrdos.net

Enjoy!
Gwendolyn

1

Of all the stupid things Laylea could be doing, running from her closest friend might be the dumbest. And yet, she couldn't force her feet to stop.

The tree roots in the school's impossible underground Jungle had no trouble stopping her. Which is how she found herself flying through the air at the rushing currents of the river.

"Look out!" KC hollered, a moment too late.

KC had signed up for Creative Writing because Laylea begged her to. In the current school climate, barely more than a week out from the wolf attack, Laylea preferred to keep KC close. If anybody found out her friend was actually a werewolf, things could get ugly.

As she plummeted toward the water, Laylea caught her reflection.

The horrified face staring back was not her own. She had suspected as much. It was why she'd run. She hadn't even slowed to give Mr. Tataryn an excuse. How could she when she was wearing another student's face?

KC had yelled some excuse as she followed, but Laylea didn't want her to see what she'd done either and ran faster. She wasn't very good at running in human form, so tripping wasn't a big surprise.

Class had convened in Caves for "inspirational purposes," Mr.

Tataryn had said. But it didn't make any difference. No matter where Laylea was, every time she put pen to paper, her mind shot her right back to the cafe. To Kyle sucking Denier's blood while the handcuffs she'd never unlocked swung free.

That was over a week ago. Pansy had immolated, Denier sicced wolves on the school, and Laylea's body lost its mind. The adults had dubbed the day P2 since it was the second time the phoenix had reincarnated on school grounds. The first time, nearly the entire city of Chicago had burned down. Last week, thanks to the newly discovered witches and dozens of students, she had only burned down one gorgeous coffee table.

The adults declared P2 no further concern for the students. But it was still the only thing on everyone's minds, as evidenced by the fact that many of the other kids in class were talking rather than writing.

Except Riva.

The sloth shifter had looked so calm, her head down over her notebook, writing diligently. Laylea just wanted a piece of that calm. She wanted a smooth, relaxed forehead like Riva's.

Like Riva's.

Instead, her face burned with the painful shifting flame. Laylea barely had time to realize what had happened when Riva looked up and saw her own smooth forehead, button nose, and big blue eyes looking back at her.

That's exactly what Laylea saw in her reflection right before she slammed into the roiling water. The only difference was that her version had a diamond-shaped birthmark glowing white on Riva's brown forehead.

The river dragged her under. It tossed her to the surface in time to hear KC yell, "Oscar! Go back. She's in the river!"

Oscar's roared response echoed from the pedestrian tunnel to Farms, disappearing as she swirled underwater again. Stone scraped her head as the current shot her through the river's tunnel. She tumbled and spun with the current, grabbing gulps of oxygen whenever she was thrown to the surface.

From the east bank, Oscar roared again, his black-on-black

leopard fur a shadow in the afternoon light. She aimed for him, kicking and thrashing with her useless appendages. Fins would be more suited to the task.

In a flash of fire, her flailing offered better results. Strangely stiff hands and feet propelled her to the surface. Her face broke through and she sucked in fresh air.

Laylea spotted the old wooden bridge as she spun. Thanks to the damage done to certain dams during the werewolves' attack, the river had risen to engulf the support posts. The current helpfully slammed her into one of them. All the hard-won breath was knocked from her lungs. Fighting the pain, she threw her arms around the post and clung on against the inexorable drag of the water.

A familiar heat tingled in her belly. Her body wanted to shift into her dog form to heal. Dog would be heaven if it weren't that her human arms were the only thing keeping her from drowning. Her fifteen-pound terrier self would have no chance against the river.

Although, fighting the river was kind of a relief. Rivers are meant to be chaotic and dangerous. It's what you expect. School shouldn't be.

Feet pounded on the bridge above her.

"Hang on, Lee!" Oscar called. "We've got you."

From farther back along the path, KC hollered, "I've got rope!"

The feet above her turned into paws and Oscar sailed into view, landing lightly on the shore. He spun and ran down toward her, though he slowed dramatically as his sleek paws hit damp ground.

Laylea laughed at him searching for a non-muddy path along the riverbank. "Hurry, KC!" she shouted. "Oscar might have to get his paws wet."

Oscar raised his muzzle and snarled at her. His long tail flicked in annoyance.

"If you can cross running water, the cat can risk moist fur," KC retorted as she leapt over the side of the bridge, landing beside the cat in question, swinging her backpack off.

Laylea argued, "I'm not a witch."

Oscar yowled at KC. She ignored him, hunkering down over her backpack. He turned to include Laylea in his complaint and froze for an instant.

She'd forgotten about her face.

Laylea dropped her head so he couldn't see and got a good look at her hands. They'd shifted into fins. Webbing connected long fingers tipped with claws that dug into the wooden post. One part of her admired them, while a larger part screeched that it was impossible. She was going crazy.

Nope, she told herself. Her mind was playing tricks to keep her from going crazy. It was just her way of dealing with the attack on the school. She had to remember that they'd survived. Her friends, the school, Chicago; they'd all—they'd almost all survived.

"Lee! Don't shift!" KC yelled at the same moment the burn flared in Laylea's belly.

Thumbs.

The thought wasn't nearly enough to overpower her shame. Her friends had already been through so much. They shouldn't have to deal with her being a freak. She absolutely could not let them see her fin-claw-hands, much less her stolen face. Drowning would be better.

The shift burned through her body, releasing her mind into the slower, calmer rhythms of her dog-self.

She realized how big an idiot she was as the current tore her tiny puppy-dog body from the post.

A sharp, sweet pain at the nape of her neck sent calm coursing through her muscles. It filled her mind with memories of her Mama lifting her to safety or tucking her in amongst her four rowdy brothers.

Oscar's growl vibrated through her body, dragging her back to the present. They jolted to a standstill in the rushing river, then Oscar flung her into the air.

Laylea thumped onto the bank and quickly snapped the elastic hairband on her wrist with her teeth. As hoped, the pain made her shift. She rolled to her human feet, already scrabbling along the bank.

Oscar flailed in the water, trying to swim to the shore but was dragged back by the current. The only thing keeping him from being swept away altogether was the rope wrapped around his torso. The rope led back to KC.

Laylea yelped at the sight and pushed herself faster.

KC had shifted. She stood on the shore, tail low, four paws digging into mud, her powerful teeth clamped onto the rope. Each step was a battle as she struggled to pull Oscar from the water.

"Go limp, Oscar!" Laylea yelled. His flailing wasn't helping.

She reached KC, wrapped the end of the rope around her body, and backed away until her feet had purchase against some rocks on the dry bank.

"On the count of three," she yelled, "I'll pull, you get a new hold."

With her mouth full, KC merely grunted a response. The ginger fur behind her ears trembled like fire against the white of her head.

"One. Two. Three."

Laylea pulled as hard as she could and fell to her butt, using all ninety pounds of herself to drag Oscar from the river. KC darted forward to get a new hold on the rope and dug in again. They repeated this two more times before Oscar's paws hit bottom.

Clearly, the feel of mud was too much for the cat. Reality shuddered around him. His fur faded to slightly less black skin as his muzzle flattened into a human face and his joints all twisted and reformed. He stood, shaking water from his bedraggled afro as he dragged himself along the rope.

KC backed up until she ran into Laylea. Oscar stumbled, trying to keep up.

When he was close enough, Laylea dashed into the water and grabbed onto his bare arms to help. She was careful to avoid the still healing scratches on his left arm where blood dribbled from the scabs.

"You gotta shift back." Oscar talked over Laylea's shoulder at KC. "You gotta shift. Tell her, Lee."

The soggy wolf's nostrils flared. Her lips curled back as she exhaled on a gentle growl, her teeth still buried deep in the blue climbing rope.

"You can drop the rope, now, KC," Laylea crooned. "He's safe. You got him."

A joyful gleam lit KC's tired eyes as the two reached her. She let Oscar take the rope, then zoomed up the bank, returning just as fast to leap at Laylea's chest, nearly toppling her. The happy wolf ran figure eights around the two of them.

"You've got to get her to shift." Oscar stepped out of the rope and began coiling it as he side-stepped their furry friend and hurried up the bank.

"I'll try." Laylea gritted her teeth against the desire to go dog and zoom with KC. "You just keep an eye out."

She dropped to her knees. She didn't have to wait long before KC launched herself into her arms. Panting, the wolf rested her one black-socked paw on Laylea's shoulder. Laylea ran her fingers through the thick, white, wet fur as she spoke quietly into KC's ear. "You're okay. He's okay. Nobody's allowed in here, so we should be safe if you want to stay furry for a bit."

Pressure grew in the air around Laylea. Her ears popped at the same moment that KC shifted. Instead of holding onto soaking wet fur, her hands were suddenly clutching soaking wet cotton. KC lurched forward and wrapped her arms around Laylea.

"That was fun," she panted, "but he's right. We can't risk it. Who knows what you'd shift—" KC stopped herself and leaned back to catch Laylea's eyes.

Laylea didn't give her the chance. "We'd better get back to class."

She leapt to her feet and turned to find an apple flying at her head.

2

Laylea threw her hands in front of her face just in time for the apple to smack into them.

"Heads up." Oscar grimaced.

"Thanks." She said it dryly but meant it with all her heart. She was starving.

Although she had no intention of wasting the food, she wound up like she was going to hurl the apple back at him. Oscar ran. Laylea gave chase half-heartedly, moving slow enough to eat the apple and fast enough to escape KC's questions.

By the time she reached Oscar under the bridge, he'd snagged a spare uniform from KC's backpack. As a matter of course, Laylea averted her gaze while he dressed. She almost wished KC still carried uniforms in her size. A dry one would be nice.

"Hey, hey, hey, stop that. Lee, hold him still." KC jogged over, yelling.

Oscar had perched his butt on a support beam under the bridge and was trying to wriggle into his uniform. He winced at KC's tone and put his hands up in surrender. The top half of his uniform dropped to drape around his waist.

Blood seeped through cracks in the scabs up and down his left arm. The weepy stitches on his chest looked worse. Laylea sat beside him and spritzed them with the numbing spray KC tossed to her.

"What are you doing here, Oscar?" KC asked, digging through her pack. "There's no way you signed up for creative writing."

"Why wouldn't I?" Oscar objected. "I have thoughts."

"You have never voluntarily signed up for a class you didn't have to take," KC retorted. "Hold still."

She slathered the stitches on his chest with an antiseptic goo and covered them with a bandage. She plastered another enormous self-stick bandage over the worst of the torn scabs down his arm. "Man, that wolf did a number on you. You sure you didn't recognize him?"

"For the billionth time, he scratched my head first and there was blood in my eyes. And I didn't recognize his voice. I only knew it was Vaughn pulling him off me because there's no mistaking Vaughn's cologne."

"It's soap," KC said, rearranging her pack.

"Soap?" Oscar asked.

"Yeah, it's not cologne. It's soap. Here." She held out a sponge and a bottle of dark makeup.

Oscar took the bottle without question and started applying it to his neck. "How can soap residue smell so strong?"

Laylea took the sponge. "Give it here," she said. "You can't even see what you're doing." She spread the makeup over the hand-shaped bruises. They'd mostly faded, but he was still sensitive about them.

"I suspect he doesn't rinse well," KC said. "It's a wolf thing."

Oscar and Laylea stared at their friend until she noticed their silence and explained. "Some wolves are self-conscious about not smelling wolf enough, so there's this super-expensive musk soap that's supposed to bring their wolf-scent out in their human form."

The rattle of a kicked stone echoed through the tunnel, raising the hair on Laylea's arms. She froze. Oscar was too intent on KC's revelation to hear it.

"Even talking about it brings up the sense memory," Oscar said. "Do girl wolves—"

Laylea tapped Oscar's shoulder and held her finger to her lips. He pulled a face but stopped talking.

It was no sense memory. Vaughn's smell was preceding him. Realization dawned in Oscar's eyes while KC lifted her backpack onto her lap, concealing them fully under the bridge.

Footsteps followed the scent. The humans were moving cautiously while one set of paws galloped into Farms, scattering dirt and stones that flew into the water when they stopped on the bridge right above Laylea and her friends. The wolf shook, its ears flapping against the sides of its head like a child's spin-drum. The air shifted and a tiny pop sounded.

Jonathan, one of the younger werewolves in school said, "Hurry up, Howe." His voice was gruff, like hers sometimes sounded right after she'd shifted. "We gotta make a plan."

"Go easy, the guy has a broken leg." Jase met Jonathan on the bridge.

Laylea shivered at the sound of the bully's voice. It was like her body couldn't help but relive the time he tricked her into eating poison.

"I suppose heroes can move as slowly as they need," Jonathan said. "You gave your all for Grandpa's fight and he's gonna reward you big time, Vaughn."

What was Jonathan talking about? Vaughn hadn't broken his jaw and leg fighting for Grandpa. They'd been broken for him by one of the invading wolves.

Oscar shot a look upwards and brought a fist down on his thigh. The bottle of makeup tumbled into the river with a barely audible splash.

At the sound, panic drove Jase's voice high. "What was that?"

KC glared at Oscar as the little bottle of concealer bobbed to the surface and disappeared one last time beneath the water.

Oscar glared through the bridge at the boys on it.

"Shit," Vaughn mumbled, his words coming out a little garbled through his wired jaw. "We're gonna get in trouble." He was still a ways down the path, but coming closer.

"Let's go," Jase hissed. "We're already not allowed to go anywhere without palming in. I don't want to have a faculty escort everywhere we go."

"Morioka threatened to give us police escorts," Vaughn reminded them.

"Chill the fuck out, you two." Jonathan laughed. "Captain Morioka isn't wasting troops on us with all the shit going down upstairs. And it was just the water, Jase. Look around, there's nobody here."

"Because Farms is off-limits," Vaughn pointed out. "We're not supposed to be in here."

"Dustin, Mo, help Howe up here," Jonathan said, ignoring Vaughn's objection. "If anybody does come in, the sound of the water will cover our voices."

Whereas anybody already crouched underneath the bridge would hear them perfectly.

The wolves gathered close, one of them throwing stones into the roiling waters.

"So, what's up, J?" Jase asked.

"I figured we gotta coordinate our plans."

Dustin asked, "What plans?"

"Tonight is the full moon. We'll finally get upstairs during Wilding," Jonathan said. "We've got to run now or we're gonna miss all the fun when Grandpa invades."

Laylea turned her head sharply to stare at KC. Oscar did the same. It almost made Laylea giggle. Except it wasn't funny. KC shook her head. She regularly lurked on the wolf net. If there was talk of an invasion, she hadn't heard about it.

"Where are you planning to go?" Jase asked.

Jase had basically declared himself the LPSS alpha after Patrick graduated. Why was Jonathan, a foot-soldier as far as Laylea knew, making the plans?

"We can get out of town, hole up in my folks' storm cellar for a few days until the heat cools," Jonathan said, "and then head up to Detroit and train with your grandma's pack."

"Train?" Jase chuckled the word.

"Yeah, until Grandpa gives us the go."

"My dad's out of work," Dustin said. "Think your grandma would let him come up and train with us?"

"My grandmother is the Detroit Alpha," Jase said, "not some military commander."

There was a moment of tense silence that Vaughn broke in a small voice. "I can't run."

"We'll help you," Jonathan insisted. "We're a pack."

"What do you plan to do about Carrie and Jimmy?" Big Mo asked.

"I don't know about Jimmy. He's too unstable to trust," Jonathan said. "But Carrie's on board. Her uncle might be able to get us some supplies before we leave the city."

Laylea almost shifted just so she could growl at that. Carrie had been sucking up to the LPSS wolf pack for information, but it was way too dangerous for her to run away with them. The scrunching of Oscar's face said he was thinking the same thing.

"Lee! KC!" Mr. Tataryn yelled for them, his voice sharp in the distance.

"Oh shit, oh shit, oh shit." Vaughn cursed in time with his crutch banging across the bridge.

"Hang on, Vaughn, I'll help you," Big Mo whispered, hustling after Vaughn. Their footsteps got softer as they reached the dirt path.

"Fuck it," Jonathan said. "What else can they do to us?"

"Plenty," Jase hissed. "Now come on."

If they were trying to be quiet, they needed more practice.

"KC? Lee!" Mr. Tataryn called, only slightly less distantly.

"Get back to your pods and pack up." Jase took charge as the werewolves ran back through the tunnel. "Dustin, help Vaughn."

The thumping crutches disappeared, and soon the footsteps did, too.

Oscar wriggled into the top half of his uniform. "You'd better get back."

KC slung her backpack on. "Go ice your knee and have the doctor take a look at your panther's injuries."

"The water was plenty cold." Oscar struggled to stand as he said this.

"Oscar Luke," KC spat. "Your knee is delicate machinery and if you don't take care of it, that limp is never going to go away."

Knowing Oscar wouldn't voluntarily go to the infirmary, Laylea said, "Or meet us in the library."

"See you there." Oscar scrambled onto the bridge and jogged off, following the wolves.

Before they left the shadow of the bridge, KC blurted out, "We don't tell anybody."

"About the wolves running?" Laylea asked.

"Yeah," KC confirmed. "We let them go. The school will be better off without them."

"But not Carrie, right?"

"Oh, hell no." KC blew a breath through her teeth. "Carrie would be eaten alive and spit out."

3

Creative Writing ended abruptly after Laylea and KC rejoined everyone. Mr. Tataryn assigned a five-thousand-word story from the point of view of their animal-selves, reminded them about mandatory dinner at five o'clock, and hustled Riva off to the infirmary. Apparently, the sloth-shifter had gone faint at seeing Laylea wearing her face. Laylea's stomach lurched at seeing Riva, too. Not having any idea what to say to the girl, she followed KC to the cubbies of dry uniforms beside the doors.

KC emptied her pockets as she searched for her size. Laylea snagged her favorite style from the bottom row. The well-worn fabric soothed her chafing skin like one of the many blankets her family had left lying around the house for her to curl up in when she was a puppy.

"Hey, Lee?" Chris, a boy who also got his uniforms from the lowest shelves stood facing sideways, as was polite when someone was changing. His ever-present sister, Krys, stood near the door, watching the other kids leaving. Laylea couldn't recall ever seeing the paired koi separated by even a foot.

Her heart jumped out of rhythm as she remembered the one time she had seen them separated.

The violent portion of P2 had just begun when Denier's interns trapped Laylea against the sealed Mer doors. Certain they were going to kill her, because they said they were going to kill her, she'd held them off with lies and witchcraft.

By the time Chris had opened the door for her, she was just saying whatever came to mind, her whole body burning with a new, searing, shifting pain. She backed into the dorm without thinking and ran for a pond. But they'd all seen her wearing that other face, that other body.

And Chris had just seen her wearing Riva's face.

What did he want? Was he going to out her as a freak? There were too many kids nearby. Somebody would hear.

She sucked in a breath, searching for somewhere to run.

The boy held up Laylea's tattered notebook. "You dropped this," he said in a small voice. With his other hand, he held up her mini-golf pencil. "And this."

Laylea stared at the items, waiting for his accusation, his threat. Chris just held the items out, quietly, patiently.

"Thanks." She must have taken too long saying the word because he thought she was asking for his name.

"Christopher."

"Christopher," she repeated mindlessly and then shook herself and took her notebook and pencil with a smile. "Thanks, Christopher."

He nodded. It looked like he was going to say something else. Every one of her muscles clenched.

"You're welcome." He jogged off to join his sister. The girl grinned at him like he'd accomplished some huge feat. As shy as they were, maybe he had.

"Library?" KC asked from behind her.

"Hm?" Laylea startled. She spun to see KC zipping her backpack closed over the deep blue of Oscar's favorite style uniform.

"Think Carrie will be in the library?" she asked.

"Yeah," Laylea said, and then corrected herself as they swept out into the corridor. "I mean, no. Carrie can't hang out in the library."

"Right." KC slapped her forehead. "Restricted students aren't allowed."

"But Brenda will know where she is, and Brenda will be in the library."

"Then that's where we go." KC hooked her arm in Laylea's and the two clung to each other through the raucous stream of kids heading the same way.

The library was Laylea's favorite place in the whole school. From the layers of rugs and pillows to the eight-foot-tall shelves filled with books, it felt like heaven.

It had become a very crowded heaven. Kids filled every table, comfy chair, and study carrel. No doubt the many group study rooms and reading nooks were also packed to capacity.

Dizzy and Ms. Crow had placed particular magical protections on the library. That was why the invading wolves had been unable to get in and do any damage. They'd been unable to get into the Dining Hall either, at first.

Most of the kids weren't sure they believed in magic. But they all felt safe in the library, so that's where they went, even kids who used to study in the Dining Hall.

A grin bubbled up from Laylea's gut when she spotted Griff DeGee at one of the crowded tables.

He leapt to his feet, yelling, "Lee!"

Ollie and Quan, two young witches rescued during P2, leapt to their feet beside him.

"Lee, we saved you a seat," Ollie called.

Quan waved. "Hi, Lee."

A blush darkened Griff's copper skin, creeping from the collar of his dark blue uniform to the brim of the knit bobble-hat he always wore. He sank back into his chair.

Laylea felt a blush rising in her own pale cheeks.

"L… Lee?" A short figure swathed in an oversized White Sox sweatshirt squeezed through the door with Oscar on her heels. Carrie's stutter would have given her away even if she didn't push her hood back. "Hi. Hi K… KC."

"Go." Oscar pushed the three girls toward the tall checkout counter where Brenda was stamping books like they'd been very bad. She glared back when she caught Laylea staring.

Brenda had been in a bad mood since pretty much forever. Laylea had assumed she'd cheer up after finding out her father wasn't really dead. She hadn't.

"Carrie wants to go," Oscar said, his tone making it clear how strongly he disagreed with her.

"Th… they think I'm harmless," Carrie said with almost no stutter.

KC and Laylea both blinked at her. Carrie lifted her chin. With her mousy brown hair hanging in pigtails down either side of her face, she looked younger than she was. Not quite as young as Laylea looked, but it was easy to underestimate her.

"You're still a Marshall," Oscar argued. "Your great-aunt is the Chicago alpha. Grandpa is never going to trust you."

"J… Jase's grandmo… m… m—"

Brenda butted in. "Jase's grandmother is the Detroit alpha and Grandpa hates her. But he trusts Jase."

Having worked in the Executive Wing since her early admission to the school, Brenda always had the inside scoop.

"Does he?" Oscar asked. "Jase's transfer was denied."

"Because Grandpa wants him here as a spy," Brenda spat in reply. "He's the one who helped Denier get his wolves in last week, isn't he?"

"But he's leaving," Laylea said.

"No he's not," Brenda argued. "Caliban got the council's approval to keep them all here."

Oscar clarified, "They're running, tonight, during Wilding."

After an instant's hesitation, which was apparently all the time Brenda needed to assimilate that information, she said, "Carrie should go."

Oscar, Laylea, and KC objected loudly. Kids on the other side of the library shushed them.

Brenda hissed, "Look at her. Nobody is going to worry about a plump little kid who can't even speak right. And Grandpa isn't worried about the Marshalls. They lost all pack cred when Sinesia got arrested last Halloween."

"And I have cousins who miss the crime money." Carrie bypassed her speech impediment by singing quietly.

"Arrgh," Brenda grunted. "I wish we had more time. Carrie, you'll have to check in on the regular. KC, you can set up a private chat room, right? Can we get her an armpadd?"

"No. We can't let her go," KC hissed. "It's way too dangerous."

"It's more dangerous to not have anybody on the inside."

"We already have somebody—" KC clamped her mouth shut a moment after the words escaped.

Brenda stared. "Who?"

It was DJ Delcampo, one of KC's brothers and Grandpa's second-favorite grandson. He'd graduated top of his class at MSC, been tight with Denier, and despite foiling the wolves wherever he could last week, he'd allowed himself to be swept up in the arrests with all the invaders. The only problem was that they hadn't heard from him since.

And they could not talk about it there in the library with everyone now watching their conversation.

Carrie took the moment of silence as her opportunity. She raised her arm and pushed her sleeve back just enough to show them the armpadd strapped to her wrist. It was an old model. She said, "I'll t... t... take Sun Tzu."

Laylea regretted teaching her the book cipher she used to communicate with her parents. She said as much.

But Brenda talked over her. "How does that work? Don't we need matching copies?"

"I got t... two copies." Carrie grinned. "The other o...one is on the M... Mer bookshelf."

KC turned on the girl. "You knew they were gonna run."

Carrie nodded. "Everyone thinks it's over," she said clearly. "But it... it's just b... b... beginning." A hint of fear shadowed her eyes as she got stuck on that last word.

"I've got this." Brenda said it as a dismissal. She cracked her knuckles. "Go away."

Laylea pulled KC from the desk, whispering. "We can't blow her cover."

KC growled at Laylea, then turned it on Carrie. She shouted, "Yeah, you would say that," then dragged Laylea to Griff's table, grumbling about wolves and the full moon.

Her rant was taken up by the group as they shuffled to squeeze the three in.

Leda followed the angry conversation with big eyes. She tucked her blue hair behind one ear as she asked, "Aren't they usually gone by now?"

"Yeah," Emerald, arguably the most classically beautiful girl in the school and inarguably the best singer, tapped the table in front of Leda. The girl untucked her hair.

"They used to have to go to Special Testing for blood draws and stuff first," Ali said. "Before Lee shut that shit down." The tribal tatt sleeve down her left arm danced as she crumpled up a piece of notebook paper and threw it at Laylea.

Griff batted the paper back at Ali.

From the far end of the table, Ahanu pulled a partial shift, the broad wings of his thunderbird form extending from his shoulder blades. He slapped the paper ball high into the air with the tip of one wing. In the process, he hit Ali, Dove, and Harper.

Ali smacked the wing. Dove swore. Harper shifted into his Rhesus monkey, knuckled his way over the table, and leapt onto Ahanu's back. The rest of the table did their best to ignore the two.

Emerald snatched the paper ball out of the air as it fell. She said, "The moon doesn't rise till six."

"They'll turn during dinner," Leda squeaked.

"No," Emerald said. "That's why dinner is—" She stood up so abruptly her chair slammed into Ali.

"Easy, Em." Ali started to complain, but then she saw what had caught Emerald's attention.

"Oh, hell no!" Emerald said, staring at the girl who had just come into the library.

4

A small girl with silky hair styled just like Em's but black, stood in the library doorway. She clutched a stack of books to her chest as she searched the crowded library with red-rimmed eyes. Chloe, Em's former BFF, or girlfriend depending on who you asked, was known for shifting when she got emotional. Laylea wished she'd gotten a few steps farther into the room so her moose wouldn't bust the smoked glass panels of the doors.

"No!" Emerald climbed over the table, scattering papers, books, and deskpadds. She shoved Griff out of her way to hop off the other side and march to the entrance. "Get out."

"Emerald," Brenda shouted from the front desk. "Keep your voice down. Everybody is equally welcome in the library, even traitors."

Kids stood up all around the room. A bunch of Mers shifted form, as they were wont to do in tense situations. Few people said anything. They mostly just stared at the moose shifter who'd let Grandpa's wolves in through the kitchen when kids tried to hide in the Dining Hall.

"They were looking for the phoenix," Chloe pleaded. "They said they were here to help."

A chorus of yells, barks, and caws shouted her down. More kids shifted.

"That phoenix was my friend." Quan DeGee yelled.

"Brenda?" Ms. Crow stepped out of the Special Collections room. Light shot across the library and back again as the glass door opened and shut.

A deafening rustle drowned out anything she said as kids resumed their seats and shushed each other. The librarian straightened her iconic blue sweater as she waited for them to settle.

While all the other teachers looked like they hadn't slept all week, Ms. Crow had an air about her as if she were more rested than she'd been in a century.

When she could be heard, she asked, despite all evidence to the contrary, "Everything okay, Brenda?"

Other than a quick, easily missed glare at Carrie, Brenda did not take her eyes off of Chloe. "It's fine, Ms. Crow."

Taking Brenda's hint, Carrie dashed past Emerald and joined Chloe. "L... let's go s... s... to the Dining Hall. There's more l... light."

Chloe didn't move.

"They should lock her in the Fields and let the wolves Wild in there," someone yelled.

Another voice muttered, "Nnete and Murph, too, since they like the wolves so much."

Laylea looked at the next table over but couldn't tell who had said it. Around the room, others agreed.

Ms. Crow flashed into her raven form and immediately back to human. The shock of seeing the librarian shift, something nobody in the room besides Laylea, Oscar, and KC had ever seen before, shut everybody up.

"Their punishment has been set by our dean," she announced. "It does not include banishment from my library. If you don't like the company, you are free to study elsewhere. Chloe, I see an open carrel by the Fiction: Mystery shelves."

Chloe shook her head violently. Keeping her eyes down, she let Carrie lead her out of the library.

Ms. Crow escorted Emerald behind the check-in desk.

"Nnete tried Testing to graduate," Ahanu confessed to their table. "Bianchi told her she couldn't graduate while on restrictions."

"How did Emerald do?" Laylea asked quietly.

A whole bunch of parents had tried to pull their kids from school after the attack. Dean Caliban told them they had to pass the tests first.

"She refused to take them," Dove said. She and her twin brother Reggie's parents were among the most vocal. "She didn't answer a single question and refused to speak in her one-on-one interviews."

"Bianchi is losing his mind." Ahanu grinned. "He has to post us all in classes that match our scores, but he knows we blew the tests deliberately."

Dove giggled, "Reggie's gonna hate his first-year courses. I'm looking forward to reviewing algebra. It makes so much more sense than geometry."

"Does it, though?" Harper asked. Human again, he had resumed his seat at Dove's side.

"I love geometry." Quan raised his hand as if looking to be called on.

Ali leaned over to Ahanu. "Why does Brenda have her hackles up? I'd be handing out lollipops if I found out my long-dead dad was really alive."

KC and Laylea both shifted so they were subtly closer to Oscar. He did not like talking about the sleepers they found in Denier's lab.

Ahanu shot a glance at the front desk where Brenda had returned to stamping books with a level of force typically reserved for tenderizing steaks. "I heard he refused to see her."

Oscar stiffened.

"No," Squirt said, looking up from the history book he'd been trying to concentrate on. For a large and growing Samoan boy, he could speak very quietly. "She went down to the sleeper lab and saw him on Tuesday. I know cuz I covered her Executive Wing shifts."

"Oh yeah, Brenda did see her dad." Griff confirmed. "But he won't let her go back. He insisted she focus on school."

"That's bullshit," Ali spat.

Griff said, his voice tight, "It's not. He looked awful and she cried. He doesn't want her to see him like that."

"Did you see Shala?" Oscar asked.

Laylea was surprised that Oscar hadn't cornered Griff and asked him sooner. It made sense he hadn't asked Brenda. Nobody wanted to talk to Brenda when she was in a bad mood. She was strong, violent, and unpredictable when she was in a good mood.

Griff had gone with when the cops took Brenda to see her father at Morioka's request. Oscar hadn't gone with them because his sister, another of Denier's victims, sent word she didn't want to see him.

"Yeah," Griff said. "You don't want to see her. She'll look better when they move up here."

"Move up here?" Ali asked. "They're bringing all the sleepers to the school?"

"It'll be easier to care for them and keep them secret here," Griff said.

"They're making Shala come back to school?" Oscar's voice broke.

"No," Griff said. "The council is building a rehab facility in the Old School."

Ahanu added, "That's why the lion habitat is surrounded by fencing."

"It is?" Dove asked.

That was news to the Mers. All the bad shifters, kids who couldn't control when they shifted between forms, got stuck in Mer Dorm. As a result, for the safety of the entire community, Mers didn't get to go upstairs very often. It was a significant point of contention among the three dorms.

Leda, still playing with her hair, said, "I thought that was just set dressing for the thumpers. You know, to explain why all the fire trucks and police cars were surrounding the zoo?"

"True-humans," Laylea said. "'Thumpers' is rude."

"Right." Milly bounced in her chair. "Am I the only one worried about the wolves running wild in the school tonight? We're all trapped in here. They could kill us."

Oscar leaned away from Laylea to push against KC. Nobody else knew how difficult full moons were for her. Actually, Brenda knew but she wasn't going to out KC or comfort her.

Laylea reached behind Oscar to grab the shoulder of KC's uniform.

"They're not gonna kill us," Dove scoffed.

"Speak for yourself, tiger," Milly squeaked. "They're apex predators. I'm a mouse."

"It's not like in the movies," Griff said. "Werewolves don't lose control of themselves just because it's a full moon. They just want to shift. That's it. Wilding is just the pack getting together and letting loose like wolves do."

"Yeah, hunting," Milly said.

Squirt tried to calm the more hysterical kids. "It's more about running and howling and maybe playing harmless pranks."

"I've seen Jase's harmless pranks," Ali said, ice in her tone. "I'd as soon they were nowhere near here when they shift tonight."

Ali's tatts glowed in the way they did before she shifted, but the intensity just washed down her arm and away. She held form.

It was comforting to imagine Ali swooping down and raking her talons along Jase's fur. Adrenaline spiked through Laylea at the thought followed by a searing pain in her hand. Her eyes shot to it. Hideous, yellow dinosaur hide covered the four toes now gripping KC's uniform with long, black, razor-sharp talons.

She snatched her arm away and shoved the hawk foot under her thigh.

"I just wish the true shifter of the prophecy would hurry up and get here," Squirt joked.

"That prophecy is a myth." Em's voice cut through the arguing as she rejoined the table. She shoved her way back to her seat, adding, "And there is no such thing as a true shifter."

In rapid succession, Leda asked, "What's a true shifter?" and Ollie asked, "What prophecy?"

Squirt handled both questions. "A true shifter is a shifter who can turn into anything, and the prophecy says that one will come here, to LPSS, then we'll all be free."

"Free from what?" Ollie asked.

Em scoffed. "From hiding."

"It's a myth. There is no such thing. Nobody is going to free us but us," Dove declared. Her words were greeted with cheers from around the table.

"It doesn't sound like the wolves are hiding much anyway if they Wild every month," Quan observed.

Ali cried out, "I say we Wild tonight!"

All attention turned to her. The kids were sharply divided between loving that idea and hating it.

"Kidding," Ali shouted, throwing her hands up in surrender. "Kidding! I promised Caliban we wouldn't, not till the new moon, at least."

The conversation split up into the kids focused on the full moon and those grilling Griff and Ahanu about the new rehab facility.

Laylea listened to both while she desperately tried to make her hand shift back to normal.

She knew what to think about to need a tail. That usually worked to transform her to dog. She laughed at herself, out loud. The laugh invited strange looks from her friends, which tamped down her joyful realization that shifting to dog would solve the problem just fine. And when the joy was tamped down, so was her need for a tail to wag out that joy, which kept her firmly in her human form.

Her brain had been doing that a lot lately. It just flew off into unwanted trains of thought, like Ahanu shifting into a thunderbird whenever he couldn't handle the problem in front of him. She needed to focus. But who could focus when talons that did not belong on a normal person's hand were cutting into the back of your thigh and everybody was staring at you?

"Shut up!" Oscar slammed a chemistry textbook down on the table.

Everybody stopped talking. True to form, Ahanu went avian. He leapt into the air to avoid hitting anybody with his wings. Ali's tatts glowed. This time she sparked and her hawk-self soared up to race the thunderbird over the stacks.

Dove's chair slammed into the people at the next table, her tiger form too big for it. She leapt onto the table, scattering books and padds. Harper lifted the chair back into place with his monkey tail before swinging onto Dove's back.

The noise and violence startled Laylea into her dog with barely a flash of warmth in her gut. She howled with relief before hopping into Oscar's lap to comfort him.

Squirt stared down at his notebook. "I'm sorry, Oscar, I shouldn't have said that about the sleepers."

"I was bitching about the other councilmembers," Leda said. "The wolves, not your dad."

"I'm sorry Shala wouldn't let you see her, Oscar. She is going to be okay," Griff insisted.

They all thought he was mad at them.

They didn't see the twinkle in Oscar's eyes as he twisted Laylea's ears around his fingers. He'd slammed the book down to make her shift.

"Not all wolves want to hunt and kill all the time, Leda," Oscar said. His voice was calm. "You're new to the shifting world, so you only know the people here. But like, you know Car—" He lifted Laylea and buried his face in her fur as if he were overcome with emotion and not just stifling his near error. Carrie might have been only pretending to be a bad wolf, but not everybody knew that.

"My aunt Shauna is a wolf," Griff said. "She never lost control at the full moon."

"She was one of the councilmembers who ran away to Grandpa the day after the attack." Ali landed on human feet behind Griff. Harper used his tail to toss her the uniform she'd left on her chair. "We're not using her as a good example."

"She went to negotiate with him." Griff said.

"Negotiate? For our lives?" Ahanu asked, settling back in his chair. "That doesn't make any sense."

"None of it makes sense," Leda cried. Tears trickled down her cheeks.

"She came back." Griff had been defending his Aunt Shauna for days. He wasn't backing down. Laylea crawled over her seat to Griff's lap.

"And the council ousted her for treason," Em pointed out. She pulled a tissue from a pocket and handed it to Leda.

"And all the wolf faculty joined Grandpa, too. They know us, but they're on his side?" Leda wailed into the tissue. "Why? Because wolves are criminals."

"Mr. Barrett stayed," Oscar objected. "He's still here and he's pissed."

"One wolf," Milly pointed out.

"Conner," Squirt began.

"Hid in the dorm all night," Ali said. "And did nothing to stop his buddies."

"Denier's wolves aren't Conner's buddies," Squirt objected.

"Isn't it just safer to hate them all?" Leda's comment shut them up.

Before anybody could reply to that gem, the dinner bell rang. The library erupted into the chaos of dozens of growing kids scrambling after the promise of food.

5

Students at the Lincoln Park Shifter School could sit anywhere they wanted to in the Dining Hall. The great room featured ten long, heavy tables. There was plenty of room for everybody to spread out, but the kids sat scrunched together at the same three tables. Sphinx dorm kids generally sat together at the table closest to the great glass entryway doors. Mers and Centaurs mixed a bit more at the next two tables over.

Jase herded the restricted wolves to the kitchen end of the Sphinx table, regardless of their dorm. Jimmy sat with them, but as close to his Mer friends as he could get. He hadn't said a word throughout dinner and was fidgeting as it got closer and closer to moonrise.

"There, I'm done." Emerald tossed her spoon into the middle of the table. "Can we find out who all those strangers are at the faculty table now?"

"Yes, your majesty. If you are done, we are all done." Rehyan pushed his empty pudding bowl to the middle of the table.

Laylea grabbed it, stacked it with hers and KC's, and stood. As expected, a half dozen other kids shoved their bowls at her. She stacked them all and stuck the spoons in the top bowl, bowing as she took Emerald's. "Well, for starters, the one sitting in a chair made from her own branches is our new dean, your majesty."

She made her escape as the rest of the table held up their glasses and yelled, "Dean Caliban!"

Up on the crowded faculty platform, the teachers and their guests stacked their own dessert plates as a steaming carafe and tea bags were passed around.

"Shake a leg, Lee." Daniel, a lanky Centaur kid, held the dirty dish hatch open for her.

"Thanks." She dumped the plates and turned to head back to the table.

"You looking to get flattened?" Daniel yelled as she walked away.

A second later, Mr. Bianchi's voice rang from the rafters. "Five minutes."

Laylea yelped and raced back to the hatch. Students exploded from the tables to grab more pudding before Chef Tod closed the line.

"Thanks. You saved my life."

"Nah, you'd've shifted and got kicked out the way 'fore you got crushed," Daniel drawled.

Laylea squinted at him, trying to figure out if he was making fun of her.

"Say, though, since I did save you from getting booted, think you could wrastle me one of them red crane things so as I can see Ms. Crow's sister?" He stared up at the faculty platform where Dizzy was spiriting dirty dishes away, making it clear which of the adults had magical protection totems and which didn't. "To me, them dishes is floatin'. Well, hell. Griff's dad don't even have one?"

Laylea blinked. Douglass DeGee's double-rung mustache vibrated with his laugh as Dizzy danced his empty plates through the air as she stacked them. He wasn't faculty or on the council. What possible reason could he have to be in the school?

"Professor Wanja is making the totems. But I'll put in a good word for you."

After nearly two hundred years stuck in a time loop, the professor had acclimated quickly to modern fashion. He'd ditched his suits for a pair of forest-green linen pants and a toffee-colored t-shirt. Even with his new twists taking away the extra inches of height his afro had given him, Wanja still towered over the new doctor sitting to his left and Ms. Muldoon on his right.

"Lee," Brenda grabbed Laylea as she passed. "Sit here."

Brenda shoved Ali aside and the whole bench shifted to make room.

"You know who's up there?"

Dizzy resumed her seat beside Ms. Lagat. The two fell to whispering, their eyes on Caliban's even smile as the new dean listened to Angelica deRio.

It was strange to see Caliban out of uniform. The practical-yet-flowing, Katherine Hepburn quality of her outfit implied that Ms. Lagat had loaned her clothes. She was the only faculty tall enough for Caliban to borrow from.

And, no shade, Caliban was pulling off the look. Everything about her would scream confidence to a stranger, but Laylea knew her. She saw her nervousness in the orange and yellow leaves sprouting from her long, ash blond hair.

Angelica deRio, head of the Midwest Shifter Council, selected a tea bag with clear distaste and a comment to Caliban. She touched a hand to the mounds of braids arranged on her head like a crown, paying no attention to Cal's response.

Brenda snapped her fingers in Laylea's face. "Do you know who they are?" she asked again.

Laylea shot a confused look at KC and Oscar before she answered. "Griff's dad is the old Chinese guy with wild eyebrows," she said, watching Angelica hold her cup up as if expecting Caliban to fill it. "And the Black woman playing power games with Caliban is Angelica deRio."

"Head Councilmember," Ali inserted.

"A wolf," Brenda growled.

Laylea grinned as she recognized the next guy. "The big guy on Caliban's left—"

"Enormous guy, you mean," Milly corrected, drooling.

He wasn't as large as her friend Ned, but Laylea conceded the correction. "I don't know his name, but he was the bouncer at the council meeting Junior and I snuck into."

"That's Bitters," Junior called down from the end of the table. "He and Ned work out at the same gym."

"He and DeGee have the same barber?" Daniel murmured this observation with awe, stroking the peach fuzz on his own chin. Both Douglass DeGee and the bouncer sported fancifully-styled beards and stashes.

"I don't know the guy in all black sitting between Bitters and Dizzy." Laylea sat up as she realized how silly it was that Brenda was asking her. "I just found out about shifters a year and a half ago. Why are you asking me?"

"You have a lot of friends," Brenda said pointedly. She added, "They've all eaten, so I know they're not vampires."

"The young blond guy in black is Lake Marshall," Rehyan said from across the table. "He was the emcee at The Music Shoppe club till last Halloween."

Milly whispered, "When the Marshalls got kicked out of Chicago pack leadership."

"And then voted right back in," Conner added. He was one of the few wolves not on restrictions. "His aunt is the alpha."

"So, what the fuck is he doing here?" Brenda asked.

"Hold up. Marshall, like Carrie's family?" Ali asked shooting a glance over at the restricted wolves.

"I don't know." Rehyan shrugged. "I just know him from the club."

Brenda confirmed. "Yeah, like Carrie's family. Her parents tried to force the school to move her out of Mer dorm. They were embarrassed by her."

A general uproar of offense arose at the table on Carrie's behalf. Laylea caught Brenda's eyes and saw her grimace at her own mistake.

"Bet they're proud now," she added, loudly.

"I bet they're in Montana." Conner's comment went nearly unheard.

Mr. Bianchi's voice rang out again. It was unusual for him to use the primitive microphone that hung from a grid high over the faculty table. "Your attention, please."

A general shushing washed through the tables that was at least twice as loud as their talking had been.

"We have some special guests tonight, as I see you've noticed," Mr. Bianchi began. He paused for only an instant and then spoke over the ensuing affirmatives from his audience. "I am going to hand the microphone over to Councilmember Angelica deRio."

A smattering of applause and some boos greeted the councilmember as the faculty passed the microphone down the length of the table.

"Thank you, Enrico." Angelica deRio stood, wrapping her perfect manicure around the mic to pull it close. "With all the uproar in the community, the Midwest Shifter Council wanted to come assure you that we are addressing the issues of last week."

She went on for a while, spouting platitudes as she reported the arrests that weren't news to the kids who had been there to see the special police known as the Four-Four dragging werewolves out in handcuffs and muzzles.

"Did Delcampo really pull his protection from the Midwest?" a kid yelled.

Mr. Barrett stood so quickly Dr. Fenn's replacement, Dr. Tippleston, had to catch his chair.

He didn't bother with the microphone. "Mr. Luis Delcampo declared himself the Alpha of the Americas. That's not how packs work. He has no official relationship with Chicago, the Midwest Shifter Council, or any of our local packs. Within LPSS, I am the alpha—as chosen by the mature wolves of our pack." He swept an arm out in a fierce gesture that invited them to note the only other wolves at the table were Angelica deRio and Lake Marshall, not faculty. "I protect our pack, and I will not stand for insubordination." That last was addressed directly to the restricted wolves.

The dining hall sat in perfect silence as the lone wolf faculty member glared at the students.

6

Silence stretched across the dining hall after Mr. Barrett declared his position as school alpha.

The sociology teacher sat, heavily. The buttons on his shirt flashed reflections of the candlelight that decorated the faculty table as he struggled to calm his breath. He turned his gaze on Angelica, giving her permission to continue speaking.

She glanced along the table to Ms. Lagat, the oldest-looking faculty member, for confirmation. Ms. Lagat looked to Caliban.

It took a moment for the dean to notice and another for her to encourage Angelica with a gentle, "Please, go on."

Angelica ignored the chatter that rose at the lower tables as the students commented on that little bit of theater.

"A meeting was held last Tuesday." She paused, took a breath, and lifted her chin. "A vote of those shifters present and those joining remotely was taken and a new council was elected. I am no longer head of the council. That honor goes to Oliver Luke."

There was murmuring at the head table. This was news to them, which struck Laylea as significant. It was also news to Oscar, based on the sudden commotion around him as he shifted to leopard and right back again. KC helped him straighten his uniform.

"Mr. Luke was unable to join us this evening as he is busy with new councilmember Siobhan Linnehan, weregrebe." She paused to emphasize the point, that Linnehan was not a wolf. "Oliver and Siobhan are meeting with federal agents to discuss the many charges of abduction, endangerment, and murder against Adrien Denier." She took a sip of water as if she needed to wash the name out of her mouth.

Mr. Barrett glared at the restricted wolves, daring them to say anything.

"The council must be a fully representative body," Angelica went on. "Our community considers the Lincoln Park School and you students vital to our future. As proven by their election of Councilmember Delilah Crow."

Dizzy stood and sketched a bow, a broad grin across her face. Laylea jumped to her feet along with Oscar, KC, Quan, and Ollie. Ms. Crow checked in with Professor Wanja before the two of them stood as well. The general applause was mixed with some confusion, particularly among the restricted wolves. None of them could see Dizzy and nobody had bothered to tell them about the librarian's long-lost, invisible twin sister.

"Thank you." Dizzy took the microphone. Around the Dining Hall, those with totems repeated Dizzy's words to those who couldn't see her. She spoke slowly to accommodate the translations. "In addition to promoting the school's interests, I look forward to helping ease the integration of our community's long-hidden witches."

As she released the microphone, Dizzy took her sister's hand. Together, they began dancing, their feet clicking in fantastic rhythms on the raised platform. Glittering magic filled the air around them with blue and orange sparkles, growing brighter until Laylea had to look away.

The tapping sounds grew louder. And closer.

All around, glasses, uncleared plates, silverware, even school books danced in rhythm with the sisters' feet.

Quan and Ollie leapt from their seats, screaming and shouting.

They held hands and the magic shot to them, propelling their feet in the dance.

The Crow sisters rose, their feet still flashing as they danced on air. With a flourish, all the objects flew up as the sisters kicked their legs high in front of them, smacking one foot against the other to create one last deafening beat.

The tableware and books plummeted back down as Dizzy and Ms. Crow landed neatly in a bow. The student body went absolutely berserk. Many of the faculty and most of the guests joined them.

The sisters retreated to their benches as Angelica called, unheard, for silence. A shrill whistle sounded from the head table. In the shocked silence that followed, Ahanu yelled, "Nice pipes, Dr. T!"

The fit new doctor stood, her apple cheeks plumping in a grin as she bowed in his direction before gesturing for Angelica to continue.

"And finally, Councilmember Lake Marshall—" Angelica had to pause a moment for the grumbling from the students and some faculty. "—representing the Chicago Wolf Pack's commitment to the entire shifter community."

There was a mixed response to that announcement. The man in question's face paled.

He hurried to take the microphone. "Uh, yeah, no. I'm not on the council as a wolf. I'm on the council as a shifter. I was in Centaur dorm." He lowered his voice and chanted, "Don't be a dick."

A whispered echo of the Centaur's totally-not-official dorm cheer went up from the table where most of the Centaurs had gathered.

"I've got two little shifter babies with my true-human partner, Tara, and we just want to help rebuild after the mess Delcampo made of things. Send me your thoughts. Ms. Crow, oh, Ms. *Elizabeth* Crow," Lake clarified this with a glance at the librarian, "knows how to get those letters to me. Please, reach out. That includes you guys on restrictions. Any physical letters to me won't be read by the school administration."

Angelica deRio waited, her expression devoid of opinion, as the kids and faculty reacted to all of that information. Laylea shot a look at the kids around Carrie. Most of them were rolling their eyes.

Without looking at her, Angelica gestured at Caliban. "In that same meeting, the council approved the nomination of Caliban Meilissene to the position of Dean of the Lincoln Park Shifter School."

Students and faculty alike leapt to their feet.

Brenda cried, "Whose dean?"

"Our dean!" They all replied. Nearly all.

The cheers and applause went on too long for Jimmy. He tugged at his neighbors' sleeves. "C'mon, it's almost six," he pleaded.

Caliban raised her glass and the kids settled, much to Jimmy's relief. "One hundred sixty-nine years and eight days ago, a phoenix shifter accidentally reincarnated in the Old School, causing the infamous Chicago Fire and killing hundreds of people. Eight days ago, that same phoenix shifter reincarnated again. Thanks to the efforts of many of our students and our faculty, the P2 fire killed no one."

She took a drink and set her glass back down on the table while the school cheered.

"While flames may not have filled our halls," she went on. "I maintain that P2 did set our school on fire. It has set our entire community on fire."

A murmur of agreement hummed through the students. She let them have the moment, her gaze searching them, letting them know that she was listening. She turned to be sure the faculty and administration were listening, too.

"I'm a werelinden, and much older than anybody in this room." She let her gaze drift to Angelica deRio, pass over Ms. Lagat, and land on Professor Safiri Wanja. "I've lived through fire before. I was born from fire. To a grove, fire means necessary change. I intend to foster the changes that are coming, starting with inviting any adult in the community to come teach symposiums in subjects they believe should be covered and currently aren't. The first Life Symposium will be called 'Move for Life, Move for You' and will be taught by our new Council enforcer, Mr. Veryl Brewster."

The bouncer struggled out of his too-small chair and waved at the students who gave him a stony response. "Temporary," he said. "Temporary enforcer. You can call me Bitters."

Gently, and with a quickly hidden grin, Caliban told him, "They'll call you Enforcer Brewster."

"Right." The big man shook his head as if reorienting himself. "That's cool, too." He sat. It was a process.

"Enforcer Brewster," Caliban resumed with emphasis, "will be teaching the class in various locations, including upstairs."

"Booooooooooo!" A chorus of Mers shouted. If a class was taught upstairs, they weren't allowed to take it. The disappointment was real, but expected, so there was little heat in the booing.

Caliban had been a Mer. Her next words showed how much she understood. "It is not fair to exclude certain students from upstairs classes," she said. "Which is why I asked Professor Safiri Wanja to find a solution. Professor Wanja is a witch."

"Amazing," Mr. DeGee interrupted, his voice filled with the excitement of a little boy. "He tells me my son could be a witch, too, if he studies hard." He turned his gaze out to search for Griff among the kids.

"You, too, Mr. DeGee," Professor Wanja said. "Magic isn't only for the young."

Griff's dad buried his fingers in his fancy beard as if holding himself in his seat. "We shall have to talk later, sir. Please, call me Douglass."

Much to Angelica deRio's annoyance, Caliban didn't rush the exchange. The dean sipped from her drink as tufts of white flowers blossomed in her hair and along her fingers, curling around the glass.

"Wow, deRio really hates Caliban," Conner hissed.

"Oscar's dad traded his vote to keep Angelica on the council in exchange for her vote to approve Caliban," Brenda whispered in reply.

KC didn't whisper. "She doesn't see Cal the way we do. She thinks she's just a skinny little girl."

The Mers, at least, knew that Caliban Meilissene would literally plant herself and grow to surround the school with her roots and branches if that was what it took to protect them. Every kid in LPSS had a story about Caliban standing up for them at one time or another.

Caliban gestured for the old witch to stand. "It's only right that Professor Wanja introduce his own creation." She shifted one arm into a branch and grew it out to slide the microphone to him at the far end of the table.

Her nerves showed again as she sat. Despite the open smile she offered Angelica, crispy leaves shed from her hair into a pile around the feet of her self-created stool.

Mr. Bianchi showed the professor how to use the microphone by singing a note into it. Around the room, members of the choir, including Oscar and KC sang out complementary notes. Emerald trilled a run in her angelic soprano voice. This also annoyed Angelica deRio.

The microphone squealed on the professor's first words. He took a breath and began again. "Stasis bands will be worn by any student going upstairs, regardless of shifting skill level." He took an object from his pocket. It resembled a thin, silver dog collar with no tag or leash rings. Wanja straightened the band and then slapped it firmly against his arm. It wrapped around his wrist and held there. "Once slapped around your wrist," he said, "you will not be able to shift."

Mers screamed their approval, culminating in their dorm cheer, "Mers desperately want to see the sun!"

Laylea didn't join in. She couldn't. She'd shifted so her tail could wag her excitement. A stasis band would solve all her problems. All she had to do was get one.

"What's wrong with your legs?" Ali asked.

Leaves and flowers sprouted from trunk-rough legs rather than brown and fawn fur. Her toes reached like roots around the bench. Laylea yelped. She saw the glow of Ali's tatts and tumbled under the table as her friend spread her wings and leapt into the air.

7

Her cheers followed Ali as the hawk soared around the room. It was just the distraction Laylea needed.

Though she'd fallen under the table, her roots didn't want to let go of the bench. They'd simply lengthened, wrapping around the place where she had been seated and extending to her as she lay in the midst of her friends' feet. She could feel them, holding on to the bench just like she wanted to hold on to her human form.

From the faculty table, Mr. DeGee yelled out, "Ali, we didn't need proof you need one."

How did Caliban do it? She'd take a breath and plant herself in her certainty. But when it came time to release, how did she let go?

A stasis band would save her life. Laylea had to get one. But first, she had to shift before anybody saw this misshapen tree-dog that wasn't her.

She groaned in her mind. The answer was right there on Professor Wanja's wrist. If Laylea could fly like Ali, she could go steal it and everything would be fixed.

Sparkling heat tingled along her back. She didn't have time to think, "what now" before her body raised off the floor. Two miniature hawk wings flashed in her peripheral vision, flapping for all they were worth. She wanted to scream. Then she was screaming. She slapped both human hands over her mouth.

Ali screeched as she thumped down onto the bench. Laylea yanked her legs to her chest just in time to avoid Ali's claws. Small as she was, she still jostled legs as she slapped her hands at her own back, twisting to be sure the wings were gone.

"Here, we have some difficult students," Madame, the language teacher, droned. "Your bracelet will work on them?"

Ali chirped a rude response.

Over the laughter, Professor Wanja said, "It works for everyone."

Laylea scrambled to peer out beneath the bench. She didn't dare resume her seat between Brenda and Ali, not that there was room. She needed to keep an eye on that stasis band.

Mr. Bianchi removed the band from the professor's arm. He examined it a moment before slapping it onto Mr. DeGee's proffered wrist.

Griff's father reached up for the microphone, admiring his new silver jewelry. "Ha Ha! This clever device would have saved me from a lot of embarrassment during my years in school."

Ali screeched agreement. Around the room, voices echoed her.

"And I am thrilled that this will allow more of you— Oh! I'm sorry, Dean Meilissene, may I share my news or..." Mr. DeGee bowed his upper body in Caliban's direction.

She waved him on, flowers leaping from her fingers and floating toward him. Bitters caught a sprig and tucked it into his beard. He handed another to Mr. DeGee.

Needing both hands to tuck his flower into his lapel's buttonhole, Mr. DeGee continued without aid of the microphone. "The council has decreed—" DeGee's deep voice didn't carry well and after a few words, Mr. Bianchi stood to pull the microphone down to him. "Thank you, Rico. The survivors of Adrien Denier's sleep labs are going to need time and a safe place to recover, as will the many shifters who have become addicted to that vile drug, Enhance."

Kids inconspicuously peeked over at Jimmy who had come to the school in the throes of addiction. His recovery had been forced and unpleasant and restarted when Jase tricked him into taking N again.

For the first time that evening, Jimmy sat up straight. He stuck two fingers in his mouth and whistled his approval.

"Yes!" Mr. DeGee shielded his eyes with a hand, searching for who had whistled. "Come talk to me if you want to get involved. Incidentally, we also needed an excuse for all the emergency vehicles surrounding the zoo last week," he added. The look on Angelica's face might have burned him to ash. "Since I had my crews erect fencing around the lion house as though it had been damaged, the council is transforming it and the portion of the Old School beneath it into a rehabilitation facility! I am donating some supplies and my own time, but my workers must be paid, and it is going to be a big job. Dean Meilissene has enthusiastically volunteered the school to host an enormous New Year's Eve party right upstairs to raise the money!"

He clearly expected the announcement to receive thunderous applause. It received dead silence. Most of the students were too shocked to react. Oscar blinked back tears. He leaned longingly toward the doors, then simply slipped into his leopard form and slid off the bench to join Laylea under the table. His uniform, already stressed from his last shift, popped buttons and puddled on the floor.

Brenda growled at the Mers around her, "Fuck yeah." She leapt onto the table, screaming, "Yes! Bring them home!"

Mr. DeGee applauded her enthusiasm as he searched the faces at the head table. "Do we have any faculty volunteers?" he asked.

Hands went up around the table. Professor Wanja's a close second to Ms. Crow's, followed by a half dozen other teachers including the new doctor and Mr. Bianchi.

Griff's father grinned, the double curls of his mustache bouncing with his excitement.

Ali swooped over Mr. DeGee's head, screaming an ear-piercing cry. She landed on the table over Laylea's head, in violation of a dozen rules, and popped human. Her excited caws turned into a whoop. She yelled, "And Mers can help because of the stasis bands!"

The feet around Laylea sparked, flashed, melted, and shifted into hooves, claws, paws, and talons. Laylea howled, her joyful tail having taken over her body. She bounded to Oscar and snagged his ear in her teeth like a puppy. He lapped at her head and did his best meowing attempt at a howl.

Amidst the cacophony of crows, barks, screeches, and howls from the out-of-control Mers, Mr. DeGee shouted to be heard. "Yes, thanks to the professor, everyone can join in the fun."

The human-shaped Mers responded as one with their battle cry, "Mers desperately want to see the sun!"

The cheering quieted slowly to a dread silence. Kids shushing each other. Many of them popped human again and hurried to pull their uniforms straight.

Laylea scurried into the alley between tables to see what had damped the celebration.

At the head table, Mr. Barrett stood. It wasn't so much his raised hand, requesting silence, as the somber darkness of his bowed head. Mr. Barrett was never bothered by uproar. He courted impassioned arguments in his classes. The last few voices died when he raised his head and showed his cold eyes.

"Not everyone," he said. "Those on restrictions will not be permitted upstairs under any conditions."

"Except for full moons!" Jonathan yelled.

A rustle, as dry and cold as a snake slithering out of old skin, filled the next heavy seconds as nearly three hundred creatures turned to glare at the werewolves.

KC stared up.

Beyond the leaded glass ceiling set in its intricate metal frame, a handful of stars peeked out of the darkness. The sun was down. The moon would rise in moments.

The thigh of KC's uniform bunched beneath her white knuckles. They weren't just white. They were furry. A growl rolled deep in Laylea's throat as if she could scare KC out of shifting. With the school staring daggers at the werewolves, now would be the worst time for Grandpa's great granddaughter to out herself.

The growl got her attention.

KC's hands flashed human.

Laylea tried to bounce over to her and slipped on too-big paws.

Her body hit the floor with a thump she felt through her skeleton. It might have worked out okay if she'd hit her head harder. But when her vision cleared from the light knock, she saw the horror.

Her impossibly adorable, little, fawn-colored dog paws had thickened into round, white wolf paws, one with a black sock. Her whipcord tail twitched, thick and fluffy with black speckles shining through the white fur. Still about fifteen pounds, she judged, she had shifted into a miniature version of KC.

She desperately needed to get her hands on a stasis band.

8

A stillness hung in the air as nearly everybody in the Dining Hall stared at the restricted werewolves, afraid to even breathe. If they breathed, something bad would happen.

Laylea attempted to scuttle back under the table before anybody saw her, but her paws were huge, her legs put together all wrong. Her tail was thick and heavy rather than the delicate one she'd wagged all her life. She slipped on the polished wood floor, barely reaching the bench beneath Ali.

From the dark forest of uniformed legs, Oscar chittered, deep in his throat. He dashed out and dropped on top of Laylea. She swallowed a grunt. He was a heavy kitty. It wasn't a fix, not for long at least.

"You can't keep us down here." The sneer in Jonathan's voice made Laylea's wolf-hackles want to stand on end. But they couldn't, because of the giant cat crushing her.

The single remaining faculty werewolf repeated himself. "Those on restrictions will not be permitted upstairs under any conditions."

Laylea cowered at Mr. Barrett's steel tone. A deep and primal part of her wanted to lick his muzzle and apologize.

Jonathan did not have the same instinct for self-preservation.

"Except for full moons when we have to go Wilding." He made it sound like a medical necessity. Like the wolves would explode if they couldn't get upstairs and run in the moonlight.

The sneer in his voice terrified Laylea. In her mind's eye, since her real eyes couldn't see anything but velvety blackness, she pictured Mr. Barrett leaping from the faculty platform, shifting wolf midair and devouring Jonathan.

Far from red-hot rage, the teacher's voice dripped ice as he said, "No, Mr. Umemoto, not except for full moons."

"We have to Wild," the idiot argued. "It's mandatory."

"It was mandatory," Angelica announced, "when Luis Delcampo held sway on the wolf packs of the Midwest. He has removed himself from our influence."

Audible shock rippled across the Dining Hall. Benches pushed back as students presumably struggled to see better.

Oscar took advantage of the commotion. He bit Laylea. He wrapped his enormous muzzle around half her head and chomped down like he was planning to eat her. Laylea's howl of outrage turned into a human whimper of pain, and in a flash the pain was gone, along with the white fur, wolf tail, and weight on her back.

Snagging a uniform from KC's backpack, Oscar hissed, "Look at deRio."

The councilmember had raised her arm. Below her gold-dusted, gem-encrusted manicure, a shining silver band hugged the tough werewolf's delicate wrist. She waited another moment until the gasps and whispers had completely died. "I will not be Wilding tonight," she said. "And neither will you."

Angelica startled as the bench and the table were gently but inexorably jostled by the new dean's roots. Caliban flowed out of her seat to standing. Her bottom half remained a trunk. It was a form every student knew meant she was not to be messed with.

"Restricted students will report to their dorms," she said, her voice as delicate as ever. "The school has special stasis bands for you, leather anklets that will keep you safe and take some of the pressure off those who struggle with the moon's influence."

Dustin's whine was so wolf-like, Laylea feared he'd shifted. If he had, it would have started a riot, not that Dustin was smart enough to realize that. He wasn't even smart enough to keep his mouth shut in front of the entire school, the new enforcer, and three fifths of the Midwest Shifter Council.

"No fucking way. We gotta wild," he whined.

A beam of light flashed across the room and retraced its steps as someone came in through the great glass doors. An unnatural pressure came with them.

Doom descended on Laylea's senses. She felt herself scrunching into as small a space as she could take up in her human form. Her body decided it wasn't enough. The burn spread from her gut out into each of her limbs, all the way into her fingers and toes, filling her head with fire until she popped from human to dog.

Her fur wasn't safe enough. Even with her tail tucked tight against her belly and her velvet ears pasted back, her primal instincts demanded better armor. She stood her front paws on the bench beside KC to hop into her lap for comfort. Farther down on the bench, Benny shifted with a snapping sound. Leda pulled the turtle onto her lap and stroked his shell. What Laylea wouldn't give to have that kind of armor.

Mid-leap, an unbearable burn shot down her spine. She fell backwards, clattering on the wooden floor. Oscar dove for her. His legs got tangled in the uniform he'd only half struggled into. He fell, caught himself on four paws, and batted at her.

His attempt to pull her into safety backfired miserably. Laylea spun, paws waving uselessly in the air as she slid under the bench on a turtle shell. Another swipe from her well-meaning friend sent her spinning down the length of the table, between feet and hooves.

What was totally mad was that Laylea knew that doom. It shouldn't scare her. She'd felt it many times before. There was one other person in the room as familiar with the intense presence as she was.

Sure enough, Junior yelled, his fourteen-year-old countertenor cracking as he did. "Yaksha!"

He was the only person in the room who would dare call Captain Yaksha Morioka by her given name. It was a mystery who could have given her the name as the demon was older than the ice age.

Kids spun to stare alternately at Junior and at the great glass doors. Feet kicked Laylea along the floor like a marble in a pinball machine until following turtle instincts, she stretched her long neck out of the shell and snapped her teeth onto a bare toe.

"Ow!" Riva screamed, kicking out. Of course, it had to be Riva she bit.

Kids burst into tense laughter. They startled as the table jumped from the force of Laylea's soft side slamming into a support post.

Burn shot from her gut and she bounced off the post in full dog form, landing on the floor in a crouch.

Riva reached down to feel the bloody damage to her foot. Laylea scuttled forward to lick her hand in apology. Oscar's paw smacked her down before she could reach it. He snatched her up by the scruff of her neck and slunk away to the borrowed combat boots KC had acquired from Ali. After dropping Laylea in their friend's lap, he curled up at her feet.

Angelica deRio stood from her seat. Her voice had a tremor to it, poorly hidden under her officious attitude. "Captain Morioka, we didn't expect—"

She stopped speaking. Her mouth hung open.

Laylea needed to see. She stood her front paws on the table. Nobody would even notice, much less care about the breach of etiquette with Captain Morioka standing in their Dining Hall.

Terrified student faces reflected in the mirrored sunglasses Morioka wore even after sunset and two stories underground. Her trench coat flapped against her legs as she strode down the length of the Sphinx table.

Logically, Laylea knew that she was a smaller woman than many of the students. Physically, any of the wolves could probably take her down if she'd really been the little Japanese woman she appeared at first glance. But honestly, once you'd seen the demon in dragon form, her visible shape didn't particularly matter anymore. The dragon was an experience that burned into your soul.

Every set of eyes and one set of stalks followed her step by step.

Junior grinned at Laylea. Their mutual friend Diejuste had named them family with the captain, a trio of brownies, and a banshee. They weren't afraid of Morioka. At least, Laylea hadn't thought she was afraid of her. Her body's reaction seemed to be saying different. She shivered.

KC wrapped her arms around her. Something sharp poked her neck.

KC held an uncapped pen, the business end drawing blue lines beneath her fur.

"Swear to phoenix, if you shift, I'm stabbing you," KC whispered into the top of Laylea's head and then kissed it.

Laylea nodded carefully, like she really had any choice in the matter.

The captain stopped briefly beside the restricted wolves, her glasses reflecting each of them in turn. Jase was the only one brave—or stupid—enough to return her examination. The slightest of nods acknowledged him before the demon rounded the end of the table. She glanced over at Chloe, sitting alone, before striding between the tables toward the front.

"Thank you for the invitation, Dean Meilissene." Morioka's voice vibrated Laylea's skull like the start of a headache. She was in a bad mood.

As if they'd dared not breathe while her back was turned, the entire student body sucked in air when she turned to face them.

"Your dean has pled your case to keep my officers out of the school, for now," she said. "Whatever your thoughts, it is your actions that will decide your fate. Adrien Denier bled hundreds of shifters for Grandpa Delcampo's drugs."

The plural of "drugs" sent a flurry of intrigue through the ranks. Enhance, N as it was known on the street, was only one of the drugs Delcampo had commissioned. He'd also ordered the development of a more lethal drug he called 'End.' That wasn't terrifying at all.

"He bled dozens of shifters dry," Morioka said. Her black feelings about those murders thrumming through every brain in the room, judging from how every body reflexively leaned away from the demon. "The rehab facility will act as a memorial for those lost. I expect you all to help with the project in every way you can. Such help will go a long way to evading my attention."

Junior muttered, "Nice stick." He said it quietly, but Laylea could hear the raised eyebrows in his voice, and disappointment.

Morioka continued, "Mr. DeGee will be arranging college scholarships to reward those who offer substantial help." She turned her reflective gaze on Junior. "Carrot."

He applauded. Laylea howled her support. Nobody else so much as breathed.

"If you are done with announcements, Dean Meilissene?" Morioka asked in that manner of hers that was an order, never mind that you could hear the question mark.

"We aren't quite—" Angelica's attempt to stand was hampered by nobody else on her bench moving.

"We are," Caliban said. "Restricted wolves, for your safety, we are going to escort you to your pods—"

Chaos broke out at the Sphinx table. Kids screamed in fear and anger. Benches screeched and clattered as nearly everyone scrambled to get away from the small, dun-colored wolf standing on the table, ready to pounce, his teeth bared at Captain Morioka.

9

"It's a full moon!" Dustin Huono leapt to the bench beside Jonathan, screaming, "We Wild!"

It was unimaginable, but Dustin was holding his human shape. Nobody would have accused him of being smarter than Jonathan. But then nobody could have imagined anyone being stupid enough to challenge Captain Morioka. And yet, Jonathan stood on the table in full wolf, teeth bared at the demon.

Kids stampeded away. Laylea couldn't see anything through the press of bodies abandoning the Sphinx table and those climbing up to see over the heads in front of them.

Sparkles flickered around Lisa Sclero. Her lanky limbs extended while her body bent forward and her neck lengthened. Brown-spotted yellow fur covered the whole of her giraffe-self. Her neighbors climbed on her to see better.

A sharp prick of pain shocked Laylea from her focus.

"Stopit stoppit stoppit." Saliva splattered from KC's lips onto the yellow and brown-spotted yellow fur of Laylea's too long neck. "I will stab you," she threatened while actually stabbing her with the pen.

Laylea yelped as the pen broke her skin. Fire shot from her gut to the wound and her view changed. She could no longer see the action. She barked.

"I'll hold you up," Oscar hissed, taking her from KC. "But if you shift, I'm dropping you. Got it?"

She barked her assent, and he lifted her to his uninjured shoulder.

From her new vantage point, Laylea could see Big Mo squeezed against the wall by the Sphinx table. He held Vaughn like he'd lifted him out of the way. Jase hadn't backed away. He crouched right next to Dustin and Jonathan, as if ready to leap to their support, but waiting to see what Morioka was going to do.

A wave of doom shot over the room as the trench-coated captain of Chicago's supernatural police forces exploded into her dragon form. Like a koi, she grew to fit the space available. Her wings scraped against the walls and her long, sinuous tail knocked into the faculty platform.

The adults held onto their seats.

Foam gathered in the corners of Morioka's muzzle. Two rows of razor-sharp teeth glinted in the warm dining room lights when she opened her mouth to release a noise that vibrated Laylea's very skeleton, from the inside.

Her forked tongue darted like a snake from between the forest of teeth. It was too fast to follow, but Jonathan howled in pain. He shifted human and smacked a hand to his neck.

"Wilding is prohibited for restricted students." Captain Morioka, the tiny, imposing human, said.

Blood welled behind Jonathan's hand. It wasn't spurting or anything, but a bead grew between his fingers, traced a path around his pinkie, and dripped to the collar of his uniform. He searched the faces around him for support. Finding none, he bent to climb, one-handed, off the table. He shoved Dustin away. That was no way to treat the only person who'd backed you up.

"I encourage all wolf students to remain in your dorms until the morning." Light as a breeze, Caliban's voice filled the shocked room. "Restricted wolves will remain in their pods until the moon sets at seven twenty-nine a.m."

"That's imprisonment." Jonathan's objection came out garbled, with little confidence behind it.

Ahanu's muttered, "Dude, shut up," was echoed by a dozen other kids.

"I would escort you to prison, Jonathan Umemoto," Morioka began, a shadow of wings spreading silently from her shoulder blades to fill the width of the room with green-tinted darkness.

Caliban interrupted, all breathiness gone, "Captain—"

"But I have made a deal with your dean," Morioka finished. Without another word, she folded the nearly invisible idea of wings and walked to the door.

"Wolves who are on restrictions, please join Captain Morioka, Mr. Barrett, and myself in the foyer. Nnete, Murph, and Chloe, you'll speak with Ms. Lagat in the night kitchen. All others, take your seats and remain until Mr. Bianchi releases you." Caliban said a few words of farewell to the councilmembers, the new enforcer, and Mr. DeGee. Then she stepped off of the platform by extending branches and using them to lift herself over the table and down to the main floor.

Bitters broke into wild applause at the stunning display of controlled shifting. Professor Wanja and Ms. Lagat, the shifting teachers, joined him, more sedately, followed by many of the other adults. Ali put two fingers in her mouth and whistled, releasing the rest of the Mers to scream approval of their former dormmate showing off.

It was the cue they needed. The show was over. They could all relax. Mers shifted human and lazily found seats again, as did the Centaurs. The Sphinx kids raced to their bench to avoid the wolves making their way to the glass doors.

From the front of the room, Caliban said, "I've been considering teaching Shifting as an Art Form. What do you think?"

"As a dance form," Milly yelled over the approving voices around her.

Not usually one to enjoy being the center of attention, the new dean dropped into a grandiose bow. Her hair fanned out as she stood again, snapping her head upright. The locks extended and turned into tree branches. Sprays of flowers burst from each branch like bio-friendly confetti.

Heat rose in Councilmember Angelica deRio's cheeks. For a moment, her eyes bugged out, then she dropped her gaze and focused on straightening her blouse.

Meanwhile, Caliban's branches dropped to drape down her back as hair once again. She walked, like a true-human, to the great double doors. Morioka held the door as the last of the restricted wolves squeezed through single file, unwilling to get any closer to the demon than was absolutely necessary. Caliban had given them the chance to leave without everybody watching. She showed off her shifting skills not to impress Angelica, but to distract the school from Jonathan's walk of shame. It was better than he deserved.

Mr. Barrett hustled down the stairs and followed Caliban through the door with a nod to Morioka. The wind of whispers that followed the demon out of the Dining Hall turned into a tornado when the doors closed behind her.

A smattering of tiny purple flowers rained down around Laylea. Oscar dragged her paws off the table. He bent over her, wrapping an arm around her head so she couldn't see anything but her bark-covered paws. He held his other hand out to KC. "Pen."

Laylea yelped in protest. She did not want to be stabbed again. It hurt. Nobody had seen the flowers in the chaos following Morioka's exit. It wasn't a big deal.

She searched for the burn and fanned the flames in her belly until it sparked through her nerve endings. Muffled by Oscar's armpit, she cried, "No more stabby!"

Oscar released her. He was even gentle as he helped her slide from his lap to the bench. But he and KC squeezed her tightly between them to have a private conference without her input. Even though nobody could hear them through the din of everybody talking, they kept their voices low.

"Can we talk about it now?" Oscar hissed, as if continuing a conversation.

KC hissed back, "Not here."

"Library?"

KC glared at him. "Full moon, remember?"

Mr. Bianchi coughed softly into the microphone in a first step to getting the kids' attention.

"I trust your self-control more than I trust hers." Oscar tapped Laylea's forehead like she was an object.

She needed to shut that down. There was nothing to talk about. She'd had a few weird accidents. It was probably something that happened to all adolescent shifters. She'd just get one of those shifter bands from Professor Wanja and wear that. Problem solved. No discussion needed.

"Let's take her to one of the music practice rooms," Oscar suggested.

KC nodded, "Yeah, that's better. They're soundproof."

"Uh, woof," Laylea interrupted. "KC and I need to get back to the dorm for book club."

"Lee." KC frowned.

Oscar sighed.

Laylea pretended she didn't see either. "I just need to talk to Professor Wanja real quick and then it's you, me, and full moon book club, KC."

Up on the only slightly less gossipy faculty platform, Mr. Bianchi moved to step two in the playbook. He cleared his throat and said, "Settle down, everybody."

The kids stopped talking. Many of them sat. The sudden silence made a dozen kids giggle and a dozen more shift.

Mr. Bianchi's sigh at the inevitable resumption of chatter echoed through the mic.

"Lee," KC growled. "We're not idiots."

Oscar said, "We know what's going on."

Well, that was nice for them. Laylea had no idea what was going on.

Neither did Angelica. While the faculty chatted happily, one eye on the student body, the former head councilmember stared daggers at Mr. Bianchi.

The music teacher stood at his seat, one hand resting on the hanging microphone. He listened to the chatting of the adults around him and waited with no urgency for the kids to settle.

Angelica spat, "Tell them to be quiet."

Mr. Bianchi and a few of the other faculty chuckled. He said, "That's not really how we do things around here."

The councilmember sank into her seat and began an urgent conversation at the new councilmember, Lake Marshall, either not noticing or not caring that his attention stayed on the glass doors, concern written in the wrinkles around his eyes.

Mr. Bianchi pulled the mic to his mouth and said, "They'll be there in a minute, Chef Tod."

KC pulled herself together as kids glanced to the back of the Dining Hall. An uncharacteristically human Chef Tod leaned beside the kitchen door, sipping from a steaming mug. Pressers were supposed to be helping him clean. His presence quieted some of the many conversations.

KC leaned around Laylea to whisper in Oscar's ear. The three of them were seated so close together, Laylea heard every word. "She was raised by thumpers."

"Oh, yeah." Oscar's eyes grew wide. "She doesn't know what a true —" KC glared. "—what that is." He sighed. More gently than before, he said, "We're gonna go talk after dinner, Lee."

Laylea shook her head. She had more immediate concerns. "I am not going anywhere until I get one of those stasis bands," she insisted.

KC sat back. She glanced up at the head table. "That's not a bad idea."

"It is a bad idea right now," Oscar insisted. "She's out of control. What happens if someone sees?"

"Someone other than Riva, you mean?" KC asked, her tone dry.

Oscar and Laylea turned to see Riva staring, slack jawed, at their not-so-private discussion. With no warning, Riva dropped into her sloth. Milly squealed and picked her up. Riva wrapped her furry arms around her friend and snuggled her face into the crook of her neck. It was too cute.

Fast upon the thought, Laylea's skin began to tingle.

KC stabbed her.

10

Laylea howled. Fury burned through her as she shifted human to see a dark blue dot marring the pale blue of her uniform, right over her heart.

"Stop that," she complained.

"You first." KC brandished the pen.

A low hum vibrated through the speaker system. A single note, increasing and decreasing in volume, pulsing, simply existing in a way that calmed Laylea.

She felt a smile climbing onto her face. She really liked Mr. Bianchi. Here he was, one of five wolves in the room on a full moon and he was just calmly trying to keep order and unity in the school.

It probably helped that almost nobody knew he was a wolf.

His hum modulated to a new quality. It sounded like… Laylea stared at her teacher. She cocked her head to the side in that way that helped her understand things better when she was a dog. Mr. Bianchi was singing two tones. That couldn't be possible. How was he singing two different notes at the same time? Was it a shifter trick?

Slowly, student conversations modulated as well. They all started asking the same questions that were spinning through Laylea's mind. One by one, they quieted until only Milly still chattered away.

Mr. Bianchi's hum danced around a vaguely familiar melody. When that didn't get Milly to stop flirting at Ollie, the choir director opened his mouth and sang the opening bars of a song Oscar and KC had been working on for choir. Milly and the rest of the choir immediately joined in. It was rocky, but still beautiful, wrapping up with a chorus of actual songbirds.

Mr. DeGee stood and applauded wildly. He yelled, "That's it! That's what we do for the New Year's Fundraiser. We'll end it with a concert put on by the school!"

Mr. Bianchi dropped his head in a sigh as Mr. DeGee's words riled the kids up again. He yelled, "You are dismissed."

Angelica was the first out of her seat, followed by the KP pressers who hurried back to Chef Tod, eager to tell him everything that had happened as if he hadn't watched it all from the back of the room.

Laylea slipped off the bench, crawled under the table, and wriggled up and over the other bench. Oscar and KC yelled. She ignored them, ducking through the press of kids so they couldn't see her.

The visitors had begun descending from the raised platform. The teachers, knowing there was no escape until the kids had cleared the way, stayed where they were, drinking and chatting.

Laylea reached the base of the platform at the same time as Brenda.

"Mr. DeGee." Brenda stared up at him with her hands on her hips. "We're gonna need money to throw a big festival on New Year's. I've got ideas."

Ms. Lagat stood to introduce them. "Douglass, this is Brenda Samborsky."

"Well, it is simply a joy to meet you, Brenda. Your father taught some of my older kids and they spoke very highly of him."

This stunned Brenda for a moment, giving Mr. DeGee the time to walk down the steps to the main floor. He turned to offer a hand to Ms. Lagat, stealing the prerogative from Professor Wanja who stood by, waiting to walk her down. Once the old shifting master had thanked Mr. DeGee, she headed for the back of the room and the three restricted non-wolves.

Mr. DeGee turned his full attention on Brenda. "I'd love to hear your ideas." He sat on the edge of the platform, indicating he meant what he said.

"What do you think about a Halloween party in the zoo to raise funds for the fundraiser?" Brenda asked through gritted teeth. She made no reply to Mr. DeGee's mention of her father. But there was a shimmer to her eyes like she was holding back tears through sheer force of will.

"Ooh, I love that idea." Lake Marshall joined the group. He had abandoned Angelica who looked a little lost. "We could make it a safe space for shifter kids to trick or treat."

"Yeah," Brenda agreed. "Plus games and stuff and cocktails for the parents."

"Lee?" Mr. Bianchi lowered himself to sit on the edge of the platform. "Did you need something?"

"I want one of those stasis bands." She needed one, but she wasn't going to tell a teacher that, even Mr. Bianchi.

He laughed. "I told you the Mers would love them, Safiri."

"I still don't understand why you put all the challenged shifters in the same dorm." Professor Wanja joined them, lowering himself to sitting with a bit more effort than Mr. Bianchi.

"I suspect it's as much for commiseration as anything, Professor." Dr. Tippleston dropped gracefully into a cross-legged seat, pretending to arrange a skirt though she was wearing lime-green jeans. She stuck her fist out in Laylea's direction. "We haven't been introduced. I'm Dr. Tippleston."

Dr. Fenn, the former doctor, had not returned. Who could blame him after Junior's father broke into the school and frightened the man so badly he had a heart attack. She hoped he was okay.

Laylea bumped the teacher's fist. "I'm Lee. Woodford."

She added her last name as an afterthought. It wasn't her real last name. It had been her true canine brother's name. Her mental tail drooped, remembering how he died. She focused her mind on an image of Woodford shoving his nose into Old Lady Rucker's rosebushes to keep from going dog. But that just made her want to wag her tail. Burning filled her body. She grunted and lifted both of her thumbs, wiggling them in front of her face like a couple of puppets.

The not-so-gentle pressure of a pen poking into her back shoved the burn right down. She shot a grateful look at KC.

"Is dinner always so exciting?" Dr. Tippleston asked, her eyes on Laylea.

"No, ma'am," Oscar answered from right behind her.

"Oh dear, no. We can't have that." Dr. Tippleston held a hand up as if physically blocking Oscar's response.

Professor Wanja and Mr. Bianchi laughed.

"What's that, ma'am?" Oscar asked.

Dr. Tippleston groaned and called out, "Bitters, I'm feeling your pain."

"What's going on?" The big man hopped down the stairs. The entire platform shook.

"You must punish this young man. He just 'ma'am'ed' me, twice."

"Ooh, harsh."

"I'm sorry, ma'am." Oscar flinched at his own words.

"That sounds like a parental issue to me." Bitters cut himself off mid-laugh. He asked Mr. Bianchi, seriously, "It is, right?"

"No, no. No punishment," Dr. Tippleston held her fist out to Oscar. "Call me Tipp."

Oscar bumped the doc's fist and let out a breath that was almost a laugh. "Yes, Tipp. I'm Oscar."

"I'm Enforcer Brewster." Bitters said it with an enormous pout. "Werearachnid." He held his fist out to each of the kids. They bumped it in turn.

"Excuse me, Bitter—I'm sorry." Mr. DeGee tried again. "Enforcer Brewster. Brenda here has some ideas for Halloween that we'd like to run by you."

"I'd love to help." Bitters hopped over to them with none of the seriousness expected of a terrifying enforcer of rules.

Laylea couldn't take it anymore. She wanted to talk to Professor Wanja privately. But that wasn't going to happen. She could feel sparks and tingling all over her body. She needed that bracelet.

She asked, "Can I get one of those stasis bands, Professor?"

"Absolutely," he said. "Everyone will get one when you go upstairs."

"I mean, like, now," she pushed. "Like I could really use one all the time."

"I know it's hard with Ms. Syperek leaving, but you'll settle into my class just fine. I promise, with practice and patience, you'll develop more self-control."

Laylea sucked in a breath, held it, and counted to ten. Switching shifting teachers wasn't hard. It was glorious. Ms. Syperek was a masochist. That's why Caliban had fired her even when the school was hemorrhaging wolf and wolf-sympathizer teachers.

"We're gonna have to go upstairs to help Brenda plan this Halloween thing," KC said, finding the excuse that had been eluding Laylea.

"And you'll get stasis bands when you go up," the professor assured her. "Don't worry so much."

Easy for him to say.

Mr. Bianchi, who had been half listening to Brenda and Mr. DeGee's energetic conversation suddenly sat up. "KC, how would you like to put together a strolling madrigal ensemble for the fundraiser?"

"I quite like madrigals, myself," Professor Wanja lit up. "I didn't imagine you'd still sing them now."

"Bu-y, buy buy bu-y. See what you want before you buy." KC and Oscar broke into a round they sang all the time. Professor Wanja and Mr. Bianchi joined in.

Laylea knew all the words. She knew when to come in. She just couldn't match the notes that she heard. She stood up straight, like Mr. Bianchi, and lengthened her neck. Was there something about the shape of his face that made his voice so rich and beautiful?

She suddenly noticed a bubbling burning on the skin of her upper body. Oh gods, had she shifted? Did she look like Mr. Bianchi? Why hadn't KC stabbed her?

Because KC was singing. She wasn't paying any attention to Laylea.

Embarrassment and shame gurgled in Laylea's gut. She shot a look at the doorway. Most of the kids had cleared it. She could get away quick. But she hadn't gotten a stasis band yet.

"Stress can make it challenging to hold shape." Dr. Tippleston said this quietly. "I can't even imagine what P2 was like for you."

Laylea took in a breath to say something, but she let it out again, having no idea what to say.

"Nobody's talking about it?" The doctor asked.

"No, everybody's talking about it, all the time," Laylea burst out. "Students at least."

"We're talking about it, too," Professor Wanja assured her, dropping out of the round.

The tingling was gone from her skin. Laylea felt solid. The doctor had distracted her and stopped her from shifting with her innocent question.

"You helped catch Denier, didn't you?" the doc asked. "And you saved the phoenix, with your friends."

Wanja leaned in to Dr. Tippleston. "She helped rescue me and my students, as well."

"And you saw how chaotic it is with me shifting all the time." Laylea took her shot. "A stasis band could stop all that."

"It may feel uncontrollable, but you're probably shifting for a reason," Professor Wanja said, gently. "You need to solve that riddle, and wearing a stasis band won't help with that."

"Safiri." Angelica commanded the witch's attention from across the platform. "Can I have a word?"

Professor Wanja slid off the platform with an effort. "I'll see you in class, Lee. You'll master shifting, I promise."

The professor might not be wearing his ornamental robes, but he walked with a swinging stride as if he were. Angelica reached out a hand to him. The gesture was equal parts welcoming and demanding. The gems on her long nails sparkled in the candlelight from the faculty table. Were her fancy clothes, elaborate hair, and bejeweled nails the secret to her confidence?

Laylea could never have her hair, but those nails. Her hands stung as if she'd dunked them in ice water. She looked down.

Her heart pounded. She'd shifted. She had Angelica's nails. And worse, her hands had Angelica's skin tone as well. She shoved them into her pockets and turned to run.

Dr. Tipp stopped her with the most bizarre question. "Do you have long toes?"

11

The question was so odd Laylea wondered if she'd heard right. She wiggled her toes as she tried to think of a polite way to say, huh? Her toes were kinda long, compared to KC's at least. Although KC wore shoes since she'd never had a problem losing her clothing.

"I'm sorry," she asked Dr. Tippleston, completely forgetting she was planning to run away. "Did you ask about my toes?"

"You're thinking about them. I can tell, because you wiggled them." Tipp's thrift-store Crocs wriggled as she wiggled her own toes. "We walk around totally unaware of our toes or our shoulders or butt cheeks." The adult giggled. "Until we need to be aware of them."

Laylea found she was suddenly aware of them all. Her shoulders were up near her ears. She relaxed them. She clenched and unclenched her butt. And she giggled.

Dr. Tippleston tilted her head. She considered Laylea's face long enough that Laylea felt heat rushing up her neck, followed by that familiar burn in her gut.

"Can you feel your birthmark?" the doctor asked.

Not thinking, Laylea raised a hand to her face. It was the usual color and her nails were short and unpainted.

The doc stopped her. "No, like you felt your shoulders, with your mind."

Laylea couldn't actually feel the white of her diamond-shaped birthmark. But she became aware of the space between her eyes. She rarely thought of it, not nearly as often as she thought of her butt.

"Good," Dr. Tippleston said, even though Laylea hadn't done anything. "Now, take a stylus and trace around the edges."

For no good reason, the stylus that popped into her head wrote with a thick white tip. She outlined the white diamond in white. When she was done, she didn't so much look at Dr. Tippleston as become aware of her. She'd been staring into the woman's face the whole time. It must have been creepy to see from outside their conversation.

There was something about Tipp that reminded Laylea of her and Bailey's landlady. Madam Hu had the same ability to calm Laylea, no matter what was going on. Tipp wore just as much makeup as Madam Hu, too. Only hers was realistic, in shades of bronze and pink to highlight her features. Madam Hu painted her face like it was a canvas, completely eliminating her eyebrows or lips sometimes.

"Stay with me, Lee." The doctor quietly pulled her attention back. "Now, carefully, how does your gut feel?"

It was fine. It was better than fine. Her gut was more relaxed than it had been in a week. Her whole body was relaxed. She took a breath and felt it fill her torso, like Mr. Bianchi always instructed.

She smiled. "No burn." Her smile faded as the word ignited a desire to shift. She flared her nostrils. What was wrong with her body?

"Is your diamond still white? Or did you outline it with glitter?"

Laylea blinked. In a flash of thought, the imaginary white line she'd drawn around her birthmark glittered gold like Angelica's nails. Her grin returned. And her body relaxed, gut included.

"How did you do that?" she asked, searching the doctor's face for answers.

Tipp's eyes narrowed. Her lips spread in a wide, warm smile filled with pride. "You did that. I have a birthmark, too. I put all my worries and feelings into it and then draw a door that can open either out or in."

That was silly, and woo-woo, and kinda genius.

"Oscar," Dizzy called over. "Can you come help us with something?"

The little concert that had grown while Laylea was focused on Tipp and her birthmark ended abruptly. Oscar shot KC a speaking look and then addressed Laylea. "I'll be back. Don't go anywhere."

Laylea smiled sweetly. She had no intention of being there when he got back.

From the faculty table, Ms. Crow called, "Oscar, bring KC with you." She turned back to Angelica to say, "KC is a whiz with tech."

KC hooked her arm in Laylea's to drag her along. "Don't make us face deRio alone."

"Actually," Mr. Bianchi said, "I'd like a word with Lee. If you don't mind?"

KC and Oscar both frowned, but they didn't argue. They dragged their feet up the steps, watching her over their shoulders as they went.

"I have an appointment with Benny," Dr. Tipp announced, accepting Mr. Bianchi's help to hop off the edge of the platform. "Take her away, Enrico." She waved one hand imperiously, wafting the scent of rosemary over Laylea. Dr. Tippleston smelled like Madam Hu, too.

"Are you wearing rosemary perfume?" she asked.

The doctor's face fell as if she were appalled to be asked such a personal question.

Laylea backpedaled. "I'm sorry. I didn't mean anything. A friend of mine—who's fabulous—just always smells like rosemary. She's into homeopathy. I thought maybe you—and there's this dog in my neighborhood named Tippy, so that got me —"

"Lee," Mr. Bianchi interrupted her babbling, ushering her away from a laughing Dr. Tipp. "Let's step outside where it's quiet."

The doctor called after them, "Come by the infirmary any time, Lee."

Sure. Make a total fool of herself and then drop by for a chat. Like that was going to happen.

"You've missed two lessons." Mr. Bianchi launched straight into it as the great glass doors closed on the din in the Dining Hall.

Laylea swore as loudly and creatively as she could in her mind. Her cheeks flushed and she stuck her hands into her pockets as she mumbled an apology.

"You're not in any trouble." Mr. Bianchi lowered his voice with a glance at Daniel and Theresa across the foyer. "I hope you're not avoiding me because of what you saw outside the café."

Laylea felt herself pale. She'd probably looked just as horrified when Mr. Bianchi had partially shifted after rescuing her from Denier.

"No, Mr. Bianchi. It's not that, I swear."

He had to know she wouldn't avoid him just because he was a wolf.

She was avoiding him because since her body had started going haywire, she got calluses whenever she even thought about playing guitar. He'd see. He'd know she was broken.

"It was just really hard last week and music is so emotional, you know?" she said, instead of the truth.

"It is. And I'm glad you're not scared of me."

"Wh… I... never," Laylea sputtered, appalled he might think that.

Mr. Bianchi nodded at that, a grim smile on his face. "You know, music can be a healthy way to express your emotions," he said.

She did know that. Which was why she played every night.

Across the foyer, Theresa shouted, "Daniel! You never listen," and stormed off.

Daniel shot them a grimace as he ran a hand through his perpetually messy hair. "Sorry 'bout that, sir, Lee." He shifted into a seven-thousand-pound elephant and lumbered after Theresa.

With an inward sigh, Laylea faced Mr. Bianchi. She didn't even have a good excuse. When in doubt, the truth often worked. "I'm not scared of you. I love our lessons. I know music could help. But, I've really got to learn how to shift better, sir. Which is why I need to quit private lessons so I can fit more shifting classes into my schedule."

The silence lasted so long she eventually raised her eyes to see his reaction.

Rather than disappointment or anger, she saw concern in his deep brown eyes. And understanding.

"Lee, I know about secrets. If you ever—"

Light spilled into the foyer as the glass doors opened. KC dashed through, jaw clenched, gripping the straps of her backpack like she was holding herself down.

Mr. Bianchi called out, "KC?"

KC whipped her head around. Her face was a rictus of fierce, untamed anger, tears welling in her eyes, just tipping over when she saw them.

Mr. Bianchi followed as Laylea ran to her friend. "What happened?"

"Luis Delcampo sent lawyers to get Denier released."

Laylea's entire body went cold, like a ghost had just embraced her.

Mr. Bianchi hastened to say, "They won't succeed." He sounded certain.

"Luis Delcampo gets whatever he wants," KC told him, sounding just as certain.

"No. The federal judge refused bail." Mr. Bianchi said "federal" like it made the judge all-powerful.

"Is there a federal prison that's prepared to hold a werewolf?" KC yelled.

The music teacher tried to sooth her. "I'm sure Captain Morioka has federal resources."

But KC shook her head. Her nostrils flared. "He also declared Gerbrand the national enforcer."

"His great grandson?" Mr. Bianchi asked.

Her brother.

"Denier was evil because he was made by Delcampo," KC spat. "Gerber was born a Delcampo."

"So that makes him evil?" Laylea asked, cutting to the chase.

"Doesn't it?"

KC was trapped in her head, in her horror that she could be just like them. Laylea could spout everything she'd done and risked to save the school. She'd stood right beside Laylea through every fight, never once considering her own safety first. KC wouldn't hear it. She was so selfless she could never see her own actions as an argument against inherited evil. But she'd die before she let anyone speak ill of her friends.

"Walter dissected living puppies to see what we were made of." Laylea struggled to get the words out. "I'm his blood."

KC's face fell. She grabbed Laylea's hands. "No, Lee, you're not evil. You fight evil."

Laylea squeezed back. "So do you."

In a small voice, very much unlike him, Mr. Bianchi suggested, "Evil is about choices, not bloodlines. And you both make powerful choices. You have your eyes open. You see the world as it is and strive to change it, to improve it for everyone."

The music teacher was lost in his thoughts, as if searching for the words. Laylea knew that halting tone. KC must as well. They both used it often enough, figuring out what they could say without revealing their secrets.

He looked at each of them, his eyes searching KC's face a little longer, noting her dyed blond hair, her blue contacts.

He cleared his throat roughly. "You inspire me."

With that, he walked away.

A part of Laylea wanted to run after him, to comfort him, and to find out what he was hiding. KC wanted to hide.

"Let's get out of here before Angelica deRio comes out." KC dragged her toward Mer dorm. "I don't know what Mariella sees in her. Mariella is so kind."

"They say opposites attract," Laylea offered, though she didn't mean it. Angelica had a bit of a superiority problem, but she had to be under a lot of pressure, being a wolf and all.

She searched for a way to cheer KC up. "Hey, we should work up matching costumes for Halloween."

"Ugh," KC groaned. "I hate Halloween. Everybody dresses up like monsters, while we spend our lives dressing up like we're not."

"We're not monsters."

"You're not," KC said. "I'm a werewolf."

Laylea automatically searched around to see if there was anybody in earshot. KC didn't bother. Seeing no one, Laylea stopped trying to change the subject and stood her ground. "KC Dells," she said firmly, reminding her friend that she'd renamed herself. "Are you saying that you want to shift and tear me to pieces?"

"No." KC's eyes sparked with offense.

"The full moon is up. You can feel it," Laylea pushed. "But you don't want to wrap your fangs around my head, shake until you've broken my neck, then run around the school displaying your trophy to Mr. Bianchi and Jase and Jimmy and Jonathan?"

By the time she was listing the wolves, KC was nodding along, conceding the point. "No."

Laylea didn't need to say *You're not a monster.* But she did need to give KC space to talk about her brother maybe being a monster.

After another look around, she asked, "You can't be all that surprised about Gerber, can you?"

The tension in KC's body drained away. She fell into Laylea's arms. "No," she wailed. "I can't. But I can't hate him either."

Laylea held on tight. She understood. There was nothing Bailey could do that would make her love him any less than with all her heart.

Strings of guilt and relief twisted like DNA inside Laylea. She'd gotten out of guitar lessons without an argument, and it was clear that KC had forgotten all about the little conversation she and Oscar wanted to have with her. But they'd remember eventually, particularly if she couldn't get control of herself.

If Professor Wanja wouldn't give her a stasis band, she would just have to find a way to steal one. She'd volunteer to help with Halloween. Then, she could just drop the stasis band in her pocket when she came back down and claim she lost it. By the end of the month, she'd have a stasis band of her very own.

Then she'd be safe.

12

Laylea and KC tumbled along with the stragglers heading into the Old School on Halloween morning. They stopped just inside the Grand Parlor as much from shock as from running into the back of a line of kids.

The room had changed dramatically since Laylea had last been there, almost exactly three weeks earlier. It wasn't so much the furnishings. The couches, chairs, and chalkboards were all there. They had just been pushed back against the bookshelves that lined the walls. The burns outlining where the clothes closet had been hadn't even been cleaned up.

New doors had been hung to replace the ones that were blown from their hinges.

The charred floorboards left behind when Pansy immolated from her beautiful phoenix form into an egg had been covered with a huge new rug. But the biggest change was the atmosphere of the room.

For two centuries, the space, originally intended to welcome new students and their families to the shifter school, had hosted only six witches and a phoenix. Now, it was filled with rowdy, excited teens and preteens. They gathered in clumps, waiting their turn to go upstairs and set up their booths and games for the shifter-only celebration. The clumps formed a ragged line spanning the room. Kids dressed in costumes and carrying all sorts of supplies chattered about their plans for an unprecedented day of joy for littler kids.

The school had been talking about nothing else for days. No one had ever heard of a shifter-only event before, other than council meetings. When it was announced that the zoo would not only be closed to the public, but also hidden from them, the ticket sales had skyrocketed.

"Haunted Hayride characters, gather up!" Emerald yelled from somewhere on the far side of the room.

A pack of kids in their animal forms picked themselves up from where they'd been lounging. They were all dressed like silly ghouls and monsters. Dove's tiger prowled over the carpets covered in colorful webs like she'd run through a field of cotton candy. Her muzzle dripped with the stuff. She'd attached lollipops and licorice to her fur as well.

KC poked Laylea. "Look at Dove's wrist."

A silver stasis band glinted from around the tiger's front left paw. Each of the other shifted students already wore stasis bands as well.

"Should have volunteered for the Haunted Hayride," KC muttered. "You, too, could be rabid from too much candy." *And it would have been much easier to steal a band,* went unsaid.

Brenda didn't know a whole lot about Halloween. Before her dad was stolen away to Denier's sleep lab, he'd been a teacher at LPSS. As a single dad with no support, he'd raised her in faculty housing. Brenda had never lived upstairs. She'd only heard of trick or treating and read about it in books. It didn't make any sense to her. Life had never given her candy for free. And she couldn't understand why anybody would want to be frightened. So, at her Halloween celebration, scares were minimized, silliness was centered, and kids had to earn their treats.

At KC's booth, for example, she was going to help kids make plaster keepsakes with their paw and handprints. While the plaster was drying, kids could guess which animal made which print to earn tickets for food, activities, or handmade plushies.

Laylea wasn't working a booth. Oscar had put himself in charge of the walls and volunteered her to help. She didn't mind at all. It meant that she and Oscar had gotten to make several trips upstairs in the week and a half they had to plan the event. Every time they went up was another chance to examine the stasis bands. And with her friends being busy and Dr. Tippleston's trick to help her hold her shape, Laylea had managed to avoid any difficult conversations. About her shifting issues, at least.

Difficult conversations about wolves were impossible to avoid. Classes were constantly being sidetracked with the issue. In chemistry, Rehyan got Ms. Muldoon talking about the breakdown of wolfsbane. It had been trés easy for Ali to get Madame to lecture on the history of the loup-garou in French film. The most interesting and most dangerous discussions were happening in Mr. Barrett's sociology classes since he was questioning everything he'd been teaching for decades.

Wolves hadn't been invited to the party. At least at first. But after Carrie had a private word with her, Brenda conceded that they couldn't punish wolf pups for the actions of adults. Though none of the restricted students were allowed to go, of course, Jimmy had recorded some eerie music for them to play, and Big Mo and Vaughn had built frames for the temporary walls.

Like Mers, many shifters would shift randomly and uncontrollably throughout their childhood. Brenda's wall made it so they could do so without consequences since they would only be seen by other shifters. Chef Tod had even whipped up treats for the kids to enjoy in their other forms. And it freed the student volunteers to create startling elements to their booths.

KC poked Laylea and drew her attention to Christopher and Krystal, the koi twins standing ahead of them at the back of the line. The twins' turn-of-the-last-century outfits faced the entryway. Their heads faced the opposite way.

"Are you cosplaying owl shifters?" KC asked.

Christopher turned. His face was painted to look like a rotting skull. A stripe of blood along his neck dripped realistically onto his collar. "We're the headless horsemen."

Krystal's face was painted like a jack o'lantern. She'd shaded her neck so it looked like her pumpkin head was sitting on a stick.

KC leaned in to look at the blood. "That's awesome."

"Nice." Laylea grinned.

Krystal ducked her head. Christopher bumped her with his shoulder. They both turned away again.

Laylea felt underdressed in her white coveralls, even if she expected to be much more colorful by the end of the day.

Laylea muttered, "Is everyone in school here?"

"Nearly," KC replied. "Brenda can be very persuasive."

Laylea rolled her eyes. "It helps that she knows everybody's secrets."

KC laughed.

She stopped suddenly when a black kitten landed on her backpack. "What the—" KC spun around in confusion.

Tessa leapt back to Miro's shoulder, flicking KC in the face with her tail in the process. She settled around their neck where she blended in with their black sweatshirt. The rest of Miro's outfit consisted of black pants and cat ears. They'd even drawn whiskers on their face.

Belle asked, "Is this the line to get stasis bands?"

Miro stared at their sister.

"Wow!" Laylea took a step back to get a full view of Belle's stunning costume. The tight bodice of her eighteenth-century ball gown was topped with lace to disguise her lack of cleavage. Not that anyone would be able to take their eyes off her towering white wig. She'd tucked flowers, pearls, and even little birds into the elaborate curls.

Of course, it was safe for Belle to wear an elaborate costume. She didn't even need a stasis band. Laylea had never seen her shift. Miro shifted often enough for both of them.

"Marie Antoinette?" KC asked.

Belle used one gloved hand to pull down the red choker to reveal a line of Frankensteinesque stitches around her delicate neck.

A choked laugh came from behind Laylea. She turned to see Christopher pointing at his own bloody neck. He and Belle grinned at each other.

Miro interrupted the moment to reiterate their sibling's original question. "Stasis bands?"

"Don't know." KC turned to Christopher. "Is this the line for stasis bands?"

He shrugged.

"We'll go find out." KC grabbed Laylea's hand. "Save our place?"

Belle and Christopher nodded. Tessa meowed, which could mean anything. Miro echoed her with a laugh.

KC dragged Laylea along the line of kids. As they neared the front KC stopped short. Laylea slammed into her, popped into a dog covered in downy, owl feathers, and back to human again.

"That wasn't there before," KC said.

Laylea looked up from straightening her clothes and kicking a few feathers away from her feet. She blinked stupidly.

The last time she'd been in the Grand Parlor, the only exits were the main entrance, an open archway leading to classrooms, and the swinging door to the kitchen. At the head of the line, Emerald stood examining her nails in a hallway now revealed where two bookshelves had been opened like doors.

Laylea muttered, "Where's that go?"

KC gripped the shoulder straps of her heavy backpack and tapped Harper with her foot. "Where's that go?" she asked.

"To the Old School classrooms. That's where they're building the downstairs part of The Phoenix. Also…" Harper smirked. He waggled his eyebrows. "There's a new way upstairs."

"Time for a party at Toby's," Reggie said around the bandages over his face. His entire body was wrapped to look like a mummy.

"No," Kara said. Reggie's girlfriend flung her cape out of the way so she could cling to his bandage-wrapped arm. She lisped a little around her vampire teeth. "It'th too dangerouth upthtairth right now."

"But you're going up," Laylea pointed out.

"Not now now, like, day now," Kara scoffed. "At night, it'th a different thtory. It's not thafe."

Theresa leaned forward to say, "Not since Grandpa took away all his protections."

That started a whole argument.

"Come on." KC hitched her pack higher on her shoulders and strolled back along the line, looking at all the faces. Laylea had a good idea who she was searching for.

There were three people Laylea would ask if she wanted details on the latest gossip. For something scandalous, you go to Milly. For anything going on outside of the school, Brenda. And for stuff that mattered, Benny.

Sure enough, KC stopped beside Benny. "Benny, what are you in line for?"

"To get a stasis band and go upstairs," he said, spitting bits of his Charlie Chaplin mustache out of his mouth. "Professor Wanja showed Ms. Lagat a lift going up into the Lion House, which used to be the teachers' entrance to the school."

"He showed her while they were on a date," Milly chimed in. Her spit curls and sparkling headband made Laylea squeal. Lina Lamont was the best character in *Singin' in the Rain*. Milly had the white, fur-trimmed cape, and her nineteen twenties make up was spot on, though she'd done nothing to hide the healing scratches on her face.

Beside her, Riva rocked a koala onesie. It wasn't much of a costume, but it looked comfy and warm.

Laylea said, "Hey, you look cute."

Before she'd finished the sentence, Riva squeaked and shifted. She wrapped her lanky arms around Milly's neck and buried her cute face in her friend's faux fur.

Laylea automatically brought a hand up to be sure she was wearing her own face. She touched her cheek with the three long claws of a sloth hand. She stared at it for an instant before hiding her hands behind her back and looking around to see if anybody had noticed.

Milly's head was down over Riva as she comforted her friend.

Benny shuffled awkwardly, putting more weight on his one good foot and the cane.

KC focused on Benny. "Should you be standing on that foot so long?"

He'd graduated to a boot and a cane rather than the crutches he'd been using, but if it still hurt as badly as Milly's face looked, he probably shouldn't be standing.

"Oh, it won't be much longer," Benny demurred.

Milly rolled her eyes. "They've been saying that for like an hour. The bands aren't even here yet."

"If there aren't enough, we might not be allowed to go up," Benny said.

A spike of concern zipped through Laylea. She needed a stasis band. Fur stood up on the back of her neck, which was particularly concerning since the rest of her was human. It was a ridiculous response. She didn't need to be bigger than anybody. She needed speed to get to the front of the line. Her thigh muscles tingled.

No, she thought, *not in front of everybody.*

But it was too late. The shift flashed heat through her lower body. From the waist down, Laylea was a kangaroo.

13

Why a kangaroo? Laylea asked her body. Did she think she was going to hop her way to the front and magically make the stasis bands appear?

From the other side of the line, Ali cried out, "Mers desperately want to see the sun!"

A cheer went up, with most of the kids, Centaur and Sphinx included, repeating the Mer war cry.

Laylea took advantage of their distraction. She tried to snap the hairband on her wrist and only scratched herself. The result was the same: pain.

She leaned into the pain and let her body take over. The way-too-familiar burn shot out from her gut, down through her powerful kangaroo legs, up through her feathered owl ears, and out through the tips of her sloth claws, transforming all of her into the little fawn mutt she preferred to be.

Everything felt right when she was a dog. Her muscles relaxed. Her brain relaxed. Just to be sure, she traced whorls around her birthmark in her mind. It was silly, but probably healthier than scolding herself.

Leda pushed through some cheering kids to ask Benny, "You think they won't let us go upstairs without stasis bands? We're not all Mers."

Benny shrugged. "It's the new policy."

KC scooped Laylea up. "That's silly," she said to Benny. "The zoo is closed off to the public. There's no reason to keep anybody from going up."

"She's right." Milly added. "It's not like they're giving stasis bands to the guests."

"Come on, Benny. Let's go sit while we wait." KC turned away without waiting for him to agree. She called over her shoulder, "You don't want Dr. Tipp to catch you breaking her orders."

Dr. Tippleston did have an uncanny habit of showing up all around the school. Dr. Fenn had never strayed far from the infirmary or his classroom unless he was called. Dr. Tippleston had been sitting in on classes. She'd even taken a pop quiz in Mr. Vronumraju's intro to physics class for fun.

KC dumped Laylea onto the long blue sofa and shrugged off her backpack. While she was setting it on the floor, a white figure dove past Benny and scooped Laylea into his lap. Griff wore another bleached uniform, though he also wore his ubiquitous bobble hat. He'd tied the dangling bobbles under his chin as if afraid it might come off.

The two of them bounced as Benny dropped onto the cushion beside them. He reached over to give Laylea's head a tentative pet. She rolled to her back and lifted an arm. He did not take the hint so she dropped her head backwards off the edge of Griff's thigh and gave Benny as close to the evil eye as a puppy could manage.

"She likes to have her neck scratched," KC plopped beside Benny and reached over him to demonstrate.

Benny took over and KC rubbed a thumb between Laylea's eyes. Laylea sighed and melted into the attention. No one ever showed this kind of affection when she was human.

"Is your neck really comfortable like that?" Benny bent close to her face. She wffd at him.

"I call that position 'Dalí doggie'," KC said. "I thought you'd be one of the first upstairs, Griff."

"No way." Griff kept petting Laylea as he responded. He was good at multi-tasking. She liked that about him. "My dad's walking the council through the zoo. He'd make me go with them. I'd never get free."

Laylea cringed. She'd give anything to spend a day with the Dad. Not her biological father, her real dad. She'd give more than anything to never meet her biological father again.

"Oh, phoenix." Griff stopped petting her. He shot guilty looks between her and KC. "I'm sorry. You don't have dads. You must think I'm the worst. I do love him. He's just... You've met him, Lee."

She had. He'd saved her butt twice and she adored him. She growled at Griff.

"Oh yeah," he muttered, running a hand down her side. "You're a fan."

Her tail flopped against his leg. She was, but she also understood how it could be difficult to be his son.

KC shot Laylea a grimace. Griff thought that both of them were orphans. There were a lot of orphaned and abandoned kids at LPSS. There were a lot of liars, too. KC and Laylea were only two of them. It was baked in to shifter culture. The very fact that they wouldn't have to lie was why so many shifters were coming to the Halloween party.

Voices raised near the entryway and the line parted to let a tall, awkward, deep pink flamingo stalk through. Like Dove, Rehyan's feathers were draped in wispy cotton candy and dotted with colorful nerds. A rope of black licorice circled his three-foot long neck like a barber's pole. He also wore a silver stasis band around the base of his neck. It glinted in the light from the torches.

As soon as he was clear of people, Rehyan spread his wings and half-hopped, half-flew to the front of the line where Emerald scolded him and shooed him into the mysterious, dark hallway.

"You're late," she told him. "They're gathering at Toby's."

A cheer rose by the entryway and moved along the line like a wave crashing on the shore.

"Yes, yes," Professor Wanja said, his voice easily carrying over the noise. "Sorry to keep you waiting."

The crowd parted, with more respect than they'd shown for

Rehyan, and Professor Wanja strode in, his magician's robe wafting in his wake. Quan and Ollie tripped over themselves trying to keep up.

"But you knew," Ollie said. "You knew and you never told us."

"I did tell you, just now." The professor swept through the room. He waved at kids and greeted many by name, but didn't slow down. Laylea almost missed it when he nodded at her because her eyes were glued to the box in his hands. Firelight sparkled off the silver bands piled high inside it.

"When did it reappear?" Quan demanded.

"It reappeared when it was needed." Professor Wanja glared at Quan over his shoulder as they reached the new doorway. "Emerald," he said in greeting. "I'm sure Brenda has a process?"

"You know it." Emerald pushed off the wall and led them away.

"I'm just saying we should have gotten to use the lift first," Quan muttered.

"You are getting to use it now," The professor retorted, his voice fading as the three headed away down the new corridor.

"Are you excited?" Griff's tone dripped with sarcasm. He stared at Laylea's tail which was thumping against his thigh.

She growled at her butt. As easily as shifters lied, her tail had never gotten the memo.

"Of course she's excited." KC bounced in her seat. "She shifts all the time. For the rest of the day, she's not gonna have to worry about it."

"And why are you so excited?" Benny asked her. "I've never seen you shift."

KC spluttered, trying to come up with an answer.

For the first time, it occurred to Laylea that KC might want to steal a stasis band as badly as she did. Whatever was going on with Laylea might just be a thing all shifters went through, like acne. But if KC ever shifted in front of anybody, they'd know she was a wolf, and it wouldn't take long for them to figure out she was the Delcampo daughter who was meant to show up the same night Laylea and KC did.

Laylea wriggled to the edge of Griff's knees and rolled off. She shifted human before she even hit the carpets. An extra pair of bleached uggs sat beside Griff's feet.

"For me?" she asked.

He blushed.

"Thanks." She pulled the boots on while talking over her shoulder. "KC, you make sure Benny stays here until Milly and Leda get to the front. I'll go hold our place behind Chris and Krys."

"I'm fine, you guys," Benny whined, but Laylea noticed he didn't try to stand up.

"You go with her, Griff," KC ordered. A look passed between them that Laylea couldn't quite read.

Griff popped up off the couch and hurried toward the line.

Laylea tugged on the second boot and tripped after him. "What was that?"

"What was what?" Griff searched the crowd, avoiding her eyes.

"That," she repeated. "KC gave you a look."

"Really?" He offered a quick quizzical look before darting in behind the koi. A few kids raised a fuss at the cutting. Griff said, "Just pretend I'm KC."

Laylea turned to Tessa, Miro, and Belle behind them. "You were saving our spot, right?"

Tessa meowed at her unhelpfully.

It was little Belle who shouted, "We were saving their spot. Jeez. It's upstairs. There's room for everyone."

"Thanks, Belle."

"No problem," the girl said. "You need one more than I do."

Laylea rotated slowly, not believing that little Belle Suttrick had just dunked on her. The glint in her eye confirmed that she had. Laylea repeated, dryly, "Thanks, Belle."

What was the world coming to with Belle, who couldn't shift at all, making fun of Laylea who couldn't stop shifting. She'd grown up some thanks to the wolf attack. They all had.

There was something about standing up for yourself that changed a person in a far more permanent way than just shifting.

14

A blast of wind off the lake blew Laylea's hair back as she jetéed between a group of little kids and the temporary wall. She cried, "One giant leap for shifterkind!"

The kids squealed. The paint they'd thrown at the wall hit her as well. She landed and ran at them, threatening to hug them with her paint-smeared arms held wide. Two dropped their empty paint buckets and ran away. A third flashed into a tiny sparrow and flew after them.

The fourth, a four-year-old werewolf named Reata, completely ignored Laylea's antics. She wandered through the spilled paint and chalk, her little paws leaving tracks around the crayons, glitter glue, markers, and paintbrushes to swipe at the fresh paint that had made it past Laylea's body to the wall. Reata had a vision and nobody was going to keep her from leaving her mark. She'd confided to Oscar that her parents didn't like messes. Oscar assured her that her art wasn't a "mess," and he loved her work. She'd refused to leave his side since.

When Brenda assigned Oscar to build a privacy wall around her Halloween event, she did not expect him to turn it into one of the most popular attractions.

Oscar, Laylea, and Griff collected every kind of art material they could find. When the event opened, they invited kids, and not a few adults, to paint, draw, and decorate the walls and their bleached white uniforms. As Oscar deemed each panel complete, they moved the supplies and drop cloths to the next one.

Deciding that her lizard foot protection charm would interfere with the stasis band, Professor Wanja had made Laylea take it off. She'd felt naked without it, but once she started leaping through paint, she was glad it was safely downstairs. By lunchtime, Griff, Oscar, and Laylea were covered head to toe in color. Mr. DeGee had painted a gold star on each of them before dragging Griff off with him.

For a hot minute, Laylea had hoped she might be able to use the paint to hide her stasis band when they went downstairs, but the paint had flaked off as it dried.

Time was running out. None of the kids she'd asked were able to remove the band from their own wrist or anybody else's. Her own attempts had all failed; water, force, heat, even a blade stolen from Chef Tod's baking booth made no dent. All she had to show for her efforts were bruised knuckles, three annoying cuts, and a delightful apple cruller.

She was getting desperate as the sun started dipping below the tallest of the buildings to the west. They'd circled the party arena and reached the final panel beside the entryway maze.

The only way in or out of the zoo was through the maze. It served a dual purpose. First, it forced everyone to get into the spirit of the party. Second, it prevented just anybody from wandering into the zoo.

The maze and Griff's mom, Inika.

"...like art. You can jump right into the festivities here with Oscar and Lee." Inika emerged from the maze guiding a late-arriving family. "Angel, Malik, let the girls explore. Everyone is here to be sure they have fun and nobody will blink if they shift."

The three daughters, ranging in age from barely verbal to early teens, vibrated with excitement, their butterfly wings and deeley boppers bouncing wildly. Angel's smile was genuine but exhausted. Her stained scrubs and Malik's wrinkled pilot uniform gave the impression of long work days rather than costumes.

"You are coming home with us, right now." An angry voice pulled everyone's attention from the latecomers.

Mr. Betts dragged his son along with a white-knuckled grip on Reggie's puffy jacket. He toed Dove in her hind quarters as she roared and struggled against her mother pulling on the leather leash around her tiger neck.

Laylea felt a zap on her wrist that squelched the burn in her gut. She wanted to transform and bite the Betts parents' ankles. It wasn't just that they put a leash on their daughter. Laylea grew up on a leash. That wasn't so bad. But her parents would never drag her like that. Dove's neck would be bruised.

She scanned the pile of art supplies, already knowing there wasn't anything there that could slice through leather.

"Dad, watch out." Reggie saw the butterfly girls and jerked aside to avoid them.

His father snarled and yanked him back, sending him crashing into the family.

Malik swung the littlest up and out of harm's way. The middle child transformed mid-fall into a gorgeous deep-blue butterfly. The oldest girl smacked her head so hard even the Bettses heard it over their squabbling.

Reata screamed, shifting human. Oscar scooped the little artist into his arms while Inika tapped a sequence on her armpadd. Alarms echoed across the zoo in response.

"Hi, I'm Lee." She rushed to the teen and stopped just short of her. The mother got there first.

Angel examined the girl with a skill that made it clear her scrubs weren't a costume.

"Hi, Lee." The girl raised a hand but didn't move otherwise. "I'm Calliope. This is my mother, Angel. That's my sister, Coy." She pointed at the butterfly balancing on Angel's piled braids.

The whole side of Calliope's face was scraped up. She winced when her mother touched a swelling bruise on her forehead, but distracted herself by wiggling her fingers at her baby sister. "That's Leticia."

"Candy," the littlest girl protested, loudly, over Dove's growling and Reata's cries.

"That's Candy," Calliope corrected herself with a roll of her eyes.

Candy squirmed in her father's arms as Malik yelled at Mr. Betts, "Let those kids go."

Mr. Betts snarled back, "They're my children. Stay the fuck out of it."

"Hey," Oscar bristled. Reata's face was buried in his shoulder, but that barely muffled her sobs.

Inika stepped forward, waving Oscar back. "This is a family event, sir," she said, her eyes glued to the collar straining against Dove's ears. "Please watch your language."

"Fuck off," Mr. Betts growled in the woman's face. "I'm taking my kids out of this school and you're not going to stop me."

He shoved past her, fighting to drag Reggie toward the maze entrance.

Mrs. Betts took up the diatribe. "The fact that you allowed wolves at this event and didn't tell anybody is appalling."

Inika straightened to her impressive height, her voice iron wrapped in velvet as she replied, "We're not going to punish children for crimes committed by some adults who happen to be wolves."

Bitters stepped out of the maze. He spread his considerable weight evenly on his feet and took stock of the situation.

Mr. Betts yelled in his face, "We pay for our kids to go here. You can't keep them against our will."

"I can't speak to that, sir. But you are treating these shifters with unacceptable levels of violence. As the—"

"They're our children," Mrs. Betts informed him the way some people said, "It's my dog."

Bitters went on as if she hadn't interrupted him. "As the Council Enforcer, I must ask you both to release these shifters and come with me."

Mrs. Betts whined, "That stupid tree wouldn't let them leave."

"We haven't graduated!" Reggie grunted this, still trying to free himself.

"Don't you speak to your mother like that." Mr. Betts slapped his son across the face.

Bitters stumbled back as if he'd been struck himself.

"She has no right to keep them against our will," Reggie's mother insisted, as though nothing unusual had just happened.

"They're not pressers." Mr. Betts spat "pressers" exactly the same way Jase said "thumpers."

"You're right." Reggie spoke quietly, all his rage focused in his balled-up fists. He raised one, eyes locked on his father.

"Don't you dare, boy."

Bitters stepped between them, his voice startlingly gentle. "Let him go now."

Reggie drew his arm back. In a flash, he swung. Dove roared as the blow connected with the enforcer's jaw. Every human gasped—except Bitters.

Bitters hid his smile with a fake cough as he easily broke Mr. Betts' grip, twisting the man's arm behind his back. "He's pressed now. And you're under arrest. Ma'am, let go of the tiger."

Coy launched herself from her mother's hair and flapped her little self over to Reggie. She settled on his shoulder.

"Get that thing off my son!" Mrs. Betts pointed at Coy as if her finger could shoot lasers. Doing so left her holding Dove's leash with one hand.

Big mistake.

Dove snatched the leash out of her mother's hands and made a dash for the entryway, where she ran smack into Laylea's friend, Ned. Built like two gorillas glued together, he caught the tiger and whispered something only Dove could hear. She quieted, letting Ned hold her like a kitten. The remaining floss on her fur tangled with his beard.

"Students aren't allowed to leave zoo grounds without permission," Bitters mentioned, as if she wasn't aware. "You're pressed, too."

"This is Dove Betts," Ned said, startling their parents. "Which would make you Reggie?" he asked Reggie.

"Yes, sir."

The "sir" right after he punched the enforcer got a variety of reactions from the adults. The uniformed police officer who had slipped into the zoo behind Ned outright laughed.

While Ned and Bitters worked things out with the cop, Angel helped her eldest daughter get to her feet. She looked torn between focusing on her kids and standing up for Dove and Reggie.

Oscar stepped in. "We're just over here making art. Could your girls come help us?"

"I can watch them, Mom." Calliope brushed herself off. "Hi." She smiled at Oscar.

He tripped in his haste to offer his hand. "Oscar," he said, recovering. "And this is Reata. She's worried about you."

Calliope coaxed the little girl to look at her. "I'm okay, Reata. It's just a bruise." She blushed as she met Oscar's eyes. "I'm Calliope."

"I'm Oscar," he said, again.

"Callie!" Candy stretched out of her father's arms, reaching so hard for her sister that he nearly dropped the little girl.

Angel still looked torn, so Laylea added, "Oscar Luke and I can look after your girls."

"The head councilmember's son?" she asked. His last name did the trick. Angel's concern was wiped away by recognition and then compassion.

Oscar looked over from where Reata was touching the bump on Calliope's forehead. "Yes, ma'am."

"You must know what the plans are for this rehab center. I want to help." Angel rescued Candy from her father's arms and carried her over to Oscar.

"Are you a doctor?" Oscar asked. He tried to focus on Angel, but shot a few disappointed glances at Calliope as she backed away.

"I am," Angel confirmed. "And I have particular skills."

Calliope kept backing away from her mother until she reached Laylea.

"We've lost her," Calliope told Laylea. She yelled, "Coy, let the cute boy go and come play with me."

The butterfly fluttered over, did a figure eight around Calliope's two buns, and flitted away to explore the art supplies. Calliope blew a raspberry after her and winced.

"Does that hurt?" Laylea peered at her scratched up face. There wasn't any blood, but the lump on her forehead wasn't the only bruising.

"Yeah," she admitted, "kinda."

"Can you shift to heal it?"

Calliope grimaced as she shook her head. "I haven't pupated yet."

Laylea wasn't sure what to say to that. She decided to let her dog instincts take over and simply said, "I don't know what that means. I didn't grow up in a shifter family."

"Really? Mami isn't a shifter either. Pupating is a butterfly thing. I just turned fifteen, so I might not ever," she explained with a frown before changing the subject. "Think they're going to first aid?"

She watched Ned as he walked away from the still-arguing Betts parents with their daughter in his arms.

"I hope so. You wanna go to first aid?"

"Don't tell my mom," Calliope clocked her mother and her father, both too busy to hear her, before she admitted, "but, yeah."

"I won't tell." Laylea led her after Ned.

"I heard there are caramel apples?" Calliope said hopefully. "Maybe we could stop there first?"

Laylea switched directions. "Good choice. I know right where they are."

Calliope called over her shoulder as she followed, "Mami, I'm running away with the circus."

Angel called back, "*Si, cariño.* Be careful around the elephants."

15

Sugar-high kids raced through the zoo, competing at some booths and crafting at others, gathering items for Benny's scavenger hunt, and generally losing their minds with freedom from parents and from fear of shifting. The sheer number of animals running free in the zoo, even if they were popping in and out of human, made Laylea feel warm and fuzzy. This was how a zoo should be.

Though it was all making her body want to go hog wild, literally as well as figuratively.

She would almost feel grateful to be wearing a stasis band if it didn't keep electrocuting her. The little sparks weren't actually all that bad. It was the lingering feeling of distress that built up with each zap. There was a chance her plan to steal one and wear it all the time was a bad idea, not forgetting Professor Wanja didn't even believe it would work with her collar on. Considering it never shifted with her like her other clothes, he might be right.

An elephant trunk nudged Laylea and Calliope aside. Daniel trumpeted at them as he, Lisa, and Theresa galloped by, children clinging to their backs and squealing for them to run faster.

"Is it like this downstairs?" Calliope asked through a mouthful of caramel apple. "In school?" she clarified.

"Not exactly." Laylea recalled the first non-wolf Wilding. The zoo sparked with a similar we're-breaking-rules kind of joyous energy. "Why aren't you in school?"

Calliope shrugged. "I might not be a shifter."

"Because your mom isn't?" Laylea asked.

"Right. And if I am, my parents want me to pupate at home, in our garden. You never know how long you're gonna be in the chrysalis."

"The what?"

Calliope laughed. "Cocoon, basically. Coy pupated for months. When she came out, she insisted we celebrate all our birthdays and the Fourth of July since she'd missed them. Gram says Poppa pupated for two years. He emerged to find he had a whole new baby brother."

She kept talking as they strolled along the path between the Waterfowl Lagoon and the South Lawn stopping to watch the competitions. At the pace they were going, the party would be over before they ever made it to First Aid. Laylea got the sense that Calliope was talking to cover her fear that she would never go butterfly.

When Calliope took a breath, Laylea confessed, "I thought I was just a really smart dog until I was eleven. And then I thought that I only turned human because my brother did a spell on me. He's a witch."

"Oh my god. It is so fun that everybody knows about witches and magic now!" Calliope squealed.

"You knew?" Laylea asked, genuinely surprised.

Calliope opened her mouth to respond and shoved the caramel apple in instead. Her face scrunched up as she chewed.

"It's okay. I get about not sharing someone else's secrets." That was an understatement. "It is cool to be able to talk about it. Although, I didn't know that shifters didn't know, so everyone downstairs thought I was crazy when I mentioned magic."

Calliope laughed. They stopped to watch Harper improvise a puppet show with some kids and the puppets they'd just built at Raederie's booth.

"Hey," Calliope said as they moved on. "My friend says that black cats screw with magic. But Oscar Luke was wearing one of those bracelets. How does that work?"

Laylea stopped walking. It was an excellent question. "I think," she began, "it works because he put it on when he was human."

But Tessa had hers on her cat paw.

Brenda had insisted it was good luck to have a black cat at a Halloween party. How she'd bribed the introvert to pose with kids and pumpkins, Laylea had no idea.

Maybe Tessa could help her get her stasis band off.

"Hi. Wanna cast your hands and your paws or talons or claws?" An adorable boy with a crooked smile and caterpillar eyebrows stepped into their path. Laylea had never seen him before.

"Cast them in what?" Calliope asked.

"Plaster," the boy said. He stepped back to show them the rows and rows of plaster prints curing on a table in KC's craft booth. "Or would you like to attempt identifying animal feet in exchange for tickets? If you win enough, you could even visit Wizard Wanja's Magical Costume Emporium."

"Who are you?" Laylea blurted out.

The kid laughed. Despite looking about the same age as them, his blue eyes sparkled with as much wonder as the littlest kids. "I'm Norman. KC just rescued a kid from the swans. She's taking him to first aid, or the primate house. I'm not sure which."

Norman ran a hand along the short braids on the back of his head as he glanced down the path both ways. His light brown curls were plaited in two double pigtails just the way KC wore her hair before she cut it. It wasn't really long enough and loose hairs stuck out everywhere.

"What's Wizard Wanja's thingie thingie?" Calliope asked.

Impossibly, Norman's eyes glistened brighter. He bent close to them, said, "That," and pointed.

The center of the South Lawn featured a platform hidden with curtains. Animals of all shapes and sizes cavorted on the lawn dressed in decadent fabrics with gems in their fur and feathers. A winged horse pranced and soared around the platform, preening at his rainbow-colored tail and mane in the many mirrors arranged on the lawn.

"Is that a..." Laylea began.

"Pegasus?" Calliope screeched.

They were across the path and stumbling through the grass before Laylea realized they were moving.

Griff emerged from the tent, shoving his knit hat on over his feathered head. He looked up at a pair of girls circling higher and higher, their arms spread wide, flying-squirrel membranes fluttering at their sides as they soared up over a third girl dancing on goat legs and strumming a lyre.

"Not so high," Griff yelled.

The sky flashed and the squirrel-girls screamed, more with glee than fear.

With Professor Wanja's help, Dizzy and Ms. Crow had created a magical ceiling to keep planes and the people living in high rises nearby from seeing into the zoo. Apparently, it also kept kids from flying away.

"What is going on?" Calliope's awe matched Laylea's.

"I've never seen anything like this." She yelled, "Griff!"

He spun so fast the bobbles hanging off his hat hit him in the face.

"Hey, Lee!" Griff waved to her. "I've found my people!" He gestured at the mythical satyr playing pan pipes for the pegasus.

"I see."

As they reached the platform, Laylea explained to Calliope, "Griff is a gryphon."

"Is that your real name?" she asked, giggling.

Griff nodded ruefully. "My mom thinks she's funny."

Calliope moaned in sympathy. "She should meet my mom."

"What," Laylea asked, "is going on?"

Before Griff could answer, a thump inside the pavilion drew him away.

He quickly returned, helping Dr. Tippleston navigate her way through the curtains without messing up her elaborate Chinese head-dress. Her face was painted white in the same Japanese Noh fashion that Madam Hu favored.

A pang struck Laylea at the thought of their landlady. She'd invited Bailey to the party, but her brother was too busy with his new internship.

The curtains kept fluttering behind the doctor until she moved forward, freeing her fluffy dog tail to wag through her wide pant legs.

Laylea gasped. That annoying spark bit her wrist and she clawed at the stasis band. Why hadn't the doctor told her she was a domestic dog shifter, too?

"Thank you, Griff." Dr. Tipp kept hold of Griff's hand as enormous dragonfly wings spread from her shoulder blades. They caught the breeze and she floated down from the platform while Griff took the stairs. He had to steady her when her hooves hit the grass.

"Is she a true shifter?" Calliope breathed, awed. "I thought they were a myth."

Laylea didn't answer. She couldn't speak, couldn't move.

"Lee," Dr. Tipp released Griff's hand to run her hands along the high waist of her hanbok. "Are you having a fabulous day?"

Laylea could only nod.

The doctor spun around. "I'm amazing, aren't I?"

"Yes, ma'am." Griff caught her as she stumbled. "Use your wings."

"How is this possible?" Laylea's question came out a bit hysterical. She gestured wildly at the mythical creatures surrounding them, at the doctor's wings, tail, and hooves.

"Quan said this is a thing they do at witch funerals," Griff explained. "It takes a lot of emotional energy to do this kind of magic, I guess."

"And he rightly assumed we'd have enough energy here, today," Dr. Tippleston said, the joy dimming in her eyes as she saw something on the path. "Not all happy energy," she added on a sigh.

A pack of barely-costumed preteens jeered and threw handfuls of popcorn at a passing parade of toddlers dancing around a wheelchair. The middle-aged woman in the chair snatched a kernel out of the air and popped it in her mouth, shouting a thank you.

"What's their problem?" Calliope asked.

"The little ones are all wolf kids," Griff answered. "Mariella deRio volunteered to babysit them."

"Where are their parents?"

Laylea knew that one. "Councilmember Angelica deRio is hosting a cocktail party in the Conservatory."

They watched Mariella distract the young werewolves by popping into her hummingbird form and darting through their ranks. Two of the older littles fought over which of them got to push the empty wheelchair. In the end, despite how spare the chair was, it took both of them.

After a beat, Griff said, "Quan said it takes all the emotions to dress a person in the right masquerade."

Calliope turned to Dr. Tipp and gushed, "You're like every Asian fashion 'do' all rolled into one!"

"Well," Dr. Tipp said, "a few." She added solemnly, "To honor all my ancestors. Ooh." She grimaced when she caught a look at Calliope's face. "We should get you cleaned up. What happened to you?"

"I fell. Can I go in there first?" Calliope asked, her eyes glued to the magically glittering curtain.

"How many tickets have you won?" Griff asked.

"Calliope and her sisters just got here," Laylea explained.

"I'm Dr. Tipp." The doctor introduced herself. "Come with me. We'll win you some tickets on the way to first aid."

"Thanks." Calliope stuck her fist out. "It was really nice to meet you, Lee."

Laylea bumped it with her own. "You, too." As the girl followed Dr. Tippleston, her costume wings bouncing beside the doctor's temporarily real wings, Laylea called out, "I hope you pupate soon so you can come to school."

Calliope walked backwards to reply, "I hope I pupate at all."

"See ya." Laylea glanced over at KC's booth where Norman was helping a small elephant delicately step in a bucket. She asked Griff, "Do you know who that is?"

"No. Never seen him before. He's been helping KC for a while. You and Oscar need me?"

"Yeah, he might," Laylea said, her mind turning back to her quest. The party was ending soon. She needed to figure out a way to steal a stasis band before she went back downstairs. "Right now, I gotta go find me a black cat."

"Oscar is—"

"I'm looking for a different cat." As she said it, a cloud of pink rose in a flutter from the Waterfowl Lagoon. One candy covered flamingo chased after a pack of little kids who were, in turn, chasing after a tiny black feline. "That cat. See you later!"

She dashed across the lawn, tracking Rehyan following the kids chasing Tessa.

16

Running through the zoo was more fun in dog form. Brenda was always harassing Laylea to work out in her human form, but it was too boring. Not to mention when she tried to run with only two legs, she had a tendency to fall on her face.

Chasing Rehyan in his flamingo form, she was wishing she'd listened to Brenda. When she lost him, rounding the Kovler Seal Pool, she followed the sound of the screaming children.

If those kids managed to catch Tessa, the poor introvert was going to explode from cuddling. That worked perfectly for Laylea's plan. She would rescue her from the kids. In gratitude, Tessa would break the stasis band magic, allowing Laylea to take it off. Then she would sneak down the seal pool stairway and stash the band in her pod before returning upstairs to help take down the temporary walls.

If she could only catch up to them.

She rounded the seal pool stadium, panting, and darted through a pack of adults two-fisting it with candy apples and hot cider. They startled at her cry of delight upon seeing the kids turn left down the path to the bear enclosure.

The bear, Toby, was her favorite resident of the zoo. He'd saved her life a few times, was nice to her friends, and he was protecting the phoenix egg like it was his own.

Laylea lowered her head and ran.

She only made it a few yards before smacking into Rehyan.

The two tumbled to the grass. Rehyan's wings fluttered, sending pink feathers flying. Laylea rolled until she smacked her head against the statues of KC's ancestors. The wolves stared at her with frozen bronze judgment. They clearly disapproved.

Her wrist sparked, shooting ache through her body.

"Sorry." She came to her feet spouting profuse apologies. "Sorry, Rehyan."

The lanky bird hopped forward and knocked her over again. He cawed a crackling sound that was definitely a laugh, then ran down the path and launched into the air. Flying low, he wove through the trees back in the direction of the waterfowl lagoon.

Laylea stood, again, and brushed herself off. Her head spun; the spot on her skull where she'd hit KC's uncle throbbed. That was a flaw in the stasis band design. Without it, she'd have shifted and healed.

She wasn't accustomed to pain lasting more than an instant. Was this how normal people felt? Her eyes watered as she stupidly poked at the bump swelling beneath her hair.

The path was the only way in or out of Bear Hollow, so she didn't bother running. She made a new plan as she walked.

The kids would more than likely circle the play area and come running back toward her. She could distract them, giving Tessa a chance to escape. But then she would have to track her down again. Better, she could scoop Tessa up and point the kids toward Rehyan. Of course, that would involve holding a testy cat.

Laylea stopped walking. Neither idea was very good. She was normally much better at plans. Had she injured her brain?

Up ahead, Toby roared.

The panicked cry cut off suddenly and then a dozen little kids in filthy, sticky costumes came screaming down the path. They tore past her, some yelling warnings, most just giggling. No cat led them. No cat followed.

Bear Hollow felt unnaturally silent as Laylea approached. Miro sat on one of the log benches, gasping and furiously massaging one thigh. On the far side of the chain link portion of Toby's enclosure, the bear stood, arms in the air and so still he might have been on display at a hunting lodge. Only his eyes gave him away as the bear tried to follow Tessa's progress, clawing her way up his chest and across his shoulders, sniffing him.

"Tessa, you've met Toby before, haven't you?" Laylea asked, trying with her teasing tone to let the bear know he needn't be so nervous. He didn't relax.

"I haven't," Miro panted. "I've heard about him though."

"How did Tessa get in there?"

"She climbed the fence and jumped onto the bear's head."

Toby's white ear twitched. Tessa batted at it. The bear's eyes shot wide.

"Tessa, you want some help getting out?" Laylea hurried to the fence. "Hi Toby. She won't hurt you." As she passed Miro, she noted that he was staring at his stasis band in annoyance.

"You injured?" she asked.

Miro grunted.

"Why not have Tessa glitch the stasis band?" she suggested in what she hoped was a casual tone.

"Can't," Miro mumbled. "Wanja tested them on her."

Laylea growled, deep in her human throat. She rubbed at the bump on her head. Mistake. Grimacing made her head hurt even more.

"Ow." She told Toby, "Pain hurts."

He stared back at her, still wisely not moving a muscle.

"So much of life is learning to handle pain." Professor Wanja strode into Bear Hollow, his long, velvet robe glittering from more than the beaded designs.

Without her collar, Laylea shouldn't have been able to see the many colors of magic coating his clothes, skin, and hair, but there it was glittering like the dusting of snow they'd cleared from the paths that morning.

"Hi," she said. Her mind raced through possible ways of getting the witch to give her a stasis band.

"I've been looking for you, Lee."

Tessa leapt from Toby's head to the top of the fence. She clambered over, lost her grip, and fell. Being a cat, she landed buttered side up and tore past the professor with Miro hard on her heels. Her fur stood up like spikes, making her appear twice her size and fearsome to touch. Laylea was willing to bet Tessa wouldn't mind looking that fierce all the time. People rarely made the mistake of calling her cute twice, but still.

"Can't blame her," Wanja said, watching the two flee. "I'm told magic feels like an ice storm to cats in general. I imagine it's worse for the mythic black ones, what with their inherent power."

"Black cats are like natural-born witches?" Laylea asked. Her interest distracted her from her wounds and the repeated shocks from her band.

Toby had dropped to his butt once Tessa disappeared from sight. He looked up as if he were curious to know the answer as well.

"Rather the opposite," Wanja said. At her confused look, he appeared to consider how best to explain himself.

With the Tessa solution off the table, Laylea was in no rush. Standing wasn't sustainable though. Her legs wobbled in time to the throbbing in her head, so she sat in the warm spot Miro had left on the log bench.

"Have you studied Newton?" This was a question that Wanja wouldn't have asked her if she were a boy, but he was learning.

"Yes." Laylea nodded and regretted it. Her vision wobbled

" 'For every action there is an equal and opposite reaction.' "

"Yes." The mere wispy beginnings of an idea blossomed. Maybe she could convince Professor Wanja to give her a stasis band by engaging him in a discussion of science and magic, a topic she knew a lot about thanks to her mother who ascribed over half her magical accomplishments to science when everyone around could see that didn't make sense.

She blinked. Professor Wanja had asked her a question. "Yes." It seemed a safe enough answer.

And it was.

"So, because nature gives most creatures common magic," he said, "she gifts a few rare creatures uncommon magic. And like natural witches wear their magic close to the skin, so do black cats. But because they are so rare, their magic is stronger. When common and uncommon magic meet, it's like oil and water, if the oil were on fire."

Toby suddenly howled like he was on fire. The sound and the description tore Laylea back through time to a sterile lab when pain was common in her world, her puppy body strapped to a cold metal table.

Licorice filled the air, turning her stomach. The furless face of Walter blocked the burning brightness of the Eye light.

"Stop howling, Rhemy." The licorice breath turned away to waft over the pen holding her brothers. Laylea relaxed, too young to know that a face turned away didn't mean the person had gone away. Walter shot a burning slime into her thigh. Laylea howled. Her blood boiled, racing back to her heart, failing to outrun the injection. Rhemy's howl broke to a pitiful, wannabe-fierce barking.

Walter bent between her and the light, his licorice breath also smelling faintly of apples.

"Lee, have you gone on safari?" Professor Wanja's dark face filled her vision, blocking out the lights coming on in the city.

Toby cried out again, shaking the fence.

The professor sat beside her. "I can go on when I get to talking magical theory."

Laylea raised a hand to her head as the memory faded. The memory was proof that she had felt pain before. Shock that she could have forgotten was quickly followed by fear. Could Walter have done this to her? Was he the reason she kept shifting into other animals?

The Narnia-esque streetlamp in the middle of the clearing turned on. It startled Laylea awake. She blinked her vision clear and made a vague reassuring gesture at Toby. Her band sent a reflection of the lamp's light flashing across his curious face, illuminating a spot of red on his white ear.

"Stasis bands are made with common magic," she muttered.

"Yes," the professor confirmed, peering at her with concern.

The silver band felt suddenly heavier. She could feel the wrongness of it irritating her skin, but just barely. How much worse was it for Tessa?

"Her stasis band must feel awful. Why would she agree to come upstairs?"

"Tessa? Oh, hers is different, as is Oscar's," Professor Wanja reassured her. "I wouldn't ask that of them anymore than I would ask you to wear a bracelet of spikes."

"I hit my head," she said, out of nowhere, realizing only after the words were out that she was attempting to play on his sympathy. "I usually shift and heal when I get hurt."

"Yes, that must be unusual. If you need to go downstairs and shift, you should go."

"Couldn't you just take it off for a minute to let me shift and shift back," Laylea asked, desperately, her hand going to the bump again. She barely stopped herself from touching it.

"Alas, I cannot," Professor Wanja tucked his hands into the pockets of his robe and sighed. "Remember, when you put it on you agreed it would not come off while you are upstairs."

While she was upstairs.

All she had to do was get downstairs and she could steal the band.

17

As Laylea's mother Sher had explained it, Will magic depended on the target's desires, whether acting against them or in line with them. Will magic was always enacted on the witch herself or another sentient creature. She'd used a lot of Will magic on the super soldiers she created for the Consortium.

For her protection, her brother Bailey had trapped Laylea in The Office with a spell that wouldn't let her leave as long as she wanted to. She'd accidentally defeated that spell by falling asleep in Ned's knitting bag. It wouldn't have worked if it had been her intention for Ned to carry her out while she was asleep because that would have been her will.

But she didn't have to defeat the stasis band. If she could sneak past the guards and get downstairs, she could just take it off.

She stood up. Bear Hollow spun around her. Toby darted to the fence, the motion throwing her more off balance.

She sat. Toby gripped the chain-link wall of his cage as if to climb over, his eyes pinned on Laylea.

Professor Wanja laid a gentle hand on her back. "Would you like me to escort you to Dr. Tippleston?"

"No, thank you."

Laylea kept her eyes on Toby. She had to. Her vision had tunneled down so that she could only see his nose. The spot of blood from Tessa's claws had already dried and flaked away.

She had to make a plan. But it was hard to think with the throbbing in her head and the ache seeping through her bones.

Getting downstairs only meant that she could get the band off.

She didn't want to take it off. She wanted to wear it permanently.

Thoughts crowded her head in that way that invited a shift to slower, simpler dog thinking. The band sparked her wrist. She wrapped a hand around it and took a slow breath.

That worked. She found the answer. When she got the band off, she would move it to her ankle and then start wearing socks to hide it. It was such an easy solution. She grinned. Her shoulders dropped and she consciously relaxed the rest of her body.

Toby grumbled. The fence rattled as he removed his claws and lumbered over to the fake rock.

"I heard this gentleman is called the depressed bear."

Laylea jumped at Professor Wanja's voice. She'd forgotten he was there.

She really did need to get downstairs and heal her brain. Maybe she could have KC put the band on her dog leg and she could stay dog. But dogs didn't wear socks.

She tried to focus as the professor added, "The poor soul looks haunted."

"Toby is depressed and haunted," she said. "The whole zoo is haunted."

"You can see ghosts?" Professor Wanja asked, his gray eyebrows lifting and brightening his whole face.

"Only when I work at it." She needed to work at standing so she could get downstairs.

"That is a type of magic I have never been good at. I wonder if you'd be willing to do a presentation on it in my magical symposium?" His tone held a hint of a larger question, but Laylea couldn't quite understand what.

"Sure, it's just a ritual of refocusing. It's hardly magic at all."

With a glint in his eye, he asked, "Would you like to learn new types of magic?"

"What do you mean?" She'd definitely like to learn how to defeat Will magic or how to heal like her mom could or how to see what Grandpa was up to.

"I'm tapping you to join my magical symposium, Lee." Professor Wanja said with a laugh. "Caliban gave me permission to invite a limited number of likely witches for the class."

"Oh. No, thank you." Laylea stood. She wanted to run, but stayed where she was, hoping the spinning would stop. "I think I need to go downstairs and shift."

She absolutely could not join his symposium. It wouldn't be hard to hide a stolen stasis band from other teachers. But she didn't think she could hide it from a practiced witch like Wanja. For that matter, she was going to have to find a way to swap out of his shifting class.

"This is... a... rare opportunity, Lee." He stumbled on his words, shocked. "You obviously have a powerful family, and you learned their techniques as another child might learn a parent's mother tongue."

Laylea wasn't sure what to say. She couldn't join the symposium if she wanted any hope of keeping a stolen stasis band. But more than that, she didn't want more magic in her life. She'd grown up with two witches, both of whom had hurt people with their magic, hurt them badly. And the Mom and Bailey were both good people.

A new voice in the deepening gloom put words to her feelings.

"I don't want that kind of power over my friends and neighbors." Ned Biggerson said as he and Bitters came around the last turn of the path.

"Well, neither do I." Bitters replied. "I'm a bouncer by trade, a bodyguard. I'm trained to physically intervene." Without looking around, Bitters walked straight to Toby's enclosure, telling the bear, "You know what I'm talking about, don't you, Toby?"

Toby shuffled to the far side of his rock.

"He doesn't," Ned said, joining the enforcer at the fence. "He wasn't trained. He was born to physically intimidate others, like me."

"Sure," Bitters conceded. "But you don't."

Ned said sadly, "I do."

"At least you're not poisonous."

"That I know of," Ned retorted. "Never bitten anybody. And you've never poisoned anyone."

"I've paralyzed a few."

Ned scoffed. "Temporarily."

"And you're leagues smarter than me," Bitters said, changing tack.

Ned grunted, "Am not."

"More thoughtful, at least. I don't..." Bitters took a breath, let it out. He leaned his forehead against the chain link. "I don't want to be the enforcer."

That was it.

Laylea faced the professor. "I don't want to be a witch."

Bitters spun around. His cheeks glowed with embarrassment. With a wry chuckle, he said, "Didn't see you there."

Still facing Toby, Ned said, "Team Wyrdos could use a witch, don't you think?"

"They've got Bailey," she retorted. Although they didn't, really. When Diejuste had appointed the team members, Bailey had not been tapped by the goddess.

Ned knew it. He turned, adjusting his knitting bag on his shoulder as he did. When he caught her eyes, she looked away.

"I've seen what that kind of power can lead to," she said. "Even accidentally. And I don't want it."

"The fact that you don't want the power, is one of the things that makes you worthy of it," Enforcer Brewster told her.

She rolled her eyes, forgetting he was an adult and had the power to order her disenhanced. "You're just saying that because it makes you feel better about running away from responsibility."

Bitters' mouth dropped open. Ned nearly smiled, then his face drooped with angst. He turned back to Toby.

The bear climbed onto his rock. He tilted his head the same way dog Laylea would, as if it could help him understand what they were saying.

"The symposium won't give you more power," Professor Wanja

told her. "It will simply teach you how to control the power you do have."

" 'The more magic a witch learns,' " Laylea quoted, " 'the more easily they are able to access the power in the world.' I was raised by a witch, Professor."

The professor blinked at her, his mouth open as if to respond, but couldn't find the words.

"I don't think you're allowed to talk to the enforcer that way," Bitters finally responded.

"Ms. Crow said we should always tell the enforcer the truth," Laylea responded, the pressure in her head apparently draining her sense of self-preservation.

"Hard to argue with the dog," Ned muttered. "You'll learn."

"She's the dog shifter?" Bitters' eyebrows rose into his hairline. "Morioka's friend?"

Laylea looked up, automatically. No dragon. No bat.

Her head spun, but she didn't dare sit down. She'd never get up again. She headed for the fence, wrapping her hand through chain link right above where some troublemakers had planted catnip. Still hunched on his boulder, Toby looked up into the sky, too.

Morioka was a literal demon. But she managed to use her power for good.

Laylea's eyes latched onto the bear's white ear, shooting her back once again to the cold, anesthetic rooms where she and her brothers were born, where they were trapped, where they were tortured.

That was what her father had chosen to do with his power over them. If there was any chance that sort of evil was inherited, Laylea couldn't risk it.

She was no Morioka, not yet.

She straightened, facing the two big men. "Either one of you would be a vast improvement on the last enforcer. I get why you don't want the job, Bitters… Mr. Brewster. I'm just scared that someone who does want the job will get it if you don't stay."

She turned to Professor Wanja, the movement making her head swim. "Thank you for the compliment. You seem like a really good teacher. I just... I'm afraid and fear leads to bad choices." Sher was in her head again. "At least that's what my mother said. So, how about instead of no, I say, not now?"

"I can respect that," the professor agreed, though his eyes dulled with a frown.

"Thanks. Send my love to everyone at The Office," she said to Ned, releasing the fence. She grabbed it again when the world tilted. Covering, she called, "Be safe, Toby."

To her surprise, Toby rumbled in response. He pounded his paws on the hollow boulder.

Ned and Bitters backed away.

Startled by their reaction, the bear slumped again, hanging his head.

"Do you need help getting downstairs?" Professor Wanja asked, standing.

"I can make it." Laylea pushed off the fence. Her first steps were not straight, but she didn't let that stop her.

"What's wrong?" Ned looked closely at her for the first time. "You look pale."

She tried to joke, "I live underground. Of course I'm pale." It sounded hollow to her ringing ears. But the men all accepted her denial, or at least respected her independence. She walked away, muttering mainly to herself, "I just need to shift."

The stasis band sparked and that all-over ache increased.

Step one, make it to the end of the path. Then it was a quick right and down the ramp into the Kovler Seal Pool.

Luck favored her. Entering the seal pool, she passed the young wolf pack with the guard stationed there helping Mariella shoo them up the ramp from the underwater viewing arena.

As soon as they were past, Laylea doubled back and took two short sets of stairs down to the ladies' room foyer. She ignored the restroom, instead facing the dank alcove under the stairs and an old, splintered door. Though the door promised to lead only to a closet with cleaning supplies, it was protected by a chain with an ancient metal sign stating "employees only" for anybody who didn't get the message from the chain.

It was exactly the sort of disguise that would keep anybody from finding the secret entrance to the empty Gryphon dorm.

Slipping under the chain should have been easy, but her head pounded and her stomach threatened revolt when she tried it. After a few breaths to steady herself, Laylea sat on the cold floor, crawled under the chain and on through the swinging grate at the bottom of the door. Tears blinded her. Flares of brightness filled her head. But she made it.

She curled up on the worn floor at the top of an endless circular staircase and let the smells of well-used wood, wrought iron, and countless feet, paws, talons, and shoes wrap her in a comforting scent-scape.

Once her heart had slowed to a reasonable gallop, she pulled at the stasis band.

It didn't come off. No matter how she dug at the layers of bracelet or at her skin, she couldn't free herself.

She wasn't really downstairs yet.

After a quick and quiet grumble at the unfairness of it all, she rolled herself to a sitting position.

Ignoring the strange sharp pounding of her heart in her skull, she used the wrought iron railing to pull herself to her ungainly human feet.

She tackled the first step of the winding staircase.

The heel of her comfy, paint-splashed uggs caught on the upper step as she shifted her weight.

Grabbing for the railing and missing, Laylea tumbled, ass over teakettle, down the stairs.

18

Drums woke Laylea. In all her adventures—flying to wooded wonderlands with the Dad, napping with sick animals in her mother's clinic, even solving supernatural crimes with Team Wyrdos—Laylea had never before been woken by a drum corps. She thanked Diejuste, the only god she knew personally, that there were no bugles.

A few more breaths into wakefulness brought an awareness of deep cold and pain throughout her human body. That realization shot her into full consciousness.

She never woke human. She rarely went to sleep human.

One boot was gone. Her bare foot had caught in the decorative swirls of the guardrails halfway down the wooden steps. A new lump had mirrored the original on the other side of her skull. Each knee and knuckle throbbed along with them in time to her heart, which itself was the cause of the drum corps' poor performance. Her heart jumped and struggled to keep pounding.

Laylea really needed to shift. Breathing deeply, she turned to memories to dull the pain of the present.

She focused on her brothers' heavy bodies squirming against hers as they all fought for a place against their mama's warm belly. The scents of sweet milk and musky brothers gave way to lavender soap, plane fuel, and safety in the Dad's lap ten thousand miles in the air, which gave over to the heavy warmth of well-worked wool, stale beer, spicy glög, and contraband rawhides snuck into her dog bed in the back of Seb's bar.

The comfort of these memories carried her on as she dragged herself from one smooth wooden step down to the next, and the next.

Stars lightened the darkness from the skylight overhead as twilight deepened. It would be a while before she was missed. Oscar would wonder where she was as he painted a clear topcoat over the kids' art. But he knew her goal for the day and wouldn't ask anybody other than KC.

She hadn't seen KC since lunchtime when they'd run from booth to booth like little kids themselves, trying their hands at the games and contests. Griff had said the strange guy, Norman, had been helping KC with her booth all day. But he hadn't been there at lunch time. Was he a kid she knew from before? If so, why hadn't she ever mentioned him?

Norman would tell KC that Laylea had gone to the transformation booth. Professor Wanja would tell her… what? That she'd left to go downstairs? If they were worried, they'd start looking for her in the Medical Wing. Nobody would ever think to look for her in the stairwell above Gryphon Dorm. If she didn't heal herself, she was going to die, right there, alone.

She had to shift. In order to shift, she had to get the stasis band off. In order to get the stasis band off, she had to get downstairs. And she wasn't convinced it would come off even then.

Her thoughts were circling. She paused in her descent, leaned against the cold iron railing, and breathed in a memory of the first time Griff held her hand: the earthy scent of the sub-basement, the pressure of his fingers entangled with hers, and the giggle in her chest echoing the sparkling magic all around them.

She opened her eyes to find three doors swimming in her vision. She focused on the middle one, following Jimmy Stewart's guidance from *It's a Wonderful Life* as she tugged off her remaining ugg, then dragged her aching body down the final steps.

Slipping her hand into the wooden glove of the locking mechanism, she felt each of the knots with her fingers and thumb. Then she took a breath and squeezed. The lock clicked. She snatched her hand away as counterweights lowered on either side of the door, raising it to reveal a tunnel of dirt and stone. With a whimper of relief, Laylea slipped through into darkness.

She walked the walls of the thin tunnel with her hands, keeping herself upright. A dim light grew as she progressed until she stood at an archway. Before her lay the criss-crossing beams, stained glass, and treetops of Gryphon dorm. She stepped forward.

And was thrown backwards. She lay on the ground, twitching and desperate.

She had to shift to exit the tunnel. If she couldn't remove the stasis band, she was going to die there.

Warm, comforting memories wouldn't help. She needed the power of the Mom. The Mom, who kept her alive when she was a puppy, who was fighting to destroy the Consortium not only to stop them using her work but to stop Walter from capturing Laylea and her brothers. The Mom who, despite the protective cage around her heart, had loved Laylea so much she made a lizard stuffy to comfort and protect her.

Laylea rolled to her belly. She closed her eyes and breathed in the scent of the lizard made from the Dad's old bandana. She exhaled her desire to remove the band and shift, to be free of pain, healed, whole, her original canine self.

The silver band unwrapped from her arm and snapped closed again around her canine wrist. All the pain vanished. She opened her eyes.

Before her lay the criss-crossing beams, stained glass, and treetops of Gryphon dorm.

She leapt to her paws and bent in a celebratory downward dog, opening her jaws wide and adding a squeaking yawn to the full-body stretch.

The lingering memory of the drum corps made a sliver of Laylea want to curl up and nap. But she was a dog. She had succeeded. She made it downstairs, and she had a stasis band.

Her tail thumped once on the packed dirt and stone of the tunnel. She launched herself out of the passageway and ran along the beams to the ladder formed by tree branches and clambered down, awkwardly, ungracefully, and joyfully, falling the last ten feet onto a mound of mossy Scottish grass.

She rolled through lakes of leaves, leapt to her paws, and kicked at the ground in a show of dominance. She had survived. She'd saved herself and stolen a stasis band. Laylea Hillen could not be defeated!

Her stomping, kicking dance awakened the fresh green scents of the moss as well as the rich death-scent of fallen leaves. She reveled in the crackling sounds and zoomed from pile to pile, bouncing off tree trunks, occasionally shaking to feel the flap of her own velvety ears and to send the sticks and leaves stuck in her fur flying.

The ground rumbled. Laylea froze, mid-dance.

A not-so-distant set of gears groaned into motion, operating the official entrance to the dorm.

Over on the non-forest side of the dorm, a wooden panel in the stone wall split in half and slid open, revealing the school corridor outside. Laylea dashed farther into the trees. She ducked under a bush behind a wide trunk as the distinct smell of wolves wafted into the courtyard.

"Howe, stop being a pup. Get in here." Jonathan's aggressive pheromones crushed the triumphant smells of infinite rebirth Laylea had kicked up from the trees.

Her tail tucked tight against her belly. Adrenaline spiked through her, preparing her to run despite there being nowhere to go. The old, long-repaired wound to her hip pulsed a reminder of being kicked. She burrowed deeper into the bush, where she could see the wolves but they couldn't see her. As humans, they shouldn't be able to smell her either, especially with the reek of unregulated anger coming off Jonathan.

"What was that noise?"

"Howe. Stop being such a chicken," Jonathan chided. "You're a fucking predator. Act like it."

Laylea scoffed in her mind. Like a predator wouldn't be aware of their surroundings. If Vaughn's human ears were good enough to pick up the whisper-quiet brush of leaves on fur over the ruckus of other wolves entering the dorm, Laylea would rather go hunting with him than Jonathan any day.

"Nobody ever comes here. Right, Big Mo?" Jonathan took in the gorgeous stained-glass ceiling that gave Gryphon dorm the illusion of a sky. He goggled at the rope bridge that crossed over a pond twenty feet down at the center of an amphitheater-like circle of wide tiers arranged with chairs, couches, pillows, and tables for lounging or studying.

In contrast, Mo circled, scanning the dorm with his available senses. "Nobody."

The final werewolf leapt through the opening into the dorm just before the door panel slammed closed. Jase landed on four paws. Laylea cringed. If he were as alert at Mo, his wolf nose couldn't miss her scent, so out of place in this abandoned dorm.

Jonathan jumped at the noise of the door.

Jase jumped in mockery of him. To Laylea's great relief, he shifted human. "Never been to Gryphon before, Jonathan?" he asked, feinting a punch at the younger kid's gut.

Jonathan tackled him.

Big Mo faced the woods, staring nearly directly across the bridge to Laylea's hiding spot, while Jonathan and Jase wrestled on the uneven paving stones of the courtyard.

Laylea took slow, deep breaths, wishing she hadn't shaken the dirt from her champagne-colored fur.

After three breaths, Big Mo walked away. "We can sit over here, Vaughn."

Mo helped Vaughn to the near side of the multi-layered lounging area around the Gryphon dorm pond. After the smoke out last July, kids had been brought there to recover. Empty, the place looked smaller. Vaughn struggled to turn on his crutches. Mo waited patiently and stood ready to catch him as Vaughn lowered himself to a plush if dingy chair in need of reupholstering. Mo took a similar chair beside him.

Vaughn leaned his crutches against the arm of his seat, but they immediately slid to the ground. Carrie dashed in and repositioned them. She kept an eye on the wrestling match between Jase and Jonathan.

Laylea's tail popped up and nearly gave her away. She hadn't seen much of Carrie the past weeks since she'd been busy preparing for Halloween and the wolves weren't allowed to attend.

That hadn't stopped Jimmy from helping. In addition to the eerie music he'd composed and recorded, he'd made treats with Chef Tod, cut out stencils for Benny's pumpkin-carving station, packed supplies for Ali's cookie-decorating booth, filled a hundred balloons with colored chalk, and put finishing touches on dozens of costumes.

Carrie had clearly been otherwise occupied. She'd been working out with Brenda and the Double Deltas since before P2. But whatever she'd been doing since had finally melted the baby fat from her cheeks. She looked sallow, lean, hungry. Laylea realized that she hadn't heard anybody complaining about Carrie stealing food in ages.

The little Mer wolf had cut her hair butch-short and dyed it in shades of white and ginger, reminiscent of KC's wolf fur. Carrie's own pelt was a bright, multi-colored array of tawny shades like Laylea's champagne. Dustin's hair was dyed the same colors. So was Jonathan's.

A sudden blur of motion and sound had Jonathan pinned to the ground.

Carrie shifted. Dustin and Big Mo leapt closer to the fight, though they didn't interfere.

Human Jase's chest heaved with effort. His right arm ended in a paw, claws extended, poking into the flesh of Jonathan's exposed neck.

Blood welled at the point of one sharp claw.

Tension filled the air of the Gryphon courtyard. Laylea's bum hip begged to be stretched, to be flexed, to be iced while she lay in her brother's lap as he read her a book.

She didn't dare move.

Jase growled deep and low, his eyes glowing yellow.

Vaughn's crutches clattered to the stones. Vaughn followed them, crying out in pain.

"See to him," Jase snapped, not taking his eyes off of Jonathan.

Big Mo and Dustin hurried to obey.

Jonathan turned his head, looking away from Jase's eyes. If he'd been paying attention to anything other than the claws at his neck and his own humiliation, he would have seen Laylea's big brown puppy eyes staring back at him from the far side of the pond, only thirty yards away.

As silently as she could, she retreated back under cover of the bush, cursing the curiosity that had almost given her away.

Finally, Jonathan slapped the paving stones twice with an open palm. Fear poured off him along with the anger he'd strolled in with.

Jase's claws disappeared in a flutter of reality and he stood, deliberately turning his back on Jonathan. He strolled over to join the others and draped himself over a swept iron bench with no cushion.

Everybody relaxed, except Jonathan.

19

Laylea breathed deep and quietly where she hid watching the wolves. The air in Gryphon dorm stunk with testosterone but it was fading as Jonathan picked himself up and brushed himself off, trying to hide his humiliation from the others.

Despite his victory, Jase's voice betrayed annoyance as he asked, "Why are we here, Jonathan?"

The defeated wolf hurried to answer. "I got a message from my mom," he said. "The loyal wolves are going to stage a protest in the city next full moon."

Some of the wolves leaned in, eyes darting at Jase who appeared to be examining the ceiling.

"We'll use the distraction to go upstairs and run." Jonathan spoke with confidence, but he remained at a distance, stretching against the bridge. "You got a message out to your grandmother, right Jase?"

"I told her what's going on."

"Great."

Not great. If all their communications were being monitored, how did Jase tell his grandmother what was going on? How did Jonathan get a message from his mother?

Jonathan swiped at the blood on his neck. He only succeeded in spreading it to look as gruesome as Belle's Marie Antoinette makeup. "So, we'll head up to her compound and prep for Grandpa's invasion from there."

"Did you get confirmation?" Dustin asked, bouncing on his toes and shadow boxing at Jonathan as he joined them on the tiers. "Grandpa's really planning to invade Chicago? When're they coming? Are we going to take out the thumpers, too?"

"Of course he's planning to invade." Jonathan scoffed, finally regaining his confidence enough to stroll closer. "But he's not going to write his plans down for anybody to intercept."

"Or tell kids," Jase pointed out, reasonably. "Do you have a plan for handling *this* little problem?" Jase raised a foot in the air. The leg of his uniform fell back, revealing a wide strip of leather wrapped around his ankle. "Cuz we know we can't get them off."

"Magic is bullshit." Jonathan leaned against one of the many statues dotting the tiers. "These don't do anything."

Jase agreed a bit too readily. "Okay. Magic isn't real. When is the next full moon?"

While Jonathan didn't notice Jase's tone, Mo and Carrie both stiffened at his casual reply. Mo raised a hand to the scars on his neck where Ms. Crow had magically healed a ghost wound. He believed in magic.

"November eighteenth, two weeks from Sunday."

"Vaughn, buddy," Jase rolled to look at the wounded wolf who was ashen, both hands gripping the fabric of his seat. "You'll be all healed in two weeks?"

Vaughn shook his head. His nostrils flared as he sucked in a breath. His voice came out as tight as the cords on his neck. "No, Jase. Might get a mobile cast in four weeks. Might get surgery."

"So, how does Vaughn get upstairs, Jonathan? How's he climb the trees, balance across the beams, maneuver through the forced shift tunnel," Jase paused at the groaning grunt Vaughn let out at the word "shift" and then went on, "climb three stories of smooth-as-marble circling stairs, and then make it past the guards and out of the zoo?"

The question hung in silence.

"You know they're watching us, right?" Jase drawled. "Hell, for all we know, Delilah Crow is in here with us now, listening to every word."

Dustin looked around.

Laylea stifled a laugh.

"That's why we need to go sooner rather than later," Jonathan insisted.

"I," Jase retorted, "am not leaving Vaughn behind."

Vaughn caught the emphasis. "You were gonna leave me behind, Jonathan?"

Jonathan straightened from his indolent pose, glaring at Jase.

Jase saved him from having to answer. "Next full moon is gonna be as bad as this one. With you idiots dying your hair to look like Grandpa's fur and all y'all stomping around like toddlers who didn't get a bone, I'd be surprised if they don't stick us in holding like the council wanted."

"What?" Dustin stopped bouncing up and down the steps of the arena.

Everyone except Carrie was equally surprised. Laylea's tail wagged at her success. She tamped it down. Carrie had made that up to keep the wolves from causing too much trouble.

Jase sat up. "Caliban made them agree to the pods."

"Oscar's d… dad was f... fur…" Carrie took a breath and tried different wording. "…real mad."

Benches groaned as the wolves shifted uncomfortably. Being isolated might be unpleasant, but it was better than not being able to shift.

Dustin growled, "Maybe we should tie Oscar up somewhere, see how his daddy treats us then."

His suggestion shocked them all into silence for a beat.

Then Jonathan laughed. Everybody else stared at Dustin in disgust.

"What?" Dustin asked, shifting his weight defensively. "He was all buddy-buddy with us when Denier abducted his daughter."

It was true. It was the reason Mr. Luke used to vote the way

Grandpa wanted, that and the fact that the wolves were keeping Mrs. Luke addicted to N.

But Oscar didn't know any of that when he came to school. He thought the wolves were his friends.

Jase drawled a bland, "Where you thinking of hiding him, Dustin?"

Carrie's face glowed red, but she dropped her gaze as if there were something intensely important at her feet. Mo, for his part, betrayed nothing of what he was thinking.

Vaughn opened his mouth to say something but looked away at the last minute. He adjusted his leg to relieve some pain and only made it worse. The torture on his face hid any other feelings.

Laylea sympathized. While her hip was an old injury, it was twinging like it hadn't since she was eleven. She moved to straighten the leg. The bush rattled.

She froze.

Jase sat up.

Nobody else heard. Jonathan, following Jase's lead, mocked Dustin. Dustin, in turn, handed credit for the idea to his dad. Mo pointed out that the council was reading all their mail and listening in on calls, so why would his dad suggest something so asinine where Councilmember Luke might hear.

Jase stared into the forest.

His nostrils flared.

She closed her eyes and held very still. There was nothing she could do about her scent. She'd just been frolicking about spreading it everywhere. A little extra fear and pain weren't worse than the triumph already all over the grass with bits of her fur.

If she could only shift into a tree, she could really hide. Trees didn't smell like their emotions, so far as she knew. Her fear wouldn't reveal her to Jase, if she were a tree.

Laylea filled her mind with Caliban's pale bark, her wide branches, and tiny pink flowers, then reached for the burn.

"Here's what we're going to do." Jase turned away to face the others.

Jase hadn't seen her. She was safe. She didn't have to shift.

Hope surged in Laylea.

So did the burn. It smoldered and grew, deep in her bones.

"I'll get a message to Grandpa," Jase said. How was he in contact with Grandpa? "Lay it all out for him, what's going on."

Laylea tucked her beloved tail tight against her belly and breathed, deep and slow.

"Since everyone else ran or got arrested, we're all he's got here," Jase went on slowly, making sure they all understood. "He might want us to join him, but he might want us to stay."

The spinning ball of heat in Laylea's bones didn't care that she didn't have to shift. It spread to her muscles, through her blood.

No, I don't want to shift, she thought. *I take it back. I want to be me.*

"We won't go anywhere until we get his orders. Until then, we play nice. Really nice. We volunteer to help with this New Year's party, act like good pups. Carrie, Dustin, Jonathan, fix your hair."

The burn hit her hip. She held her breath to stifle a cry.

The pain would mark her with a scent no predator could ignore. There was no way even the distracted, human-shaped wolves could miss it much longer. She had to calm down.

Her tail drooped as she focused on relaxing her muscles. Thinking about her butt muscles reminded her of Dr. Tipp's trick for unwanted feelings and worries. It might work for pain, too.

Closing her eyes, she imagined the diamond over her third eye and drew a doorknob on it. With a deep, slow breath, she shoved at the memory of steel-toed boot hitting bone into her birthmark and slammed the door. Hardknock hadn't known who he was when he did that. He hadn't meant to hurt her. The crazy hermit had saved her life once, too. She focused on that, on his good intentions.

"We buckle down through this full moon, behave, voluntarily confine ourselves to our pods," Jase was saying. "So when Grandpa calls for us, we'll be able to escape. Now, get back to your dorms before Barret-face comes looking."

They were leaving. She heard them standing, grunting, gathering themselves. She traced a silver line around her birthmark and inhaled.

Everything was going to be okay. They'd go away. She'd shift. The pain would go away.

"W… w… where are you g… going, J… Ja… Ja—?" Carrie's stutter increased made her nearly impossible to understand.

"I gotta take a piss." Jase's voice was closer to her.

Laylea's eyes shot open to see Jase not leaving.

Not leaving.

He was crossing the bridge that led to the trees, to her side of the pond.

"It's a dorm, Jase," Big Mo shouted. "They have urinals in the podroom."

"And gr.. grass," Carrie added.

"What are you, my mother?" Jase shot over his shoulder, not stopping. "Fuck off."

Laylea had to run. She couldn't run. If she moved, Jase would see her. He'd pounce on her like he did Jonathan. He'd kill her. But if she didn't move, he'd find her and kill her anyway for overhearing their plan, for spying on them.

The flames in her brain made it hard to think. She didn't know what to do. Her dog instincts wanted to run, to hide, to fight, to cower. Adrenaline shot through her system, readying her for whatever option the logical, intelligent part of her chose.

But she couldn't think. Her body was being torn apart, like she was a newborn again in Walter's lab, the scientists strapping her down, trapping her. Her mind pulsed with memory after memory of freezing chemicals shot into her bloodstream, of stinging blades cutting her flesh, tape tearing fur from her legs, and the never-ceasing stench of licorice and liver.

She tucked her tail, flattened her ears, and scrabbled mentally at the door she'd drawn on her birthmark. The memories had to go away.

Jase reached the edge of the trees. Twigs snapped under his boots.

The snap broke her control.

Fear took over. It sent her skittering backwards.

Jase saw her. "What the fuck are you do—"

The hard core of the bush stopped her retreat. She hit it dead on with her tail, hearing a crunch as her spine shattered all the way up to her skull. The fire blazed. Her body exploded as slowly and painfully as the first time she ever shifted human.

Her skeleton twisted, grew. Her muscles stretched, broke, and realigned. Her brain melted to pulp and reformed. The blinding new scent-scape smacked her nose with smells she couldn't even imagine as a dog.

One overwhelming scent could not be ignored. Laylea unfolded her new limbs and pushed up on all fours, bursting out of the remains of the bush to face a bitter cloud of wannabe-alpha aggression.

Jase's mouth dropped open. His pupils blew wide.

Laylea, the bear, curled her new lips back and huffed right in his face.

20

A torrent of odors assaulted Laylea. She covered her nose with giant, sweet-smelling paws against the riot of competing scents. Rich mossy trees surrounded her, the air marked with the tang of joyful puppy though there were no dogs in sight. Distantly she sensed musk, soap, and the coppery rot of broken bones.

She backed farther into the trees, knowing she mustn't let those humans see her.

But one of them already had. She huffed at him.

The nutty, sweet reek of her own breath washed over the bitter fear of the small human daring to encroach on her space.

"Tob… Toby?" Jase sputtered. His pupils blew wide with fear and confusion.

Laylea huffed again. Jase's hair blew back, but he didn't retreat. Her thick, slow brain did not understand. The tiny creature should run from her. This was her grove. Hers.

But the fear faded while his eyes grew wider still. "No," he said. "Toby's ear is white." He took a step forward, into the grove of trees.

This was her place. Not his. She was here first. Laylea stood to her full height. She swiped an enormous paw at a tree, slashing four parallel gashes in the bark. It was hers. She claimed it. He had to go away.

"You've got a white diamond," the boy whispered, "on your face. Like Lee."

She rolled anger in her throat, forced air from her powerful gut in three pulsing growls.

"It's true," the puny werewolf gasped. "The prophecy is true. You're her. You're the True."

"What are you playing at, Jase?" Jonathan called. "Who's back there?"

Jase ran. As he should. His boots hit the bridge, his senseless cry of, "Spiders," lost to the chaotic yelling of his pack.

"Spiders?" Vaughn asked, panic raising his pitch.

Jase yelled, "Spiders. And..." He broke off, gasping for breath.

"And what? What's worse than spiders? Open the door," Jonathan ordered.

Laylea slammed her claws into the tree to hold herself still. Something from deep within her told her she shouldn't give chase. She should let the wolves run. She cried out a moaning bawl to hurry them away.

"And there's somebody coming through the forced shift tunnel," Jase cried. His footsteps pounded across the courtyard stones.

The ground rumbled. Laylea toppled, crushing bushes beneath her bulk. Twigs snapped and leaves crackled around her, their scents bursting into the air.

Voices overlapped with hushed questions and demands. She understood only a few clear phrases.

Jonathan's high-pitched screech: "Hurry, Vaughn."

Jase's deep, clear order: "Pick him up!"

The scent of their fear comforted Laylea. They were leaving. They wouldn't hurt her.

"I've got your crutches," Carrie sang.

Adrenaline spiked through her system, the stench of her own fear filling the grove. Carrie shouldn't be with those predators. They would hurt her.

Laylea wrestled out of the foliage, branches slapping against her thick fur. She burst from the trees, grunting and huffing.

But she was too slow.

The wooden panel door slammed shut.

They were gone. Carrie with them. The little, harmless wolf was gone, carried off by the predators who had invaded Laylea's school, who had tried to stomp her friends, who had wanted to kidnap Oscar and use the phoenix as a weapon.

Laylea roared. And ran.

Two lumbering steps out, she tripped on her ungainly legs. Four-legged running was better anyway. It was always better.

She galloped across the bridge, wood groaning beneath her weight. Picking up speed, she rammed into the wooden panel the humans had taken her friend through.

It did not open.

She hit it with one broad paw, claws scoring the wood. She slammed it with her shoulder.

It did not open.

She shook her head, trying to find some air that wasn't thick with the stench of her fear, their fear, their sweat, her musk, and... everything. She could smell wood, steel, glass, and the history of shifter children, of blood spilled on the tiers, of trees calling to other trees, of rotting nests high in the metal rafters.

Through the chaos, a tiny voice inside her told her not to go outside. If she went outside, others would see her birthmark and they would know, like Jase did, that she was the true shifter. Grandpa would come and, like Walter of the licorice breath, he'd bleed her. He'd cut her.

He'd kill her friends.

She backed away from the wooden panel. She needed to hide.

Dizzied by the onslaught of smells, Laylea forgot the many tiers of the arena. She stepped back with one enormous, ungainly bear paw onto empty air. Time slowed.

Then gravity kicked in.

Her stubby arms pinwheeled, impossibly trying to regain her

balance as all four hundred pounds of her fell to the next tier landing on half a dozen wooden chairs, crushing them all. Splinters the size of knitting needles piercing her flesh, though she barely felt them through her layers of fat and fur.

The broken edges of the hand-crafted wooden furniture bit into the sensitive skin between the pads of her paws. She shook them with each step as she scrambled out of the mess.

Scared by the droplets of blood flying from her paws, she darted away from them. Bits of broken chair tumbled with her over the edge down to the next tier.

Her left hip took the brunt of the landing. She squealed in pain and scrambled away, iron chairs and perches scattering before her.

Gravity and panic sped her down the last three tiers, leaving a trail of destruction, blood, and fur in her wake.

Though it all hurt, her bear form took the punishment in stride. There was not even the hint of burning in her gut. She searched for it, tried to force it to come alive. A tiny piece of chair stuck out of one paw. She pounded it on the ground, shoving the splinter farther into flesh.

Pain blinded her, but still, she didn't shift.

Instead, she bleated like a cub calling for her mother.

The water ran from her breath. Wrinkles spread across the surface of the pond, racing away from her voice. Laylea tried to stop them.

She pulled her paw back in shock. Then she crawled into the pond, holding her paw out to be soothed by the cold water.

The ground gave way beneath her and she tumbled, splashing, into the depths. She came up shaking, sending water, wood, and blood flying in an arc that sprayed the bridge overhead.

Above water, human thoughts and worries poured into her, sending her nerves into a panic. She dunked again, staying under until her lungs burned for oxygen. The deep, clean, scent-stuffed breath she took filled lungs larger by far than dog or human lungs. She took another, then dove into the water and stroked her way as far down as she could go. Four hundred pounds of fat and fur took her deep.

Without her collar, she couldn't see through the magical boundaries into the sub-basement of the school. She could believe she was alone in a mountain lake far away from squabbling werewolves or tortured family and friends. There were no scents, no sound except the pulse of her heartbeat in her ears.

It was calm.

She hadn't been calm in so long.

She played in the water until her mind cleared of thoughts and fears. She dove and floated until her bloodstream was free of adrenaline. She swam until exhaustion forced her to the shore.

There, she lay in the short grasses and stared into the water. She did look like Toby; long snout, adorable ears perched on top of a wide head, with eyes the same chocolate-lab-brown as her dog and human eyes. Her birthmark stood out stark white against the deep chestnut and black fur.

She tried to trace the birthmark on her reflection and sent ripples circling out toward the opposite shore.

She watched the water drip down her claws as her new brain put everything together.

She was Laylea.

She'd been a dog. Then a human. Now she was a bear.

She could also be bits of everyone else.

Oscar was right. She was the true shifter, the true shifter that Grandpa wanted to find. The true shifter who was supposed to somehow free everybody.

Free them from what? And how?

Laylea lay her muzzle on one huge paw and stared out over the water letting her thoughts run wild until exhaustion claimed her.

It didn't take long.

21

Voices muttered around Laylea. Many voices.

She usually woke in KC's pod. KC wasn't a morning person. She didn't talk. When she woke, she'd quietly pop her pod open so Laylea could hop down and trot to the grassy patch in the bathroom.

The thought woke Laylea a bit. She didn't need to use the grass, though, and her body sunk back down, reaching for the Milkbone she'd been battling Toby for in her dream.

"How did she end up here?" The voice was familiar, but new. It took Laylea a moment to identify the speaker as Bitters.

The realization pulled her from her dream. If the enforcer was there, she was in trouble. Would he disenhance her for stealing a stasis band?

No, they wouldn't recognize her as a bear. They'd arrest her for breaking into the school.

"I assumed Lee would go down the lift." Professor Wanja brushed a hand along her ribcage. Magic tingled from him, sparkling through her tiny canine body, soothing the ache in her bum hip.

Joy that she wasn't a bear anymore made her tail twitch. She sent it a stern warning, but it had never been under her control. It thumped once before obeying. She sighed. She'd have to face the music.

"I love it when puppies dream," Bitters whispered. He accounted for her tail's rogue wag better than she ever could have.

"Of course you did," Caliban reassured Professor Wanja. "She should have."

"She said she was injured. Hit her head, I think?" the professor said. "I should have taken her to first aid."

"Is she cut? I can help," Bitters offered. "Spider silk is antiseptic, you know."

Professor Wanja said gently, "I didn't think Brazilian Wandering spiders spun webs."

"Oh, I'm a wolf spider on my Mom's side. It doesn't come naturally, but Gramps taught me how. Paralytic venom is my gift," he said bitterly. "That just doesn't seem useful in this situation."

"Lee heals when she shifts."

Laylea almost wagged again at the sound of Ms. Lagat's voice. She should have known she was there. Ms. Lagat's long skirts spread the scent of her lavender laundry detergent everywhere she went.

"That's why she wanted to get downstairs." Bitters crouched near Laylea's head. The faux woodsy scent of his beard oil wafted over her as he bent close.

She held her breath, realized that was dumb, and let it out slowly.

Ms. Lagat suggested, "She probably thought the seal pool would get her down more quickly."

"How does she even know about that entrance?" Wanja asked.

After an awkward silence, Caliban filled him in, cautiously. "You weren't a student here, so you wouldn't be aware. The students have a lot of time to explore."

Caliban knew, of course, about the secret upstairs gatherings in Toby's hollow. Apparently, all the faculty knew that the students knew how to get outside on the sly. That would put a wrench in the wolves' plans.

On the heels of her thought, Professor Wanja asked, "Do the wolves know about the secret exits?"

The ground rumbled as gears shifted to open the dorm's door.

Bitters sighed. "Yes. I see your point, Professor. I'll talk to the Council about putting more eyes on the secret exits."

"Lee?" Ms. Crow's cry was followed by a clicking croak. A pair of talons clicked onto the stones by her head. Ms. Crow's worry was a light tang over her raven's solid musty-book scent.

The gentleness of the scent reassured Laylea. She risked opening her eyes.

"Lee. Hi." The raven croaked the words, tapping her on the forehead before she shifted. "Just sleeping, were you? Not dead?"

Laylea couldn't help the wuffle of air through her teeth that sufficed for a laugh.

"May I pick you up?" Ms. Crow asked. "We'd like you to see Dr. Tippleston."

Being carried sounded nice. Laylea stretched long, throwing her head back in an enormous yawn. Her tail joined in the full body waking and thumped freely against Professor Wanja's knees. Everything seemed in good working order. Even her bum hip felt tip top. The tip of her long, pink tongue curled at the end as she squeaked into the stretch.

The adults around her laughed.

"I mean, that is just the cutest thing," Bitters cooed. He caught himself. "Sorry, Lee. Sorry."

Ms. Crow waited for Laylea to finish her stretch. She didn't wait for her to get up, just scooped her into her arms, on her back, like a baby. It wasn't a particularly dignified position, but Laylea was too comfy to care.

"Dizzy, tell Tipp we're on our way to her." Ms. Crow climbed the steps that connected the tiers as her sister swooped past them, feathers dripping.

Bitters bounced past Ms. Crow to the wall beside the door. He was still searching for something on the stones when Dizzy settled on a sconce placed, oddly, above the wooden panel door.

When the rumbling of the gears shook the floor, he snatched his hands back. "I didn't do anything!"

"Dizzy opened the door, cherie," Ms. Lagat assured him. "This was the bird dorm back in the day."

Laylea raised her head to bark a thank you to her feathered friend. Dizzy cawed back as she flew out before anybody else could slip through the slowly sliding panel.

Laylea stared at the dark circles under Ms. Crow's eyes. They'd nearly gone after she found out her sister was still alive. Why were they back? Was she that worried about Laylea or was there something else?

Something besides the self-proclaimed Alpha of the Americas essentially declaring war on the Midwest with her school being his primary target? Laylea scoffed at herself. Probably it was that and not her going missing for a few hours. Ms. Crow didn't know that Laylea was the key to Grandpa's genocidal new drug.

But Jase knew.

Her heart pounded in her chest and she tucked her tail, shivering.

"You go ahead, Lizzy," Ms. Lagat called. "Don't wait on us."

Permission granted, Ms. Crow hustled through the doorway and down the hall.

Behind them, Bitters exclaimed, "Oh, should I have punished her for—"

Ms. Lagat shushed him before he could say whatever he thought he might have needed to punish Laylea for.

"He is not made for this job," Ms. Crow mused. She grinned at Laylea. "Lucky for you."

Laylea dropped her chin in a doggy grin. While anyone was better than Denier, Bitters was a bit of a gift.

The trough lighting in the corridor was dimmed a deep blue that was barely light at all. That meant it was still night. She hadn't slept very long.

She wished she could ask what time it was. But that would mean shifting and Laylea was perfectly happy remaining a dog for as long as her body would let her. She'd rat out the wolves whenever she got her teeth on a golf pencil.

"Are you sure you're okay?" Ms. Crow asked as she hurried. "Jase didn't hurt you?"

Laylea blinked awake. She blew air through her lips in a question.

"Yes, I know they were there. Dizzy has been following them. When she heard Safiri tracked your stasis band to Gryphon dorm, she raced for me. Caliban has too many things going on to have to worry about Jase's vendetta against you."

Laylea's eyes shot to her legs and her hopes plummeted. They'd taken her stasis band. Not that it mattered if Wanja could track them. She'd never have gotten away with stealing one. She grunted in frustration.

"Oh, don't you worry, Lee," Ms. Crow assured her. "Rico and I will keep a close watch on the boy."

Enrico Bianchi had secrets of his own to keep. He shouldn't have to put time and energy into protecting Laylea. But she was grateful, even though Jase was unlikely to harm her as long as he believed she was Grandpa Delcampo's true shifter.

"That sligh nut poisoning is in your medical record, so Tipp will know to be prepared." Ms. Crow looked ahead as she talked. That could be because she was focused on walking quickly and safely in the dark. But Laylea suspected Ms. Crow was working through her thoughts out loud more than she was actually talking to her.

"Not that she's ever unprepared. There is more to Tipp than meets the eye." She chuckled, Laylea bouncing against the staccato breaths. "Her resume is pure fiction. Still, she has no love for Delcampo and is more knowledgeable than any shifter doctor I've met before." Her steps slowed, her eyes darting about as if she were reading her thoughts on the corridor walls. "But that's the problem, isn't it? It seems remarkable that this highly skilled woman would appear now, right when we need her." She picked up the pace again, her shoes tapping along the corridor with metronome precision.

It sounded very much like Ms. Crow meant suspicious when she said remarkable. Was she right? Should they be wary of the new doctor? Tipp seemed nice to Laylea. She was the first person in school to offer her any practical advice on not shifting.

Ms. Crow muttered, “Addie says the universe provides, but I don’t know. Right when we need her…” She trailed off and went silent as though her thoughts were still churning, but she’d run out of breath to voice them.

A giggle bubbled in Laylea’s tired brain. You couldn’t call old, wrinkled, wise, proper Ms. Lagat, “Addie.” Laylea flashed on a picture she, Oscar, and KC had found of when Ms. Lagat first came to school as a little girl with a giant bow in her hair. She imagined the old teacher she knew wearing that bow.

Her tail popped out and thwapped Ms. Crow’s chest. It picked up speed when she heard a familiar voice yelling in the distance and getting closer.

“But where is she?” KC demanded. Her voice bounced along the stone walls of the main corridor.

Ms. Crow called out, “She’s right here.”

KC squealed. Her borrowed boots pounded down the corridor almost as fast as Laylea’s tail.

22

Footsteps like a herd of horses announced Laylea's friends approaching along the corridor.

KC, Oscar, and Griff slowed as they turned the corner and saw Ms. Crow holding Laylea like a baby. Ms. Crow didn't slow a bit. The three spun easily and hopped along beside the librarian, vying for the best position to see their friend.

"Lee..." KC drew the word out in a way that told Laylea she had a million questions. "Oscar's pissed," she said instead. "He had to clean up all by himself."

"I'm not pissed," Oscar protested, shoving KC out of his way. "Norman and Griff helped."

Norman. Laylea's ears swiveled at the name. He was that cute boy manning KC's booth. She raised her eyebrows at KC and the way her friend blushed told her everything. Maybe she could risk shifting human, if only to grill her.

"Ned said you got hurt." Griff reached over to scratch her chest. "Was it Jase?"

His question sobered her. It wasn't. But it would be.

She licked his hand.

KC stopped chattering. She shot Oscar a look that made Laylea realize how intimate her gesture had been.

A blush crept up Griff's neck to the goofy grin on his face. He caressed her fur once more, then stepped away.

Laylea dropped her head back over Ms. Crow's arm, letting her tongue fall out of her mouth in a goofy expression, trying to pretend she hadn't just kissed Griff.

Oscar scoffed. He and KC fell to teasing Griff, nudging him silently. They lost pace as Ms. Crow continued hustling through the dark school.

Laylea's tail tucked in embarrassment, or tried to. She couldn't really do it with the way Ms. Crow had her cradled, belly to the wind. Laylea yearned to just curl into herself like a potato bug. A gentle warmth swirling along her spine suggested she probably could, if she really wanted to. She closed her eyes and mentally decorated her birthmark with glitter and gems, like Councilmember Angelica's nails.

The air swirled and filled with a croaking and clicking.

Laylea's neck suddenly went heavy with the familiar weight of her collar crushing her fur. She opened her eyes to find Dizzy walking beside her sister. Some fear and tension fled Laylea as she was reunited with her magical protection lizard.

"...thought you'd want this," Dizzy said, her cries turning to words halfway through her sentence. "I'm not sure how the clasps work."

"I've got it." KC danced over, leaving Griff. The sing-song of her voice made it clear she wasn't going to let that lick go. But that was fine. Laylea wasn't going to forget to ask her all about Norman, either.

"Tipp's on her way," Dizzy reported to her sister before asking Laylea, "Were you in the dorm at the same time as the wolves?"

Laylea barked.

After a second, Oscar told Dizzy, "That's once for yes."

"Did they know?"

She barked twice.

"They're going to find out," Ms. Crow told her sister. "She left Bear Hollow at four-thirty. The wolves met right after dinner. Word is going to get around."

"They'll kill her." KC jerked from smoothing Laylea's fur as if she wanted to tear her from Ms. Crow's arms and run away. "We need to spread a story that she was somewhere else."

"But she was. Instead of helping me," Oscar declared in a faux-aggrieved tone, "Lee and Griff were making out in the reptile house."

KC barked a laugh. Griff grabbed the pompoms hanging from his hat as if he could make the hat cover his face if he just pulled them hard enough.

Oscar continued, "She ran down through Gryphon to get away after Enforcer Brewster caught them, right Griff?"

Ms. Crow sighed. "Enforcer Brewster isn't the best liar," she said.

"And Griff was with his dad during cleanup, remember?" KC added. "Pretty much the entire council saw him."

Griff didn't say anything. He shot her a begging look, his blush growing deeper.

"Oh good, you found her." Dr. Tippleston appeared out of the darkness with no warning.

Oscar screamed and all the kids giggled.

Laylea tilted her head in bafflement. She hadn't noticed the doctor approaching. Rosemary filled the air along with the dull thump of Dr. Tippleston's boots approaching. She wasn't a quiet presence, like Ms. Crow, to be sneaking up on people. And Laylea was primed to sense rosemary from however far away, thanks to Madam Hu's generosity with dog treats.

"Shifting trouble?" The doctor asked, her voice low.

"No," Ms. Crow answered.

"Yes," KC corrected. "She got hurt and couldn't shift to heal."

"Gryphon dorm was the fastest way down," Oscar said.

"Unless you're a bird," Dizzy told him dryly, "Gryphon is never the fastest way down."

He retorted, "It was the closest to Bear Hollow."

Dizzy inclined her head as if to concede the point.

Dr. Tippleston stepped in front of Ms. Crow, stopping the head-long rush through the halls.

"She was found in Gryphon?" Dr. Tippleston asked, alarmed. "Were you there when—"

Laylea barked.

"But if the wolves find that out," Ms. Crow said carefully," she'll be in danger from them."

"Yes, you've made that clear," Dr. Tippleston nodded at the librarian with the hint of a smile. "Which is why I lied when Ali came looking for Lee in the infirmary."

"What? How did you guess?" Dizzy asked.

Dr. Tipp went on as if she hadn't heard the question. "I made sure that Vaughn Howe overheard me tell Ali Lee came to see me after she left Mr. Biggerson, Enforcer Brewster, and Professor Wanja." Dr. Tippleston laid her hands on Laylea's skull, searching for injuries. "I said I was escorting Lee to the infirmary when she ran from me."

KC hopped a few steps, declaring, "Of course. Because the last time she was confined to the infirmary, Dr. Fenn tried to feed her to a bear."

Ms. Crow bristled. Laylea's body bounced with her huffing breath. "He did no such thing."

"He kind of did," Dizzy corrected her. At her sister's appalled look, she amended, "It wasn't his idea, but he didn't stop it."

"Toby would never eat a student," Ms. Crow argued.

Laylea growled.

"Toby would never eat anyone," KC accurately voiced Laylea's thoughts, and in an appropriately aggrieved tone.

"She was hallucinating from sligh nut poisoning," Dizzy reminded them, her tone as stern as her face. "And she didn't know Toby, then."

The doctor stepped between the sisters, stopping the argument. "I'll take the patient now."

Ms. Crow hesitated, but after a nod from Dizzy, she handed Laylea over as if she were made of china. The doctor showed less concern. She held Laylea up with one arm, allowing her to see everyone.

As they managed the transfer, Dr. Tipp commented, "It was my assumption that she ran from me because she had an important date she didn't want to miss." She turned her twinkling eyes on Griff.

"Anybody could see Griffin was trying to get away from his father. At least that's what I told Ali, in front of Vaughn."

Laylea whimpered a question at Dr. Tippleston.

"He'll be okay," she assured her. "But not if he isn't more careful. I told Carrie and Big Mo as much when they brought him in. Carrie said there was a fight and Jase schooled Jonathan," she added to the Crow sisters.

KC and Oscar stopped poking at Griff long enough for the three to exchange surprised looks. No other faculty would talk so openly about pack politics in front of students.

"How badly was Jonathan hurt?" Ms. Crow asked.

"Not so bad that he came to see me," Dr. Tipp told her.

"He's got some minor puncture marks on his neck." Dizzy waved away their concern. "Look, for her safety, we need the whole school to know that Lee was not in Gryphon dorm until well after dinner."

"Why would they think she was?" Dr. Tipp asked.

Dizzy straightened her sweater, visibly restraining herself from rolling her eyes. "Gossip spreads faster than the plague here."

"That's how we do it," Oscar laughed. "All we have to do is give Milly some hot gossip at breakfast. The wolves will know about it by lunch."

Griff sighed. He released his hat and stepped forward. "We were gonna have a picnic at the seal pool, but I got there late, like way after six, and we fought," he said, raising his eyebrows to ask Laylea if that story was okay with her.

Laylea's tail thumped slowly against Ms. Crow's chest in regretful approval. He'd made himself the bad guy. That wasn't fair.

"Upset, she ran down to Gryphon dorm," Dizzy continued the story, "and cried herself to sleep."

Griff's face fell.

Laylea sang out, trying to reassure him.

KC caught the exchange and squeezed Griff. "Don't worry. It's good goss," she said, nearly interrupting herself to cry, "Hey, I'm on the breakfast shift. I'll remind Chef Tod he packed a picnic for Griff."

Dr. Tipp chuckled. "The chef will lie for you?"

"Chef hasn't cornered you yet about his nutrition-as-health program?" KC's face contorted through a whole series of shocked and doubting expressions.

Dizzy raised a hand to slow KC and turned to assure the doctor. "Chef Tod was particularly offended by Jase using food as a weapon against Lee. He'll play along."

Ms. Crow nodded her approval of the plan. But her hands clutched her cardigan, obsessively adjusting it. "Will Lee be safe in the infirmary with Vaughn there, do you think?"

"She heals when she shifts," KC pointed out, looking to Oscar to back her up. "Why does she need to go at all?"

"Because she's a healer and she's not accustomed to the stress of pain. I just want to keep an eye on her as a precaution," the doctor assured KC. For Ms. Crow, she added, "Vaughn is on strict bed rest. That means no visitors. Trust me, Lizzy. I'll keep her safe."

Ms. Crow did not look comforted. "What's to keep Vaughn from harming her?"

"His leg is broken in several places. His jaw is wired shut. He's ripped opened some stitches," Dr. Tippleston began.

"He was beaten by other werewolves," Oscar cut to the chase. "He's a basket case, but he's not dangerous to anybody but himself."

"Plus," the doctor said, "I've given the poor boy something to help him sleep. Which I will order for you all if you don't get to your pods and your perches." She turned a particular eye on KC. "If you're still tired after your presser shift in the morning, come to the infirmary. I'll cover for you with your teachers."

Laylea's tail smacked loudly against something jingly in the doctor's pocket.

KC giggled and scratched Laylea's ears. She whispered, "I'll see you in the morning. I have so much to tell you." She turned and grabbed Griff's hand to drag him away. "Let's go spread some rumors. This is going to be so much fun."

Laylea howled. Poor Griff looked back at her with a tortured grin that turned to pure panic when Oscar plucked the hat from his head and stuck it on Laylea.

With an evil laugh, he tore past KC and Griff, crying "And to all a good night," over his shoulder.

Dizzy bumped Ms. Crow with a hip. "She'll be okay. Let's go tell Cal and get to bed."

Ms. Crow's brows knit.

Dr. Tippleston adjusted Laylea on her hip. Griff's hat fell further over Laylea's eyes as she did.

"Captain Morioka made a point of telling me how important Lee is to her," the doctor said gently. "You don't know me. But you can trust I won't do anything to make Captain Morioka upset."

Ms. Crow tilted the hat back and tied the dangling braids under her chin, petting her at the same time. Her chuckle confirmed how ridiculous Laylea must look. "Lee is important to me, too."

The librarian squared off with the doctor. She reached down and took her sister's hand, just as they had in the Dining Hall. Laylea's ears perked up, knocking the hat askew. There was a threat and a promise in Ms. Crow's eyes.

The doctor shifted Laylea to her left side. Heat radiated into Laylea as Dr. Tipp's hand spread to hold her more securely. She offered her right hand to Ms. Crow.

When Ms. Crow took it, Dr. Tipp said, low and serious, "I'll guard her like she's my granddaughter."

Laylea barked reassurance. She was no fan of the infirmary by any means, but there was a very good chance Professor Wanja had left some stasis bands there for emergencies. She could examine one and figure out how to reproduce it.

"And don't worry about Jase, Lee," Dizzy said. "I'll keep an eye on him."

Apparently satisfied she was safe, the sisters shifted into their matching raven forms and soared away down the hallway.

Dr. Tippleston broke into a lope, jogging through the dark, quiet corridors of the school. The jolting pace disguised Laylea's trembling.

Her friends could cover for her all they wanted. Deep down, she knew it didn't matter. Jase had seen her. He might already be figuring out how to contact Grandpa.

Griff's hat slipped down over her eyes again as she tucked her muzzle against Dr. Tippleston's shoulder. The cedarwood scent of him failed to calm her racing heart.

Unless she could stop shifting, Grandpa would find her and bleed her. It was only a matter of time.

23

Moonlight brightened the library nook enough that the trough lights had dimmed completely. Or maybe they had dimmed because it was so late.

Laylea lay on the carpets, watching motes of dust and smoke floating through the moonlight. Her brand new gills flapped helplessly, failing to suck oxygen out of the air. Distracted by the crushing weight of her too-big collar, it took a moment for her body to recognize death was imminent. Then the burn that once knocked her on her butt with pain shot soothingly through her veins.

She sucked air in through her muzzle and released it on a growl. She'd never shifted into a fish before. It was not a pleasant experience. It was possible her body was warning her to stop inhaling the smoke of failed potions.

Potion work could be dangerous even with guidance. Hell, Bailey had burned his eyebrows off the first time he tried to make a potion with Sher standing right beside him. Knock on wood, Laylea hadn't done much worse than annoy her lungs.

After nearly dying for reals on the stairs to Gryphon, she'd given up on trying to steal a stasis band. For the two weeks since, she'd focused instead on making a band or any other kind of totem. She absolutely could not risk shifting anymore.

If she could just hold her shape, she'd be safe. Jase might think she was the true shifter, but with no proof, he'd be mocked mercilessly. Nobody believed the myth was real. She'd asked around.

If he got word to Grandpa, it would be game over.

Only, he couldn't get a message to Grandpa. He'd lied to the wolves when he said he had.

The instant Dr. Tipp had set Laylea down in the infirmary, she'd grabbed a pencil in her teeth, spilling the pack's plan to Wild in the city as a distraction for the kid wolves' escape.

Dr. Tipp had woken Mr. Barrett who'd come to grill Laylea for details and share a few. It turned out that Jonathan's mom had been arrested at P2. She was in the special Four-Four jail and wasn't talking to anybody, much less making escape plans for her son. Plus, the Midwestern wolves loyal to Grandpa were converging on Detroit for the next full moon, not Chicago.

He'd told her not to worry, like that was possible. Worry was just about all she did.

Except when Griff was around. The story of their bad date spread so well, even Mr. DeGee heard about it. He sent Griff a book about how to be a gentleman that was making the rounds of the dorms to everyone's amusement.

Griff had apologized grandly with a speech stolen word-for-word from the book, then sat beside her for dinner every night since. And he hadn't taken his hat back. Since it covered her entire dog's head, she wore it in her human form.

Laylea sighed and rolled to her paws on the library carpet. Holding Griff's hand was a great reason to stay human. She should try to put that in her potion.

Creating a stasis band had been a pipe dream. It required a magic- and/or love-filled object that she could attach to her person. Her lizard foot overflowed with love and magic, but she wasn't about to risk it.

Oscar was gifting his mother's homemade red paper to people

after reading the letters she'd written on them in magically-hidden ink. Quan would then charm the paper to offer protection from magic, allowing them to see Dizzy.

Laylea couldn't ask Oscar for a red paper when she already had her lizard foot. It wasn't fair to Dizzy. So she'd started trying potions.

Whispering voices carried down the bookshelves to the nook. Laylea sat up. She shook from head to tail to get her blood moving.

"But what if she gets hurt again and we're not there to—" KC interrupted herself. "Hey Dizzy, that's a lot of books."

"Over a hundred years in this school with nobody to talk to, and I have read all the books here," Dizzy grunted, "except the ones on civic duty and shifter law."

Oscar's voice perked up. "Oh, you're gonna want to read—"

Dizzy cut him off, mid-yawn. "Can you make me a list? I'm a little overwhelmed with what I've already got."

"Yeah, sure." Oscar agreed. There came the sound of shuffling books. "This is a good solid overview of the North American council system."

"Thanks."

The footsteps resumed their quiet progress across the library toward Laylea.

"That's what I'm talking about, KC."

Laylea hopped to her paws. Beakers and ramekins of potions littered the carpet around her Bunsen burner hearth. She dashed around, nosing them all into a clump. Then knocked a pillow off the bench to cover all her failed attempts.

"What?" KC asked.

"We don't want to overwhelm her. Maybe she just needs some space to get used to her new situation."

KC and Oscar were in the stacks, getting close.

Laylea leapt for the French chair blocking the nook, singing a greeting at them.

The trilling song mutated into an off-key warble as she landed on the velvet seat with human knees, setting the chair wobbling. She squawked and a searing pain flashed through her coccyx. Her brand new prehensile tail grabbed on to the nearby shelf to keep from falling over.

"Hi!" she said, overeagerly, twisting to hide her butt. "Are you talking about Shala?"

Oscar laughed uncomfortably and began stuttering some response.

KC rescued him. "Yes," she said, making a show of steadying the chair.

Laylea pushed Griff's hat up, out of her eyes, as she slipped off the chair and backed away, ostensibly to give them room to enter.

"Oscar finally realized that Shala needs some space to get used to being awake before she has to face the fact that her bratty baby brother has grown up to be a cute teenager."

Oscar did a double take. "Cute?"

KC side eyed him as the two clambered around the chair into the nook. "I can't tell if you're insulted or surprised."

Oscar hastened to reassure her. "I'll take cute. Does Norman know you think I'm cute?"

"Ha," KC laughed, not bothered at all by his taunting. "Norman's the one who pointed it out to me."

Laylea slapped yet another coat of imaginary paint on the birthmark in her mind. She fought to keep her face neutral as fire burned away the tail, her birthmark to the rescue again.

The thought sparked inspiration. She returned to her wildly unsafe "hearth" and started mixing ingredients.

"I'm glad you're giving Shala some space," she said, realizing that her friends were staring. "And that Norman has good taste."

"And what are we doing here?" KC asked as if she were addressing an unhinged toddler.

Laylea used her teeth to tear a thread from the mini pompoms hanging off either side of Griff's hat.

"A totem was never going to work," she said. "So I'm making a potion. I can just take a draft every night—"

"You mean morning." KC set her backpack on the bench and dug through it.

"What?" Laylea looked over her supplies. She needed something to scrape her birthmark to include it in her potion. Inspiration struck as she fingered the lizard on her collar. She unzipped one of the collar's pockets.

"If you want to stay human," KC explained, "you'd have to take it in the morning, so it would wear off by bedtime."

The Milkbone that Kyle had given her months ago was still there. She pulled it out, half listening to KC. "Why do I need it to wear off?"

"Well, every time you go to bed as a girl, you wake up as a dog," KC said, holding out a protein bite.

Her stomach yelled in approval, but Laylea needed to try this one thing first.

"Are you still trying to work Will magic?" Oscar asked.

"Yeah," Laylea paused, her hunger shutting her brain down in the face of a Milkbone and a bite-sized Chef Tod protein bar. "So?"

"So, your will wants you to be a dog all the time, right?" Oscar said. "And you can't fight that while you're asleep."

"Right," Laylea sighed. "Okay, so, I have to shift human in the morning, which I can successfully do most of the time."

KC waggled her head. "Some of the time."

Oscar raised his brows at both of them. "You mostly come to breakfast as a dog. The faculty keep scolding you for it."

Laylea growled, determined to put mind over stomach. She scraped the Milkbone against her birthmark, garnering strange looks from her friends.

"So," she said, working it through. "KC puts the potion in a bowl...grrrr. But then I'd stay dog unless I set my will while drinking the potion to become... arrrrgh."

Oscar laid a hand on her shoulder. "Maybe you could just talk to Ms. Lagat about the trouble you've been having."

"Maybe you could talk to us," KC suggested. "You really are improving. Most shifters never learn to keep their clothes and you've done that."

"I'm not having any trouble!" Laylea threw the Milkbone with her birthmark's epithelial cells into the beaker.

It exploded.

Oscar screamed in fear. Laylea screamed with frustration. KC lobbed the protein bite at her as she smothered the flames with a fire-retardant blanket.

Dizzy soared into the nook, her wings folding as she landed on the bench and shifted, also carrying a fire-retardant blanket. She threw it over Laylea and batted at her head.

"I'm fine. I'm fine." Laylea mumbled, fighting her off.

A burn threatened in her shoulders and she stopped fighting Dizzy to focus on fighting herself. She traced her birthmark, wiggled her thumbs, snapped the hairband, and breathed as best she could under the oxygen smothering fabric.

"I think she's fine," Oscar said slowly.

"Her hat was on fire," Dizzy said pointedly.

Laylea tore the blanket and Griff's hat from her head. It was singed. She groaned. Her stomach growled.

"Eat," Oscar and KC ordered her.

Laylea opened her mouth to show them the half-chewed protein bite.

"Ewww." They both recoiled in disgust. Laylea giggled.

"You're okay, though." Dizzy looked each of them in the eyes, reassuring herself. "Right? You're all okay?"

"I'm sorry. I'm sorry. It's my fault," Griff called, running through the stacks. "Lee was working on a thing for me, a trick, for my magic act." Griff stumbled on, every word clearly leaping out of his mouth at the exact moment it arrived in his brain. "For my magic act for the New Year's Eve event."

"That sounds fun," Dizzy said. "I've been looking for a way to get involved. We could work out some tricks that don't require explosions." She turned a stern gaze on Laylea. "Or fire in the library."

"Yeah, working here might have been a mistake," Laylea admitted, crumpling the hat in her hands, hiding the singed bits.

"You four get this cleaned up and get off to bed," Dizzy ordered. "You wouldn't want to miss the soccer game Sunday. Bitters is taking you all upstairs."

"Isn't that dangerous on a full moon?" Griff asked.

"The restricted kids aren't allowed upstairs," she reminded him. "And Conner is voluntarily not going."

Oscar muttered, "Because he's a chicken."

"Because there will be so many parents watching," Dizzy corrected. "Pull it together is all I'm saying, Lee."

Dizzy hopped back up on the bench and leapt into the air, shifting to caw at them before flying back to her books.

The four of them waited a minute before they burst out in smothered giggles.

Laylea bent to start cleaning and KC waved her away. "No no no, you've caused enough trouble. I've got it. Oscar, come help."

Oscar started to protest, then shut his mouth at a glare from KC.

Laylea slunk over to Griff. She smoothed his hat and held it out. "I kinda burnt it a little bit, just there." She pointed out the spot. She'd pretty much burnt the fluff off of one of the hanging pompoms. "You can have it back if you want it."

"I don't," Griff said brightly. "It looks good on you. The burns give it character." He choked on a snort and had to take a minute to pull himself together.

"You okay, man?" Oscar called over.

Griff nodded vigorously. The feathers on his head bounced just like they would on his gryphon form. "It's just my mom always says my feathers give me character. I never imagined I'd turn into my mother."

"Would you rather be your dad?" KC asked doubtfully.

"No!" Griff's eyes grew wide at the very thought. "I like being me." He giggled. "Everybody got their jokes in about my feathers that first week you had my hat, but my mom was right. I shouldn't have tried to hide. I like being myself. Sure, I'm the only gryphon. But that's cool, right?"

"Yeah," KC agreed.

So did Oscar. "Super cool."

Laylea thought about it a moment before saying, "I think you're cool. Your gryphon is kind of derpy."

"Yes," KC agreed.

Oscar, too. “Totally derpy. Do you know how hard it is to get you to focus when there is anything shiny around?”

“Like this?” KC tilted her ID band to catch the light and reflect a dot around the nook.

“I mean I'm a cat, I get the allure,” Oscar said, watching the light with an intensity he typically reserved for dessert. “But, dude.”

Griff blushed, but his smile grew wider.

“I like derpy.” Laylea grinned. She stuffed the hat back on her head, pretty sure it made her look super derpy.

KC and Oscar put the last remnants of Laylea's foray into potion-making in a trash bag. Oscar slung it over his shoulder and ran a hand over the carpet to see if they'd missed anything.

“The carpet,” Griff said, staring in awe at the unmussed rug.

“Oh yeah,” KC shoved Oscar ahead of him out of the nook. “This was the Crow sisters' favorite nook. They charmed it.”

“Magic is so cool,” Griff breathed, staring in equal awe as Laylea took his hand.

“It's good you think so,” Oscar observed, nudging him to move.

“Yeah,” KC hooked her arm in Oscar's. “Cuz, you know you're gonna have to do a magic act, now.”

“Yeah,” Griff nodded enthusiastically. “Imagine what I can do with an invisible assistant.”

24

"Heads up!"

Laylea spun around at the words and stopped the soccer ball, with her face.

Sparks bit into her wrist as she fell to her knees in the icy grass of the zoo's South Lawn. The stasis band kept her from shifting to heal so all she could do was blink away the pain making her eyes water.

"Little late on that warning, Dove," Bitters called from the side-lines. "Look alive out there."

Laylea raised a hand to let everyone know she was okay, even though Reggie had snagged the rebound and was halfway down the field. She snagged Griff's hat from where it had fallen and jammed it back on her head as she watched the game move on without her.

Bitters said his life symposium, Move for Life, Move for You, aimed to find which type of exercise a person would enjoy enough to keep doing throughout their life. Laylea enjoyed the cheering crowd surrounding the makeshift soccer pitch more than she enjoyed the game. Particularly with uncalled tears freezing on her cheeks.

She blinked and wiped them away.

"You okay?" Norman offered Laylea a mittened hand.

She took it, letting him help her up as she looked down. Her knees hurt worse than her face. Blood showed through a torn spot surrounded by grass stains.

"I can wash those off for you, if you want. I've got a first aid kit in my bag." Norman carried more in his backpack than KC did, and that was saying something.

He gestured toward the sidelines where parents had gathered.

Norman's overstuffed pack sat at the feet of a slight man staring adoringly at the giant-eyed toddler trying to eat his thick beard.

Norman did a double take and yelled, "Where'd you get the baby, Uncle Johnny?"

The man tore his eyes from the child. "The lady with blue hair gave her to me." He turned to the man making eyes at the baby over his shoulder. "I promise I'll give her back."

"Of course you will," Norman yelled. "You have me to take care of."

A silly grin spread across Uncle Johnny's face. He snorted and lost himself again as the kid grabbed the sunglasses off his face.

"He has to mean that council lady," Norman said, searching the field. "We met her in the parking lot, put air in her tires."

"Tara," Laylea said. "She's Councilmember Marshall's partner."

"I didn't know she had two babies."

Snow and violent pro-wolf incidents had kept the symposium downstairs since Bitters initiated it. When word went around the community that they'd be playing upstairs the Sunday before Thanksgiving, dozens of parents had demanded they be allowed to attend.

Bitters welcomed them. He even sent out an invitation for them to play, which was why Tara had come, despite not having kids in the school or being a shifter. As a wolf, her puppydaddy, Councilmember Marshall, stayed away out of courtesy. It being a full moon and all.

"Hey, Uncle Johnny," Norman yelled. "Her mom's name is Tara."

His uncle repeated the name at the little girl and then to the man beside him.

"Is your uncle..." Laylea stumbled on how to ask the question politely.

Norman saved her, clearly accustomed to the question. "He has intellectual disabilities. But the kid is totally safe with him. He pretty much raised me. My folks… work a lot."

"I'm sorry." Laylea acknowledged the resignation in his voice. She could say the same about her own parents.

"What do you say?" Norman asked, changing the topic. "We go wash your knees?"

Laylea considered his offer. It would get her off the field, which she would prefer. But, the kids not playing were stomping their feet and rubbing their hands together. She didn't want to be cold. Griff's hat wasn't enough to keep her warm.

Tara ran by, dribbling the ball, her little boy bouncing on her back. Clouds puffed into the crisp air with her encouragement. "Brush it off. They're just knees. Looking good, Johnny."

"Go, Tara!" Johnny bounced the girl, who squealed in delight.

It was hard to wimp out when a true-human with no special healing powers told you to brush it off.

Norman and his uncle were both true-humans. They usually spent Sundays and all their other free time cruising around Chicagoland helping people with car trouble. They'd interrupted their "rounds" so Johnny could finally meet KC after weeks of Norman sneaking into the zoo to sit with her in all of her upstairs classes.

The Foreman Pavilion, where classes usually met had been draped and had heaters installed so the construction workers could get away from the lion house on their breaks. They were respectful of the classes and teachers encouraged them to participate. Norman simply dressed like them and nobody gave him any trouble.

Somewhere, he'd picked up the code phrase, "I'm a friend of Cate's," which meant he knew Cate O'Leary. The infamous owner of the cow that started the Chicago fire *was* the cow. Laylea wasn't sure Norman actually knew that. He just knew saying it would get him and his Uncle Johnny into shifter-only events.

She turned to Norman. "Thanks. They're just knees apparently."

"Yeah," he scoffed. "It's not like they're the only knees you'll ever get."

He meant it as a joke, so Laylea laughed. But she would get four new knees as soon as she went downstairs.

She limped down the field, following the ball. Norman jogged along beside her.

Soccer was a very different game upstairs, where nobody could shift. Reggie, the unchallenged superstar of nearly every sport downstairs, was covered in grass stains and bruises. He kept shaking his hand as if that would release his stasis band and let him shift. It didn't help that he and Dove kept searching the sidelines in fear of their parents showing up.

The rest of the kids kept searching the sidelines for wolves.

KC was the only one there, other than Tara's twins. There hadn't even been any wolves in the halls that morning.

According to Carrie, Jase had given the wolves strict orders. All of the restricted wolves had requested excused absences from their classes and secluded themselves in their pods after an early breakfast. They wouldn't be officially locked in until three-thirty.

While most of the wolves were trapped underground like Mers before the stasis bands, KC had been upstairs every chance she got.

It had been barely three weeks since Halloween, when Norman had snuck in to see why the zoo was closed and stuck around to help KC with her booth. Now, he showed up and was glued to her side every minute the two could steal.

Which was why it was odd when he jogged along beside Laylea while KC played wing on the other side of the lawn.

"So, I know that you and KC are orphans and usually stay at school over the holidays, but—" Norman intercepted the ball and kicked it back to the players at the center.

"Nice kick," Laylea patted him on the back.

"Lee. What are you doing?" her team captain yelled.

Damn. Norman was on the other team. She should probably have battled him for the ball. She waved a hand at the irate Rehyan. "Sorry."

"Don't worry. You'll get it next time," Bitters yelled, raising his eyebrows in disapproval at Rehyan.

The action moved to the other side of the field, leaving Norman free to chat as they jogged back in the direction of his team's goal. "My parents should actually be home and I'd love them to meet KC and I know she won't leave you because that would be a dick move and she doesn't roll like that, so I was wondering if you would like to come have Thanksgiving at my place? With KC? Unless you already have other plans," he finished in a rush.

"Thursday?" Laylea asked, like a total idiot. Of course Thanksgiving was Thursday. It was always on a Thursday.

Norman did not point out the idiocy of her question. He didn't answer it either.

"I tried to ask KC when we were stretching, but she's being odd today."

Laylea blew air through her teeth like she was a dog. "Yeah, it's a full moon tonight." Too late she remembered KC probably hadn't told him that she was a werewolf. She mumbled, "She's sensitive?" It came out like a question as she raced to get a foot on the ball as it flew across the field in their direction.

She missed. Norman kicked the ball hard. In the wrong direction. He was razzed by his team, but didn't pay any attention.

"Okay, but like I need to know so I can tell Uncle Johnny if I'm going on rounds with him that morning and stuff."

"You should totally do rounds," Laylea said. "We're kind of both in detention until further notice."

Bailey had gotten detention a lot in school. It just meant he had to sit in a room and do his homework for fifteen minutes or so after school. She hoped it was a plausible excuse.

"Oh. Is that why she won't go to the movies with me?" he asked.

"Yeah," Laylea said, like only an idiot wouldn't know that. "She'd love to go to the movies with you."

"Really?" Norman said in a small, giddy voice.

She grimaced. KC was going to be unhappy with her.

The ball flew toward them, giving Laylea the excuse she needed to run away. She did not want to mess up that relationship. Anytime KC tried to broach the subject of Laylea's weird shifting, Laylea just brought up Norman. Subject changed. Easy peasy.

Oscar was even easier to put off. He'd become a model student since Halloween, going to see Tipp without them harassing him, studying, even taking on more science courses voluntarily.

Laylea searched for him. There weren't enough positions in soccer or enough room on the South Lawn for more than one game, so lots of students were on the sidelines with the parents. And with his knee—

Tara yelled, "It's yours, Lee!"

Laylea ran for the ball and missed. It rolled past her into the onlookers.

"Here you go." A familiar man with a close-cropped afro kicked the ball to her. She was so surprised to see Officer Garcia there that she missed it again. He didn't have a kid in school, did he? He was a cop. He was the cop who'd arrested Denier and taken him away, in fact.

"Ya doing great, Lee. Get back out der." Diejuste shooed her away. A voudon loa in the body of a nearly twelve-year-old girl, Diejuste was definitely not a parent.

"Hi." Laylea grinned. "What are you doing here?"

Diejuste's face lit up with an infectious secretive smile as she melted into the crowd.

Laylea hadn't even considered that any of her family would be on the sidelines. Bailey was too busy with medical school to even respond to her letters.

She wiped tears from her eyes, overwhelmed by the idea that her friends from Team Wyrdos had come to see her. And then her brain took over from her emotions. There would be a full moon overhead in eight hours, Delcampo devotees had declared war on non-wolves, and nearly half the school was upstairs. Morioka had brought Team Wyrdos to protect them, not to see her.

Bitters blew his whistle. "Off sides."

Another Wyrdo, Lucio, hollered from the far side of the pitch, "Get your head in the game, Woodford."

"Like you'd do any better, Lucio," his fellow brownie, Orin, called from behind her team's goal.

"One on one," Lucio cried back. "You and me, bro."

Laylea looked around for Morioka, Dee, and Amal. She found Junior, searching the crowd, too.

The cry of a dozen seagulls interrupted their familiar bickering. Their harsh calls cut through the air like alarms, stopping all chatter as kids and parents alike looked to the sky. The birds' gray forms wheeling against the grey November sky.

Half the adults on the sidelines raced away toward the sound. Both Captain Morioka and Dee were among them.

Laylea shook her arm like Reggie as her stasis band bit her, stopping her from shifting dog and running toward the danger with her friends.

25

A chilly breeze blew across the South Lawn, raising goosebumps on Laylea's human arms. Other than Norman stepping back to block the wind, no kid on the field moved. The soccer ball rolled, forgotten, past Tara's feet as she hustled toward Uncle Johnny and her little girl on the sidelines.

Off the field, adults and kids ran every which way, some running away, some running toward the screaming gulls swooping in dizzying patterns over the East Gate and Adelor, the lion statue covering a secret stairway into the zoo. They ran past the café and the construction fence surrounding the Lion House where the lift down into school waited.

The brownies disappeared, speeding off faster than the human eye could track to help karma in their own special way.

Dee, a bulb of red curls sticking out of the back of a Chicago Police Department ball cap ran across the field. "Everybody downstairs. Call it, Enforcer."

As she approached him, Bitters blew a long blast on his whistle. He yelled, "To the Lion House." In a quieter voice, he said, "Muldoon, McCobb, take over." He handed the whistle off to Ms. McCobb and jogged down the path past the Park Place Café.

Students milled about the field, staring at the flock of seagulls shrieking over the East Gate.

"To the Lion House or we'll never play upstairs again!" McCobb's threat got them moving.

"Stay close to the café as you head down the path," Dee shouted. "Head left into the Lion House through the gate. Four-Four," she yelled to the cops, "stay to the right."

While the students raced for the Lion House and the lift down to safety, their eyes followed the seagulls. Laylea and Norman followed with more than just their eyes.

It wasn't hard to slip past the herding adults in all the commotion. Where the kids turned left to duck through the opening in the construction fencing around the Lion House, Laylea simply continued on toward the East Gate. Norman followed her.

"Hey, did you see Dee?" Junior's question startled Laylea.

She jumped and slapped at the stasis band zapping her wrist.

"How'd she get in the zoo?" he asked. "She's not a—"

"Neither are you." Laylea cut him off. She really needed to ask KC how much Norman knew about 'Cate's friends.'

Junior scrunched his eyebrows in confusion. Laylea aped the gesture. He wasn't a shifter. He was the boogeyman's son. Did he not know Norman?

She turned to find Norman whispering with KC and interrupted. "Norman, this is Junior. Junior, this is KC's *true* friend, Norman."

The confusion cleared. Junior shook the kid's hand. "Hey man, the zoo is closed down. How did you get in?"

That was a great question.

Norman answered with a secretive glint in his eye, "I'm a friend of Cate's."

"Who should gather his uncle and leave before anybody checks on that," KC said pointedly.

Before he could respond, the seagulls coalesced over the East Gate archway. They dove and darted at the trio of cops marching Jase Batka back into the zoo, screeching senselessly. Despite the cops' rough handling, Jase offered no resistance. He shivered as a breeze washed over the sweat dripping down his neck, but kept his eyes down, nearly closed, as if he were lost in his own world.

Laylea's band bit her repeatedly as her body tried to shift seagull so she could understand.

"He got a letter off to somebody," one of the cops yelled at the gulls. "Go follow her."

The seagulls ignored the order. They swooped down, claws out as two red-faced humans escaped the security guards at the gate and ran at Jase. The woman shared Jase's mocking eyes, thick brows, and tall forehead. The man's bulbous nose echoed Jase's but over a luscious beard Jase could only dream of growing. Both screamed obscenities as they made their mad dash. Dad Batka was thwarted by the seagulls, but Mom Batka reached him.

"Marina!" Jase's dad called after his wife. Blood flowed down his face from gull scratches on his bald head. "You get him, Marina. They can't keep our boy imprisoned like this."

Jase rolled his eyes.

"I am not a fan of his parents," Oscar murmured, slipping up behind Laylea, KC, and Norman.

Norman scoffed, gesturing at Jase. "He isn't either."

"Look," KC breathed, grabbing Laylea's hand.

Jase's mom, Marina, kept up a stream of invectives, cursing the cops, the school, and all non-wolves. She waved one hand ineffectually at the seagulls. Her multiple bracelets clinked and jangled, drawing most everybody's attention up. The metallic sound rang sharply, covering the barely audible crinkle of paper. Few people noticed her stuffing something in her son's pocket.

Jase noticed.

Laylea and her friends noticed.

"Get your filthy hands off of me." Having achieved her real goal, Marina Batka allowed Officer Garcia to haul her away. Though she clawed his face and fought like a badger.

A woman with a long, silky ponytail falling halfway down her back from her Chicago PD ball cap joined him. She spoke a few quiet words into Marina Batka's ear and Jase's mom calmed instantly. Garcia slipped on the cuffs just as a cruiser pulled up to the curb. The woman helped Jase's mom into one side while a whole bunch of cops shoved his dad in the other.

His dad yelled, "You can't keep us from our son. He's not a presser." He said "presser" with exactly the same disdain as his son.

"That tracks," KC said quietly.

"He is now," Bitters muttered, passing the kids. He stopped and turned to scan them. "You're all students?" he asked.

Laylea's heart sped up. She stepped in front of Norman as if her five-foot-three, hundred-pound form could hide a five-foot-ten boy. Her band sparked as she held her arm up with the others, showing the enforcer that they were.

Norman held his own wrist out, a silver band wrapped around it. Laylea stared, wondering how he'd gotten one and how she could get him to give it to her.

"Alright, go on downstairs now." Bitters turned back to his main concern. "Show's over."

"Who are the people in the parking lot?" Oscar asked. "Isn't the zoo supposed to be closed off?"

The adults who hadn't stopped by the Lion House fencing to see their children safely downstairs swarmed the perimeter of the zoo and the parking lot. Many of them were dressed like Dee and Garcia, in athletic wear emblazoned with the Chicago Police Department logo. Dozens of squad cars circled the lot, rousting an inordinate number of people in balaclavas.

"Those are wolves," KC said, almost to herself. "Aren't they?"

Bitters sighed. "Get downstairs. I'll see y'all Tuesday."

Around Jase, seagulls dove and swooped, creating chaos as his escorts continued to haul him toward the Lion House. Jase kept his eyes straight ahead. He ignored them all, shoving a hand into the pocket with his mother's note.

"Adelor," Bitters ran forward to redirect them. "Take him to Holding."

Laylea spun to confront Norman. "Where did you get a stasis band?"

"It's not a real student band," KC said, with no particular emphasis on the altered name. "It's just a slap bracelet."

"Oh, yeah." Norman held his arm up between them. He peeled the band off into a long flat rectangle of silvery plastic and then slapped it back around his wrist with a snap. It was like a real band, just without the magic. "I found it at a party store."

"Shh, I can't hear." Oscar shushed them without taking his eyes off the cops around Jase.

"We can't take him through the other students," Bitters intercepted the perp walk as they reached the convergence of the paths that could take them ahead to the Lion House, left to the carousel, or back toward the South Lawn.

There was some argument between the officials about the danger of taking Jase back to the parking lot. The seagulls made their opinions known in a language understood by no one but themselves. Some of them landed on the rounded cover of the nearby trashcan to get closer to the discussion.

Bitters' gentle tone disappeared. "I am the Council Enforcer," he announced in a voice that turned all heads his way. The words held a power he'd not dared to command before, making him stand straighter, making everybody in earshot stand straighter. "Guards, to your posts."

The gulls over Jase ceased their squawking and flew away. Some perched on the East Gate archway, some on the stone wall. The rest flew out over the parking lot to harass the wolves being chased and arrested there.

As Bitters and the cops watched the seagulls, Jase pulled his hand out of his pocket and, without looking at it, tossed a crumpled piece of paper at the trash can. He missed. The paper ball bounced once on the cold pavement with a soft tap before rolling to a stop under the can.

"I've got the kid. Go round up those others." Bitters took hold of

Jase's arm and pushed through the cops, back toward Adelor, who stood open, swung off his plinth.

Nobody noticed the dropped note.

Oscar ran for it.

26

The biting air off the lake hadn't bothered Laylea when she was running up and down the field. Watching Oscar chase Jase's note, however, sent ice shooting through her veins.

Bitters had turned his back on them to drag Jase off to Holding. All the undercover cops who'd been roaming the sidelines with Dee were busy chasing werewolves in the parking lot. Most of the rest of the adults were busy hurrying the students back downstairs to safety.

Nobody should have seen him.

Oscar had nearly reached the can when an older cop with a mustache that might have been fashionable in the nineteen-seventies grabbed for him. "Hey, you!"

Oscar dove to scoop the paper up and Laylea lost sight of him behind the trash can for a moment. She, Norman, KC, and Junior all hurried to rescue him.

They stopped at the sight of Amal standing up behind the trash can, a giggling Diejuste in his arms. The cop yanked Oscar up, wrestling one arm behind his back.

"He didn't mean any harm, Officer." Amal smiled in his unflappable way, showing more reserve than the windblown little girl in his arms. "Thank you, young man. Jane could have been trampled if not for your quick thinking. Young lady." He turned a stern tone on the goddess. "I told you to stay close."

Diejuste, in a manner unlike her usual, peaceful, all-knowing self and more like the young girl she appeared to be, shouted, "Wheeeeeee!"

Amal hid his grin with a cough. He turned to the uniformed cop gripping Oscar by the arm. "Thank you, Officer. I'm sure Mr. Luke has his feet under him now." After a pause that made it clear the cop didn't recognize the name, Amal added, "His father, Head Councilmember Luke, raised him right, don't you agree?"

The cop dropped Oscar like he was on fire.

"I'll be sure he gets downstairs safely." Amal said this while setting Diejuste on the ground.

"Norman, you've gotta go." Laylea stopped talking when she turned to find herself standing with only KC and Junior. Norman had disappeared as magically as Amal had appeared.

KC sidled up close. Keeping her voice low, she said, "Norman knows when he's not wanted."

"He's not some kind of wyrdo that can go invisible?" Laylea asked with a grin.

KC smirked at Laylea. "No. He just knows how to be quiet. I guess it was a useful skill in his house." She ducked her eyes and then looked away at the scene around Oscar.

Laylea wove her fingers into KC's. Teasing, she asked, "Oh, is that why he spends so much time at the zoo?"

A blush darkened KC's face and she fought a grin as she shot back, "It used to be."

Across the way, Diejuste grabbed Oscar's free hand and walked him back to the others, saying in quiet approval, "Your sister is going through it, Oscar. You're loving her good."

Oscar stared at Diejuste in awe. She smiled up at him and rubbed his hand with all the gravity of a proud grandmother.

Then she spotted Junior and squealed, running to him.

"KC, Oscar, this is our friend Diejuste." Junior dropped to a knee to be bowled over by her hug.

"Ya look like me, now." The little girl said this without irony as she held the boogeyman's milk-pale cheeks in her dark black hands.

"Pff, I'm like fourteen and you're still only, what, eleven?"

"I am a being with no age and you are wise beyond ya zits. I ran with Amal!" she exclaimed, bouncing. "Y'all were frozen still and we ran right by ya. I have never felt that before." Her grin widened, fit to split her face.

"Let's get you downstairs," Amal rested his gaze on Junior and Diejuste as he finished in a tone dryer than the Sahara, "kids."

"Guys," Junior said, leading the way back to the lion house. "This is Amal, one of the brownies."

"A pleasure," Amal said to KC and Oscar. To Junior he muttered, "We're just telling everyone now?"

"This is KC," Junior replied with raised eyebrows. "And this is Oscar."

"Oh." Amal regarded them each more carefully.

"Nice to meet you, too," Oscar managed.

Laylea's band sparked in rhythm with her happily waving mental tail. She wished her friends were meeting each other under different circumstances, but it was still pretty awesome.

As they walked, Diejuste took KC's hand. She looked up at the werewolf, her eyes brilliant with inner sight. "Your blood doesn't matter like ya heart do. It knows right from wrong. Your brothers' choices don't need to be yours."

Blood rose in KC's cheeks along with tears in her eyes. A smile fluttered on her lips, here and gone again.

Laylea knew better than to try to interpret Diejuste's words to someone else. It didn't matter. She grabbed KC's other hand and followed the others the last few steps.

Only a few kids remained outside the gate, their parents not ready to say goodbye.

Other parents demanded to know how the school planned to keep their kids safe.

"All the wolves should be kicked out," a thin man screamed in Ms. Muldoon face.

The chemistry teacher took a deep breath, turning her hazel eyes down, spotting her bright green stocking cap in the grass. She raised a hand to her wild hair as if she hadn't noticed it fall off. Releasing her breath, she looked up at the man.

"The boy wasn't trying to hurt anybody," Ms. Muldoon informed a father tightly. "He was just trying to run away."

Muldoon was known for bouncing off the walls with excitement in her classes. Facing the parents, steam rose off the bare skin of her face and she clasped her gloved hands as if holding herself back.

Diejuste tore away from Oscar and KC to tug Laylea into a hug. "You made good friends, Lee," she said into her ear. "I like them. You should trust them."

Junior wrapped his arms around the both of them and squeezed.

While Laylea struggled to breathe in his embrace, Amal huddled with her friends. "Lee hasn't given us your secrets," he told them. "Bondye sent Diejuste to help families. That's how she knows what she knows."

"Yes, sir, don't worry," Oscar reassured him. "Lee would never. She's so careful with secrets, they sometimes eat her up inside when we're right here to help."

"Let's go," Ms. McCobb called from the gate. She blew her whistle just like she did to gather them in class.

Junior leapt up and ran through the gate, high-fiving McCobb. Oscar and KC followed, dragging their feet as Laylea pushed herself up to follow, still goggling at Oscar's words. She moved slowly, her thoughts bubbling like a stream parting around boulders.

"Be good, Lee," Amal called. With a grin, he added, "Nice hat."

"We'll keep an eye out for ya," said the little girl who was not what she appeared to be.

"Thanks." It was the polite response. And Laylea repeated it to Ms. McCobb as the teacher checked her in.

But she couldn't help wondering what they were keeping an eye out for. You couldn't spot a werewolf on sight. And even if you could, you couldn't tell which ones were dangerous, just like with any other creature. And if Norman could sneak in and out of the zoo without being caught, so could anybody.

So why had Jase let himself be caught after delivering his letter? Why had he tossed his mother's note?

His nose had been as crinkled up as the note, disgust written in every line of his face as he aimed for the garbage can. It contrasted wildly with the image stuck in her brain of his brown eyes gone big when he called her the True. Awe had lit up his face. The corners of his stupid, wispy attempt at a mustache turned up as he gazed at her.

Far in the distance, a wolf cried, "Awhoooooooo."

The howl was a taunt.

It was echoed by dozens of others.

Laylea's stasis band sparked against her skin. Kids grabbed at their wrists as every head turned to the werewolf chorus in the parking lot.

Behind them, Brenda exploded out of the door with a scream filled with fury. Kids fell to the ground from the violence of her passing.

"No." Ms. Crow dashed in front of her.

Brenda ducked sideways to slip around the librarian. Ms. McCobb grabbed at her uniform, slowing Brenda for a step.

Ms. Muldoon slammed the gate shut. It accidentally knocked Laylea into Brenda's path.

Using his powers, Amal dashed through the gate before it closed. He appeared, Diejuste in his arms, just as Brenda dodged sideways to avoid Laylea. She ran right into them.

Diejuste's reaching hands grasped Brenda's. The goddess' voice rang in Laylea's skull. "Speak."

Brenda's knees hit the ground, dirt billowing around her at the impact. Grief and terror contorted her face. "They stole my dad. They stole his life. They can't get away with it!"

Her screams faded as she buried her face in her knees. Diejuste wrapped herself around the python-shifter, humming wordlessly.

Ms. Crow knelt at their side. "They won't, Brenda. They won't. But we can't let you get hurt, too. That would destroy your father."

Ms. Muldoon put a hand on Laylea's back and ushered her past the scene. “Let’s get downstairs,” she said in a voice that wavered with emotion. She clutched her stocking cap with white-knuckled fingers.

Laylea grabbed Amal. “Her father is Brian Samborsky, from the sleep lab,” she told him.

Amal nodded. He’d been there, with her and Junior, when they first found the sleep lab. He’d been attracted to the great good karma lighting Brenda’s father up like a Christmas tree.

Amal said, “I’ll do what I can.” But his dark face was shadowed with decades of waging unwinnable wars.

As a Black man in America, he had little reason for hope. As a wyrdo in a world ruled by true-humans, often by thumpers if she reserved the word for those selfish, prejudiced, superstitious, small-minded people who deserved it, he knew better than her what it was like to be hunted. And as a brownie, he could feel the bad karma in the world as strongly as he could the good.

It would hurt him and all her dear friends if Grandpa got her.

And there was no doubt in her mind that Grandpa was coming for her.

Jase had gotten out of the school. He’d gotten all the way to a parking lot reeking of wolves. She had to assume that Grandpa knew who she was and what she was.

Amal would do what he could to help Brenda. Brenda was doing everything she could to help her dad. The least Laylea could to do was to get out of the school before Grandpa hurt them all in his hunt for her.

But she could do so much more. Her mother was a powerful witch. Her father and his friends were super soldiers. She could bring them to Chicago.

No matter how much she loved it at LPSS, Laylea had to leave.

27

Last on the elevator, Laylea and her friends stood crushed against the metal grate as they descended. Ms. Muldoon made her way through to the far side. The anger radiating off the normally ebullient teacher moving kids out of her way faster than any words.

Kids barely waited for her to slide the opposite grate open before they poured out into the Old School halls. Dr. Tippleston hurried to remove stasis bands, check kids in, and shoo them on into the Grand Parlor. Ms. Muldoon helped, but it still took ages for the volume of voices to lower to bearable. Everybody had an opinion. Everybody was angry.

Laylea was scared.

To calm the tightness in her throat and pounding of her heart, she planned.

It wasn't enough for her to leave the school. She had to be sure Grandpa found out that she had left. She'd have to tell Carrie, so she could make sure Jase found out and stopped Grandpa from invading the school, again.

She wouldn't have to tell Carrie why she was running. Laylea had been trying to leave school ever since she'd been pressed the first time. Carrie shouldn't be shocked that she wanted out.

"Ow." KC clutched her arm to her chest, breathing deep and wiggling her thumbs, the way Laylea did when she wanted to stay human.

"I'm sorry." Ms. Muldoon was only moderately more gentle removing Laylea and Oscar's stasis bands. She pushed them toward the pigeonhole cubbies beside the lift. "Get your things and move into the Grand Parlor."

Dr. Tippleston shot a glance at KC, then focused on Ms. Muldoon's harsh whispering.

As KC reached up to snag her backpack from the pigeonholes, her sleeve pulled back, dragging blood from a scratch on her wrist. Oscar helped as he toed his sneakers off and kicked them into the pile.

Laylea crouched to remove her too-large sneakers. She huddled over her feet to hide them from the others. They had grown to fit the shoes and when she took them off, they shrank again, burning as they did.

The torn and bloody knees of her uniform reminded her how much her legs hurt. Quick as the thought, the burn in her feet shot up her legs. Laylea sucked in a breath, and dug her nails into her thighs, painting glittering paisley mind designs on her birthmark. The burning dissipated, taking the pain with it.

She yanked up one leg of her uniform. Despite not shifting, her knee was whole, no scrapes, no bruising.

"Fine. Notate it however you want, Tipp." Ms. Muldoon hopped back onto the lift and yanked the grate closed with more force than was strictly necessary. As she rose out of sight, she growled, "We've got one more. Brenda Samborsky. Try to clear the place out before she can incite another riot."

Concern wrinkled Dr. Tipp's face as she watched Muldoon ascend.

Oscar took a step closer to the doc. He lowered his voice. "Brenda can't see her dad and—" he began explaining.

Dr. Tippleston gave him a speaking look. "I know," she said. And it was clear that she did.

She fell in beside KC as the three of them headed down the short hallway to the Grand Parlor. "Would you like me to look at your arm, KC?"

KC shook her head. "It's just a scratch."

"Alright," the doctor allowed. "Head back to your dorms until your next class."

Laylea put her collar on with her eyes pinned to the entryway. The doors stood open and ignored. Ms. Correnti and Mr. Tataryn were fully engrossed, examining blueprints taped to a rolling chalkboard. Kids milled around, sprawled on couches and gossiping, no doubt spreading word of Brenda's breakdown.

Laylea needed to get somewhere quiet, somewhere she could think.

She froze, her breath catching in her throat as Jase and Bitters stopped in the corridor outside. Bitters ducked down the short foyer into the room and called Mr. Tataryn over.

"Is that Jase?" Ahanu yelled, moving to get a better view of the corridor.

In the hallway, Jase looked up from his handcuffed wrists.

"Did you bring the wolves here, you asshole?" Emerald screamed.

All around the room, students exploded into their animal forms. Birds soared overhead. Ungulates stomped their hooves. Reptiles hissed. Brian pounded his chest and bellowed a roar that silenced everyone.

Bitters backed out of the room, pulling one door shut.

Mr. Tataryn slammed the other door before anybody could reach it. "The enforcer has it handled. We're going to wait here until he gives the all clear."

It was unlikely most people heard his words. But nobody could mistake his wide-legged, cross-armed stance in front of the doors. Behind the normally peacefully man, Ms. Correnti glared. Laylea didn't know anybody who'd try her.

The kids turned their energy inwards, many of them flashing human again to voice their anger a little more cogently.

Britny muttered, "I told you wolves can't control themselves on a full moon."

"Wolves can't control themselves ever," Harper retorted.

A small voice called out, "But the moon doesn't rise till four."

Laylea tuned them all out. Her mind whirled with fears. She blocked them out with plans. Planning always worked.

But every plan she could think of, she could also crush. The school was going to be on even stronger lockdown what with Jase nearly getting away. Sneaking upstairs wasn't going to be as easy as it had been in the past. Poor Toby wouldn't be having any midnight visitors for a while.

"Lee," Oscar hissed, "this way."

KC tugged on her arm, pulling her to the kitchen door and away from the chaos.

"What does it say?" KC asked Oscar, tripping over her own feet in her rush to keep up with him and hold on to Laylea.

Laylea blinked. She had forgotten the note that Jase's mother shoved in his pocket.

Oscar didn't respond. He pushed through the swinging door and held it as they passed into the quiet of the Old School kitchen. Reggie and Kara sat, entangled in each other, on the prep surface. Chef Tod would be appalled. Neither looked up. They were too deep in each other's tonsils to notice they had an audience.

"Come on." Oscar shoved the girls ahead of him toward a heavy door.

Laylea jerked her shoulder out when she tried to pull it open. KC wrapped her hands on the bar over Laylea's and it opened with a sucking sound onto a dark tunnel. They might have turned away, but Oscar was hot on their heels, eager to avoid Reggie's wrath if he caught them snooping.

The heavy door fell closed with another sucking sound, sealing them in. They hurried forward through the cold and ran into another door, just as heavy. Oscar helped them wrestle this one.

Light flooded the stone tunnel along with a pattering sound like a herd of students rushing quietly out of the library.

The three stepped into a green wonderland and stared around, letting the wet warmth and the smell of life and earth wash over them.

Laylea curled her toes into the cold dirt beneath her feet.

"This isn't possible," KC breathed. She'd taken crops 101. She'd know.

"Magic isn't possible," Oscar chuckled.

Laylea added, "Shifters aren't possible."

The entire room was smaller than the South Lawn. Fruit trees grew on islands in a swamp of rice stalks. Root vegetables grew alongside tomatoes and wheat. Everywhere, herbs filled the spaces between other crops. Water tumbled down one wall, drenching plants growing out of the stones. Vines climbed the walls on every side, reaching across the ceiling, dangling out-of-season melons and strawberries. Sunlight shone through these vines, filling the small, underground garden with light and warmth.

"I guess we know why the witches didn't starve." Oscar reached for a strawberry from the wall beside the door. Jase's crumpled message dropped from his hand.

KC dove for the paper.

"Was that his mom, you think?" Oscar asked her.

KC rolled her eyes as she flattened the paper against a thigh, muttering, "They look exactly alike." She waved the paper. "Yeah, this is signed, 'Mom.' Not 'love Mom,' just 'Mom.'"

"Are we supposed to feel bad for him?" Oscar asked through a mouth full of strawberry.

KC blinked up at him. "Actually," she said. "I kinda do."

A path of flat, wide stones circled the garden in a spiral that ended at the base of a chimera tree. Laylea hopped onto one stone.

Oscar took the note from KC and read it. "'Lay low tonight. Forces are gathering for the next full moon. Mom.'"

"But he didn't read it," KC said.

"Yeah," Oscar agreed. "That's weird."

The tree called to Laylea. She'd never seen anything like it. A real tree grew one kind of leaves, one kind of nut, one kind of bark. Dozens of different leaves sprouted from this tree in every stage of maturity. Green balls grew from one branch, spiky red pods from the branch beside that, and clumps of white flowers from another. A myriad of nuts lay at the base of the tree, waiting to be scooped up and cracked.

That too-familiar burn shot down her arms. Laylea automatically turned away from her friends.

Dark, gnarled bark crumbled off her arms as she folded them, thin yellow leaves falling from her hands.

She was out of control and couldn't imagine what was making her body want to go tree. Was it that a tree had a place to live where it felt safe and useful, where it wouldn't be hunted or used to hurt her friends?

She growled at her arms.

If she'd gone tree in Gryphon Dorm, Jase might not have discovered her or her secret. She might be able to keep hiding, to stay.

"Do you think he went up just to get that note?" KC hopped onto a stone.

"No," Oscar tucked the note away in a pocket. "That cop said he handed a letter to someone who took off, remember?"

"I didn't hear that."

"Yeah, Bitters was focused on the escape attempt, but the cops were more upset about Jase getting a message out," Oscar said.

KC groaned, "What do you think it was about?"

"It was about me." Laylea said.

Only when she turned to face her friends did she feel the tears pouring down her face. Heat rose, flushing her skin. It wasn't the burn of change. It was shame.

28

Dogs didn't blush. They didn't cry tears. They didn't have tree branches for arms or feet that grew and shrank to fit the available shoes. That burn of change rolled in her gut, flaring as she yearned for her tail.

"No!" Laylea yelled at herself.

Oscar took a step back.

KC took a step forward.

"I won't run away." Laylea shook her arms out, mentally shooting the burning from her gut to her biceps, forearms, and thumbs. She imagined her birthmark lighting up, washing her friends in a white glow. When she brought her hands to her face, they were human with pale pink skin, short nails, and smooth, callous-free pads despite hours upon hours of guitar practice.

"Lee?" KC asked quietly.

Laylea nodded, mostly to herself. She forced her eyes up. She had to face her friends and tell them the truth. "The letter Jase got out was to Grandpa, about me. Jase saw me shift into a bear. He saw me shift into Sierra." She scoffed at herself, finally admitting it wasn't the witch Ben glamouring her during the P2 attack. She'd shifted herself to look like Denier's intern beta.

"Jase knows I'm..." She choked on the words, not ready to believe it, much less say it. She cleared her throat and tried again. "I think I'm the true shifter."

She forced herself to look at her friends and face their shock.

Oscar watched her as if expecting her to say more. When she didn't, he rolled his eyes. "Finally. Now, doesn't that feel better?"

"Shush, kitty," KC admonished him. She wrapped her arms around Laylea, pulling her close. "We know you are. It's gonna be okay."

Laylea pushed away. "No," she said. "It's not gonna be okay. Grandpa needs the blood of the true shifter to create a new drug, a worse drug than N. Denier wasn't only looking for the phoenix and a way to get rid of Oscar. He was also looking for me. Well, for the true shifter. He didn't know it was me." She paused to take a breath. Her head was spinning. The stress of keeping all that shifting secret from her friends leached strength from her as she let it go.

She dropped her gaze, unable to look into KC's understanding eyes. "I didn't know it was me."

"How could you know?" Oscar wrapped an arm around her. "Your parents didn't know anything about shifters."

"You probably thought it was just puberty, finally," KC said.

They were being so understanding. Laylea couldn't stand it. She burst into sobs, wailing, "I should have told you."

KC hugged her. Oscar wrapped his arms around the both of them.

KC murmured in her ear, "I didn't tell you about Norman."

Laylea snorted. "Oh yeah, the girl who can't go upstairs for fear of being recognized is suddenly going upstairs every chance she gets? We figured it out."

"And covered for you." Oscar tapped the top of Laylea's head with his pointy chin. "Just like we covered for you, Lee."

"Yeah, we figured out you were the True," KC said gently. She pushed Laylea back to catch her eyes. "Now, all we need to figure out is," she looked up at Oscar, "who convinced you, sir, to take so many new classes."

Laylea grinned, thrilled to have the attention off her. She tipped her head back to see Oscar. "We know you signed up for a bunch of science classes."

"What's with the science, Oscar?" KC spun Laylea so they could face him down together.

"You hate science."

Oscar's cheeks flushed. He ducked his head. "KC, can I get something from your pack?"

"No."

Oscar sucked his teeth at her. Grudgingly, he said, "I'll tell you if you let me get something out of your pack."

Without another word, KC turned her back to them. Oscar dug through her pack. He handed Laylea a bag of trail mix, then pulled out the little first aid kit. He searched it while simultaneously hopping stone by stone to the wall where watercress and wild strawberries peeked out from a tumbling waterfall.

The girls followed, Laylea shoveling nuts and raisins in her mouth.

"Give me your arm." Oscar handed the open kit to Laylea to hold, retaining a clean cloth and disinfectant spray.

KC demurred. "I'm fine."

"It's either me or we drag you to see Tipp."

"I'd like to see you try." KC puffed herself up.

Laylea imagined KC's white hackles rising and had to tamp down a burning on her own back.

Oscar grinned. "You know I can. And she'll want to see you try to heal it by shifting first," he said.

KC growled. She also rolled up her sleeve. "Now, spill."

"Lee, you remember at Halloween when Dove's dad knocked Calliope down?" Oscar asked. He tucked the spray bottle under one arm to gently push KC's sleeve up. The fabric stuck to the bloody wound.

"Who?" KC asked.

"Calliope," Laylea answered, "Nice girl, our age. She isn't in school because she hasn't 'pupated' yet."

"Our age," KC repeated. She looked squarely at Oscar to ask, "Cute?"

He glanced up at her raised eyebrow and tore the sleeve free of the scratch.

"Ow!"

Blood dribbled up from the reopened wound.

"Whoops. Come here." Oscar manhandled her closer to the wall and held her forearm, bloody sleeve and all, under the water.

KC sucked in a breath but then her shoulders dropped a good inch as she released it.

"It's colder than I expected," Oscar said. "It might be cold enough to numb it." He tried to move her arm out of the waterfall, but she growled.

"Leave it."

He laughed.

"Ha ha ha." KC grabbed the chest of his uniform and pulled him toward her. "Why are you taking science classes?"

"Angel, Calliope's mom, got me talking about Shala and my mom. Angel's a doctor and she wants to volunteer at the clinic when they get it open." He moved KC's arm out of the water and dried it off with the clean cloth. "She said I don't need my sister's permission to help with the clinic."

He sprayed disinfectant along the two-inch cut. Laylea had a bandage ready for him when he tossed the spray bottle back into the kit.

"So." He lined the bandage up and wrapped it around KC's wrist, smoothing every edge to be sure it stuck well. "I'm going to learn everything I can about how we work so I can help all the N addicts and sleepers. We should get you a new uniform."

Avoiding their eyes, Oscar busily zipped up the kit and tucked it back into KC's pack with extra care. He shoved the used cloth into his pocket and snagged the empty trail mix sack from Laylea.

They watched as he hurried away from them, hopping precariously from stone to stone toward the tree.

"That's really sweet, Oscar." KC said it quietly.

It was the first time he'd talked about Shala refusing to see him. And apparently it was all he intended to say.

Oscar plucked a handful of nuts from the forest of salad greens at the foot of the tree and cracked them against the bark. "So, you think Jase wasn't trying to escape," he said, definitively changing the subject.

Laylea went with it. She needed their help if she was going to get out of the school before Grandpa came for her. "Yeah," she confirmed. "He just needed to get a message to Grandpa Delcampo."

"But he didn't give it to his parents," Oscar said, chewing.

That was strange. His mom had to chase him down to get him her "stand back and stand by" message. If he'd given them the letter, she could have given him the order then.

"Why not?" she asked out loud.

"KC, do you know when his parents moved them down here?"

"I don't. But —" She interrupted herself. "Give me your handkerchief, Lee."

Laylea dug it from her pocket. "But what?"

KC sighed. "But..." Her eyes went distant while she chose her words. "I think Grandpa has to already know. Denier's interns all saw you shift into Sierra. There's no way one of them didn't tell him."

"They got arrested. Sierra was thrown back into the mental hospital," Laylea protested.

"Because she was dithering about magic and some girl stealing her face," Oscar said pointedly. "KC is right. Grandpa would assume that meant the true shifter was here."

"Which means I have to leave. And we have to make sure he finds out that I left." She growled her unhappiness, her throat burning as it shifted to allow her a more animal response.

Laylea had hoped her friends would point out that it would be silly for her leave.

KC raised Laylea's hands to create a platform and laid the unfolded handkerchief across them.

"But you just came back," Oscar whined.

"Oscar," KC snapped.

"Can Junior whisk you out with his boogeyman powers?" he asked.

"No," KC collected strawberries into the handkerchief. "There's actually a school rule about no closets in sleeping areas because of his dad. Cal made Junior promise to respect that rule."

Oscar crouched at the base of the tree. "After he gave Dr. Fenn a heart attack, I don't blame her."

"Yeah, Junior's dad sounds like the kind of guy who'd bring wolves in, just for funsies," Laylea said.

Oscar shoveled nuts into the trail mix sack.

KC wrapped the handkerchief around the strawberries and tucked the package into the front pocket of her backpack.

"You'll just have to graduate," she declared as if it were a done deal.

Oscar laughed. He shot the girls a grimace. "Sorry. I'm not worried about the academic tests. But, if Lee wants to graduate, she's gonna have to shift… into a dog… on command."

That was going to be a problem.

29

Ten minutes from the end of Shifter Sociology, Laylea grunted and dropped her deskpadd in her lap. Not one thing on the test was going to help her graduate.

Two dozen students tapped and typed on mobile deskpadds, desperate to get their answers down before Mr. Barrett called time on the quiz. Laylea wasn't concerned. Her grade in the course wouldn't be calculated until long after she was gone, which was a good thing because Barrett's questions hadn't come from the textbook.

The man had gone off the reservation. His quizzes had started reading more like surveys than tests. She looked back at the question blinking on her padd.

If your family has different rules than your community, which are more important for you to follow?

That was not an appropriate question for a pop quiz. How would Barrett even grade it? Which community was he referring to? The shifters? The true-humans? The Delcampo wolves? Not to mention how thoughtless it was to ask such a question of the many orphans in LPSS.

Mr. Barrett was not bringing his A-game.

As the last remaining wolf faculty and token pack alpha for the school, Mr. Barrett was feeling pressure.

He hadn't been upstairs since talking to the cops the day Denier was arrested. He didn't go up for Thanksgiving or his famous monthly poker game. Instead, he played endless games of gin rummy with Professor Wanja where they discussed how different the world had been two hundred years back.

With the witches debunking the lies the wolfpack sold after the Phoenix Event, Mr. Barrett was questioning everything he'd learned and taught. Laylea had thought he was coming down on the anti-Delcampo side, but his pop quiz suggested he hadn't decided anything yet.

Not that the students were doing much better. Bitters had thought that seeing their parents would calm the kids' fears. It didn't occur to him that the parents would tell their kids about the increase in violent crime across the entire Midwest. They all brought stories back from Thanksgiving.

Britny spent the holiday cleaning up her aunt's veterinary practice in Michigan after it was set on fire. Other vets in the area had been vandalized and robbed. She said only one vet clinic wasn't touched; the one owned by wolves.

Parents passed along similar stories happening all across the Midwest. ERs were reporting a rash of "animal" attacks. The true-human government kept slinging blame but not doing much else.

A leather couch creaked as Barrett leaned onto it, peering over Milly's shoulder. She squeaked and froze. Everybody looked up. Barrett didn't notice. He moved on, strolling to the next conversation nook of comfy chairs and couches.

Ahanu flinched as Barrett's shadow passed over his padd. The thunderbird shifter wriggled closer to his neighbor on the loveseat and kept typing.

Dustin baldly watched Barrett from the chair he'd slunk into after Barrett made him move away from Vaughn.

Barrett had instituted a new rule after P2. Werewolves were not allowed to sit together. It made class unpleasant for everyone since it meant every conversational nook included a wolf and at least one kid who'd been physically injured by a wolf, not forgetting that all of the kids had been psychologically injured by them.

"Padds down."

Mr. Barrett blew his despised air horn just in case anybody was so entranced by his pop quiz they couldn't hear his voice. Four Mers popped into animal form. Their padds thumped to the carpet.

"That's a demerit for each of you, Rehyan, Thad, Peter, and Carrie. Shame on you for shifting, Carrie, when you know how concerned everyone is right now."

The fuzzy wolf hopped back onto the couch she'd fallen off of and curled up between Vaughn and Junior. She muffled her growls by tucking her muzzle behind Junior. Her twitching tail swished loudly against Vaughn's cast.

Pink feathers flew past Barrett's face. Rehyan's honking cry turned into words as he touched down on the back of a loveseat and slid onto the cushions. "That's not fair. You know we're Mers."

"Oh?" Barrett searched the room. "Belle, aren't you a Mer? And you, David? But you didn't drop your padds."

Squirt, who nobody called David, looked up from taking out ear plugs. "Sorry, what?"

Belle stood. She always stood to speak to teachers. Miro never spoke to teachers, but they said it was expected of them in their last school.

"All due respect sir, but I can't shift at all if anybody is watching, so I'm not a good example. If you weren't aware, you should know that your airhorn is really startling and many young shifters shift when startled. That was a really fun quiz. Thank you, sir."

She crouched to retrieve Thad's padd and then invited his spider self to crawl onto her hand before she sat.

Mr. Barrett stared at the small girl, his face turning red. Around the room, other kids offered their unrequested opinions on the quiz and Mers. None of them were as eloquent as Belle.

"It's the politeness that gets him," Oscar murmured.

"And her utter sincerity," KC added. "You think she's faking it?"

Laylea did not. Belle and her sibling had arrived at school afraid of everyone and everything. Something happened during Denier's attack that flipped a switch. Belle wasn't in fight mode like nearly every other student and teacher. It was like she wasn't afraid to be seen anymore.

"Carrie," Mr. Barrett snapped, turning his frustration back on her as he collected padds, yanking them out of kids' hands. "You know you can't sit beside Vaughn."

The teacher took Vaughn's padd, stared a moment at the two padds Junior held out to him before turning the other way to continue gathering in another circle of couches and chairs. Junior handed the padds to Ahanu behind him.

"She's only here as his tutor," Emerald spat. "Why even make her take the quiz?"

Ahanu did not look at Emerald as he said, "She should know what we're being tested on." He wasn't really defending Barrett, just disagreeing with his ex-girlfriend. But Barrett hadn't been paying attention to romantic gossip.

"Thank you, Ahanu. Will you collect the padds, please." Barrett scattered the padds he'd collected on the podium and started compiling the results without proposing a topic for them to discuss while he did.

Which meant every discussion arena broke out in quiet arguments.

"That's weird," Oscar muttered, staring at Junior. "Why wouldn't Barrett take the padds?"

Laylea kept her voice quiet. "Barrett can't see Junior. It's freaking him out."

Their couch jostled as Riva sat up on the one behind them, looking around.

Riva had been avoiding Laylea. It wasn't hard to do. It just meant she couldn't ever go to the library, because that was where Laylea lived as she prepped for the graduation tests. She couldn't avoid Sociology, so she'd sat directly behind Laylea so there was little chance of accidentally seeing her. Laylea couldn't blame her. Seeing your own face on someone else's body would terrify anybody.

Riva twisted to ask Oscar, "What is she talking about? Junior isn't in this class."

"Yeah, he is. Isn't he?" Leda, a strand of blue hair in her mouth, kneeled up on the cushions to search. "There he is."

Riva squinted where Leda was pointing, lips pursed in an angry pout. The expression dropped as she caught a glimpse of Laylea. Her eyes grew wide with fear before she fell back as her sloth, wrapping her long arms around herself.

KC yanked her backpack off the floor into Laylea's lap. "If you're cold, put on a sweater," she said, out of nowhere.

Laylea grimaced at her. She wasn't cold. She was never cold when squeezed into the tight seating arrangements in Barrett's class, as evidenced by her rolled up sleeves.

Laylea sighed. Her rolled up sleeves revealed sloth fur instead of nearly invisible blond hairs and pale freckles.

She rolled her sleeves down, but by the time she reached the second one, her arms shifted back to skin with only minor searing pain. Simply admitting what she was had improved her ability to control the shifting almost as much as Dr. Tipp's tricks had.

Kara leaned away from the hissing argument raging between Conner and Merrilynne to ask Oscar, "Why can't Barrett and..." Kara tilted her head at Riva rather than saying her name, "see Junior?"

KC leaned closer to Kara. "You're cool with witches, right?"

Kara blinked at the non-sequitur. "I'm in the Witch Club." Her eyes widened. "Has he been cursed?"

"No," KC lowered her voice even more. "His father is the boogeyman. So if you're scared, you can't see him."

"But the boogeyman is just a story parents tell kids," Kara said.

KC shook her head.

Kara looked to Laylea, "She punking me?"

Laylea and Oscar shook their heads. The girl's jaw dropped. She turned to stare at Junior.

"Wow." She laughed. "People are scared of *him*?"

"No, it's if you're scared of anything," Laylea said, adjusting Griff's hat. "Apparently his dad is so frightening that pretty much nobody can see him for long."

"Oh," Kara looked over her shoulder at Mr. Barrett. "So, Ferret-face is being a dick because he's scared."

That was way more insightful than Laylea expected from Kara. If only everybody was so kind.

"They can't help it." Emerald stood on the far side of the room. Her chair flew back and rammed into the wall. She clutched her skin bag to her chest. Most selkies left their pelt in their dorm lockers or pods. Ever since P2, Emerald kept hers with her. "Wolves are just violent by nature," she insisted. "They should all be sent to MSC."

Across the room, Dustin yelled, "We want to go to MSC."

Carrie barked at him sharply. Her wolf didn't stutter, even if she was trembling at the vitriol around her. Jase had ordered them to keep their heads down and play nice. Dustin glared, but he sat down.

A number of arguments rose in volume around the room: in favor of rounding up wolves, in opposition to anything wolves wanted, condemning blanket prejudice, supporting Emerald's declaration. Pretty much any opinion that could be had was being voiced.

"Not all wolves are violent, Emerald." Oscar spoke loud enough to get her attention. At the same time, he leaned forward, deliberately blocking Jimmy from Emerald's line of sight.

"Prove it," Emerald spun. Her hair, gorgeous as ever, wrapped around her arm like she was holding herself back.

Oscar sputtered, "How am I supposed to prove a negative?"

"If they haven't been violent, they just haven't been violent, yet." Emerald glared at Carrie as she said this.

"That's nuts," Rehyan yelled.

"If all wolves are violent, then all selkie are—" Ahanu was cut off by Ali.

"I didn't know you were a bigot, Em," she yelled.

Mr. Barrett looked up, finally. "Name calling isn't—" His words were lost in the shouting.

"If the shoe fits," Emerald screamed. "It's like that saying about hammers with eyes."

Confused silence fell over the room.

"Hammers… with eyes?" Brian finally asked.

Emerald growled, then turned reluctantly to Ahanu. "That thing you said. You know. When my parents said you were the reason I was being so difficult."

Ahanu folded his arms as if he were holding himself in human shape. He cleared his throat and offered, with a barely restrained grin, "To a hammer, everything looks like a nail?"

"Yes, that," Emerald crowed. "To a wolf, everything looks like a snack."

Impossibly, the silence grew even deeper.

Mr. Barrett stood directly behind Emerald. He cleared his throat.

She spun around. Mr. Barrett leaned back to avoid being hit by her hair.

The bell rang. Nobody moved.

Mr. Barrett sucked in the slowest breath ever. He let it out before saying, "We don't eat people."

The class watched, horrified, waiting to see who would move first; Barrett or Emerald.

It was Jimmy.

The boy who'd been made a werewolf against his will unfolded from where he'd basically hidden himself in the cushions of a comfy chair. With his eyes on his own feet, he walked to the door, where he raised his head.

All the color drained from Mr. Barrett's face as he looked up. To his credit, he faced Jimmy.

Jimmy didn't need to say anything. Still, in her head, Laylea heard, *but you do bite.*

30

In the deep, late-night silence of the library, Laylea's little body trembled. Her paws crinkled the pages of the book she slept on as she tried to run away from her nightmare.

In the dream, a twisted memory of her puppyhood, a table of ice sucked Laylea down, ripping fur from her side. Vaughn's cologne surrounded her on all sides. The nurses were all wolves standing on their hind legs to reach the exam table. All but Walter stared at her out of Denier's human face, the sweet copper of her blood splattered over their scrubs.

Laylea whimpered. Her brothers yelled from the pen. She couldn't cry. She couldn't or Walter would hurt them and Mama. Where was Mama? She held her breath. Whimpers needed oxygen. If she couldn't breathe, she couldn't cry.

The black edges of the world closed in on her.

Until the Eye.

Wolf Walter lowered the blinding Eye over her. Dates poured from the lamp along with the burning heat and painful light. Numbers stabbed her flesh as they fell. 1789 pierced the ice table, trapping her neck as if under a tiny guillotine. They kept coming, the months and days and years, until they buried her.

In the distance a door slithered open. Mama!

"Thank you for your help, Ms. Crow." Not Mama.

The dates, the wolves, even the ice beneath her all faded away as little white buds washed through the room on a green breeze. Air flowed into Laylea's lungs; rich, damp, forest air untainted by licorice or blood.

"Call me Lizzy, Cal."

The nightmare changed as the sound of Ms. Crow's voice drew Laylea toward safety and wakefulness. The wolves surrounding her lost Denier's face. Their lab coats morphed into cardigan sweaters in all the colors of the rainbow, their fur and faces just as delightfully varied.

"Lizzy." Caliban corrected herself with an airy laugh.

Laylea's ears twitched. Or one ear did. The other was smashed beneath her.

"Thank you." Caliban yawned and laughed. "You need to get some sleep."

Every jot of residual cold and fear vanished as Laylea woke, safe in the library at LPSS. Her heart ached with the remembered loss of her brothers, and Mama.

"Speak for yourself, Cal." Ms. Crow said, her voice coming from far away near the check-in counter. The squeaky wheel of her desk chair sang out as she sat. "I know the Mers won't mind if you plant in their courtyard for a night."

Of course they wouldn't. Many of the Mers missed roosting in her branches or cuddling into the loam raised by her roots. The other trees were nice, but Caliban was special.

Laylea sniffed. And growled, low in her throat. Her nose ached where it was pressed into the crease of the book. The more she woke up, the more she wished she were still asleep.

"Yes, I'm sure," Cal said. "And I would love that. But what would the council say?"

"It's past curfew. You could plant in the fields." The squeaky wheel came to a rest. "I'd even join you. I might sleep better."

"Maybe one day." Caliban crossed the room, her sneakers tapping dully on the layered carpets. "But the wolves aren't the only ones to fear. There are others who believe in Luis Delcampo's cause."

Mr. Luke had helped Grandpa's cause because the wolves kidnapped his daughter, got his wife hooked on N, and threatened his son. Would others still support the wolves if they knew that? Would they support them if they knew Grandpa wanted to drain her blood to create a drug that would enslave all non-wolves and eliminate non-shifters? A younger Laylea would have said not a chance.

Fifteen-year-old Laylea knew better.

She snorted.

"Lee?" Ms. Crow called out.

Caliban echoed, "Lee?"

The sound of her own name startled Laylea. She sat up and tumbled off the book, then the table. Despite the multiple carpets, she hit something hard enough to send the burn racing through her body.

"Sorry," she mumbled, her tongue settling slowly back into human. "I didn't know there was a curfew."

Standing took a moment as she sorted out her long legs and lack of tail. Griff's hat draped over one eye unhelpfully.

"It's for the wolves." Ms. Crow sighed. "Good night, Dean Meilissene. We'll talk more tomorrow."

"Good night." Caliban finished shelving a book. She rolled down the sleeves of her sweater as she crossed the library. It was still strange to see her in street clothes, or to imagine her upstairs, shopping for them.

"Good night, Lee." Caliban offered Laylea a smile as she reached the library doors.

"Hold up. I'll walk with you." Laylea gathered her books and hurried to set them on the nearest re-shelving cart. "Good night, Ms. Crow."

"Good night, Lee."

As smart as her friends insisted she was, as quick as Laylea knew she was, she was having real doubts about passing the graduation tests. It wasn't just the shifting. She was learning shifter history from scratch and neither chemistry nor calculus were turning out to be terribly crammable subjects.

And it wasn't like she was going to retain anything she learned just to graduate. Her time would be better spent letting Brenda teach her how to fight or learning everything she could about wolf culture.

Oscar and KC had both warned her that there was no way Caliban would let her leave without graduating. The council wasn't thrilled with the way Cal kept bending rules. If she started breaking them altogether, they'd ditch her for someone who couldn't possibly care as much. But it was worth a shot.

The Dad said it never hurt to ask.

Caliban held the door for Laylea. "How are you holding up?"

"I'm scared," Laylea admitted, heading down the corridor that would take them by the Fields. She amended, "Not like can't-see-Junior scared, but like anxious all the time."

"You're not alone."

An argument popped into her mind that just might work. She let her shoulders slump and slowed her steps.

"My brother is alone, though." She sighed. "Now that witches are out of the closet, I guess it's okay for me to tell you. My brother, Bailey, is a crazy powerful witch. But he's kinda volatile and my mom ordered me to watch over him when—" She suddenly remembered that she was meant to be an orphan. "—when she died. And what with all the violence upstairs, I'm really worried about him… and the city. If he loses his temper, a lot of people could get hurt."

It wasn't a lie. And that was the worst part of using it to manipulate Caliban. Laylea probably should be keeping a closer eye on her brother.

"I really wish I could help, Lee. But there are rules. As I keep telling the parents who want to take their kids home." Caliban said the last bit as if she were talking to herself but ended with a glance down at Laylea.

It was a good counter argument. The dean couldn't hold the parents to a rule she let a student disregard.

They walked in silence. Laylea sped up to match Caliban's longer stride. Caliban strolled more slowly than her typical pace.

She could just tell Caliban the truth. She'd considered it.

But Oscar and KC agreed that while Caliban might believe her, the Dean's hands would still be tied. She'd just put more guards around the school, which would create all sorts of new problems. One being that it would make it more impossible for Laylea to sneak out. Another being that it would further exhaust resources that were needed to protect the entire Midwest from Grandpa's attacks.

"Do you remember the first time we walked this way together?" Caliban asked in her quiet voice.

"Yeah," Laylea remembered clearly. "It was my first day here."

Caliban reached up, her arm shifted, the branch lengthening to brush new leaves along the ceiling. "I was testing to graduate that day."

"Which part did you not pass?"

Caliban laughed. "I passed the whole thing. I asked Mr. Bianchi not to submit the results."

Laylea stared up at Cal, her mouth hanging wide open. As if tripped up by her own bafflement, she stumbled and nearly went down. A flowering branch set her back on her feet and straightened her hat.

"I thought you might need company," Caliban said. "Like you, I had never been to school before I came here. It was very hard at first."

"You stayed for me?"

"At first. Then you discovered what Dr. Durrah had been doing, and I stayed because I knew he couldn't have done that alone. My grove is well off and very far away. And it's hard to kill a tree. I felt like I had the freedom to stand up to the faculty and to the council in a way nobody else could."

"Thank you." Laylea spluttered. She had so many questions.

"We need you here, Lee."

"What?" Laylea stopped walking.

"You see the world differently. Like me, you didn't grow up with their rules."

"Caliban!"

They both looked up to see Ms. McCobb hurrying down the corridor toward them. She held a folded sheet of paper out in front of her.

She called again, "Caliban!"

"Randee!" Farther back, just turning a bend, Ms. Muldoon ran after the PE teacher.

Ahead of them, one of the doors to Lakes cracked open and the air filled with voices shushing each other.

"Lee!" Oscar cried out as he squeezed out the door. His voice cracked when he noticed who she was with. "And Caliban—gah!"

The door was slammed shut behind him.

He covered poorly. "Dean Meilissene, hi. We were… I… I was just… you having a nice night?"

Laylea smirked at her friend, thinking it was a strange sort of respect for him to pretend he wasn't coming from the Double Delta's fight training. Caliban knew all about the group of students secretly training under Brenda. But the Dean shouldn't.

She didn't dare look at Cal's reaction, instead curbing a grin as the three of them pretended to only hear Ms. McCobb's urgent footsteps and not the Double Deltas poorly hushing each other behind the door.

31

Caliban stepped to one side of the corridor, where she could easily look both ways and see everybody coming at her. Laylea moved aside with her.

The impossible gold undertones of Ms. Muldoon's black curls gleamed in the deep blue of the trough lights as she pumped her short legs.

Ms. McCobb's blond ponytail slashed through the air like a pissed-off horse's tail as she glanced over her shoulder at the chemistry teacher. She picked up speed. "I just need a moment, Dean," she called, her voice as hard as the stone walls.

"Does nobody sleep in this school?" Caliban asked.

"I was just looking for you," Oscar said, "and then I'm going to bed."

"And what about all the other kids in the Fields who you just warned about me?" Caliban reached out one growing branch and tapped on the door. She called, more loudly, "Sleep is important for building muscle."

Veins pulsed on Ms. McCobb's temples. She'd missed a button on her shirt and it hung askew. Likewise, her normally severe ponytail jetted stray hairs like a field of weeds.

"Dean, I can't do this anymore. Please, take it." She shoved the folded paper at Caliban with barely a glance at the kids.

"No, don't take it." Ms. Muldoon cried, grasping at the paper even as she had trouble stopping. Where Ms. McCobb wore her standard sneakers, Muldoon went barefoot. She dodged to one side to avoid running over Ms. McCobb, slipped, and ended up slamming into the wall and then into Oscar.

Having seen her coming, Oscar was prepared. Neither fell. But he sucked in a breath, grabbed at his chest, and quickly shifted all his weight to his right leg.

"I'm sorry, Oscar. Did I tear your stitches?" Ms. Muldoon tried to hold him up without touching any of his bruises.

"Nah, Tipp took the stitches out." Oscar's face went blank for an instant as he quickly reconsidered. "I mean, it still hurts, though." He grimaced and held his shoulder like a Killdeer luring prey away from their nest. "I don't know how I'll be able to focus on tomorrow's test with all this pain."

Ms. Muldoon smirked at him. "That's not a problem, Oscar. I'm happy to give you loads more homework instead."

Oscar stood up straight and rotated his shoulder, carefully. "I'm feeling so much better already."

"I'll take him to Tipp, just in case," Laylea assured the teacher.

"I'm fine," Oscar began to object.

Ms. McCobb interrupted with a growl.

"Take him now," she said and turned away as if she considered them invisible after her order. "Dean Meilissene," the PE teacher said formally, "I can't do this anymore. The kids argue all the time. They demand answers that I don't have." McCobb yanked on her ponytail so hard it was like she was punishing herself before she continued in a tight voice. "I can't go upstairs without parents screaming at me. I don't feel safe. You won't get rid of the wolves, so I have to resign."

Ms. Muldoon inched closer, her clasped hands shaking as if she wanted to grab McCobb but wouldn't let herself. "Randee, don't do this. Please talk to me."

"There is nothing more to talk about. Nothing is going to change." Despite her snarling tone, a tear rolled down one cheek. She swiped it away so fiercely she scratched her own face.

Caliban did not take the letter. Instead, she buried her hands into the deep pockets of her trousers. "Oscar, what feels better for you, heat or ice?"

He raised his eyebrows at Laylea. There was an edge to Caliban's airy voice that kept him from objecting to needing either. She wasn't asking that. She was asking which he preferred.

"Heat."

She pulled a heat pack from her pocket, squeezed it until something inside popped and then shook it before handing it to Oscar. "Randee, I need the kids to get to their dorms, so give me a minute to hear Oscar out. Then we'll talk."

"No. I'm leaving." Ms. McCobb threw the paper at Caliban. It fluttered pathetically to the ground. "I won't be back tomorrow."

Ms. McCobb's resignation settled on the packed dirt.

"Randee, please. I know I was angry about the soccer game, but I'm working through it." Ms. Muldoon begged, "Don't leave me. We can change things."

"No," Ms. McCobb snapped, finally looking at Ms. Muldoon. "We can't. The wolves aren't just going after us, they're attacking true-humans, too, making more wolves. What can we do about any of that from down here?"

Making wolves. Nausea surged up Laylea's throat. She grabbed for the burn and shifted before she could lose her dinner, digging her claws into the packed dirt to tamp down her whimpers.

Oscar pressed a leg into her side. His hands balled into fists.

Grandpa's forces were biting people and turning them, just like he'd done to Denier and someone else had done to Jimmy. Turning people was so verboten that many wolves thought it was just a movie trope.

The ground shivered as Caliban's lower half shifted and broke through the dirt, reaching through the foundations to ground her to the earth or at least to the magical sub-basement. Her voice was richer but no less gentle than normal as she told Ms. McCobb, "You have a contract with the council. Would you really make Bitters arrest you?"

"I'm leaving the Midwest." McCobb shot this back quickly, but her voice shook.

Muldoon—tough-as-nails, didn't-take-shit-unless-it-was-funny Muldoon—cried. "Randee, no."

Cal tilted her head. Leaves sprouted in her hair, turned red, and fluttered down, burying McCobb's letter. "I'm going to speak with Oscar. Consider for a moment why you had no problem working with Rex Mendenkov."

"He kept his wolves-first attitude to himself."

"No he didn't," Oscar and Laylea objected in near unison disbelief, Laylea shifting without even being aware of it.

Ms. McCobb opened her mouth. Nothing came out.

"All the students knew," Caliban said. "Why didn't you?" She turned to Oscar without waiting for an answer. "Oscar. Go."

"It's Vaughn Howe," Oscar began, pressing the heating pad to his chest and shoulder. "The restricted students are required to help out with the reconstruction in the Old School. But with all his injuries, there isn't much Vaughn can do physically." Oscar took a breath and barreled on, "He's being bullied by the other restricted students for not helping and he's being bullied by everyone else for being a wolf."

"He should have thought about that before inviting his friends in to attack his classmates," McCobb said.

A black-on-black spotted leopard tail tore a hole through the back of Oscar's jumpsuit. It twitched as he fought to hold his voice steady. "All due respect, Ms. McCobb, he didn't. Denier did. Vaughn was just doing what the enforcer told him to do, like we're all supposed to. Adults keep harping on us following the rules and obeying the law. Well, one of the rules is we're supposed to do what the enforcer tells us, right? It was the enforcer's friends who attacked me, the enforcer's friends who would have killed me if Vaughn hadn't stopped them."

He broke off, his chest heaving like he'd run a marathon.

"That's how Vaughn broke his leg and his jaw and a couple ribs," Laylea put in, in case Ms. McCobb really didn't know. Her face looked like she really didn't know. She stumbled back a step. When Muldoon put a hand out to keep her from falling, the gym teacher took it and held on like it was a lifeline.

"I just wanted to tell you, Dean Meilissene," the fur of Oscar's tail settled as he turned to Cal, "that Vaughn's really good at drawing. He sketched a map of the entire zoo, to scale, when we were planning for Halloween. I thought that's a way he could feel useful."

"I'll pass that along to Mr. Vronumraju. He has regular meetings with the contractor to see how our pressed students can best help."

Ms. McCobb slipped a hand into Ms. Muldoon's. With a voice like wet fur, she said, "He should take your design symposium."

"Yes," Muldoon stared down in awe at their clasped hands. The glow of hope kindled in her eyes. "Yes, he should. Toni Correnti and I want to teach a design symposium to support the reconstruction. Do you think he'd—" She shook her head. "I'll talk to him and see if he'd like to join us, if you approve, Dean."

"I think that is a lovely idea. Randee, your master's is in exercise physiology, correct? Sounds like that could be useful in designing a rehabilitation facility."

Ms. McCobb nodded, her eyes on the ground, on her buried letter of resignation.

"Get some sleep." Caliban gave her head a shake. Humanity washed down her body. She kicked the dirt from her practical boots and put an arm on Laylea and Oscar's backs, escorting them down the corridor. "I'd like you both to see Dr. Tippleston in the morning."

"I'm fine," Oscar objected, limping.

Caliban ignored him. "Tell her all about Guppy Wilding." She used Jase's term for the non-wolf Wilding that Laylea had invented. "We have a new moon coming up and I'd like to find a way to involve the entire school in a game. Set Tipp to thinking how we can safely include those of you on the injured list."

"Yes, Dean." Laylea got the giggly words out an instant before a bubbly burn shot from her gut through her veins to her extremities and out through her frantically wagging tail.

A school-wide wilding would be the perfect distraction. While everyone was playing, she could run away. Then she wouldn't have to lose sleep over history after all.

32

Sometime after lunch, Laylea flapped her itchy ears against her head and wiped at her eyes with her paws. She flopped onto the carpet beside the deskpadd and buried her nose in the scents of lavender and Fritos.

Not even a week after Caliban had the idea for a school-wide wilding, students and faculty filled the school with laughter, replacing the awful memories of P2.

And Laylea was stuck in Testing.

Classes were canceled, meaning fewer teachers and less discipline. The teachers that lived in the school were, for the most part, playing the game, too. All that, plus the chaos of three teams racing through the school searching for flags—the Crow sisters had refused to give up more sweaters—made the New Moon Wilding a great opportunity to sneak out.

Except, the new moon fell on December fourth, a Tuesday. Tuesdays were an open testing day as guaranteed by the school charter.

A testing day included the opportunity to take the graduation sequence. So, while she suspected there was a snowball's chance in Hawaii that she would pass, especially given how exhausted she was from studying, Laylea presented herself for the sequence.

The testing had started off easily enough with science, one of her strong suits. Laylea had hung out at the Mom's veterinary office often enough that the biology section was a breeze. Sher had all kinds of texts, journals, and reference books lying around, since she hadn't actually gone to vet school. Laylea also read under Bailey's shoulder as he devoured every human biology book he could get his hands on. As the son of a genetically altered super-soldier, he had questions.

The chemistry section wasn't as smooth, but she was pretty confident she'd done well enough. Physics got iffy. But then, after a quick lunch and stretch break, she'd lost herself in the arts and literature essay questions and forgotten all about physics. She was feeling unexpectedly confident as she finished up the math section, which did not require she show her work.

When the padd flashed over to the shifter history portion of the test, it may as well have been a brick wall. Her first concern was if the test had been recalibrated since the witches from two hundred years ago had revealed the textbooks had some of it wrong. Mr. Bianchi had informed her that they had not been changed yet but the issue had been raised with the council. Her concern turned out to be moot once she read the first question and realized she didn't know the answer either way.

So, she buried her nose in the comforting smell of the carpet and let her mind wander.

She'd met Caliban right there in the back row of testing with no idea that the tree was a shifter, much less that she'd become the Dean and force the wolves to play at the non-wolf Wilding Laylea had invented.

The rules weren't exactly the same as that first game. Cal had met with Laylea about the original rules and with Brenda and Ali about the rules they'd invented for their month-long Wilding. Cal didn't want a binary us-and-them game, so she declared there would be three teams.

Each dormitory would compete against the others to gather multiple flags. Each team was given two hours to hide five flags. Then the teams had until moonset at 4:34 to capture as many of the opposing teams' flags as they could and raise them on their team's flagpole in the Dining Hall.

Dizzy's former dorm, Centaur, got orange flags and Sphinx, Ms. Crow's dorm, got blue. Caliban chose green for the Mers.

"Lee?" Mr. Bianchi's shoes squeaked as he crouched near her. "Are you okay?"

She lifted her head and nodded at him.

"Ms. Lagat is here." He stood, peering at something on his armpadd as he walked away.

Laylea shifted suddenly into a green-breasted pigeon, Ms. Lagat's other form. She stifled a thoroughly avian screech and demanded her gut flash her back into a dog. For once, it listened.

Her padd was blinking. A message flashed across it calling her to the Shifting Test and certain doom.

The burn gurgled through her, expanding her ribs, flattening her snout, widening everything. Too late, she reached for her birthmark with her mind. In a heartbeat she went from thirteen pounds to four hundred.

Why would her body make her a bear right when she was trying to be inconspicuous? Did it think she needed a reminder of why she needed to get the hell out of school before Grandpa showed up?

Well aware, body, she thought.

Before she could leave, she needed to graduate. In order to graduate, she had to shift dog or human and then go do it again in that tiny, stuffy room with Ms. Lagat staring at her.

And she had to do it soon, before anybody saw the unknown bear in the room.

Boom.

A bench fell over near the front of the room. KC cried out.

How did that fall on you, KC?" Mr. Bianchi hurried away. "Let me help you."

Oscar appeared around the corner of the last row. "Come on. We've got you." He hustled to Laylea, picked up her now carry-sized dog form, tossed her testing padd on the desk and headed for the doors.

KC limped over to join them, leaving Mr. Bianchi righting the bench with Reggie's help. "Oscar, can you help me get to the infirmary?"

"Oscar's in the middle of his test. And Lee?"

"It's okay, Mr. Bianchi," Oscar paused briefly in the doorway. "I was just keeping them company and Lee is too freaked to finish the test. We'll come again next week."

Laylea howled over his shoulder as slipped into the hall and hurried away, KC at their side. Her limp miraculously vanished the instant the door shut behind them.

"It was a long shot anyway," KC said, zipping her pack. She flung it around to her back, nearly smacking Laylea and Oscar.

"We have to find another way to get her out."

"Do we?" KC asked. "It's been two weeks. If Grandpa knew, wouldn't he have tried for her by now?"

"With Thanksgiving, he's only had like a week to get anything planned," Oscar said, slowing as they reached a bend in the corridor.

"But, I don't want you to go," KC growled, her face scrunched into a super impressive pout.

She stomped around the corner and ran straight into Squirt.

"H... hey." Carrie dashed past the two as they sorted themselves out. She bounced on her toes, looking down the empty corridor before confirming their fears. "J... Jase is in contact with Grandpa."

"We can't talk to you," KC tried to drag Oscar away.

"It's okay." Carrie grabbed hold of KC's sleeve in an uncharacteristically aggressive move. "Jase ordered all wolves to st... stay with crowds, to be seen."

"Squirt is a crowd?" KC asked.

Squirt flexed his arms like a dog putting its hackles up to look bigger.

Laylea sang out a barking howl.

"That's right." Squirt grinned. "I am the brute squad."

"Hey Squirt, you never get in trouble," Oscar said, stepping back so he could see around the bend. "But you join in every Toby party. Do you think you could sneak out now without getting caught?"

"It would be pretty tough. Aren't there guards like everywhere?" Squirt said with an intrigued gleam in his eye. "Why?"

Oscar blew out a breath so hard it fluffed Laylea's fur. "Lee's mom is a super powerful witch."

"Oscar— Oh." KC's warning tone shifted gears, her brain processing what he said a second too late. It clearly wasn't the secret she'd been worried he might tell. Unable to shove the cat back into the bag, KC made a halfhearted effort. She muttered from behind her hand, "She's an orphan, remember?"

"Yeah, but she just said that because witches were a secret, right Lee?"

He checked in with her. Laylea wasn't sure where he was going, but she trusted him. She barked once for yes.

"Plus, whatever she won't tell us about her dad," Oscar added nonchalantly.

Laylea growled at him.

He pet her head condescendingly. "If she can get to her parents, tell them what's going on, we think they can help us overthrow Grandpa and get things back to… better than normal."

That was actually a really good idea.

"Oh hells, I'm in." Squirt held a fist out to Laylea.

She wriggled around in Oscar's grasp to tap it with a paw.

He blew it up, adding, "I've always wanted to see the Dean's tunnel anyway."

"Can you think of an excuse that isn't wolf-related?" KC asked, adding, "Not that you're gonna get caught."

"For trying to leave? Sure," Squirt said. "My momdads put in another request to transfer me to NESS and I could say that I just wanted to go beg my case with the council directly."

"The council doesn't have anything to do with transfers," KC pointed out.

"Really?" Squirt widened his eyes, the picture of innocence. "I didn't know that."

"Ah, cool," KC said. "Thanks."

"I'm p... pretty sure I could get into the f... faculty stairway without being caught," Carrie suggested from behind them.

Laylea dropped her head back to see if the little werewolf was serious.

Carrie grinned. "I'd b... bet they aren't w...w... guarding the teacher's exit as w... well since it's used more."

"You're a wolf," KC pointed out.

"Yeah, but C... C... Ca... the Dean knows which side I'm on and it w... would get me more cred with Jonathan and Dustin if I p... pissed off Jase."

Laylea howled. It was a bad idea.

"Tough." Carrie glared at her. "You c... can't tell me w... what to do."

Squirt punched Carrie in the shoulder. "You're a superhero." He pushed the girl between KC and Oscar and then scooted around them, jogging backwards to say, "Tell 'em what they need to know. I'll bring you a present from upstairs."

Carrie pulled KC and Oscar in close. She chanted quietly, a trick that helped with her stutter. "Jase won't let the wolves have private meetings. He's making them communicate through me."

"Why?" KC said as Laylea barked the same question.

"Cuz everyone thinks I'm harmless and stupid," she chanted with a roll of her eyes. "He's threatened banishment on anyone who causes trouble today."

"Banishment?" Oscar asked. "You're not allowed to leave."

"We'd treat them like they're invisible, like we did to Dustin after his outburst in symposium."

"Phoen... Damn," Oscar swore. "So that's what was going on."

"Shut up. I have a lot to say." Carrie neither sang nor stuttered that.

Oscar bit his lip.

"He says the orders to play nice came from Grandpa who is planning some big rescue," she chanted. "He says Barrett is sowing chaos but is still with us."

"No, he's not," Oscar blurted.

Carrie glared.

He waved a hand in apology and then covered his mouth.

She peered up and down the hall to be sure it was empty. "Jase says the council wolves are playing along to stay in power." Carrie's chant faded into plain old speech. She didn't appear to notice. "But I know my Uncle Marshall is not a Grandpa fan, so I'm baffled. I don't know how Jase is getting messages in and out. But I will."

She fell silent, caught up in her thoughts.

KC and Oscar let her think. Carrie was taking a big risk spying on Jase. Thanks to her stutter and shifting issues, the wolves didn't consider her "good breeding stock." But that wasn't much comfort if she ended up surrounded by the kind of people who thought of women as breeding stock.

Laylea whimpered. Carrie was putting everything on the line to protect the school while Laylea was drawing trouble to them.

Carrie stepped close. She made sure to meet each of their eyes before singing, "Grandpa is coming. It won't be a full moon. Tell everyone."

Laylea yelped like Carrie had just kicked her.

Grandpa was coming.

33

Grandpa was coming to get her.

Laylea had known it was going to happen ever since she shifted to a bear right in front of Jase. But hearing Carrie confirm it straight from the wolf pack themselves made everything real. She had to run.

Flames tickled Laylea's paws. She squirmed in Oscar's arms. If the burn started in her gut, she'd be okay. Heat anywhere else meant trouble.

She closed her eyes and focused, trying to move the shift from her paws to her gut. She growled low, painting her birthmark in shades of blood.

No. That wouldn't help.

Her eyes snapped open and she growled again at her stupid imagination.

"I kn... know, Lee." Carrie twirled one of Laylea's ears in her fingers. It helped. "I'm doing everything I can."

She shouldn't have to, though. She should get to be a kid, safe in her school.

The flames shot down Laylea's tail.

"We know," KC said quickly, gently pushing Carrie down the hall. "Go, find a crowd."

"So you're not alone," Oscar added, backing away. He squeezed Laylea too tightly against his chest. When he reached the corner, he ran.

Burning zipped like lasers through Laylea's body. She burst from Oscar's arms already in full gallop. She had to get out. She had to get away so Grandpa wouldn't come and hurt her friends.

"There are no white horses in school, Lee," KC gasped, her backpack thumping as she ran after Laylea.

Oscar yowled, right on her heels. He reached out to swipe at her haunches with a grunt of pain. Laylea shifted too fast for him. She burned down into Reggie's tiger form. The only surprise to seeing Reggie racing through the halls would be that Kara wasn't with him.

"Guys, please," KC's voice faded into the distance. "Wait for me."

Laylea's gut wrenched at having to leave her friends behind. She wanted to be a kid, too, just like Carrie should be. But if Grandpa was coming, she had to go. She could get to her family, like Oscar suggested, get her many super-soldier aunts and uncles to come help the Midwest. Or she could go straight for Grandpa at the Montana Shifter Collective.

Anything other than read one more history book.

Yes, she thought, the joy of running cutting through her panic, *avoiding history was a totally valid reason for starting a revolution.*

Oxygen flowed through Laylea's tiger veins like a drug. If N made you feel this good, no wonder Jimmy had gotten addicted. It made Laylea wonder why Reggie ever went human.

Even with the worse-than-death threat hanging over her head, simply sailing through the halls filled her with euphoria. Reggie's sports mania made sense now.

The giggle in her heart slowed her. It was enough for Oscar.

He leapt, landing with his murder mittens in full death mode.

Pain lanced through Laylea. His claws sank into her neck, releasing the sharp tang of blood. As it always did, the fatal wound popped her right back into her velvety, comforting dog shape.

It did not affect Oscar's shape or their momentum.

The two flew forward, gouging a trench in the hardened ground. They slammed into a wall and shifted human as they tumbled to a tangled rest.

"Get off, you fleabag." Laylea wriggled to get out from under Oscar.

"Ha ha! I've got you now!" KC's pounding footsteps drew rapidly closer. The steps stopped. Her cry kept barreling toward them.

KC landed heavily on top of them. She grabbed a handful of both their uniforms and refused to let go.

Oscar almost got free until he knelt on his bad knee and crumpled in a heap. Laylea pounced on his leg and wrapped herself around it. KC trapped him in a headlock. She tossed Laylea an ice pack.

"I'm fine," Oscar wailed the lie as he wiggled just enough to keep Laylea from icing his knee. "It's too cold."

"We've got you surrounded."

Miro Suttrick's declaration was just ridiculous enough to get their attention.

The three rolled apart to find little Miro standing on one side of them with skinny Tessa on the other. They each held a homemade double-barreled water bazooka at the ready. Hoses led from the guns to enormous tanks on their backs supported with waist belts. Tessa had two flags tucked into her belt, one green and one blue. Two blue flags hung from Miro's belt. Of the five Sphinx flags in the game, these two had three of them, plus a Mer flag.

"Hand. Over. Your. Flag," Miro demanded.

Oscar either didn't hear the demand or dismissed it as unimportant. "Miro, you're perfect. You're invisible even when you're not a butterfly. You're clearly sneaky and devious." He said this gesturing from the flags to the guns to the tanks.

"More importantly, you've never broken any rules, that anyone knows of," KC said. "I can't see them raising the threat level if you try to escape."

Miro's face squeezed into pug-level wrinkles, asking "what" without the word.

"Lee's parents are witches with connections to powerful people," Oscar explained. "We want to get her out so she can bring an army to help us."

"But we need to see which exits are viable," Laylea put in. "I'll only get one chance."

"KC can't go because..." There was the slightest of pauses as Oscar realized he couldn't say the real reason. "She is on notice for leaving the school during P2."

"Oscar can't go because he's injured," KC put in, tossing a second ice pack right at his face.

Oscar caught it and pressed it to his chest.

Tessa scoffed. "And his father is head of the council and would fire the dean."

"I like the dean," Miro said in their ASMR voice. They added, just as quietly, "I'll go."

"No!" Belle burst out of the shadows, Christopher and Krystal on her heels. "You will not."

Miro didn't say anything. They tilted their head, knitting their brows in accusation.

"We saw the guns," Belle explained, "and were worried the older, bigger kids would hurt you taking them." Tears welled in her eyes.

Laylea wanted to hug her and assure her that nobody would hurt her sibling. But that wasn't true, was it?

Miro wasn't moved. They popped a hip and raised their brows, their disbelief clear.

Belle dropped her very convincing act. She stomped her foot. "Fine. We were going to jump you for your flags when you ran out of ammo." She turned to face the three friends still lying on the ground. "I'll go. Dr. Tipp knows I have panic attacks. If I get caught, I'll say I needed fresh air and wasn't thinking straight. Everybody knows I wouldn't leave without Miro."

"We've got others trying, too," Oscar said.

KC added, "Squirt's got the Dean's tunnel, and Carrie is going up the faculty stairs, so those exits are covered."

Christopher grinned. "I've got ideas. Let's go check some things out."

He took off running. Belle and Krystal turned to follow him.

Laylea hollered, "Be careful."

Krystal turned back to shake her head violently. Her eyes were bright and fierce as she whispered, "Today we Wild."

She and Belle bumped fists and then ran after Christopher.

Tessa cleared her throat. "Speaking of Wilding, hand over your flag." She raised her bazooka which had drooped during the conversation.

Oscar snorted. "We don't have one."

"Two Mers wrestling a Sphinx. You have a flag."

"He's not even playing," Laylea said. "He's on the injured list." She turned to him. "I'm sorry, by the way. I forgot."

"Hey, I attacked you."

"That is true."

"Hand over your flag," Tessa demanded, "or we shoot."

"I mean, Oscar's the only one who's really gonna be bothered by getting wet," KC chortled.

"You get one more warning."

Oscar dragged himself up the wall to standing. "Seriously, the flags are too big to fit in our pockets. Search us."

He tugged at his uniform, which was strangely still on him. Oscar wasn't one of the shifters who got to keep his clothes.

"How do you still have your uniform?" Laylea asked, scrambling to her own feet and snagging Griff's hat from where it had been trapped under Oscar. "And what's wrong with it?"

She should have noticed before. It was a testament to how nervous she'd been before testing that she hadn't spotted the alterations earlier. First of all, the jumpsuit was a couple sizes too big for Oscar. The sleeves had been cut off, like Ali's personalized uniforms, and the legs had been cut to just below the knee. Though, as he adjusted an elastic belt, the uniform settled lower, dropping the leg cuffs to shin-level.

"I'm too old to be running around bare-ass naked like some Mer."

Laylea's jaw dropped. KC's giggles stopped cold. The girls stared at their friend, then at each other, then at Oscar again.

"Who is she?" KC asked.

"Yeah, Oscar," Laylea said, her heart climbing into her throat at all she'd be leaving behind, "who don't you want to see your bare ass?"

KC advanced on him. "Who is she?"

"There's nobody." Oscar took a step back.

KC stepped forward. "What dorm is she in?"

"She's not in school."

"Ha!" Laylea leapt in triumph.

"Give us the flag and I'll tell you."

The three spun to face Tessa.

Oscar shouted, "You don't know."

She held her ground. "Yeah, I do."

"She knows," Miro said, "cuz I told her. And you know how I know."

The death glare Oscar shot Miro proved it was the truth.

"Tell us," KC yelled at Tessa. "Tell us. Tell us. Tell us."

Laylea joined the chant, the two of them holding hands and bouncing.

"Give us the flag and I'll tell you," Tessa repeated.

KC growled.

Laylea groaned, "We really don't have one. We've been in testing all morning. Come on."

"Tell us tell us tell us," KC repeated at speed. "Please."

Tessa turned her bland gaze on Oscar. "Give us the flag, and I won't tell them."

Oscar dropped his head to his chest with a heavy sigh. Laylea and KC grinned hopefully at Tessa.

Oscar spread his arms, raised his head, and said, "Just shoot us."

KC and Laylea had barely begun screaming "No," when they fired.

34

Glitter filled Laylea's vision.

She snapped her eyes shut in self-protection. Her mouth wasn't as quick. It filled with a gooey, sugar-fluid that resembled chalk and syrup in both flavor and consistency. She choked and shifted.

While the pads on her paws were a built-in non-slip surface, the gooey glitter shooting from Miro and Tessa's bazookas proved to be too much for them. She slipped, fell in the goo, smacked her head on the ground, and shifted back to human.

KC windmilled her arms in an effort to stay upright. If she hadn't dropped her backpack before pile driving Laylea and Oscar, she might not have succeeded. It was a near thing, until Oscar leapt.

He shifted midair and pushed off KC to launch his kitty self to clear ground, leaving her sprawled in the glitter puddle.

Miro's eyes grew large as the black panther bared his teeth right in their face. Oscar's roar blew their hair back.

Miro shifted. One second they were a small, fine-featured kid trying to bring a bazooka muzzle to bear on a too-close panther muzzle. The next, they were a multi-colored Eastern Tiger Swallowtail with mismatched wings, soaring away on the wind of Oscar's attack.

The visual field around Oscar shuddered as his muzzle shortened, his tail sucked in, and his whole body landed as gently as ever, furless and human and covered in goo and glitter from head to toe.

Tessa stood her ground, shooting KC. Laylea dove at the girl, grasping at her belt.

Just as Laylea's fingers brushed fabric, Tessa's cat reflexes kicked in. She jumped. The air spun around her like a blindingly-sparkly mini-tornado. Laylea blinked away the shadows left in her vision to find the four pound domestic shorthair version of Tessa halfway down the hall, running and leaping beneath Miro.

"What the phoen—" KC took a breath and tried again. "What the wolf is this goo?"

"It tastes like licking a tree." Oscar scraped his tongue clean with a green cloth.

"It tastes," KC corrected him, "like squirrel candy."

"My friends, you are mistaken," Laylea crowed, crawling out of the mess. "It is the taste of victory!"

She used a wall to help her stand.

"Really?" KC squinted at her, glitter dripping from her blond bob. "How do you figure that?"

Laylea grinned and held up the large, rectangular blue cloth she'd been using to wipe her face. "Because before Tessa ran, I got one of her flags."

"Really?" Oscar of Sphinx dorm asked as he sidled around the puddle toward Laylea. "You got yourself a Sphinx flag, did you?"

Laylea circled the other way, avoiding him. "Don't even try, mister."

Oscar stopped. He dropped his head and sniffed, as if resigned. "I wasn't. I just wanted to make sure I was closer to the Dining Hall than you."

"Why?" KC asked, suspiciously.

He raised the cloth he'd been using to wipe his own face. It was a Mer flag. "Cuz I got this off Miro before they shifted."

Oscar turned tail, not literally, and limped away.

Laylea shouted a wordless cry of frustration. She dashed after him. Her feet flew out from under her, landing her on her butt.

KC squished through the mess, slamming each boot down before daring to pick up the other. She held out her hand. "He's injured. He can't move fast. We can catch him."

Laylea hesitated. She looked longingly down the hall toward the exit tunnel beyond Sphinx dorm. "But Grandpa is coming."

"Not today," KC said. "Let the others find the best way out and then go. You're only going to get one shot. You know that."

She was right. Laylea let her friend help her up. With an effort, she turned her mind from escape to revenge.

As they carefully picked their way around the goo, she said, "I'm going to hug the shit out of Tessa and Miro next time I see them."

"What?" KC blurted. "Why would you hug them for this?" She gestured down at the glitter plastered on both of them.

Laylea grinned. She didn't mind the glitter. It was pretty. And the sticky was gross, but it smelled like hiking through mountains with the Dad.

"Because," she said, "while you and I love hugs..."

KC stood from picking up her back pack. "They'd hate it," she finished.

"Plus," Laylea added, weaving her gooey fingers with KC's, "it'll cover them in their own shiny sparkly fabulousness."

The corridor echoed with KC's evil laugh. "Let's get that Mer flag from Oscar and deliver all three to the Dining Hall."

"All three?" Laylea asked, holding Griff's hat on her head as she jogged to keep up with KC's longer stride.

"Oh, yeah. While we were testing, I saw Harper hide a Centaur flag under the bench I was sitting on," she said, jogging ahead a few steps to show Laylea the blue flag strapped to her pack. "That's why I flipped it."

Laylea goggled. "It was just sitting there on your backpack where Miro or Tessa could have easily taken it."

"I think they wanted to shoot us more than they wanted another flag."

KC dug through her pack before flipping it onto her back. She handed Laylea an apple as the two headed after Oscar, their shoes squishing and slipping with every step.

Laylea devoured the apple, swallowing more glitter than was probably healthy in the process. She tried to stuff the core in her pocket, but KC offered her a waxed bag to drop it in.

When Laylea squinted at her, she explained, "Britny loves apple cores," and shoved the bag into her pack.

They only caught sight of Oscar as they turned into the Dining Hall foyer. They pushed to a run as he reached for the handle on the great glass doors.

"Oscar Scott Luke!" KC yelled.

He spun. His eyes scanned the few people gathered in the foyer. He yelled, "Cake! Chef Tod's bringing out cake!"

A dozen rabid teens bolted for the Dining Hall. Laylea and KC were caught in the crush of bodies fighting their way through the door. By the time they got inside, they were too late. Oscar tossed the wadded ball of his Mer flag to Quan who lobbed it to the Sphinx flagpole keeper.

"Ha ha!" Benny caught the flag and spun it over his head.

"Hold the doors." A woman built like Santa Claus minus his jolly, plus Rudolph's red nose, trudged across the foyer. Wanda Bargo had been the school secretary through five Deans and had served on the temporary Dean team between Dean Gorse's disappearance and Caliban's appointment. She waddled along, holding Squirt by the arm with the unwarranted confidence that he couldn't easily free himself.

Laylea and KC stepped to either side, each holding a door. Squirt shot them a sheepish shrug as he was hauled past.

"Already?" Laylea blurted. It hadn't been nearly long enough since Squirt volunteered for him to even try, much less get caught.

"Ms. McCobb, I need your ear." Wanda headed straight for the health teacher seated alone at the table on the faculty platform.

"Guess you're not escaping through the Dean's tunnel," KC muttered.

On the main floor of the Dining Hall, a surprising number of kids and faculty gathered in clumps that spread like an exploding dandelion. A dozen people sat on the tables and benches in the center of the room, engaged in a conversation being driven by Brenda. Farther out from them were smaller groups of two or three, watching the conversation but not engaging. Beyond them were the solo flagpole keepers with maybe one or two companions. And, finally, isolated individuals sitting at the edges pretending to be involved while avoiding any actual interactions.

Oscar followed his Mer flag to the far side of the room, where the Sphinx flagpole stood. The half dozen Sphinx kids in the Dining Hall cheered as Benny raised his glittering flag up their pole to join the lonely Mer flag already there.

Closest to the door, the Centaur flagpole boasted two greens and a blue.

Back near the night kitchen door, the Mer flagpole stood tall and shiny, bereft of any flags at all.

Laylea and KC headed for it.

Trough lights came on along the walls, surprising Laylea. "What time is it?"

"It was maybe two-something when we left Testing," KC said. She grabbed Milly as they approached the Mers guarding their barren flagpole. "What time is it?"

"I dunno. Late?" Milly said gesturing at the darkening sky overhead before taking a good look at the pair. "Ew. Did you get ambushed in the art room supply closet?"

Laylea had momentarily forgotten they were covered in goo and glitter. Rather than explain, she waved the Sphinx flag she'd stolen from Tessa. Ali swatted as the glitter flew at her.

KC whipped her Centaur flag off her pack and waved it as well. "Centaurs tried to take us down," she declared. "But we prevailed.

"Finally!" Ali, grudgingly on the injured list, grabbed KC's flag. "Mers rule!"

Mer kids cheered as the flags inched up the pole, dripping glitter the whole way.

"How do we only have two?" Laylea asked.

"We have three," Ali said quietly. "But keep it quiet."

Milly tied off the pulley rope. "The Centaurs stole the first flag we had raised while Ali was over helping Benny fix the Sphinx's pulley."

"That's against the rules!" Laylea shot a look at the banner hanging over the faculty table listing the few rules in enormous print. "Once it's up the pole, it's out of the game."

"Yes. Which is why we're being quiet. The Centaurs think they're winning, but that top flag there?" Milly pointed at the blue flag flying high at the top of the Centaur's pole. "That is ours. Plus, they'll be docked two points for breaking a rule."

"So, we're letting them think they got away with it?" Laylea asked.

"Yep," Ali confirmed. "Brenda's orders. She says it'll make us fight harder and them relax."

"Hey," Squirt tapped Laylea as he hurried past them, heading for the night kitchen. "Come with me."

"How did you manage to already get caught?" KC asked as they fell in behind him.

Without looking around, Squirt replied, "There are desks just inside the tunnel entrance. Bargo and Muldoon were both doing paperwork. It sounds like it's not official or anything, but the faculty aren't letting anybody get near the Dean's residence without an appointment."

He pushed through the swinging door into the night kitchen where Chef Tod kept pots of stew and porridge heating twenty-four/seven. Laylea's stomach growled as the smells hit her. She went for a bowl.

"So, the Dean's tunnel is a no go. Got it." KC sighed.

"Thanks for trying." Laylea paused in scooping stew to offer him her fist. "Did you get pressed?"

"Not really. But I'm out of the game. Ms. McCobb ordered me to help Chef Tod for the rest of the day."

"I'm sorry, Squirt." KC offered her fist.

Squirt bumped it. "Nothing to be sorry about. I like cooking. And Ms. Bargo said he'd talk to my momdads for me and see if she can get them off my back."

"That's cool," Laylea said between bites.

"Yeah. Oh." Squirt peered through the porthole window in the door to the kitchen. "The Sphinx tunnel is also out. We ran into Barret-face on the way here and he had just come from this new 'information booth' they've built in the Regenstein Center. It blocks our exit."

KC frowned. "Damn."

"KC," Squirt laughed, "It's good news that our school is really well guarded. If there's no way for anyone to get in, then we don't need Lee to get out."

He pushed through into the kitchen too quickly to hear KC's response.

"That doesn't protect everybody upstairs."

She was right. Oscar's lie could be truth. Laylea's witch mother and her super-soldier father were always talking about how the refugee super-soldiers needed a purpose. This could be their purpose, at least for a time. Grandpa's forces couldn't possibly win against the team her Uncle Jay could pull together.

Belle or Carrie would find a way out. Laylea would get out to keep Grandpa from attacking the school. And then she would gather forces and stop Grandpa from hurting everybody else.

She crossed to the flatware station and snatched up a spoon.

She dropped it when the door from the corridor smacked her in the butt.

Belle burst in clutching an orange cloth to her chest. Seeing them, she cried "Water!"

Laylea grabbed a cup and met KC at the beverage urns, wondering what had gone wrong with Belle's escape attempt.

"Bigger," Belle yelled. "A bowl." She knocked the stack of bowls over with an elbow.

KC pivoted to catch one and spun back to the spigot. Water splashed to the floor as she and Laylea switched spots. More water sloshed out of the bowl as Laylea emptied her glass into it.

Belle squeezed past her, standing tall as Christopher and Krystal slid from her arms, splashing into the bowl.

35

Krystal and Christopher swam dizzying loops in the soup bowl, like a pair of hands washing each other. The instant KC set the bowl on the ground, they swirled into a water spout and stepped from the empty bowl as humans.

"That was close," Krystal exclaimed in a bright, melodic voice.

Christopher's tone was equally exuberant. "Let's go try the Sphinx tunnel."

The pair dashed for the door, each grabbing one of Belle's hands to drag her with them.

"Sphinx is a no go," KC told them quickly. "They've blocked the exit."

The twins slowed. Belle pulled them to a stop.

"Also, you nearly died," Laylea pointed out. "You have to go to the infirmary."

The two shook their heads violently. "Happens all the time," Christopher said.

"Please just go see Ollie real quick while Belle tells us what happened," Laylea begged them. "He's in the dining room."

Christopher brightened at that. Krystal blushed and ducked her head.

"You're right. I feel oxygen deprived," Christopher said.

He looked at Belle for reassurance and took her wicked grin as the answer he wanted. Without another word, he dragged his sister out into the Dining Hall. Krystal didn't fight him very hard.

Belle giggled as she dropped to her knees. Her uniform soaked the spilled water more effectively than the cloth she'd been using to carry the koi.

KC snagged a mop from the corner and tossed Laylea some rags.

"We tried Gryphon dorm first," Belle said. "But the doors wouldn't even open. You turn the torch holder, right?" She swept water towards the drain in the middle of the floor with her not-very-absorbent orange cloth.

"Yeah," KC confirmed, swishing the mop through the puddle.

"So then we tried getting to the Old School lift, but there are way too many people working in there." Belle swiped at the streams escaping KC.

"Yeah," KC nodded. "Apparently, they're working around the clock."

Belle squeezed her cloth out in the drain and wiped at the larger puddles while Laylea dried the smaller ones.

"Nocturnal shifters take the odd hours," Belle said. "I don't think you're getting out that way."

"What happened to make the koi shift?" Laylea asked.

"Oh," she said, "we were running to go try Adelor. There has to be a way to open it from the inside, right?"

Laylea shot a look at KC. There was. KC had used it in October.

"So, we took the last turn and ran into a brand new wall." She shrugged and grimaced simultaneously. "There was a splash and Chris and Krys were suddenly flopping around in the dirt. That was scary." She squeezed her cloth out again and sat back on her heels.

"I'm sure it was." Laylea agreed, joining her while KC returned the mop to its corner.

"But at least we found this." She held up the bedraggled orange cloth and shook it out.

KC screamed, "You got a Centaur flag!"

She grabbed Belle and dragged her out into the dining room. Laylea followed.

While they were in the night kitchen, the Centaurs and Sphinx had gained two new flags each. With Belle's flag raised, only two flags were still in play with just a short time before moonset.

Overhead, stars were starting to glimmer in the haze from the city lights. The trough lighting flickered like torches around the hall. Even the injured kids, resting and icing their bruises, cheered or booed as Ali raised the Mers' new flag.

Mer now flew three flags. Sphinx claimed four. Centaur had five on their pole.

Laylea strolled over to the First Aid Center Ollie had set up at the end of one table. Neither Christopher nor Krystal was anywhere in sight.

"The koi are okay?" she asked.

"Yeah, they're healers." Ollie answered her with a smile, though he kept his eyes on the gauze he was rolling. "No damage done."

Peter, his leg resting on a bag of ice, fed the gauze to Ollie as Thad, a Mer spider shifter, wove it from a spool of his own silk. The two sat on either side of the balled form of Vaughn Howe. Every now and again one or the other would run a hand through his fur.

Ollie caught Laylea staring at the unlikely trio. "It's not magic if that's what you're thinking," he said. "Emerald lit into Vaughn for nothing. He shifted wolf—he's allowed to now that his cast is off—and Peter and Thad have been protecting him ever since."

"That's hopeful," she said, feeling her heart lift.

"Yeah," Ollie agreed. "The school needed this." He grinned at the buzzing energy around them.

"I was scared the wolves would throw a fit," Laylea admitted quietly.

Ollie rolled his eyes. "They know where they stand in the school right now."

"It's not a party!" Brenda stood up. Everyone in the room fell silent. "The point is to raise money to create the best shifter sleeper and N addiction rehabilitation facility we can."

"The place needs a better name to start," Oscar yelled.

"What would you suggest?" A deep, adult voice carried across the room.

Laylea knew that voice. "What is Mr. DeGee doing here?"

"Quan's nephew snuck in to spy on the Wilding for the council," Ollie told her.

Laylea laughed. Griff's dad was Quan's descendant. "Nephew" worked as well as any description.

"Any ideas?" Mr. DeGee prompted. "The council hasn't come up with anything."

"How about the DeGee rehab facility?" Peter suggested. "Since you've put up most of the material and manpower."

Mr. DeGee tried to laugh it off. "I do expect to be paid back for much of that."

Peter pushed, "Sure, but you've spearheaded the project."

"No." Mr. DeGee's definitive answer left no room for argument.

Benny cried out, "Phoenix."

A number of kids objected to his language.

Ali stood. Her tattoos shimmered like she was about to shift. "We're not swearing like that anymore."

"No, I mean, like, you know." Benny flushed at all the attention. "It's just, I think of what Grandpa did to all those people, the sleepers, the addicts, the people we're building this for and I... I want to swear. Phoenix." He spit the word with venom. "But it turns out the phoenix wasn't a bomb or an attack on anybody. It was just Pansy, just a girl."

"Another Grandpa lie," Milly shouted.

"Yeah," Benny wrapped a hand around the Sphinx pole and pulled himself to his feet. "So, we're right to not use Pansy as a swear. But more than that. She kept bringing her brother back to life, trying to save him, right? This rehab center is the same. We're trying to bring our family and friends back to life."

"Like a phoenix," Ms. McCobb said into the solemn silence that followed.

Mr. DeGee stood. He gave a bow in Benny's direction. "I hereby dub the lion house shifter sleeper and N addiction rehabilitation facility, The Phoenix."

"Hear, hear." Ali's cry was echoed around the room.

"What if the council doesn't like it?" Benny asked.

Mr. DeGee rolled his eyes so expressively that Ms. McCobb choked on a laugh. "I really should get something for putting up most of the material and manpower."

"To The Phoenix!" KC raised an imaginary glass. Everyone except the sleeping Vaughn joined in the toast.

"To The Phoenix!" Junior's cheer, from the glass doors, came with a different, more somber tone. He may have thought they were toasting Pansy.

Laylea's heart dropped as she saw Carrie entering behind Junior. She slipped into the Dining Hall with her head down and her arms wrapped around her chest, her long sleeves tucked over her hands.

Blood dripped down one side of her face.

36

Each of the three flagpole keepers shook their poles, cheering the new name of the rehab center.

"The Phoenix!" Ali howled and swung around the Mer pole with its three glittering flags.

The ruckus had nearly calmed when Junior pulled an orange flag from under his ugly sweater and spun it over his head.

All the Mers went wild.

All the Mers except KC and Ali, who watched Carrie limping along the wall. KC darted over to her. The tattoos gleamed on Ali's arm. She soared into the air, circling the room and dragging all eyes with her, away from Carrie and KC.

After buzzing Benny at the Sphinx flagpole, Ali landed beside Junior in human form. She yelled, "Four flags! We're closing in on you, Centaurs. Mers are gonna take you down. Aren't we Sphinx?"

She threw attention to Benny at the Sphinx flagpole on the far side of Brenda and Mr. DeGee's enclave.

Benny stood on the bench and whipped his dormmates into cheers for Mer. It was an unexpected alliance. Junior danced between the tables, high-fiving and fist-bumping every Sphinx and Mer in his path.

Between the three of them, they kept all eyes away from Carrie, leaning on KC's arm. As they made their way toward Ollie's first aid station, Carrie ducked her head and wiped at the hair plastered against her face. Her eyes blew wide when her hand came away with blood on it.

Laylea moved to join them.

Ollie grabbed her elbow. "Don't overwhelm her. She's more scared than injured."

"How can you tell from here? That's a head wound."

"Her aura would be more electric, sharper, if it were primarily physical pain causing her distress."

Laylea chuckled at his explanation. "I can't even see her aura."

"You can't?" Ollie looked honestly surprised.

"I don't think most people can see auras," she explained.

"Oh, interesting." He gathered supplies as he spoke. "But you do know that an aura dims and shrinks the longer someone hides who they really are, right? Like…" He examined the space around her, then looked her directly in the eye before shooting his gaze over her shoulder. "Like KC's."

Laylea wheeled around as if she was going to suddenly be able to see her friend's aura. She couldn't. But she did get a clear look at Carrie. She gasped. Ollie took her hand and squeezed it.

"She needs your calm, not your fear," he said. And for the first time she noticed his voice held the depth of the two hundred years of time loop he'd survived.

Carrie's uniform hung unevenly from her shoulders. The fabric was torn, with one knee showing bloody and bruised through a massive rip. She shook as though she were freezing even with KC's arm wrapped around her.

Laylea pasted a smile on her face. She reached for Carrie's hand as they approached. "I'm so glad to see you."

"N... n… n… you're…" She took a breath. "I'm f… f… fine," she managed, the increase in her stutter accentuating the lie. "G... Go. Go away."

"But—" Laylea didn't want to leave Carrie, not in this condition, especially not when it was her fault.

Carrie shot her a look of exasperation, the expression begging Laylea not to make her keep talking.

KC came to her rescue. "Lee, she can't be seen with us."

Laylea grumbled, but let KC lead her away to the hot cocoa urns on the serving line.

Ollie brushed aside the hair hiding much of Carrie's face. Still-wet blood coated her temple. "Can I fix you up?" he asked.

Carrie nodded. With her consent given, Ollie led her to the bench. He moved Peter and sat her beside the warm, sleeping Vaughn.

At the serving line, Britny and Theresa doctored their cups with the many options Chef Tod had put out for personalizing the cocoa. Theresa appeared to be of the opinion more was better. Britny was pissed at Oscar's lie.

She told them, "There is no cake, if that's what you're looking for."

"As long as there's chocolate," KC replied evenly. "Oh, hey." She retrieved the waxed bag from her pack and handed it to Britny. "It's not cake, but I saved you more apple cores."

"Thanks." Britny shoved the bag into her pocket as she and Theresa took their drinks to the edge of the Brenda discussion.

"That's great. I love it!" Junior yelled. His voice cracked and after laughing at himself, he added, "Make it happen, Douglass!"

Mr. DeGee bowed in his direction. "I will do my best."

KC focused on filling two mugs. With their backs safely turned, Laylea hissed, "What happened?"

"Later." KC handed her a mug and proceeded to add peppermints and whipped cream to her own.

Laylea took the mug grudgingly, turning to watch Ali raise the Mer's new flag.

As it reached the three already flying, Junior saluted, "To The Phoenix!" and everyone toasted the name all over again.

Brenda took that as her cue.

"The Phoenix needs to be incredible. And that means we need to raise a ton of money." She took the floor by standing on a table. "We need games, craft booths, raffles."

"Snacks!" Brian yelled.

Kids started shouting out ideas. Brenda hollered for them to take turns and called on Belle first.

"We could raffle off limited edition gold passes to the zoo," she suggested.

Daniel scoffed. "The zoo is free, doofus."

"That's why it's a brilliant idea." Brenda glared at him. "We need to sell things that cost us nothing. What else?"

"My family can't afford a ticket or anything else." Britny stared into her cocoa, gripping it with both hands. "With all the attacks, they need to be ready to move or rebuild or go to the hospital."

"Yeah," Theresa backed her up. "We can't ask our families to donate all this money when they're already struggling."

"We need to invite thumpers," Squirt called as he gathered abandoned mugs.

"Nons," Junior corrected him. "True-humans and non-shifter wyrdos should all get to come to our party."

"Should all *pay* to come to our party," Brenda corrected.

"The council will never let non-shifters come to the party," Ali said. "No matter how much money they can bring."

"Why not?" Peter looked to the front of the room where Ms. McCobb was watching the discussion. "We'll all be wearing stasis bands, right, Ms. M?"

"Awwww, we can't have a glamour station then," Milly pouted.

Jeers rang from around the room. The jeers increased as an influx of students pushed through the great glass doors.

There was a moment of distraction as everybody searched to see if any of the new kids brought flags. None of them did.

A flock of birds soared in over the humans' heads with Rehyan's flamingo in the lead. They swooped around each of the poles, making the flags flutter and glitter fly before splitting up to settle with their different dorms.

Rehyan landed by Ollie and called out an insistent, croaking cry. A trio of colorful little birds harried a downy egret over to the first aid station.

Rehyan shifted human with a hop from one leg to the other. "Leda, he won't use magic if you don't want. Right?" he asked Ollie.

"Right," Ollie agreed, looking up from where he was working on Carrie's knee. "And Dr. Tippleston is in the infirmary if you'd rather."

Leda fluttered like she *would* rather, but her escorts chirped their disapproval. They hovered over her until her bright yellow feet tapped down on the table. With a belligerent squawk at Rehyan, she lowered herself and tucked her beak under one wing.

Rehyan smoothed the feathers along her neck. She shivered them out of place again. He smiled and kept smoothing.

"Birthmark," KC hissed into Laylea's ear.

"Excuse me?" Britny turned just as KC snatched the cup from Laylea's hands.

Laylea barely caught a glance of her own bright yellow, webbed feet before KC stabbed a pencil between her ribs. Heat flashed and Laylea found herself looking up at a scornful Britny. She barked. The girl turned away.

KC folded down to sit cross-legged on the floor at the end of the serving tables. She set the cocoa aside—chocolate wasn't good for dogs anyway—and scooped Laylea into her lap. "You're safer in this shape, right?" she asked into Laylea's furry head.

Laylea leaned back to lick her chin.

"Brenda?" Carrie called out.

"Yeah?" Brenda acknowledged her coldly.

"M... m... my uncle knows J... Joseph Lyman."

The name sent waves of shock and confusion through the kids. The Chicago locals knew the name, and they were impressed.

Squirt paused in his cleaning to look over at Carrie. "Whoa, cool."

Laylea leaned into KC and wuffled for an explanation.

She just said, "He's a legend."

"The billionaire?" Theresa asked doubtfully, once the furor faded.

"He's not a billionaire," Rehyan spotted the cocoa as he turned to correct Theresa. He dashed over, adding, "His company is worth billions, not him."

"If we invite Lyman," Squirt shouted, "he'll buy tickets for everyone he knows."

Someone near the Sphinx pole yelled back, "He's done it before."

"He probably would." Mr. DeGee sounded thoughtful.

"But he's a true-human," Coraline, who'd come in during the bird antics, said.

"I th... think he's a non," Carrie said carefully.

"This is your uncle, Councilmember Lake Marshall, you mean?" Mr. DeGee clarified, pointedly.

Carrie nodded until Ollie gripped her head in both hands to make her stop.

"Brenda," Mr. DeGee said. "Gather all the ideas and start planning. I'll get the council on board and Joseph, too." He stood and turned his electric gaze directly on Laylea. "*Someone* tell Griff his father loves him, would you?"

Her jaw dropped in a stress response that she hoped he'd interpreted as a grin.

With that, Mr. DeGee strode out of the Dining Hall, bumping fists and giving the claw sign with a hearty, "Grr."

Britny dragged Theresa away to the Centaurs as kids gathered in around Brenda.

"Okay, so Carrie is kinda freaked." KC kept her voice low, talking right into Laylea's ear, in part to keep things private, in part because Squirt was making an ungodly racket cleaning.

"Carrie got up the faculty stairs and into the zoo," KC said. "She was about to make a dash for the West Gate when Benniker jumped her."

"Woof?" Laylea asked. Benniker had been a guard when she first came to the school. But Kyle had scared him away.

"He's not a guard anymore." KC smirked. "He's park services. And he didn't catch her to return her. He recognized Carrie, threw her in his garbage bin, and was gonna sneak her out and deliver her to the wolves. Told her he knows how much they need 'breeders'."

A growl rolled through Laylea's chest, vibrating her entire body. She tamped it down and mentally traced her birthmark, fighting the burn in her paws that wanted to shift her into something that could tear out Benniker's throat.

"Yeah," KC agreed. "Also, Dustin's dad is organizing a rescue for the night before the next full moon. The idiot was bragging to someone on a radio with her right there." KC grinned. "That's why he didn't hear Toby come up behind him."

Laylea's triumphant howl turned to a yelp of fear as her spine flamed with an imminent shift.

37

KC scrambled to her feet, a hard thing to do with a dog in her hands and a heavy pack on her back.

Laylea whimpered at the heat running the length of her spine. Her body wanted, desperately, to shift into that too-comfortable bear form that had given her away to Jase. She refused to let it.

KC whispered as she ran for the night kitchen, "Toby is fine. He handled it. He threw Benniker into the flamingo pond and carried Carrie to Adelor."

She slammed through the night kitchen door and let herself get a little louder on seeing it was empty. "He stayed with her, waving away seagulls while she opened Adelor. Carrie said the gulls were more scared of him than worried about her. He led them out of the zoo!"

Worry for Toby kicked the flames higher. Laylea imagined ice shooting from her birthmark, through her skull, and down her spine.

KC set Laylea down near the bowl of water under the beverage station. "I can't believe the wolves are going to invade the zoo."

Carrie hadn't been caught by a guard. Which meant Laylea could get up through the faculty stairs and use the "rescue" to get out of the zoo. If she looked like a wolf.

Laylea transferred the burn from her spine to her floppy velvet ears, visualizing the ginger tufts of fur behind KC's wolf ears. She released her control and shifted.

KC screamed.

Laylea spun. And toppled over. Her new, enormous paws were awkward. She rolled upright, waving her long, fluffy tail.

"Bad dog," KC hissed, pointing the finger of shame at Laylea. Her face scrunched up as she got a good look. "Is that me?"

Laylea searched, found the burn waiting in her gut, and commanded it. She leapt mid-shift and landed on her human feet, stumbling into KC's arms. The bobble on the top of Griff's hat hit her friend's face.

"I can get out in the wolf pack," Laylea squealed.

"That is a very bad idea," KC growled at her, "that could work. But not with my muzzle."

"You'll help me?" Laylea asked.

"You shifted into me, deliberately?"

Laylea's grin could have turned her into a hyena if she wasn't laser focused on keeping her vocal cords for this conversation. "Yeah. My body wanted to be a bear, but I made it do what I wanted."

The cheer that sounded from the Dining Hall matched the joy in Laylea's heart.

"I'll help," KC agreed, "if you practice every minute for the next two weeks."

"I will. I will." Laylea bounced on her toes.

"And," KC grabbed her arms to keep Laylea still, "promise you'll get away from the pack as soon as you can."

"I promise."

The cheering out in the Dining Hall was joined with shouts of dismay. KC took Laylea's hand and held tight as the two pushed through the door to find it filled with excitement.

Kids and faculty poured through the Dining Hall doors, everyone counting the flags.

When he saw them, Oscar leapt from his seat by a curled-up Carrie-wolf. "Where have you been? It's four-thirty," he called. "Four minutes till moonset." As he got close, he lowered his voice. "Looks like bad news all around. No unguarded exits and the Centaurs have won."

"There are no winners until the points have been counted," KC intoned, like a wise old seer.

Oscar proceeded to count the flags on each pole. "Let's see; Sphinx, one, two, three, four. Mer; one, two, three, four. Centaur; one, two, three, four, five."

"Yes, dear," KC agreed agreeably. She hooked her arm in his and leaned in to whisper something to him.

Laylea thought she was telling him why the Centaurs' top flag belonged to the Mers, making it five-four in Mer's favor. But Oscar's reaction put paid to that.

"No." He spun and grabbed Laylea. "The guard was just outside the door, getting some air while Benniker cleaned the building. She would have caught Carrie if he didn't. You can't get up that way."

"If KC thinks it can work," Laylea began.

"You can't shift on command," he interrupted, voicing his real objection.

"I just did." Laylea felt like her whole aura must be glowing with her grin.

Oscar and KC engaged in an eyebrow conversation. It was probably best, with the volume of celebration and disappointment growing beyond tolerance levels.

Oscar shook his head. "I'll have to see it for myself."

Mr. Bianchi stood on the faculty platform and sang an impossibly high note into the microphone. He must have been using some twist of partial shifting to accomplish the sound. He didn't stop until everyone else fell silent.

"Two minutes," he announced before sliding the microphone to Ms. McCobb.

"Out of our way!" Reggie's voice broke over the tense hush as the doors were shoved wide. "We bring the conquering sloth!"

Centaurs near the door pushed everyone aside, making room for Reggie and Harper to scamper through, Riva balanced on their shoulders.

The sloth-shifter held two green flags in her hands. She spun them like Rehyan dancing after too much sugar. As they got close to Daniel, Riva sent one of the flags flying at him.

Theresa helped Daniel hook it up when he fumbled the clips in his excitement.

Half a dozen Centaurs stood ready as Riva arrived with the second flag. They rushed to clip the flag on and raise both up their pole.

Bells rang over the school-wide speaker system.

"It is four thirty-five," Ms. McCobb announced over the mic. "The new moon has set and the first school-wide Wilding is ended."

Laylea imagined the ground shaking under zoo guests' feet at the explosion of the school's response. The Centaurs screamed particularly energetically.

Mr. Bianchi raised a hand. Ms. McCobb simply stared at them all, her eyes sad.

Around the room, kids fell quiet in order of those who'd seen what Daniel did, those who had heard about it, then the Mers and Sphinx who intuited the sour feeling from their friends. Lastly, the clueless Centaurs quieted.

Daniel's guiltless, grinning expression twisted Laylea's gut.

"We will now tally the scores." Ms. McCobb said, her voice tight.

The Centaurs began cheering instantly, before any tally began.

Ms. McCobb brought two fingers to her mouth and whistled.

A few Centaurs began looking around, some catching the edgy mood of the others, some baffled at the need to tally anything with seven flags flying from their pole.

Ms. McCobb directed their attention to Professor Wanja.

The witch waited by the scoreboard, a chalkboard from the Old School. He fished a piece of chalk from the tray and flourished it.

"Professor, if you would," Ms. McCobb requested.

The professor made a show of counting each flag and placing the tally on the board. A gleaming blue four for the Sphinx. A flowery green four for the Mers. And a simple, white-chalk seven for the Centaurs. He stared at the seven as if surprised at its simplicity.

The Centaurs didn't notice either Ms. McCobb's somber mood or the plain chalk number. They broke into a riotous celebration, chanting, "Seven. Seven. Seven. Seven."

Ms. McCobb held up a finger, her face deadly serious.

More and more Centaurs began to notice the mood in the room. They shushed those caught up in celebrating, searching other faces and the flagpoles for a reason for the chem teacher's expression.

"The top flag on the Centaur pole originally flew for the Mers. As the rules state that a flag raised is no longer in play, that point is to be subtracted from the Centaur score and added to Mer dorm's tally."

The Centaurs' shock didn't translate into Mer joy. Instead, Ali hopped off her seat by the Mer flagpole and made her way to the Centaurs to explain what Daniel would not. Milly and Ahanu joined her, spreading the details of how Daniel had stolen the flag.

As a puppy, Laylea had been kicked in the ribs by a man wearing steel-toed boots. The air had been knocked out of her. The room, at that moment, felt just the same. Questions flew. Centaurs turned on Mers, who stood their ground, backed by Sphinxes.

Not giving the kids enough time to break out in a full-on riot, Professor Wanja made the change on the scoreboard. The chalk sang as he calculated six points for Centaur and five for the Mers.

"We still win," Daniel yelled, trying to convince his dormmates to celebrate. "We just played the rules."

"Did you forget about the penalty?" Caliban asked quietly. "'For each rule broken, there will be a penalty of two points.'"

Professor Wanja subtracted the penalty. "That's four points for Centaur, four points for Sphinx, and—"

"Yay Sphinx!" Ali yelled, interrupting him. "Great finds Brian, Oscar, Raederie, and Lisa!"

Professor Wanja tried to continue. "And five—"

"And hurray for the Sphinx who hid your flags!" Rehyan yelled. "We only found one!"

"We didn't even find that one," KC hollered. "Lee stole it from Centaurs."

That got an honest cheer.

"And five points—"

"Kudos to Tessa and Miro for those bazookas," Brian shouted. "The school is gonna glitter for a century."

Laughter rang brightly from scholarship and paid students and a bit darkly from pressers. Miro leapt away from their admirers and popped into their butterfly, fluttering over everyone's heads and on up into the rafters.

"Five points for—" Professor Wanja tried again to announce Mer as the winner.

"And to Harper," Ms. Crow interrupted the Professor, raising her glass. "How many flags did you recover and re-hide, Harper Pemberton?" she asked.

Harper, looking as disheartened and pissed as most of the other Centaurs, let some of that slide from his shoulders as his neighbors took up Ms. Crow's praise. He held up a hand, all five fingers spread. Slowly, a grin spreading across his face at the same falsely-modest pace, he raised his second hand with four fingers.

"No!"

"How?"

"That's crazy."

"He stole two of those from me!"

"And one from me!"

"What's your secret?"

All around the Dining Hall, kids and faculty exchanged stories of how Harper had tricked them.

"Huzzah." Tessa's low voice came from directly behind them. She held up a mostly empty red and white bag reading *Garret's Famous*. "Popcorn?"

"Where did you get that?" Oscar squawked.

"Garret's," she said, looking at the bag which clearly said as much, "by Music Shoppe."

Miro fluttered down and shifted. He took a handful of popcorn.

"There are stairs in the Old School, where they're building the physical therapy room," Tessa said. "They come up inside one of the lion enclosures. The door's been boarded over, but a small dog can squeeze through."

"What," KC asked carefully, "about the lions?"

"They're cool." Tessa blinked at them for another moment. Then she and Miro strolled away through the mingling Sphinx and Mer kids to join the defeated Centaurs.

A thickness in her chest made Laylea examine herself. It wasn't like the burn of shifting. Still, she traced her birthmark a few times just to be sure. The tightness remained.

"I guess you're going," Oscar murmured.

"You're really leaving," KC breathed.

Laylea grabbed their hands.

"It's agreed then?" Caliban's voice rang through the Dining Hall over the speaker system.

The crowd of kids yelled a nearly unanimous, "Aye."

Oscar grabbed Raederie to ask, "What are we voting on?"

"Big Mo suggested that Daniel clean up the glitter."

"It is decided," Caliban declared to raucous approval.

Ms. Lagat and Mr. Barrett stepped up beside Caliban as a contingent of Mers demanded the dean's attention.

The old shifting master took the microphone. "P2 taught us all that there are times when rules should be broken."

The crowd shifted, quieting at the reminder.

"But we must be very careful about choosing to do so. Daniel, you made a bad choice."

Ms. Lagat let her gaze settle on the restricted students for a moment before facing Daniel. "I hope you come to regret your choice and give your classmates reason to forgive you. Though, I suspect the glitter will be the easier mess to clean." She gestured to Mr. Barrett. "Mr. Barrett will get you started."

"What, now?" Daniel asked. His voice cracked.

Two hundred students answered, "Yes."

"There are always consequences for breaking rules," Ms. Lagat said. "They're not typically pleasant."

Daniel climbed down from the table beside the Centaur flagpole. Reggie and Harper leapt in and lowered the flags. Reggie took it another step and loosened the screws to collapse the pole entirely.

Mr. Barrett met Daniel at the end of the table. He escorted him through doors held open by Centaur kids. They closed the doors and formed a wall in front of it, as if making sure he couldn't come back in.

Caliban reclaimed the mic to announce, "The Mers have demanded a rematch."

Ali hollered, "We'll beat you next time, too. But fairly. And Sphinx, you'll play to win."

Ahanu added, "Yeah, do your best. You haven't got a prayer."

That started a round of good-natured trash talk that washed away some of the sour feeling.

"Meanwhile," Caliban's good cheer cleaned the air even further, "Brenda has demanded we all focus on our New Year's obligation. With that in mind, tonight's very special dinner, specially prepared by Chef Tod and some of our less competitive pressers, will be our fuel for a brainstorming session and not a celebratory feast."

Professor Wanja washed the scoreboard clean with a wave of his hand. He stood, head bowed, and brought his hands together in a clap that echoed impossibly in all their ears, shaking the glass ceiling. He threw his long arms wide like a bird spreading its wings.

Fiery words exploded onto the board behind him. The flames flared blue, faded through red, orange, and yellow and glittered away into gleaming golden letters spelling: The Phoenix.

38

A glob of glitter goo dribbled from the makeshift window shade on the music practice room door. Laylea kept her eyes on the glitter and off the hint of fear in her friends' eyes.

"Good?" she asked.

Two weeks of practice weren't much. She'd gotten decent at shifting in and out of the few shapes they'd focused on. But the height of adults still felt weird, and she kept scratching at the stubble on her cheeks.

"Good." KC nodded. "But avoid talking."

"And stick to shadows," Oscar added.

"And don't forget the scarf," KC said.

The two were holding back. Laylea could smell it.

She let out a breath. "What is it?" she asked. "If there's something I can do better, tell me."

Oscar was right. The vocal cords that came with Officer Garcia's face were too different. The voice wasn't hers. But it wasn't his either. She reached for her throat and adjusted the scarf hiding her collar.

"Do the wolf, just one more time," KC ordered, not answering her question.

Laylea took a breath. Her mind flashed on KC's fluffy ginger ears.

She forced her thoughts to the deep grey and brown wolf they'd designed together. She had to look like a young adult wolf, not affiliated with the Marshalls or Delcampos or Batkas or any of the many other known wolf families. KC had been insistent about that. She also had to be really shaggy in hopes her collar would get lost in her fur.

She shot the flames through her paws and shifted.

"Wow." Oscar breathed the word. "She's got it."

"Do Benniker again," KC demanded.

Laylea growled before she breathed in, summoning the scent of desperation and over-starched uniform that helped her shift into Benniker's shape. The shift was searing when she shifted to Benniker or Garcia. Hotter and more dangerous than when she shifted into herself.

"If you shake your hair into your face," Oscar said, "it'll hide your birthmark a little. It might not be a full moon tonight, but it'll be bright."

Benniker and Garcia had been Oscar's suggestion. If the wolves got routed by the police, she could play Benniker and look like she belonged in the zoo. Alternatively, she could play Garcia to look like she belonged with the police. Either way, she would still be able to get out of the zoo.

Laylea was more familiar with Dee, and it would be easier to pull off a female voice. But the thought of even pretending to be a banshee made her stomach cramp. Garcia was safe. He just talked to ghosts.

Laylea shook off the greasy taste of Benniker, letting the easy burn of her dog form swim through her veins. After a quick, comforting shake, she burned into her wispy, fifteen-year-old human shape and ran a hand through her hair.

KC handed her a bag of nuts and dried fruit. Laylea poured the food directly into her mouth.

"We should get you into place." KC gathered the empty snack bags that littered the small room. "I can see the wolfpack trying to use the bustle of all the construction workers leaving as a chance to sneak in."

"I really don't think they'll come till later," Oscar said, continuing the argument they'd been having for the past week since they started nailing down Laylea's escape plan.

Laylea chewed as he tore down the fabric he'd stuck to the window. He folded it carefully so the glittery maple glue stayed on the inside. It left residue, as it had on all the windows they'd used it on, but none of them bothered cleaning it off. Daniel would get to it eventually.

Laylea swallowed and stuffed the empty bag in KC's pack. "I should use the bustle of the construction workers leaving to sneak out. The wolves might not even be coming."

According to Carrie, the restricted wolves knew nothing about Dustin's dad's rescue plan. Laylea worried that they had to be missing something.

"You are giving them too much credit, Lee," Oscar argued. "Huono's dad is popular, not smart. He probably thinks he got a message through."

KC slung her backpack on. "With any luck, that message was intercepted by the police and Captain Morioka is lying in wait to arrest the whole lot of them."

Which sounded great, except that meant Dee would be there for the raid. And if Dee saw Garcia with Laylea's birthmark on his face, the gig was up.

It would be a matter of speed at that point. But even the fastest, most invisible animal she could think of—a Mexican free-tailed bat—wasn't going to be able to outrun Morioka in her dragon form.

While none of the wolves knew about Papa Huono's plan, all the Double Deltas did. Jase had ordered the wolves to pitch in with the New Year's preparations. The DDs were taking advantage of that order to keep the wolves busy. Brenda had quietly assigned each wolf a babysitter to be sure they were kept busy far away from any exits.

KC hauled on the door until the seal popped and the eerie dead air of the practice room was replaced with the redolent, cool of the music wing.

"I can't believe Brenda really got Reggie to babysit Jonath..." Oscar trailed off.

A haunting melody captured them, stopping all thought. It rang from the open door of Mr. Bianchi's private lesson room.

"What is that?" KC whispered the question as if she didn't want to stop listening to the music even long enough to ask.

Laylea didn't answer right away. She wrapped an arm around each of her friends, pulling them close as the tragic longing of the final ringing note faded away.

"That," she said, "is Jimmy, on the floor harp."

"He doesn't have an assignment?" KC asked, quietly.

Wolf Jimmy leapt out of the room. He dropped to his belly and then his side, whimpering and groaning as the air shimmered and sparked around him.

Human, huddled in the fetal position, he told them, "This is my assignment."

Oscar left the girls to help Jimmy stand as Mr. Bianchi came out of his room.

"Don't worry. Emerald is Jimmy's babysitter," he told them. "We're writing new music for the New Year's celebration." He turned a warm smile on Laylea. "It's good to see you, Lee. I miss our conversations."

"Yeah, me too," Laylea admitted, honestly.

"Sorry, Mr. Bianchi, we've got to go," KC said, dragging Laylea away. She turned back to say, "That was amazing, Jimmy."

"It really was," Oscar gushed. "I wish you could play that at New Year's. I wish I could hear it again now."

"You can't," KC yelled over her shoulder.

"Yeah," Emerald agreed as she stepped out of the lesson room. "We have work to do."

The tone in her voice was enough to send Oscar chasing after Laylea and KC.

Laylea stumbled. She was going to miss Jimmy's music. And her guitar. And Mr. Bianchi's lessons.

KC didn't slow until they reached the main corridor.

The corridor was mostly empty. Daniel was still crouched down near the turnoff to physics row, scrubbing the floor with Big Mo helping.

Mo waved. Laylea waved back.

For her own reasons, Brenda had assigned each of the boys to watch the other as if it were an important favor they were doing for her. Certainly some kids weren't being as mean to Daniel now that Big Mo was working with him.

Oscar's footsteps slowed as he reached them and asked, "Lee, you quit your private lessons?"

Rather than answer, Laylea sped up. "It's getting late."

KC grabbed the back of her uniform. "You loved those lessons."

Oscar blocked her path. "Why?"

Laylea faced them. With a grimace, she held up her delicate, soft-skinned, short-nailed, little-girl hands. "When I pick up a guitar—" She stopped mid-sentence.

That was all it took; the word, spoken so close to the practice rooms. Her fingertips tingled a little, not really enough to be called a burn, a minor smolder, maybe. They simply changed. The nails on her right hand stuck out beyond the fingers, strong, square, and just long enough for picking. She clawed her fingers a bit so her friends could see the hardened flesh of her left fingertips; solid, embedded calluses years in the making, with nails cut nearly to the quick.

KC's face melted into the pity that was the very reason Laylea hadn't told them.

Oscar's mind somehow leapt from that revelation to another enormous regret. "You sure you don't want to say goodbye to Griff?"

KC hit him.

Laylea spun around and stomped away. For good measure, she wriggled her thumbs, imagining Broadway lights around her birthmark.

She still had to fill her pockets with nuts and Chef Tod's protein bars. She couldn't do that if she went dog. And if she couldn't control her form when her friends irked her, what chance would she have in the middle of a wolf pack?

She sucked in a breath and held it as she skirted around Daniel, Mo, and the mess they weren't making much of an inroad on.

"Lee," Oscar jogged after her. "I'm sorry, Lee. I just… you're gonna miss him."

Oscar needed to stay out of her love life. Just because he was pining after someone didn't mean he had any business judging her avoiding Griff.

"She's leaving us, too. Don't you think that's hard enough?" KC panted as she chased Oscar chasing Laylea.

"You're the one taking classes you hate just so you can go upstairs and see your boyfriend every day." Oscar's taunting tone stopped Laylea in her tracks.

She waited for the two to catch up and reached for a pompom that wasn't there anymore.

Without facing them—she couldn't risk crying—she said, "I am going to miss everyone. I don't—"

She didn't want to go. But she couldn't say that. Saying that out loud would make it real and that would make leaving even harder.

"I'm coming back. I just have so many phone numbers and emails and maps in my head that I can't—" Again, she stopped herself.

She didn't want to admit any weakness. If her friends sensed doubt, they'd stop her from going. So, instead, she told them the truth.

"I saw Griff last night. I didn't tell him anything, just gave him his hat and asked him to look after you guys."

She grabbed their hands. Their skin felt hot against hers. Almost like all the practice had leached the heat from her skin to supply it to her shifting.

KC shuffled sideways until their arms were touching. "We'll look after him, too."

Oscar squeezed her hand and moved closer step by step as they headed on through the school to the Dining Hall. "But if you don't come back," he muttered, "he's fair game, right? Because those little top feathers, they're starting to grow on me."

Laylea snorted.

"And that hat," KC added, humming her appreciation. "There's just something about a man who wears pompoms."

39

Moonlight streamed through the glass ceiling of the lion enclosure. Laylea attempted a purr with her canine throat to assure Roxy that she was plenty clean enough. Either she'd got it wrong, or the lioness didn't care. Laylea closed her eyes against the pain of the giant tongue rasping the wrong way along her short fur.

"Good night, everybody. See you tomorrow." Finally, the zookeeper completed her round of thoughtful chats with each of the big cats.

Several voiced growly good nights in return as the overhead lights snapped off. Roxy raised her head to grunt a series of grumbly calls which the other lions responded to with grunts, grumbles, and puffs of breath.

Laylea snagged her chance and army crawled out from under her new friend. The cool air bit at her wet fur and love-raw skin, but she didn't dare stop to shake herself back into order. As soon as she was free, she leapt for the low wall and squeezed through the bars to the visitor's walkway. She turned to pff at Roxy, since it was a sound she could make, and seemed a polite response.

Roxy offered Laylea a view of her tonsils as she grumbled an unhappy farewell. Laylea imagined she didn't get too many visitors inside the enclosure.

The Dining Hall had been nearly empty, with most of the school off building booths and decorations on Brenda's orders.

It hadn't taken much for Oscar and KC to convince Chef Tod that kids were going to forget to come to dinner and it might be a good time for him to do a burrito run. While he was chatting with them, Laylea slipped through cold storage and ducked behind tubs of tomato sauce to the little hole in the wall that was just barely big enough for her to wriggle through. After a minute of fear that she had just voluntarily crawled into a freezing cold trap, the tiny tunnel opened into a much taller one.

As Tessa had promised, the new tunnel opened out into the Old School kitchen. She simply walked across the Grand Parlor and through the plastic curtain by the lift into the disarray of the construction zone. From there, it took a little sniffing around to find the physical therapy room and the spot where they had boarded up the entrance to the stairwell.

Tessa's scent filled Laylea's mindscape as she nosed around the loosened slats. The tips of her whiskers stung for an instant like the tips of incense sticks. Then her collar hung loose, smashing black fur into her skinny kitty neck.

For all Oscar's constant bragging on feline directional skills, *up* wasn't too much of a challenge even for a canine, so Laylea had shifted back to her familiar paws and bounded up the multiple short flights to the door near Roxy's resting spot and her unexpected tongue-bath.

The lions' rumbling faded as Laylea wove around the half-walls leading deeper into the new rehab facility. Following Tessa's instructions, she snuck through the echoing construction to an unfinished new doorway and on out through a maze of building supplies covered in blue plastic. The ground and tarps glittered with fresh snow. It was more than a little dusting, unfortunate for anybody who wanted to keep her paw prints hidden.

Laylea leapt and danced her way to the fencing, taking a circuitous route. She wanted it known that she had left school, but not until she had actually left.

A final squiggly dash landed her at a dented section of the fencing. Tessa had scented it better than she had described it. Safe between the chain-link and a tarp, Laylea rotated her ears in all directions. Not hearing anybody moving around, she dropped her jaw to utilize the scent receptors on the roof of her mouth and focused on isolating the myriad scents of the zoo and construction.

All the human scents were fading with the deepening dark.

Laylea stuck her nose beneath the tarp. It crinkled in reaction to a thick musk gathering far to the east.

With the way clear, she ducked under the tarp and crept quickly and quietly south. Her muscles craved speed. Every nerve sang for her to run, but running was more likely to draw attention. Her pale fur was bad enough. Her canine scent worse. Running would get her caught.

At the south end of the construction, which had been a cafe before the rehab project swallowed it up, Laylea closed her eyes. She reshaped her body in her mind, filling her senses with rich, aggressive, wolf-musk. The flames sparked in all her most sensitive and stinkiest spots. Under her legs, beneath her tail, and deep inside her throat, fire burned so harshly she cried out.

The sound emerged a strangled half-yelp that she buried in the fur of her enormous wolf paws.

But, like a twig snapping in a silent forest, her cry rang through the zoo, silencing the insects, the birds, all the little creatures whose voices make up the ambience of the outdoors.

She had to move.

Laylea lowered her head, flattened her ears, and fled to the bushes lining the path outside the primate house. The bushes rustled and twigs actually snapped as she ran headlong into them, rather than skidding beneath into the shadows. She'd forgotten how big her wolf-self was.

She shook her head clear and then snarled. The helicopter flapping of her ears was even louder than her yelp or collision with the shrubbery.

A wolf howled north of her. A dozen others joined in.

Laylea froze. Her heart raced.

She didn't need to run, she reminded herself. She was one of them.

Another wolf howled a deep, commanding, alpha call. This time, return cries rang from throughout the zoo. Two wolves appeared around the corner of the primate house, loping along the path. A feral part of her laughed at their civilized ways. Carrie would have bounded straight through the grass and over the flowers, reveling in the feel of dirt on her paws.

One of the pair chirped an order at her. Laylea dropped her tail in submission and fell in behind them. She shouldn't have hesitated to answer the alpha call.

Her heart pounded faster in time with her feet, driving blood to her muscles and every single terrified hair follicle judging by how they were all standing up. The closer she got, the more thankful she was to have set her shifting off of scent. There was no shortage of aggressive, over-saturated wolf-musk.

It was the ocean of wolf that made the human scent she'd dismissed earlier smash through her pounding fear. The tang of his terror bit her nose so painfully Laylea had to fight to keep from shifting human just to dull it.

"Nice wolf," Norman said.

The terrified human was KC's Norman. What the hell was Norman doing in the zoo?

Without any conscious thought, Laylea raced past the elder wolves leading her. A wall of fur and teeth slowed her body but not her panic.

The alpha crouched at the head of the pack, snow dusting his fur as if he'd been lying in wait for a long time. Rust-furred ears lay flat against his white head. The rough skin of his nostrils cracked audibly as he made a show of sniffing the air. As if Norman's fear wasn't drenching every inch of the little alcove by the carousel.

Norman chuckled nervously. Hysteria edged his voice. "We should get you back to your cages."

Somehow, in the universe of things the skinny Polish boy could have said, he landed on one of the worst.

Hackles rose on every wolf and the musk scent sharpened. A deep grumble rolled through the ranks, starting from the alpha. He took one step back. The wolves on his tail tripped over themselves scrambling out of his way.

Norman misread the alpha's apparent retreat. Nylon crinkled as his puffy coat resettled on his relaxing shoulders. "Good wolf."

How could KC be attracted to such an idiot? Laylea barely had time for the thought.

Ancient lupine hormones flooded her system. Saliva dripped from her fangs. Her wolf body responded to the alpha and to all the other wolves, insisting she take down the mouthy food.

Rumbles, chirps, and roars of need burst from the wolves like kernels popping over flames. Slowly, inevitably, the sounds increased until it was a symphony of warning that dropped into a low growl more felt than heard, like the rumble of a race car straining against its chocks.

At long last, Norman cottoned to the mounting danger. "Sorry," he muttered. "I'm so sorry. I shouldn't be here. I… I thought I could help. Look, I'm all muscle. I wouldn't be a good meal. Uncle Johnny says we should be strong if we can be strong so that… so we can help those who... who can't be strong."

The growling grew as the alpha leaned back into a crouch.

"Please," Norman begged, changing tactics as if anything could save him. "My uncle has intellectual disabilities. He needs me. I... please… I'm in love," he exclaimed with total sincerity and a joy that was out of place. "I just met the most amazing girl. She doesn't think I'm weird and she's like, super smart... Please." The plea came out on a sob. He took a breath, slowed his words. "I know you don't mean to scare me. It's just your instincts."

He was wrong. These cruel wolves, who in the light of day were humans, had made the human choice to torture him.

Laylea ducked her head and backed away, barely aware she was doing it. The elder wolves who had chastened her earlier closed ranks in front of her. She must not have looked as adult as KC told her. They'd only protect a youngling.

Norman kept babbling. His words had no effect.

The growling engine revved, only held at bay by the alpha's will. Any second, he could release them. The pack would explode out of their trembling crouch and bury Norman. There wouldn't be a scrap of him left.

She had no choice.

She couldn't count on Toby leaping from the bushes to save Norman as he had Carrie, as he had her. She would have to be the Toby.

Laylea dragged herself from the trance of the pack growl. She released the heat from her gut, sucked a breath deep into ursine lungs, and stood tall on thick hind legs.

Too late.

The alpha's red ears trembled and folded back. With no other warning, a young man stood where the wolf had been.

Norman blanched. He stumbled back, his rambling pleas falling silent as his throat seized up in fear.

The alpha growled, "Mine."

40

"Mine."

The man who stood in the puddle of saliva that had been dripping from the alpha's fangs was barely an adult. The skinny beard tracing his jawline did little to disguise his youth. Any good it did was undermined by the thick, black, double ponytails hanging down his back. It was just how KC wore her hair before she cut it off.

Laylea blinked. The alpha's round cheeks and wide brows also mirrored KC.

A wolf near the front whimpered. KC's doppelgänger snapped at them as if he still had a wolf's jaws.

"We'll get the True," he spat.

Her. He meant her.

His eyes sparked yellow as he turned back to growl at Norman. "First, I'm gonna have some fun."

The words turned into a wolf's growl as the alpha dropped back into his lethal form, disappearing from her view.

Norman's vocal cords abruptly released. His screams shattered the ice in Laylea's veins.

She roared. Wolves spun.

A voice yelled from far away in the zoo, "What a pack of goobers!"

More wolves turned. Their eyes slid right past the bear in their midst.

"Wolves are a waste of fur!"

Laylea recognized the voice. She roared again. What was Daniel doing upstairs, trying to get himself killed? She was already pushing it, thinking she could rescue Norman. There was no way she could save both of them.

Options raced through her mind as Daniel continued his taunting, coming closer with every panted word.

"Grandpa ain't no wolf," he yelled. "Boy's a chicken. Has to send minions to fight his own battles."

The insult to their revered Alpha of the Americas was the last straw.

The stench of the hunt sent Laylea stumbling away from the pack on her awkward legs. She dropped to all fours as they exploded around her.

Norman's screams faded to desperate, confused wails.

At last, the alpha appeared, bringing up the rear. He stopped by Laylea to throw back his head and howl through bloody fangs. Daniel got a teasing reprieve as the rest of the pack joined their alpha. Then the monster snarled and the chase was on.

One final wolf appeared as the pack raced away. The skinny Maned Wolf bounded through the trees and over the grass. He slowed near Norman and looked up at Laylea. Moisture sprayed from his nose as he puffed out a breath of air, acknowledging her presence. She might not have been certain who it was if it weren't for the leather cuff circling his ankle.

Big Mo lowered his head and rocketed around the curve of the carousel and out of sight, away from Daniel and the hunting pack.

Laylea ducked behind a tree. She turned into her girl self with barely a thought. It would be safer to look like Garcia or Benniker, but Norman knew her. He wouldn't be scared of her.

"You're okay," she called quietly as she circled the tree. "It's KC's friend, Lee."

A quiet, wet sob crept from Norman's throat. He raised his hands as if to ward her off, but in the same moment, his knees gave out and he grabbed her instead. It took an effort for Laylea to will strength into her own legs. If she hadn't, they would have both gone down.

"I came to help you," he whispered, holding on to her for dear life.

"To help me?"

"I know how to get out of the zoo."

Horrible sounds came from the South Lawn. The featherlight footsteps of two dozen wolves rained around the desperate, thundering drumming of Daniel's elephant feet running away.

Norman stared, glassy-eyed, at the trumpeting, snarling, snapping battle. His grip weakened and he nearly fell.

A lone seagull screamed. Laylea prayed that meant they were gathering troops. She dragged Norman beneath the trees and leaned him against a trunk. They needed to get out of the zoo now, while the guards were distracted and before the cops arrived.

"How do we get out, Norman?" she asked.

He didn't answer. His hand grasped for the tree trunk.

Daniel roared. It wasn't just scared. He was hurt. She had to get help.

"Norman. Do you have an armpadd?"

When he didn't respond, she reached for his arms. His coat squished where she grabbed him. The sleeves were drenched in blood.

She wiped at it, trying to find where he'd been hurt. Her heart jolted as her brain caught up. "Norman, did the wolf bite you?"

A whimper squeezed through her shrinking hope. How did it work? Did it have to be deliberate? Would one wolf bite turn him into a monster or did the maker have to mean it?

"I just wanted to help," Norman breathed. "She told me they were dangerous. But…" he broke off in a choked sob.

"It's okay," Laylea tried to pull herself together. She tried to think straight.

Sirens screamed their approach to the zoo. Her window was closing. But where could she go? Where could she take Norman? How badly was he bitten? Could he make it as far as The Office? Could they even get to The Office with him bleeding or would they be stopped and picked up? Was there even anybody at The Office who knew how to heal a werewolf bite?

No. There wasn't.

Norman sucked in a shuddering breath. It stuck in his throat. The desperate sound hit her like a slap.

Laylea's mother was a doctor. Her father was a soldier and a survivor. They had taught her better than this.

Laylea blinked the haze from her eyes as she wiped the blood from her hands onto her uniform. His puffy jacket wasn't spitting feathers or cotton or anything. His face was pale leaning toward blue, but clear of blood. She ran her hands over his neck and then took his hands. They were slick, but that could be from him touching the wound.

She asked him, "Where did he bite you?"

Her new tone cut through whatever shock had frozen Norman's mind. His eyes cleared as he watched her search his body. "I… my leg. He bit my leg and my arm."

"Raise that arm above your heart," she ordered. Her eyes spotted the black stain spreading over his jeans as her hands felt the ragged edges of the bite.

He hissed.

"Sorry," she said, mentally reviewing her supplies.

She hadn't prepared for injuries. It was a serious oversight. But she did have her handkerchief. It wouldn't be long enough to wrap, but it was something. She dug through her pockets, scattering protein bars and snacks. Something thumped to the ground after bouncing off her big toe. She bent to retrieve it.

KC hadn't wanted her to take the pocket knife. They'd fought over it. But the Dad said a good pocket knife and a bandana could get you out of most tough spots. He was a genetically engineered super soldier though, and she'd been a dog, so at the time she'd taken the advice with some doubt.

She stood to look Norman in the eyes. He was following the sounds of the battle and she had to shake him to get his attention. "Daniel is keeping them on the run," she said to reassure him. "Elephants have really thick hides. He'll be okay," she said to reassure herself. "I need you to lean on the tree. I have to let you go. Okay?"

It wasn't. He wasn't.

He grabbed at her. "Don't leave me."

"I won't. I need to treat your wounds, like your Uncle Johnny would."

It worked. He nodded.

"Okay, Norman. I'm gonna sit you down."

As she helped him to the ground, Laylea averted her eyes. She couldn't let him see her frustration.

Sirens closed in on the zoo.

The alpha had confirmed her fears. Grandpa had sent them to take her. He knew who she was, what she was, and where she was. She had to leave.

But she'd chosen to help Norman instead.

She was risking the school, her friends, and the entire community for one boy.

It was the wrong decision. But it was the only one she could make.

After a quick slice with the knife, the leg of her uniform tore away cleanly.

She wrapped it around his thigh as human footsteps thundered into the zoo from all sides. Gulls screamed overhead, not seeing them beneath the trees. While she tied her handkerchief around his upper arm, voices rang out, calling orders to each other.

Wolves howled and barked and growled. An eagle screeched. Magical wards flashed and yelps were followed with the stink of singed fur.

A wave of wolves washed past them.

Laylea threw herself around Norman, wrapping him in thick, dark arms, hiding him with a bear body. She leaned into the fear, anger, and desperation, letting it overwhelm her, flooding herself with an acrid stench that might conceal Norman.

She needn't have risked it. The wolves didn't slow. Their own mindless determination to escape drove them right past the enticing copper scent of bleeding prey. They leapt the fence beyond the carousel, some leaving fur on the spiked uprights.

Laylea roared. She shook, trembling right back into the familiar small human who could sob, helpless to escape either her own nature or Grandpa. Norman reached for her. She screamed at him, a wordless cry of terror and frustration through gasping breaths she couldn't stop.

But she had to stop. Norman was bleeding.

She had to raise his arm. She had to put pressure on his leg. She had to find a healer who knew about wolf bites.

She had to run.

She had to run. She had to hide. She wouldn't survive another lab, more experiments, and endless bloodletting.

The first six weeks of her life had been a hell of needles and torture. Her mother had abandoned her to save her from that. The Mom and Dad had abandoned her to save her from that.

If she didn't run, Grandpa would get her. If he didn't drain her dry, he would drain her weak enough that she'd never be able to escape her bio father a second time.

"No," she screamed. "I can't do it."

A downdraft of freezing air drove her to her knees. Gooseflesh pimpled her skin.

"Run," Norman slurred. He pushed at her weakly. Blood covered the silver plastic of his non-magical wrap bracelet.

She shook her head. She couldn't abandon him.

"I can't do it."

She took his bracelet and shoved it in her pocket, then pushed to her feet, leaving bloody handprints on her uniform. She stared at the trampled bushes, the paw prints through the snow, the fur fluttering from the fence.

With trembling knees, she stumbled out from under the cover of the trees.

"Help!" she screamed. "Morioka!"

Another blast of air froze the tears on her cheeks. A darker-than-night shadow blotted out the moon.

The dragon backwinged, landing on the path with just a tap of leather-soled shoes. Morioka's trench coat billowed behind her as she ran to Laylea.

Morioka ran. Laylea had never seen the demon hurry, ever.

"Stand up." Morioka tapped Laylea's head with one hand as she passed her. "I'll get the boy."

Norman put up no fight. Shock was taking over. He stared from one to the other as Laylea and Morioka helped him limp up the path.

"Captain." A uniformed police officer called to them just as they passed under the sweeping sculptured arch of the East Gate. "I've got another escapee."

"Lee, you're..." Daniel cut himself off, glancing first at Norman and then at Morioka. "Let me help, ma'am."

He rushed away from the cop and was pulled short by her grip on his upper arm. "You're not going anywhere, kid."

"Ow." Daniel glared at the cop.

"He won't run from me." Morioka intoned this in that way she had of filling words with meanings they didn't literally hold.

The cop heard the "let him go," interpretation as clearly as Laylea did. She dropped Daniel like he was on fire.

Daniel rubbed his arm as he took two steps sideways. "Just healing, ma'am," he said before shifting.

Laylea's ears popped so hard she could hear her own heartbeat.

Daniel flung his trunk high and trumpeted at the gulls. Then he shifted human again.

Unable to let go of Norman long enough to cover her ears, Laylea grimaced at the repeated popping.

"Thank you for coming, Captain Morioka." Big Mo tripped along beside the small cop pushing him harder than was necessary. His hands were trapped behind him.

At a look from Morioka, the plainclothes removed the cuffs. They gleamed in the moonlight, prettier and more delicate than the handcuffs Dee carried.

"Ma'am." Daniel raised a hand to get Morioka's attention. "Mo only left the zoo because I figured his anklet would alert you. I take all the blame."

Morioka took his measure. "That will be up to your enforcer. You are all pressed. Take him to Holding. Ms. Crow will meet you."

"He's been bitten." Laylea warned as Mo moved to help her with Norman.

"The boy's best chance is Holding." Morioka cut off any further discussion by bursting into her dragon form.

Norman gave a little yelp. His head fell back as they watched her soar over the parking lot, fold her wings, and dive.

A wolf's yelping followed them all the way down the steep stairs.

41

Of the many secrets in the Lincoln Park Shifter School, Holding was one of the biggest, even as it was one of the smallest rooms. Big Mo could barely stand straight in the low-ceilinged Victorian cell. So he sat, deep in thought between two of the three cots against the west wall.

"Who the hell was he?" He'd been muttering that same phrase over and over.

Daniel paced the single-lane walkway between the two rows of cots squeezed against the curving stone walls. He tapped the pocket door of the boys' locker room, crossed the little room, tapped the rough wooden door of the water closet, and did it all again.

Laylea lay with her muzzle under the pillow of a cot on the east side, wondering how it had all gone so wrong.

All but one of the six cots were made up with white sheets, a white pillow, and a grey wool blanket. The sixth cot stood naked. The bare yellowed mattress showed stains that reminded the three conscious kids that this room had a long history. Norman hadn't been the first to bleed all over it.

After cleaning up his wounds, Dr. Tippleston declared them "not so bad." She'd given Norman a tetanus shot and a sedative, and seen him and his freshly wrapped bites tucked cozily into fresh sheets on another cot.

Ms. Crow had helped her strip the bloody bed. Daniel held the pillowcase open while they stuffed the sheets inside. Big Mo folded the grey blanket, bloody side in.

He was the only one brave enough to question the adults. "Is he gonna turn?"

"Not tonight," Dr. Tippleston's answer came after she and Ms. Crow exchanged a nervous look.

"Is it a good idea to leave us in here with him?"

Ms. Crow took the blanket from him, saying, "It's a safety precaution."

"How y'all figure we're safe trapped in here with a turning werewolf?" Daniel squeaked.

Ms. Crow had laughed ruefully at the question. On her way out the door, she muttered, "The school's safety, not yours."

Dr. Tippleston was more reassuring. "The room keeps you in your natural form. It should keep Norman from changing."

The room kept Laylea a dog. It had shocked the staff her first night in Holding. After that, she figured her natural form was dog. But this time felt different. This time, she didn't feel like she had to stay a dog if she didn't choose to.

She thought about this for a while after the women left as she circled a few times in each direction and curled up with her muzzle under the pillow.

She'd nearly made it out of the zoo. If the wolves had just focused on their hopeless rescue plan and left Norman alone, she'd be gone. But she wasn't. And she hadn't even saved Norman.

Across the room, he moaned. Laylea unburied her nose. His fever was getting worse, but he still smelled one hundred percent human. Unless the change was being masked by Big Mo's glaring wolf musk.

The cot creaked as Laylea stretched. She did a down dog, an up dog, and then flapped her ears against her head and sent the shake all the way down to her tail. With a puff of breath through her teeth, she hopped off the bed and landed on the old rag rug with two bare human feet.

"Dang." Daniel leapt away from her and banged into a cot which slammed into the nightstand beside it. Water sloshed from the bowl, soaking the toothbrush and washcloth waiting there. "How d'you—"

"What were you two doing upstairs?" Laylea cut him off before he could ask. She could shift because she was a true shifter. Any form was her natural form, apparently. Though she suspected she would shift back to dog when she fell asleep. She always did.

Big Mo glared up from his seat on the rag rug by Norman's cot. "Shh."

Laylea matched his glare but lowered her voice. "What were you doing?"

Big Mo cut his eyes to Daniel as if telling her to ask him.

Daniel knelt with the washcloth. Instead of soaking it up, he'd wiped the water from the stand to the floor, creating a puddle that was slowly soaking through the rug.

Laylea stomped over.

"Well?" she asked.

Daniel grumbled, "Saving you." He sat back on his heels with the washcloth dripping all over his dark blue uniform.

"Why did you think I needed saving?" she hissed. She'd been so close. She could have made it out. She should be on a train heading west right now.

"He looked like somebody in school, didn't he?" Mo asked, off topic.

"Who?" Laylea asked.

"The alpha. I know him. I know all the Midwest wolves."

Laylea grabbed the washcloth and dragged Daniel to the washroom.

"This isn't going to help your reputation much," she told him. "Did you think about that?"

"Shows what you know." Daniel pumped cool water into the basin.

Laylea glared at him. "What does that mean?"

A choking snort accompanied Big Mo's approach. He tossed a

warm wet washcloth in the basin. "It's all over school that you have connections to an army of robots on the outside. Daniel believes it."

Laylea tried not to react. The widening of Mo's eyes told her she failed.

Daniel squeezed the cool cloths over the sink and handed them to Mo. "Yeah it sounds nuts. But that's none crazier than anything else going on upstairs. And then you and Oscar and KC were saying goodbye, and I figured…" He pushed Mo out of his way and squeezed past the both of them, wiping his clean hands on his dirty uniform. "Well, I figured if everybody else believes Lee can stop Grandpa, then—" He stopped talking as he realized what he'd said right in front of Mo, one of the wolves who had fought for Grandpa.

Laylea held her breath.

Mo took the washcloths to Norman. He lay one gently on the boy's head, brushing wet hair out of the way. The other he spread on his chest. If he noticed their discomfort, he didn't mention it.

"Seriously," he said, once he'd settled on the floor again. "This is important. I know that guy. You didn't think he looked like somebody's dad?"

They both shook their heads, not moving otherwise.

Mo reached down and twitched the hem of his uniform over the leather anklet. "Huono's dad was there. Jonathan's dad was waiting in a van in the parking lot. Well," he chuckled, "until he got arrested. Jase's folks were the pair right up on the alpha's tail, showing their bellies. No Marshalls, no deRios."

With a grunt, he sat up and took the washcloth from Norman's head, folded it outside in, and replaced it.

"Maybe I met him when he was a kid. Well, a littler kid. He can't be much older than me, now." He flung his hands up. "Which means he isn't anybody's dad."

Mo disappeared into his own thoughts.

Daniel picked a cot and lay down on the covers. He shut his eyes, like that was it, he was going to sleep.

Laylea kicked the frame. "Why did you come upstairs?" she asked, again.

Daniel sat up. "I figured if everybody in school believes in you, they might go lighter on me if I helped you."

He'd risked his life to be more popular.

"Have you tried apologizing?" she asked. He hadn't, as far as she knew.

"That's what I suggested," Mo whisper-sang.

"And why did *you* come up?" She spun to face the werewolf. Seeing Norman twitching, she lowered her voice. "You're already restricted. How much more trouble do you want to get in?"

"Good trouble?" he asked with a glint in his eye. "Lots. Like you said, I'm already restricted. Caliban doesn't believe in disenhancement. What more can they really punish me with?" He crossed his legs, rolled forward into a down dog, then stood to face her. "Brenda assigned Daniel to watch me. He can't afford to have her pissed at him, so when he went up, I went up. When the idiot ran out and," he sketched a bow at Daniel, giving him credit, "effectively distracted the pack, I ran for the gate so my anklet would alert Morioka before you or Daniel or Toby got… eaten."

He dropped his head on the last word and turned to refresh the washcloths in the bowl on Norman's bedside table.

Laylea watched him, speechless for a moment. He said Toby. He thought the bear was Toby. He hadn't recognized her. He didn't know.

One after the other, the washcloths splashed into the bowl like Christopher and Krystal diving into the Mer's freshwater pond at bedtime.

Laylea snagged another cloth and joined him. She dunked it in the bowl and slipped to the far side of Norman's bed, kneeling to hold the cool cloth on his wrist. Steam rose.

Mo kept his eyes on his hands as he replaced the cool cloth on Norman's head and slipped another behind his neck. "I didn't believe," he admitted slowly, "there were really packs who do stuff like this."

"What was he even doing in the zoo after hours?" Daniel wondered out loud, clearly not expecting an answer.

Mo said, "He's KC's boyfriend."

"Boyfriend?" Daniel screeched. "She's dating a thumper?"

Laylea would have hammered him for the slur, but another voice squeaked out, "Boyfriend?" Norman stared up at her with glassy eyes and a shit-eating grin.

She pat his shoulder. "You're dreaming. Shut your eyes."

Norman flopped his head to the side to address Mo. "She called me her boyfriend?"

Mo grinned at him. "How you feeling, Jackson?"

"I'm Norman," said Norman.

"Yeah," Mo chuckled. "It's just a thing my Papa calls people."

"My Uncle Johnny calls 'em 'boss'." Something sparked in Norman's brain. He blinked, trying to clear his eyes. His voice came sharper as he tried to sit up. "Uncle Johnny. He'll be worried."

"No, it's fine," Laylea pushed him back down. He offered a token resistance, unable to really fight her. "Ms. Crow is going to tell him where you are."

"Remind him to eat dinner. He forgets to eat." Norman faded back into a half sleep, murmuring, "Boyfriend."

"That's it, boss," Big Mo murmured. "Go to sleep and dream of KC." His face glitched. "He looked like KC," he said and immediately contradicted himself. "No." He went still as if the facial recognition search took all his computing power.

The alpha had thick, smooth hair, just like KC's. It was the first thing she'd noticed about him. She shook her head. No, that was wrong. She'd seen his wolf form first. The first thing she'd noticed was the spray of ginger fur behind his ears.

Her heart plummeted to her gut. Before she could throw up, she shifted.

"How're you shifting in Holding?" Daniel asked from his cot.

Mo sat up. "He had red ears."

"Well, it was cold out," Daniel said.

"Naw, he had red ears as a wolf," Mo insisted. "Like all the Delcampos."

Daniel sat up.

"It's true. Grandpa sent his militias to cause trouble in the Midwest." Mo's chest rose and fell like he'd just run a marathon.

"How do you figure?" Daniel asked.

"I didn't recognize a lot of those people, and I haven't seen that guy since he went off to MSC and became best beta, Grandpa's body man, and finally one of his top lieutenants."

"Who is it?"

"That asshole was Gerbrand Delcampo, Grandpa's favorite great grandson."

Gerber. KC's big brother. Her boyfriend had been bitten by her brother.

Mo slumped back down against the stone wall. He covered his face in his hands. "I've been such an idiot."

"Yeah," Daniel agreed. "I told you so."

Laylea hopped onto Norman's cot so lightly, it didn't move. She picked her way over his legs, circled three times to the left, twice to the right, and settled herself in a tight ball.

Gerber's human face appeared before her closed lids. His human face that looked like a douchebag version of her best friend. She opened her eyes.

She had to go. It wasn't just about keeping herself out of Grandpa's hands anymore. The lie that Oscar had spread should be the truth. The Dad and all the other conditioned force soldiers her parents had rescued were good people. Mentally unstable, for the most part, but well-meaning, strong, and literally unstoppable. Add to them her witch mother, witch brother, and Team Wyrdos and an undisciplined pack of brainwashed werewolves had no chance.

She had to leave. She had to do it without telling anybody else about her plan so that nobody else got punished or hurt. And she had to find a way to do it without using any of Norman's secrets since he'd promised Ms. Crow to tell her all about the weaknesses in the zoo's heightened security.

"Hey," Daniel asked them, "you think Dean Caliban is gonna ban us from going to the New Year's party now?"

That was it. The zoo would be crowded at New Year's. Everybody would be busy with the fundraising games and crafts and the concert. She could get herself assigned to clean-up duty as punishment for this evening's disaster. She could clean her way around the park to one of the secret entrances that Norman used and slip out while everyone else was at the concert.

And then she'd gather her magical robot army and go after Grandpa Delcampo, and Gerber Delcampo, and anybody else who tried to hurt her friends.

42

aylea tripped off the faculty stairs into the hallway behind Cafe Brauer's upstairs banquet hall. Griff caught her with an arm around her waist.

"Careful." Norman turned to be sure she was okay.

It was ironic. She'd spent much of the last week comforting Norman, curled at his side in her dog shape. He liked dogs.

"I've never been up this way before," she said to excuse her clumsiness. No need for Norman to feel bad for keeping them all awake last night. He felt awful in so many other ways already.

The bright midday sun streamed through tall windows as she and Griff followed Norman, KC, and Jimmy into the banquet hall. It was hard to believe it was the same place that the Shifter Council had held their community meeting just before P2.

The vaulted beams were draped with garlands of fresh-cut fir branches. Rainbows danced around the room as sunlight glittered off a hundred clear globes hung from the rafters where chandeliers had hung in October. Wreaths and banners in the colors of all the many winter holidays decorated the walls between the windows.

Chef Tod served hot food from a table set up in front of the half-built New Year's Eve stage, while families gathered at a dozen round tables draped with blue and silver tablecloths.

Kids typically went home for Christmas week, if they had a home. But with all the violence in the Midwest and Gerber escaping the cops after biting a true-human, shifters weren't in the holiday spirit. Most parents figured their kids were safer underground. For those who wanted to celebrate Christmas together, the school arranged for a small gathering inside Café Brauer and a whole lot of security outside of it.

"The stage looks great," Laylea said. "Why aren't we just holding the concert in here?" Having everyone inside would make it much easier for her to sneak away.

Griff laughed. "Way too small. And Dad wants eyes on The Phoenix, reminding the guests why they're here."

"I don't see my uncle." Norman searched the room with his eyes. The last week was apparently the longest he'd ever gone without seeing his Uncle Johnny in his life.

"He'll be here." KC tangled her fingers in his.

"He's got to be worried," Norman fretted. "I don't like to worry him."

Jimmy shot Laylea and Griff a worried look as Norman's band sparked visibly. They'd all had to wear them to go upstairs, and Professor Wanja had hoped it would give Norman some relief from the constant, agonizing shifting. It didn't appear to be working all that well. Much like Holding, the stasis band might be hurting him worse.

Morioka had been right. Norman hadn't turned in Holding. But his fever never stopped climbing. Early in the morning of his second day there, Dr. Tippleston called it. She and the rest of the faculty had reached out to every authority they knew. The only person with any answers was Jimmy, the only other wolf they knew who'd been turned by a bite.

Or the only one who would admit it, he suggested.

The turning was awful. Norman's bones had all broken. His flesh twisted in tortured ways as his body went through the shift for the first time. Jimmy sang to him, demanded Chef Tod keep the infirmary supplied with protein-rich foods, and made sure Norman knew he wasn't alone.

"Norman." Ms. Crow spotted them and hurried over. "Now, you're sure you're up for this?"

Norman laughed. "You couldn't keep me from my Uncle Johnny if you tried, Ms. Crow. I've seen you with Other Ms. Crow. You get it."

She nodded. "He has been inconsolable. Though we have certainly tried to reassure him since you came through everything okay. Mr. Barrett has been doing the 'rounds' with him and making sure he eats." She peered at him, her eyes clouding. "Are you sure you don't want us to tell your parents?"

"No. They don't need to know. And I'm eighteen." The sparking from his band broadcast his distress better than his tone. He sighed, looking down at it. "They're litigious people."

"Won't your Uncle Johnny tell them?" she asked.

Norman face hardened with an anger for an instant. His voice came out cold and sad. "They won't believe him."

Ms. Crow took his hands and held them tight. "I'm so sorry, Norman."

"Don't worry," Jimmy reassured her. "He's got us."

By "us" Jimmy could have meant pretty much the entire school. Every kid in the room had been watching them since they came in.

"Uncle!"

Across the room, Dizzy came through the front doors with Uncle Johnny Gorman.

Norman broke from the group to race to his Uncle. Johnny met him halfway, sobbing and crying his name.

Jimmy and Griff chased after Norman but kept a respectful distance from the two.

KC and Laylea would have followed, but Ms. Crow blocked their path. She lowered her voice to a near whisper. "KC, I'm not sure you should be coming upstairs now that your brother is in town. If he sees you…" she trailed off, unwilling to put words to her fears.

KC stared at the librarian, her mouth actually hanging open in shock.

It was Laylea who had to ask, "What are you talking about? KC is—"

"An orphan. Yes. KC Dells is an orphan," Ms. Crow agreed. "Who just happened to get pressed in the parking lot the very night that Karly Carlotta Delcampo was expected to show up."

To her credit, Ms. Crow looked around carefully as she said KC's real name.

"You remember that you weren't keeping secrets around your invisible raven friend, Dizzy, right?" she added, raising her eyebrows at the both of them.

Laylea had forgotten that. From how pale KC's face turned, she'd forgotten as well.

"Why haven't you turned me in?"

"For what?" Ms. Crow looked offended. "We respect chosen names here."

KC scoffed. "Haven't my parents been looking for me?"

A pall passed over Ms. Crow's face for a moment. She cleared her throat. Then answered quietly, "No."

Laylea's throat closed up. Her stasis band sparked.

KC looked off at Norman and Johnny holding each other as if they would never let go. Before the tears that had welled up could fall, she nodded curtly at Ms. Crow.

"Thank you for your concern," she said. "I'm not letting them trap me downstairs. I'm not letting them trap me anywhere."

She left, stomping just a bit.

Hurriedly, before KC could get too far away, Laylea assured Ms. Crow, "We'll keep her safe." Then she chased after her friend.

There were a lot of people who needed safety. The entire school and all of the Midwest shifters for a start. Hell, Norman hadn't been a shifter. So, just make that all of the Midwest.

She caught up to her just as Norman started introducing his new classmates.

"Johnny, Jimmy. Jimmy, Johnny."

"It's a pleasure to meet you, sir." Jimmy held a hand out.

Johnny pulled Jimmy into a hug, crying, "Norman's emotional-support wolf!"

Jimmy was not the kind of guy who invited hugs, at least not in human form. He buried his face in Johnny's shoulder and held on tight.

"KC!" Johnny opened his hug to pull KC in.

Jimmy took the opportunity to grab Laylea into the group hug as well.

After a solid squeeze, Johnny released them all to peer at Laylea. He bit his lip and asked, "Lee?"

"Yes. Hi," Laylea confirmed. "You're really good with names, Johnny."

A broad smile lit up Johnny's face.

"He is." Norman said, his voice tight. A wave of tension washed through his body.

Griff stepped up, drawing Johnny's attention away from Norman. "I'm Griff."

Uncle Johnny stared at the crest of feathers on Griff's head in awe.

Griff brushed a hand over them, ducking his eyes. "I'm part eagle on my mom's side. I usually wear a hat."

"Lee," Dizzy called from the front doors. "You have a guest."

The door opened behind her and Laylea squealed just like Norman had.

Bailey stood there. He looked around, taking in the families exchanging gifts and working on the stage. While the sight of him made her want to dance for joy, he did not look good.

It wasn't like he was underweight or sallow-skinned. His whole appearance was an illusion, so he could hide anything like that. There was just something off, like he was weighed down by something awful.

"Go." KC shoved her.

Coming in the door behind Bailey, Dee did the same to him.

With her stasis band sparking, Laylea ran to hug her brother.

"Hey, Lee."

"Hey, Bails."

He neighed. And some of the heaviness lifted. "Nice hat. Aren't you just gonna lose it next time you shift?"

"Thanks. My friend Griff gave it to me," she said, bouncing on her toes. "Would you like to meet him?"

Instead of answering, he pulled a thick envelope from his jacket pocket. "I brought you a present."

Laylea took the letter reverentially. Her heart skipped a beat as she realized that she would actually see their parents soon. She grinned at Bailey, wishing she could tell him her plan.

"Are you coming to New Year's?" she asked instead. "This rich guy bought two tickets for every student."

"I'm sorry, Lee, I can't. I got an internship and the whole team is heading to Nevada to help tamp down a viral outbreak. In fact, we're leaving in an hour. Dee's gonna drop me at O'Hare after she checks on how the sleeper relocation is going."

Sleeper relocation? Laylea's heart had gone on a whole journey during Bailey's little speech. But his last words stopped her cold. She thought she'd misunderstood. "Sleeper relocation?"

Dee cut in between them. "Give your sister a hug, Bailey, and then we've got to go."

"No no no," Laylea stepped back when Bailey leaned in. "The sleepers are being moved into The Phoenix today?" she demanded. "Like right now? Shala and Sanna and Mr. Samborsky and Deanna are…" She stopped, looking around the room for Oscar and Brenda.

"Lee, no," Dee snapped. "They're doing it today to keep it quiet. Say goodbye to your brother."

"Is Jeannie Nellwin here?" Laylea asked, wondering if the doctor could help Norman at all.

Dee ignored the question. She turned and opened the door. "Morioka and I are coming to New Year's."

"You can't drop by for five seconds." Laylea grabbed Bailey's wrist and hung on. "You're supposed to be looking after me."

It didn't make any sense. She hadn't seen him in months and she was taking off in a week. She'd be back with her parents and they would definitely include him in their rescue plans.

But seeing him changed everything. She wanted more time.

"Lee, this is a great opportunity for me," Bailey peeled her fingers from his arm. "You're busy with school. You won't even notice I'm gone."

Laylea released him. She wrapped her hand around the stasis band which wouldn't stop stinging her.

"Fine." She shrugged, eyes down. "Be safe."

"Hey." Bailey grabbed her head and zerbeted her cheek. "I love you."

"I love you, too, Bailey."

He turned away then and followed Dee out.

Laylea tucked the letter carefully away in her pocket. Her parents never wrote anything important in their letters. They never said where they were or what they were doing. The notes were more like a lot of words just saying "I love you."

Thinking of Shala Luke and Mr. Samborsky, trapped in sleep, kept from their families, she stuck her hand in her pocket to touch the letter. Maybe saying "I love you" was important, too.

Oscar and Brenda weren't in the room. They were in the fields, training because Mr. Bianchi had suggested a Double Delta training session would be a good distraction. They only assumed he meant a distraction from the ruined holiday.

Should she tell them? Or would it be even worse knowing their families were so close and didn't want them to know.

The door opened again and a frantic Ms. Lagat hurried in and past her, straight to Uncle Johnny and the kids surrounding him.

"Mr. Gorman," she began, then stopped to calm her voice. She attempted a smile. "I am Adele Lagat, a teacher here. I was wondering if, in your travels, you'd seen a..." she licked her lips and adjusted her glasses. Her hand trembled more than it usually did. "A bear. Have you seen a bear around in the past few weeks?"

"Toby?" KC asked.

"He's gone missing," Ms. Lagat said curtly.

KC shot Laylea a look. Toby had led security guards away from

Carrie during the school wide wilding. She said they'd chased him out of the zoo. Had he never come back?

"I haven't seen any bears, Adele," Johnny said solemnly. "Is it a friend of yours?"

"We can look for Toby tonight." Mr. Barrett broke through the circle they'd made around Johnny. "If you don't mind me taking Norman's seat again?"

Norman cried out. He turned his back to his uncle, bending double over his sparking wrist. He struggled to remain standing as his body convulsed, needing to shift.

"Norman, what's wrong?" Johnny searched the worried faces around him. He didn't question Norman's pain or tell him it would be okay. He looked at the crowd of strangers with complete trust. "Help," he begged.

And they all did.

KC wrapped an arm around Norman's shoulders, giving him her other arm to squeeze.

Jimmy led him in a rhythmic, growling chant.

Griff ran to the buffet to grab the plate Chef Tod had ready.

Ms. Lagat took Johnny's flailing hands in hers. "Norman needs to shift. His body is still changing."

"Shift, Norman," Johnny insisted, his eyes wide and terrified. "I won't be scared."

"He can't shift up here. Students aren't allowed to," Mr. Barrett explained.

"And family can't go downstairs," Ms. Lagat added, before Johnny could make that suggestion. Her tone made it clear she disagreed with that rule. She and Mr. Barrett hovered over Johnny. The man would be cared for as carefully as Norman.

A line of shifters stood ready to help Norman get wolf as quickly as possible. Dr. Tipp stood at the top of the stairs, waiting to remove the stasis band. Griff held the stairway door, a plate overflowing with food in one hand. Jimmy stood chanting with his arms spread wide, as if he could be a wall to protect Norman from staring eyes. Laylea sidled over to help KC hold him upright.

"We'll take good care of him, Uncle Johnny," KC said, quietly. "I promise."

Norman gasped, spinning to wrap his arms around his uncle. For the first time, he seemed like the child in the relationship. "You'll come next week?" he begged.

Johnny held Norman gently as he reassured him, "I'll be in the front row."

43

A giggle of little kids ran by, squealing and leaping for the bubbles Diejuste and Calliope shot at them from plastic blasters. Kyle's little true-human daughter, KJ, ran hand in hand with Angel's butterfly shifter daughter, Coy.

Far off in the direction of Café Brauer, a deep handbell rang. A dozen other, higher pitched, bells echoed from throughout the zoo, alerting the guests it was time to take their seats.

The New Year's Eve party was already a wild success. Adults ate and drank, bought silly trinkets, bid on donated art, danced in Café Brauer, and crowded the magically and prosaically heated Foreman Pavilion as kids ran wild, hopped up on caramel corn and hot chocolate. Shifters mingled peacefully with true-humans and wyrdos. The few werewolves in attendance made their alliances clear, draping themselves with the fiery Phoenix-branded scarves sewn by the Orbweavers club and sold at exorbitant prices.

Residual warmth from the heaters and the comfort spell the Witch Club had placed on the South Lawn barely reached Laylea as she cleared the last empty plates from a pub table onto her tray and moved on to the next.

Brenda had the stage set up in front of The Phoenix with chairs, benches, and couches arranged on the expansive South Lawn for the audience. The two halves of the audience were split by a runway of raised plywood to save heeled and wheeled guests from getting mired in the grass. Big Mo, Daniel, and Laylea had spent the morning laying it in place, complete with off-ramps for the expected wheelchair users like Angelica's wife, Mariella. The aisle was painted red so Mr. DeGee could market the party as a Red Carpet Event. Not that they'd needed to market it after Joseph Lyman had been invited.

The enormous lights loaned to the school from the Music Shoppe snapped on as a signal to students to shut down their booths and gather onstage.

It was also Laylea's signal. Once everyone was focused on the stage, she could slip away.

"Lee, do you know that girl?" Ollie startled Laylea so badly she dropped her tray.

Cups, glasses, plates, and crumpled napkins spilled everywhere. Some wit in the distance yelled, "Opa."

"Opa!" A duo of little voices repeated, laughing.

Diejuste and Calliope's coven of kids bounced between the stage and the seats. All of them began chanting, "Opa, opa, opa."

"Sorry about that." Ollie set his tray of snacks on the pub table she'd just cleared and dropped to his knees.

"It's not your fault," Laylea mumbled. "I was stuck in my head."

"Who's that girl? I haven't seen her in school." He was staring at a dark-skinned girl with the most fantastic braids-on-braids mohawk. The sides of her head were shaved back in a way that complimented her long forehead. It was the school uniform that made Laylea think of her as a girl, but the weight on her shoulders and exhaustion in her face made her too old to be a kid.

Laylea frowned. "She's not a student."

"She looks familiar." He lifted Laylea's filled tray to the table.

Laylea tilted her head, squinting. He was right. She looked really familiar.

The woman turned to laugh as a white-haired man with glittering eyes chugged the last of his cider before slamming the mug, upside down, onto her tray.

Laylea gasped. "That's Shala Luke."

"Oscar's sister?" Ollie asked. "I knew she was alive, but it's been so long."

So much had happened that Laylea had forgotten Shala found the witches, too. Denier had kidnapped her as she was leaving to tell someone about them. They saw her conked on the head and carried away.

"Hey, she's one of the sleepers." Ollie shifted gears. "That might explain her dusty aura."

"What's wrong with her aura?"

"It's angry. That's to be expected, right? The problem is on the, I don't know, edges? A gray dust..." He tilted his head and squinted, just as Laylea had done. "Is that magic?"

Laylea took his hand and dragged him toward Shala. She searched the crowd for Oscar and spotted him and Brenda harassing Councilmember Angelica deRio. They'd been advocating for the patients being invited to the concert. It looked like they were still at it. It just didn't seem right for them to not be invited to a party that was being thrown for them.

Apparently, Shala felt the same way.

"You should buy another, Mr. Lyman," Shala said. "Just five dollars."

Joseph Lyman shook his head, frowning. "Ten dollars is highway robbery. How much for two?"

Shala sized him up. "For you, sir, I'll give you two mugs of cider for twenty-five dollars. A steal at twice the price."

"A steal, you say?" Joseph peeled a hundred off his roll of cash and stuffed it in a mug filled with fives. "Then I'll just steal them."

He snagged her last two full mugs and ran away giggling.

Shala set her tray on a nearby pub table and emptied the mug of cash, folding the bills with Joseph Lyman's hundred on the inside.

"Excuse me," Laylea approached before Shala could move off. "I'm Oscar's friend, Lee."

Shala's laughing expression dropped into wariness.

Laylea barreled on, "This is Ollie, one of the—"

"Ollie," Shala cried. Tears sprang to her eyes. "I'm so sorry."

Ollie hurried to her. "No, it's okay. I'm so glad you're alive."

Shala wrapped her arms around herself. "I don't feel like I'm alive."

Ollie nodded like her answer wasn't terrifying at all. "Do you know you're being muted with dark magic?"

Shala blinked. Her mouth dropped open. She snapped it shut. Her tone was colder than the air as she informed him, "I am a black cat."

"Which could be why the curse can't get past your aura," Ollie replied, not put off in the least. He planted his feet, then ran a hand through the air about a foot in front of Shala.

She stumbled back, sucking in a ragged breath and shook herself, exactly as Oscar's panther shook. Her pupils blew wide, briefly flashing yellow. The heaviness and exhaustion Laylea had noted earlier fled.

"What did you do?" Shala asked.

"I cleaned away the curse."

Shala grabbed Ollie's hand. "Come with me."

After a moment of stunned shock, Laylea tripped over her own feet to catch up with them.

Shala led them to the unfinished side of The Phoenix where she slipped through a break in the fence hidden by a row of trees.

As Ollie followed her, Laylea spotted Griff waving. He jogged over.

"I finally got away from my dad," he joked.

"Hey, go get Quan and any witches you can find." She kept her voice low.

"Sure." His eyes lit up. "What's going on?"

She grinned at him. "Something magical." She kissed his cheek and ducked away into The Phoenix's courtyard.

Wide walkways had been poured around tiled seating areas enclosed by trees. Lights had been strung up throughout the little courtyard just as in the zoo. Her eyes marked a bench deep in shadows before she spotted Shala leading Ollie through an open doorway and chased after them.

People in chairs and tripled up on beds filled the foyer beyond.

Laylea stumbled as she scanned the faces. She knew some of them from when she, Junior, and Amal had snuck into the Starwood sleep lab. They looked better, awake. But they didn't look good. Every one of the patients had sunken cheeks and dull eyes. Not a one of these people looked able to sit up for the length of the concert.

"Leenie." Dr. Jeannie Nellwin strode over. Her skin was ashen. Her dim eyes brightened as she pulled Laylea into a hug.

"Hi." Laylea spoke into Jeannie's shoulder. "I just saw KJ. She's having fun."

"Yeah, we heard," a young, white-haired girl called from a chair. "Opa, opa, opa."

"Shh. You're gonna get us in trouble, Deanna." Shala wrapped her long fingers around the girl's head as if she would crush it.

Deanna sat up straighter, her face brightening as she chant-whispered, "Opa opa opa!"

"They all have the gray," Ollie muttered.

"What's that?" Jeannie asked.

"You're all cursed," he told her.

Laylea might not have been quite so blunt.

The doctor smiled gently. "They were cursed," she agreed. "But we found them and everyone is getting better." She said that last to the patients themselves, as if convincing them of it.

"No, ma'am, Dr. Nellwin," Ollie insisted. "You're all cursed." He raised a hand in front of Jeannie and brushed it through the air like he had done with Shala. His hands moved slowly, as if trying to brush away tar.

Jeannie gasped.

So did Ollie. He bent over, hands on his knees to hold himself up.

Shala grabbed Jeannie. "Feel better, don't you?"

Jeannie's brightened expression said it all.

Shala turned to the room and shouted. "He can heal us."

Sanna Luke buried a shriek of joy in her neighbor's hair, hugging the poor woman tight enough to strangle her.

The neighbor straightened at Sanna's touch, just like Deanna had at Shala's. Her face filled in to merely underfed rather than emaciated and she hugged back with more strength than she'd appeared to have.

Patients surged from their seats, everyone reaching out to Ollie.

"Slow down." Laylea's warning was lost in the chatter around them. She clutched at Jeannie. "It's too much for him. He can't heal everyone right now."

Jeannie turned away. She held her arms up. "Sit down, everybody. Ollie, sit."

He didn't argue but let Jeannie help him into a chair. A shiver wracked through him when she let go.

"I'll get you a sweater." Deanna trailed a hand along the wall until she reached a closet. It held a variety of sweaters, wraps, and coats.

Laylea's mind took a break from all her other concerns to worry about that. When they'd first come in, some patients had been sleeping. That meant the boogeyman could get at them.

"I can heal them," Ollie insisted.

"You just can't heal them all right now." Professor Wanja strode through the doorway and straight to Shala, wrapping an arm around her with a wide grin.

Shala's jaw clenched with emotion. She dropped her head to hide it.

"Professor, it's so good to see you again," Jeannie cried, rushing over to embrace him.

"And you." Professor Wanja kissed her cheek.

Laylea breathed back her frustration that their new witches hadn't been helping with the patients' rehabilitation. She didn't have time to wallow. "I think Shala and Sanna can help make the healing easier." She turned to Oscar's mother. "Sanna, hug that guy beside you."

Oscar's mother hesitated.

Laylea squinted at the man. "Mr. Samborsky?"

"Brian." Brenda's father wrapped an arm around Sanna's shoulder. "I'd love a hug," he assured her.

Sanna folded into him, holding on tight. His body relaxed. He kind of brightened. Laylea couldn't say exactly what she saw, but Ollie saw it, too.

He leapt from the chair. "You're a black cat, too?" he asked.

"A leopard," Sanna said proudly.

Ollie grinned. "Hug everyone you can reach."

Without questioning the bizarre request, patients around the room began hugging each other.

"Not—" Ollie cut himself off. "Okay, that's fine." He turned to Oscar's sister, the only one not joining in. "Shala, you too. And Oscar when he comes. And Tessa."

"Slowly," Professor Wanja murmured. He took Ollie's hands when the boy raised them to wipe another patient clean of the curse. "We need to know how to help."

"The black cat magic repels the curse," he said. "See how the gray, clumpy, dusty particles soar to the outer edge of their auras when Shala or Sanna hug them?"

With the Professor's encouragement, Shala crouched to hug a woman in a wheelchair.

"Ah," he exclaimed. "And then you just need to wipe the aura clean."

With a gesture, he did just that. And slumped, the hem of his long coat brushing the floor. "Oh dear, that is still too much. We need help."

Laylea nodded. It was the perfect opportunity. She backed away to the door. "I'll go find Oscar and Tessa."

Tessa would hate having to hug strangers.

It was a good thing for her that Laylea wasn't really going to fetch them.

44

The din of the orchestra warming up hit Laylea with a reminder of the beautiful chaotic life she was leaving behind.

It took everything she had to make herself dash to the shadowed bench on one side of the Phoenix courtyard where she'd hidden her collar earlier in the day. Clasping it around her neck, she hurried to a good tree. Doubt niggled at her. Professor Wanja could be wrong. The lizard totem on her collar might not affect the stasis band at all.

Her worries vanished when she reached for the burn and instantly shifted into her tall bear form. Though most conscious thought also vanished, she reached for the lowest branch as she'd planned. It creaked as she wrapped her enormous paws around it, then sprang upwards as she shifted back into her tiny human self to swing up.

Once crouched on the branch, she fired up a burn in her shoulder blades, flexing until they sprouted wings and her entire body twisted into the shape of a seagull. Brenda's insistence that she strengthen her core translated surprisingly well to the bird form. Wobbling a bit, she spread her wings to keep her collar from falling down her small body, and found her balance.

The cacophony of clashing instruments silenced. A single note rang out from a plucked guitar string. Jimmy, for sure. Then Emerald sang the same note octaves higher and the choir joined in from all around the South Lawn. Their footsteps added a percussive accompaniment as they marched along the plywood center aisle, up the four steps of the proscenium, and onto the stage singing the same old campfire song her friends had sung the first time she had been invited to join a party at Toby's enclosure.

It was a perfect departing anthem.

Laylea leapt from the branch.

Adjusting her father's flying lessons to her own bones and muscles took effort. But soon enough, she rose above the wall and caught a current that flew her over the heads of the choir, the orchestra, and the audience of shifters, wyrdos, and true-humans. A few faces glanced up, but most didn't notice the single seagull stuttering through the dark sky.

She pumped her wings to rise higher, wanting to avoid any seagull guards, though she couldn't see any in the air or perched anywhere. There was movement beneath the trees lining the path beyond the South Lawn. That was fine. She was going the other way.

She would borrow a zookeeper's coat from coat check, then fly straight to Union Station and catch the first train to Oregon.

As she flew over the primate house and the carousel, she saw more figures skulking across the grove where Norman had been bitten. It was surprising there would be so many guards and none in the air. She hadn't seen that many while she was working the party.

Once over the gate, she landed a little roughly in the bushes behind the coat check shack.

Her nose crinkled the instant she shifted dog. Her hackles shot up. The scent of blood filled the breeze.

And musk.

Deciding to check it out quick, she dashed to Adelor's plinth and crouched against the bottom step, twisting her ears every which way. There was no sound other than her pounding heart and the distant traffic on Lake Shore Drive. No sound was not good.

Another whiff had her scrambling up the steps. On the far side of

Adelor, Officer Jharrel Garcia lay unmoving, draped off the edge of the plinth. Only the rise and fall of his chest kept her from howling with grief.

Garcia's broken body was coated with a slimy grey sheen that she could see but not feel, like magic gone sour. Just the tips of his fingers remained clear where they reached for a red, origami crane that lay beneath the shattered remnants of his armpadd. The sheen shied away from the crane. Until he dropped it, Garcia had been protected from magic. Was that why he was the only guard in sight?

She grabbed the totem in her teeth and dropped it into his hand, then turned to the wounds she might be able to do something about.

She shifted human without a thought and tore open his shirt to find four shallow slices across his chest.

Wolves.

Her scalp prickled as her hair stood on end.

The wolves weren't at the gate. They were already inside the zoo.

She had to warn everybody.

Her fingers shook as she scrabbled at Garcia's utility belt. His radio was gone. So was his gun.

Laylea shoved down the voice in her head telling her there was nothing she could do, that she should run and gather the magical robot army that could defeat the wolves in one fell swoop.

But that would take too long. What use would any army be if there was no one left to save?

She was all they had. She had to be enough.

With a quiet, desperate whimper she leapt from the plinth and exploded in fire. Flapping madly, wings smacking into her collar with every beat, she shot back toward the concert as the fastest, most invisible animal she knew.

Her bat nose dulled the terrifying scent of blood that had been driving her into a panic. A new, unfamiliar sense put her on a different kind of alert. Letting instinct take over, she cried a series of chirps and listened. Movement pinged her from the parking lot.

Her chest swelled with hope that there were cops there to help.

"Leave him. That's good enough," a voice hissed from the trees.

A young woman, her blond hair poorly covered with the hood of a black coat, instantly dropped a body. Before it landed, she shifted into an Arabian wolf and bounded over the still, magic-coated bodies of uniformed guards and officers, clearing the fence in a leap that landed her behind the primate house.

The thud of a head hitting pavement pummeled Laylea's bat ears, pushing her little body as if she'd been physically propelled away from the still figures of the zoo's protectors.

Something had gone terribly wrong.

The adults had gotten it wrong. Clearly Grandpa didn't care about true-human witnesses. The wolves had come and somehow broken through the Council's every protection.

Laylea cleared The Phoenix and darted over the audience as Mr. Bianchi's voice rang out from the speakers surrounding the South Lawn.

"A special thank you to Mayor Colbrook and Governor Battles for joining us tonight." He held for the applause as the two politicians raised their drinks, toasting with Caliban and Oliver Luke.

The rest of the shifter council kept a lower profile, sitting with their families and Enforcer Bitters a few rows behind the vast DeGee clan.

Mr. DeGee stood, taking pictures of Griff, who huddled at the base of the proscenium steps, top hat in hand, ready to run onstage after Mr. Bianchi's speech.

Faculty gossiped together just behind the front row raffle winners. Lyman Corp employees sat at the very back. Even the parents had arranged themselves in a separate cluster, the wolf parents isolated on one side.

The adults had sorted themselves as clearly as the sopranos, altos, tenors, and basses on stage.

Ms. Crow stood to one side of the choir's risers, upstage of the orchestra, ready to act as Griff's lovely assistant. Dizzy waited on the other side. She was his invisible assistant and the secret to all his tricks.

Laylea folded her wings and the weight of her collar dragged her to the ground beside the stage. Shifting dog, she scurried into the dark shadow of Dustin Huono's upright bass.

Adults wouldn't listen to a kid. She'd have to borrow an adult face. She chose the face and form of the most powerful woman she'd ever known, the Mom, dressing herself in a turtleneck so her collar wouldn't give her away.

Rushing for the stage, Laylea made it past Griff and up three steps before falling flat on her adopted mother's face. Sher would be mortified. Laylea didn't have time for embarrassment.

As Mr. Bianchi hurried to help her, she scrambled to her feet and shoved past him to the microphone he'd abandoned at center stage.

"The—" Laylea realized as she yelled that she couldn't exactly say that the wolves were coming. There were true-humans in the crowd. That's why she had wasted time not flying directly to the stage. But the words were out before she could stop them. "The wolves are in the zoo."

Half the crowd laughed, thinking it was part of the show. Half argued with her in shock and denial, yelling, "Impossible," and "We were told we'd be safe."

Near the back of the audience, surrounded by the brownies and other Office regulars, Dee and Morioka stood. Too late.

All the laughter and shouts turned to shrieks as black-clothed militia raced out of the shadows to surround the South Lawn.

"Too fucking late, lady." Gerber Delcampo strode up the center aisle. His combat boots echoed dully on the red-painted plywood.

Every inch of Laylea wanted to shift dog, tuck her tail, and hide. With guns on every side, not even a dragon-shaped demon could stop the wolves without getting innocent people shot. Still, Morioka and Dee remained standing, turning slowly to scan the attackers.

Following their lead, Laylea stood her ground in the spotlight.

Behind her, instruments twanged as they fell. Kids leapt to their feet. Brenda hissed orders that were passed in whispers through the performers.

Jonathan shoved through the choir to the stage floor, crying "Wolf power." He stumbled off the last step and plowed headfirst into the trombone section. Thanks to their fear, almost nobody saw Junior trip him.

"Gerber," KC growled from her place amidst the altos. Her eyes glowed yellow. Oscar grabbed her hand.

Dustin howled from behind his upright bass, pumping a clawed hand in the air.

One of Gerber's black-clad militia howled back, from his looks, Dustin's dad.

"That's right," Gerber called out. The wolf's voice carried over the audience as though amplified. "We have the power."

"Hello. Mr. Gerber?" Junior stepped into the spotlight.

Gerber didn't hear him. He replied to Dustin's salute with one of his own, howling along with his militia as they shoved their own clawed hands in the air.

"Yoo hoo," Junior tried again. Again, no response. "Good. You can't see me."

"Why not?" Laylea asked, quietly, off the mic. "What does he have to be scared of?"

"You. And me. And Grandpa," Junior said, racing down the steps. "Bullies can almost never see me. Keep him talking, lady. I'll go get the cops."

"No, wait," Laylea said. "The cops are cursed."

But Junior was already rounding the corner of the stage, heading for the East Gate. Laylea grabbed the mic and yelled. Too loud. Her cry was drowned in feedback. She tried again, controlling herself, "Junior!"

"That's Lieutenant Delcampo, to you," Gerber spat, his attention fully back on the stage.

Mr. Bianchi pulled Laylea out of the spotlight. "Ma'am, don't get yourself killed."

Gerber marched down the aisle like a little boy playing at soldier. "I am here on orders from your Alpha, Luis Delcampo."

On stage, kids quietly moved into squads if they had been training with Brenda or to their friends if they hadn't. Big Mo shot Brenda a look as he and Vaughn boldly joined Dustin. The horn section kept Jonathan from even getting to his feet.

"Show them what respect looks like," Gerber shouted to his militia.

The hair on Laylea's arms stood at attention as sharply as the werewolves on the perimeter.

"Yes, sir, Lieutenant Delcampo, sir!" they cried as one, rattling their guns.

"Understand your position, now?" Gerber asked. "There is no escape, no help is coming." He sneered at the people standing to protest.

Even those standing kept to their protective bubbles; politicians isolated from true-humans, true-humans isolated from shifters, wolves isolated from everybody. It was all just like Grandpa wanted it.

If they only knew the skills their neighbors had, they could work together. The shifter birds could fly for help. The witches could connect and reverse the curse on the cops. The true-humans could create distractions.

Gerber announced, "Listen close. I will not repeat myself."

"I bet he will," Rehyan muttered. Kids laughed.

"None of this is funny, children," Gerber spat.

"Says the seventeen-year-old." KC's words came out as cold as her eyes.

"You will obey. My guns will see to that." Gerber strolled up the aisle, enjoying himself.

Laylea sought out Dee's face in the audience. She would know how bad things were going to get.

Back to back with Morioka, Dee, who despised killing, crossed her arms like she was bored, not cold. It was a good bet she was reaching for her shoulder holster. Their two guns were vastly outnumbered. Pulling them out would be just as disastrous as Morioka going dragon.

Amal started to stand, but Morioka stopped him with a gesture. He and the other brownies stayed where they were.

That wasn't good. It meant she thought there were too many wolves for even the brownie's karma magic to handle.

Gerber stopped beside Bitters. It was a foolish choice. Standing near the physically enormous and well-loved man only made Gerber look like more of a child.

The enforcer didn't notice Gerber staring at him. He had moved to protect Angelica deRio. His attention was down on Angelica's wife, Mariella, whose wheels blocked him from the aisle.

"Sit down, Enforcer Brewster."

Bitters' fancy facial hair fluttered as he sucked in and released a deep breath. He said nothing.

Angry and unnerved, Gerber yelled, "Sit!"

Bitters didn't move.

"Sit." Gerber reached for a holster strapped just an inch too low on his leg. He fumbled, struggling to draw it one handed. Once he got it out, he pointed the nasty-looking weapon at Bitters' head.

Raising his hands to show Gerber they were empty, the enforcer said, "Let's take this somewhere else, away from all these innocent people."

"Fuck that, thumper-lover. You want to keep 'innocent people' safe? You sit the fuck down."

"I could just… change." Bitters said this so quietly Laylea could barely hear him.

Gerber snorted. "You can't break the law. You're the enforcer." He sang the title like it was a playground taunt.

"Which only means I would be the one to punish myself." Bitters kept his voice low. A grin quirked one side of his mouth.

All laughter and mocking dropped from Gerber's face. He lowered the gun to Mariella deRio's temple.

She trembled, her wheelchair rattling with her fear.

"Keep pushing me, and this cripple dies."

45

Bitters' shoulders slumped. Where he'd faced Gerber's gun fearlessly, he backed down when it was pointed at someone else.

With a hand on Mariella's shoulder and his eyes glued to Gerber, he sat.

Gerber swept his gaze over the audience. More adults sat.

"That's better." With a smug grin, he holstered his pistol and continued up the aisle. "We're here for the True. We know you're hiding him in the school. Give him to us."

Most of the audience had no idea what he was talking about. Students openly, if quietly, mocked him. Laylea's heart leapt at the pronoun.

Him.

Gerber didn't know that Laylea was the True.

Despite herself, she looked to where Jase crouched amidst the front row tenors, his attention laser focused on Gerber. His eyes flared yellow and the tight line of his jaw suggested he was working as hard as she was to stay human. But that didn't make sense. Her eyes shot to his wrists. He wasn't wearing a stasis band.

Beside him, Riva wasn't either. All the singers had bare wrists.

The shock threatened her control and Laylea raised a hand to touch her birthmark. Riva saw her do it. She turned her eyes front, her expression turning steely hard.

"Give me the True," Gerber said, "and no one has to get hurt."

"Liar," Big Mo and Daniel shouted as one.

Faculty hissed from the audience. Seated beside his Uncle Johnny in the front row, Norman sobbed.

Gerber laughed. "Smart kids," he said. "We are here for the True, though. The Alpha wants him alive."

He waited, eyes on the stage, eyes on Laylea and Mr. Bianchi. "No?" he asked. "None of you is willing to hand him over? One kid to save everybody else?"

Nobody stepped forward.

Jonathan voiced the general opinion, his face crinkled in bafflement as he said, "The true shifter's not a real thing."

"Okay, troops." Gerber ignored Jonathan, if he heard him. He turned in a circle, speaking to the menacing perimeter of werewolf militia. "Find the True. Kill anybody who gets in your way."

Riva stood.

"Don't hurt anybody," she yelled. Her voice shook. "It's me. I'm… I'm the True."

"A girl?" Gerber scoffed, though triumph suffused his face.

Over in the soprano section, Krystal stood and raised her hand. "No, it's me. I'm the true shif—"

"I'm the one you're looking for," Christopher called from the tenors.

Rehyan grinned as he stood, brandishing his violin like a sword. "I'm Spartacus."

Ms. Crow dodged around a baffled Dustin, yelling fiercely, "I'm the True."

Kids' voices rang out, each shouting louder than the next as they claimed to be the true shifter.

In the audience, Mr. DeGee's bellow drowned them all out. "I'm the true shifter. Take me."

Everyone fell silent when Caliban stood.

"You don't know us." She laid a restraining hand on Oliver Luke's shoulder. "You don't know which of us is the True, so you can't kill any of us."

"Actually." A short woman stepped out of the ranks flanking the lawn. Her thick brown hair was tied back in double ponytails, just like Gerber's. The last time Laylea had seen her, she'd been disowning KC. "That one's the dean," Mrs. Delcampo said. "You can kill her." She raised her rifle as if she would do it herself.

"Drop it!" KC screamed.

KC's mother dropped her gun into the grass. The shock on the woman's face showed she hadn't dropped it by choice. She'd responded unnaturally quickly, magically quickly. Just as the militia had when Gerber ordered respect.

The risers shook. KC stomped down them, Oscar on her heels. "Caliban was a student when Denier was stealing our blood," she yelled. She shoved her way through the scattered orchestra seats to stand at the top of the proscenium steps. "So, no, you can't kill her."

The murmuring in the audience grew. The adults' whispers turned angry. The words "stealing" and "blood" rose in volume with every repetition.

Gerber didn't seem to hear them. His eyes were glued on KC, seeing past her blunt-cut blond bob, stacked boots, and stuffed bra. Despite her careful makeup and blue contacts, he recognized his missing sister.

Invisible to most of the audience, Dizzy soared over the choir. Landing in human form, she planted herself between KC and her brother.

Gerber stared daggers straight through her. "You don't tell us what we can't do." He spat every word.

Clearly he hadn't seen his mother obey KC's orders.

"We are superior to you in every way," Gerber yelled, turning from her. "It has been proven over and over. Just look at you, cowering to us. This is the natural order of things."

He went on. Laylea stopped listening. The werewolves could be defeated, even with their weapons. If only everybody wasn't afraid to show what gifts they truly brought to the table. If only they knew what their neighbors could do.

The thing was, they might not know, but she did.

Laylea stepped back, bumping Bianchi.

"Hold still," he whispered. "You don't want to run from a predator."

"Oh, I'm not. Just moving away from the mic." Laylea patted one of his hands on her arm. "Dizzy, you can't stop a bullet," she said, keeping her eyes on Gerber, his back to her as he yelled about superiority and the natural order of things. "But you can tell our friends Brenda's plan." She did not look at Brenda as she asked, "You have a plan, right, Brenda?"

"You know it," Brenda answered.

Dizzy flashed back into her raven and flew to Brenda.

To distract from their conversation, Carrie moved to the far side of the stage, whooping and cheering Gerber's continuing nonsense. Jimmy joined her. And then Big Mo.

To the east, Junior ran through the militia line and straight for Dee and Morioka. Not one of the werewolves saw him.

"The cops are down," he yelled. "Cell service is down."

Laylea launched herself at the microphone. "There's a bedroom closet in The Phoenix," she yelled.

"Yes!" Junior threw her a thumbs up as he conferred with Team Wyrdos before racing away to get help.

Gerber sneered her way, barely interrupting his diatribe about wolves and their superior genes.

Another idea sprouted. "Professor," she said, speaking directly to the witches she'd left in The Phoenix, hoping they were still there. "Professor, our guards have been cursed."

Gerber stopped talking mid-sentence.

"Take the cats and help them." Laylea kept going. She was on a roll, her brain sparking with ideas on how to save them all without sacrificing herself. "Hey, neighbors." She spoke to the audience and the militia. "News flash. Magic is real. Some people are going to disappear now. Don't freak."

Gerber raised a hand, crying, "Troops—"

"What?" Laylea asked him. "You gonna command them to shoot anybody who turns invisible?"

He turned to her, as she'd wanted.

She lowered her voice, staring into his eyes as best she could under the spotlight. "You're using magic," she said, making it more of an affirmation than a question.

Not even realizing he was doing it, he nodded.

Sher had never taught Laylea magic, per se. She had taught Bailey behavioral conditioning. And Laylea had paid attention. It didn't work well without physical contact, but maybe wearing Sher's body would loan her some of Sher's power. She didn't need much. Just enough to keep Gerber focused on her.

"Do you know about brownies?" She put a little emphasis on the word, hoping the brownies would take the hint.

Muffled screams from the audience assured her they had. Hope surged in her chest as sounds of alarm rang out across the South Lawn. Grandpa's militia would be learning the hard way what tricks brownies could play with bad karma.

"Lieutenant Gerber Delcampo," she crooned, using the most basic trick in the book to keep his eyes on her. "You have the power. And you're not going to hurt anybody, like you said. Otherwise my friend, the banshee, would be shivering. Still, animals react to intense feelings like what's going on here. Who's to say which ones might not be able to stay in their cages."

There was no way to tell if the shifters in the audience caught her suggestion, but Gerber sure did. He broke eye contact and wheeled on the audience. "I'd better not see anybody shift here!"

Right at his elbow, Diejuste puffed up, moving her tiny, eleven-year-old body in front of Coy and Calliope as if she could protect them.

"Diejuste," Laylea said, dropping her conditioning voice. "Gerber's mother is here." She didn't mention his sister.

"Gerber," the little goddess, protector of families, drawled in her deeply comforting accent. "It must be hard f' you, bruddah." Diejuste stepped into the aisle. "Having to prove yourself just because a who ya great granddaddy is, pretending to be older than you are." She held a hand out to him.

It should have worked. Bondye had sent her to protect families. Gerber's mother was backing him. He'd found his lost sister. Diejuste's words should have constrained him to listen to her. But they only made him angry.

His roar issued from a throat that wasn't entirely human. Claws sprouted from a half-shifted hand as he snatched up little seven-year-old Coy. A trickle of blood dribbled from her neck onto her fluffy, pink dress-up coat.

Norman wrenched himself from his terror to scream, "She's a kid!"

"Let her go!" Oscar cried, his hand white in KC's grip.

"You don't want me to hurt your friends, Karly?" Gerber asked his sister, ignoring Norman, Oscar, and everybody else. "Tell me who the True is."

Coy's sister climbed on her chair.

"Calliope," Dizzy screamed. "No!" Reality twisted around her as she half-ran, half-flew at Gerber.

Calliope launched herself a moment later.

Screaming a war cry, Mariella deRio rolled up the aisle aiming her chair like a missile at KC's brother.

All three hit him in rapid succession.

Sparks exploded around Gerber, leaving him untouched.

Mariella's chair slammed into the crowd, scattering people and chairs like bowling pins while Mariella flashed into her hummingbird form.

Dizzy was flung through the air. The dead weight of her human form tumbled onto the DeGee family.

Coy and Calliope disappeared completely.

"You can't touch me," Gerber crowed. "I am a wolf!"

46

Ignoring the sparks that flew from Gerber along with Dizzy and Mariella, Dr. Angel Lopez wailed and lunged at Gerber.

Her husband wrapped his arms around her and Candy, holding her back. The toddler drooled on his hands from her baby carrier. He shouted something in Angel's ear then pointed to a deep-blue butterfly flitting safely away from Gerber's claws.

Coy was safe. But where was her sister?

"What did you do to Calliope?" Oscar cried, stumbling forward on the risers with KC holding tight to his hand.

Gerber screamed, "You can't touch me. I am a wolf!"

Many, but notably not all, of the wolves screamed and hollered and hooted.

"A wolf with some kind of magical forcefield around him," Rehyan muttered.

Coy fluttered over Joseph Lyman, who lay in the aisle, his arms wrapped around his chest. She stayed close as a dozen hands reached to help the man to his feet.

The effort pushed him too close to Gerber and he was flung into his rescuers with another blast of sparks, stench, and despair. The rich man kept his head down over his folded arms.

Sparks flew yet again. Hummingbird Mariella was flung away. Angelica caught her wife as those around her continued to wrangle the mangled wheelchair into the aisle.

Bitters could have lifted it with one hand, but he leapt at Gerber, disappearing just before sparks flew off the shield near Gerber's feet. He must have hoped his spider-self could get through the shield.

"He's vaporizing them!" Mayor Colbrook yelled, standing to point at Gerber. Her finger shook with terror, but she shouted the warning anyway. "Don't touch him!"

"Siddown!" Spittle sprayed from Gerber's mouth. He pulled his gun. "Wolves, shoot anybody that moves."

Every werewolf raised their weapon instantly. While they did, some faces showed they were less than enthusiastic about the order. But, they had no choice. It was magic.

Adults and students froze in place. Sobbing cries were silenced with harsh, scolding whispers.

Grandpa's tactic of division was working. Even loved ones were turning on each other in fear.

"I guess we're doing this the hard way," Gerber said, smoothing his hair. "Shauna, you're up."

He finger-gunned at a woman holding her rifle with shaking hands. She'd removed her many earrings and shaved off her thick braids. Former councilmember Shauna DeGee had opened Adelor for Laylea in October. She'd had plump cheeks and a fire in her eyes. Both had diminished.

"Separate the thumpers from the shifters. If anybody moves, shoot 'em."

"No!" Rehyan yelled.

Emerald screamed, "You're insane!"

Oscar growled, "Give us the go, Brenda."

"Don't do it, Aunt Shauna," Griff begged from the lawn. "You can't follow an order like that."

"I have no choice," she whimpered.

"Of course you do."

He took one step in her direction before she fired.

His body flew backwards, the bobble on top of his hat exploding into bits. He hit the ground and lay deathly still.

"No!" Cries of rage and horror rang out from the audience and the stage.

Laylea found she couldn't pull in enough air to scream. She couldn't make her limbs move much less run.

"Griff! I'm sorry," Shauna croaked. Tears poured down her face. "We have to obey."

Norman stared in horror as his Uncle Johnny dove from his front row seat to throw his body over Griff's.

Amal flashed into sight. He handed Norman a red bag imprinted with a white cross, then disappeared again.

Bullets pinged the ground around Griff and Johnny. Not one hit. Several weapons failed to even fire. The wolves examined them, fear and anger written in grooves on their faces.

Gerber didn't notice the failure. He gleefully danced in the aisle.

This was her fault. Gerber wanted her. All she had to do was give herself up.

You're an idiot, she told herself. *Gerber wants violence. You're just the excuse.*

If she didn't speak up, everyone in the zoo would die. But if she did, Grandpa would imprison her in a lab to make a drug that could kill everyone in the world he didn't approve of.

There had to be a way to stop him. Too many people had died already because of her. She had to stop it.

Her mind spun as tears froze on her cheeks.

"Lee!" Dee's cry demanded her attention.

Across a sea of terrified humans huddling together, Dee and Morioka sat still and straight in their seats.

A hint, a shadow almost, of wings floated behind the captain.

"Lee, look at me," Dee cried, fluffing her red curls. "Look at me."

Her red curls.

Griff wasn't dead.

If Griff were dead, if Calliope were dead, Dee's hair would be white. They'd be having this standoff in the middle of a raging storm.

Stars shone above in a clear sky.

Nobody had died.

Just as a rare smile graced Dee's face at Laylea's understanding, a shiver ran violently through her body. The smile fled.

Laylea's heart sank again.

"One last chance," Gerber hollered, prancing in place like he was a show pony rather than a wolf. "Give us the true shifter or we'll kill you all, starting with the thumpers."

"Shut up." The words shot from her mouth unbidden.

"Excuse me?" Gerber asked.

As one, KC and Oscar growled, "Shut up."

Blood roared in Laylea's ears. She faced a war. It was a frozen war at the moment, her side reorganizing in the face of the surprise attack from Grandpa's side.

She wouldn't call it "the werewolves' side," because it wasn't werewolves versus everyone else. Not all werewolves were self-centered supremacists. Or brainwashed, she amended, trying to be kind.

The wolves might have magical protections on their side—Gerber seemed to be counting on that advantage—but her side had a whole pack of witches and all kinds of different creatures. They had a demon. And a tree. They had brownies.

Grandpa's wolves had claws, teeth, and self-righteousness. Her side had all the wolf weapons and more. Her side had every shape imaginable. She could hold every shape imaginable. She could do magic.

"Come away," Mr. Bianchi said, his voice quiet.

She glanced at him. And at the apparent chaos behind him. It wasn't chaos, though. Double Deltas had formed into units, just as they had practiced. They may look like terrified children, huddling together for support. And they were that, but they were also warriors, ready to fight for their community.

Mr. Bianchi laid a hand on her elbow. "Please, Miss. Don't attract his attention."

But that was exactly what she needed to do.

She'd already set things in motion, the brownies and small shifters were doing what they could, Junior was off fetching help, the witches and cats were rescuing the cops. She shot a look at Oscar, ready to go at a word. She shot a look at KC, quivering with rage.

Laylea leaned in to the mic. "We don't say 'thumpers'," she scolded Gerber. "'Thumpers' is a rude word."

Gerber's face twisted. It reminded her of the pained rictus of Jimmy's expression every time he shifted.

Werewolves blinked, their hooting falling quiet as they turned to see how their alpha would respond to her challenge.

He responded by raising his gun and pointing it at her.

Laylea's heart galloped. The burn tingled over every inch of her body. Every hair stood on end. But she held tight to Sher's shape.

"We call them true-humans" she said, cursing her voice for shaking.

She didn't want to die. Not now any more than when she thought fifteen was as old as she would ever get.

Though if she did die, Grandpa couldn't create End, and that would save so many other people.

And when she died, Dee would explode into her full Banshee form and bring a storm down on their heads.

It would be a great distraction.

"I told you magic is real," she said to the audience, her voice unnaturally calm to her ears. "So are banshees. There is one among you and when he kills me, she'll raise a storm in mourning. Use it."

"Shut up," Gerber growled, moving again, toward her.

"No. Death is coming."

If it was hers, so be it. She was going to make sure that everybody knew Gerber was killing the one thing Grandpa wanted more than anything.

She had tried everything. Dee was shivering, her face impossibly pale. Any second, they would reach the point of no return. Somebody would die.

It was time to stop hiding.

47

The heat seared the tips of her ears almost before Laylea called for it. Standing in front of hundreds of shifters, true-humans, and wyrdos, full in the spotlight where Gerber's shot couldn't miss her, she shifted.

Her wolf's hackles stood up all the way down to her stupid tail, which tucked under her belly, giving away her fear.

Screams and gasps rang through the audience like a thunderstorm. Some stood to run but found nowhere to go. She'd terrified them; true-humans and shifters alike. That wasn't what she had wanted. Revealing herself as the true shifter was supposed to free them.

On the upside, she had stopped Gerber from shooting her.

He froze. The muzzle of his gun dipped. He shot a look at the shock and terror around him. He'd had the shifters' first rule ingrained into him from birth. And Bitters' defeat had confirmed it.

That ingrained secrecy made him lean in to hiss, "You're one of us. Why fight for the losers?"

She had him off balance. This was her chance to use his own magical spell against him.

Mrs. Delcampo had obeyed KC's order. Shauna had obeyed

Gerber. If the militia were cursed to obey wolves, she could control them.

At a thought, she conjured the odor of starched uniform and rose to two feet wearing Benniker's weaselly face. He was a low rank wolf, but a wolf.

"You don't have to fight for him," she said. "Lay down your weapons."

The wolves did not comply.

But they responded. Their shouted threats drowned the appalled voices of shifters denying what they had just seen her do.

The prophecy said the True would come and save the day. They needed to know for certain that she was the True.

In desperate need of Toby's courage, she shot flames down her spine and shifted into the bear form that fit her like a beloved coat, then immediately dropped into her familiar teenage girl self.

Gerber raised his gun, holding it with both hands to keep it from shaking.

"Go ahead, Gerber, shoot me," Laylea said, her voice steady as a rock. "You think Grandpa will thank you for killing his true shifter?"

Her heart raced as she watched Gerber's every violent thought flash across his face.

Shock and panic of every flavor bubbled through the audience and the militia. Kids argued with Brenda to take advantage of Gerber's distraction, though only two moved, their footsteps giving Laylea courage as they dashed to her side.

"We're right here," KC murmured in her ear.

Laylea's heart swelled. Of course she wasn't alone. She'd never been alone. She grabbed her friend's hand and squeezed.

Just as quietly, Oscar observed, "They do what he says."

He was right. That was the answer.

Feeling more in control with her friends at her back, Laylea studied Gerber's thick, carefully styled hair and round face, so like KC's. She reached inside herself to find KC's familiar lupine warmth and twisted it, shooting fire through her biceps to form Gerber's unwieldy muscles.

She shifted.

The militia yelped in alarm. Mr. DeGee barked a laugh. Gerber's face, the one on the real Gerber in the aisle, glowed with anger.

"Retreat," she ordered into the mic. "Lay down your weapons and go."

The wolves did not comply.

KC swore.

"Why didn't that work?" Oscar muttered.

Around the circle, militia growled. Laylea blinked to find a number of them had actually taken wolf form. All she'd achieved was freeing them to shift, too.

She'd revealed herself to be the true shifter but nothing had changed.

Dustin Huono's dad broke formation, pounding up the plywood aisle. "Protect the alpha! Kill the abomination!"

"You shut your mouth," KC cried.

Mr. Huono's jaws snapped shut.

He was so shocked he face-planted on the plywood. The big man lay unconscious and unmoving.

"It's blood magic," Ms. Crow breathed, excited, "They have to obey anyone with his blood."

In a dread tone, Mr. Bianchi spelled it out. "They have to obey Delcampos."

KC could stop the militia.

That's why Mrs. Delcampo had dropped her weapon when KC ordered her to and why they hadn't responded to Laylea. She'd looked like Gerber, but she was still herself. She didn't have Delcampo blood.

KC, however, could control them all. Every wolf in Grandpa's militia had to obey the girl who'd been terrified they'd discover who she really was.

Gerber's pupils shot wide at the words.

Despite the gun in his hands, Gerber ran for the stage.

As he leapt the steps, KC grabbed the mic. "Dro—"

Gerber reached her. He tried to snatch the microphone, but KC wrapped herself around his arm as if the mic were a basketball and this was all a game.

Mr. Bianchi dove in and was blown back. He knocked Ms. Crow into a pile of orchestra chairs.

That slowed the two dozen Double Delta kids running to launch themselves on Gerber.

They had to negate the forcefield. Laylea didn't know enough about magic to figure it out. But then, she didn't have to. They had a black cat on their side. She yelled, "Oscar!"

He was already on the move.

As smooth as his panther, Oscar slipped past her and touched Gerber. No sparks. No stench.

Before he could get a better grip, Gerber slashed at him with a shifted hand.

Oscar cried out. He released his grip as he jerked away.

An instant too late, the Double Deltas hit Gerber's renewed shields and Laylea got knocked back with everyone else as the sparks and stench sent them flying. Her head smacked an abandoned viola and knocked her out.

The sharp scent of fear brought her back to consciousness.

"Karly, I didn't mean it." Gerber's horrified voice reverberated over the speakers. His grief and shock made him sound like a little boy.

What did he not mean? What had he done? Laylea struggled out of the tangle of chairs and instruments, her blood running cold at the unexpected feeling in Gerber's words.

KC and Gerber stood frozen in the spotlight, the microphone gripped between them.

KC's forehead wrinkled in confusion. Her mouth hung open. She stared at her brother's hand, his claws buried in her chest.

Bile stung Laylea's throat and every inch of her blazed, trying to shift her into the form that could stop this moment from existing. Bear? Panther? Python? Bat? Dragon? She was the true shifter. She was meant to save everybody.

But she couldn't even breathe.

KC's glazed eyes slid from Gerber's hand to the microphone between them.

Blood sprayed the microphone as KC dipped her head to gasp, "Drop your weapons."

Guns thumped to the ground all around the South Lawn.

"Go!" Brenda's order freed the Double Deltas to launch from the stage.

"You bitch!" With that cry of rage, Gerber the alpha returned. He wrenched the microphone from her boneless grasp and screamed, "Kill everyone."

Following his own order, he wrenched his claws from his sister's chest. Bright red blood sprayed out.

Laylea howled, terror drowning out all other thought. Her mind filled with the iron taste of blood, bringing with it the impossibility of life without KC. Moving without conscious thought, she raced to her friend. Her friend, her pod mate, the bravest, most selfless girl she'd ever known.

Far away, in another reality, the South Lawn erupted in gunfire, howls, and screaming.

In front of her, KC crumpled to the stage. Laylea's paws slipped in her blood.

"Not you." Gerber snatched her up, his clawed hand wrapped around her neck. The fabric of her collar tore and she smelled her precious lizard soaking up KC's blood from his claws.

She yelped, squealing her fear until Gerber squeezed hard enough to cut off her air.

"I need you alive." He swung her out, as if displaying her would somehow cow the shifters. It didn't work. The shifters couldn't spare any attention for him or for her.

Or for KC.

Ideas tumbled through her mind like tossed dice as Gerber shook her.

The very first time they met, KC had saved her butt and Laylea had saved KC right back. Their entire relationship had been based on lies and secrets that kept them safe. Now her brother was attacking them and KC had stood by her side yet again, risking her own secrets. And she'd been stabbed for it.

The wide battle flashed in a panoramic blur before her eyes as Gerber swung her to face the primate house.

Some of the militia had recovered their weapons. Others had simply shifted. They rampaged through the audience, drooling like rabid creatures.

The Double Delta squads pushed the werewolves back, teachers getting in their way as they tried to protect their students.

All across the lawn, audience members were working together. Shifters with true-humans. Some were protecting each other. Some fighting.

A reindeer galloped at three human-shaped werewolves gathered in formation. They shot her. She fell, shifted human, shifted reindeer, and attacked again.

And was shot again.

These people weren't trained to fight, not like Grandpa's militia. They were going to lose and die and it was all her fault.

Gerber swung her back to face the flamingo pond. One claw slipped from her collar and bit into her neck. It didn't hurt as much as seeing KC's blood pooling on the stage.

"I've got your True!" Gerber yelled, as if he thought they would do anything to save her.

"Careful!" Jase yelled from upstage where he huddled by the risers, holding a flute like he was going to drink from it. "Grandpa wants her alive."

"Fido!" Brenda screamed from the grass. She smacked the gun out of a man's hands with a folding chair and then kicked him backwards into a uniformed police officer. "Save Fido."

Dustin Huono stepped over the unconscious Jonathan to dive off the stage at Brenda. Daniel, defending fallen bodies at the base of the steps, shifted. Dustin bounced off his elephant hide.

Laylea grabbed at the inspiration. She shifted into Daniel's twin, cringing as the clasp on her collar snapped.

Her bulk knocked Gerber down, but his shield blasted her upstage.

She shifted dog, then human, and then spider as she saw Gerber dashing to grab her up again.

An earsplitting, earthshaking roar competed with thunder rolling overhead to deafen them all. It drowned the sound of Oscar's yowl as his sleek black figure soared out of the night at Gerber.

Gerber tumbled, nearly crushing her tiny form as he crashed to the ground. Going on instincts that came with eight legs, she buried her fangs in his hand. A flood of cold something rushed out of her. Then she was flying through the air as he shook her off.

Gerber let his own instincts rule him as well. He shifted, spinning and cowering as the sea of abandoned instruments and scattered chairs parted. A terrifying, colossal wolf rose from the mess, red-tufted ears pasted against his white skull. Drool dripped from vicious fangs as he loomed over Gerber. With one massive paw, he swiped the microphone from the stage, then shifted human.

With blood dripping from an open wound and matting his thick black hair, Mr. Bianchi sucked a breath deep into his gut and yelled, "Freeze."

His voice rang over the field, no amplification needed.

Apparently, Laylea and KC weren't the only ones hiding their true selves.

The militia complied. They didn't just stop moving. They literally froze. Frost bloomed on their guns, on their skin, hair, and fur. Ice formed at the sweat on their brows.

Howling with rage, Gerber snapped at Bianchi, tearing his tuxedo pants. He launched off the stage and into the battle, Oscar on his heels. With barely a thought, Mr. Bianchi shifted and gave chase.

Laylea skittered to KC's side, turning human on the way. Her hands were too small to effectively press on all three wounds, so she shifted them larger. Blood still pumped, hot and sticky, through her fingers. Fat tears splashed in the deep red puddle soaking KC's jacket, leaving hot streaks down Laylea's cheeks.

Laylea could shift into anything. But was there any form that could save KC's life?

KC's face lit up with a weak smile. Her lips parted as if she would speak, but it was too late. Her eyes closed and her head fell back.

Lightning exploded across the sky and rain began pelting them with great drops, flooding the back of her throat with ozone. A freezing wind slapped Laylea's hair into her face as she struggled to stop the bleeding.

Deep in the battling audience, some creature keened in distress.

Laylea's head snapped up. That wasn't an animal.

Dee stood, head thrown back, arms spread as if fighting to stay upright. Grief poured from her mouth on a high-pitched wail that pierced Laylea's senses like a tick. Dee's red hair turned white. It grew straight and long, whipping about in the rising wind of the storm.

"No." Laylea whimpered.

KC couldn't die. Laylea wouldn't let that happen.

She needed a doctor, a witch, anybody who could save KC.

"Help!" she yelled into the storm. "Please, somebody help me."

48

ightning crashed to the earth like strobe lights. Each flash froze the chaos on the South Lawn into a series of horrific paintings.

Crack.

Governor Battles, arms wrapped tightly around a baby goat, blood seeping through her fingers, back-to-back with Mayor Colbrook whose fierce eyes followed a tiny whirling figure wearing a trench coat and the shadow of wings. Morioka's katana glowed as if the lightning came from it.

Crack.

Gerber, mid-spin, human arms out straight, one shoulder thrown back from the recoil of his gun, his lower half still mostly wolf. A trail of broken and bitten bodies lay in his wake. Johnny arching over Griff's still body as though protecting him. Norman, sprayed in blood, rain plastering his long hair to his face, catching an unconscious Mr. Bianchi.

Crack.

KC's pale face. Her dyed-blond hair stained with blood. Her body splayed on the stage. Still. Cold.

Her brother had done this.

Heat flowed over Laylea's skin as she tried to hold KC's blood in with her inadequate hands. All the screams, shouts, howls, cries, caws, and gunshots faded to background noise against Dee's piercing keen.

That horrible sound said someone had died. It could be anyone. It could be Griff.

Deep down, Laylea knew Dee was mourning KC. And that meant there was nothing she could do.

But it didn't mean she wasn't going to try.

"We need help!" she cried out through a throat throttled by fear. She took a deep breath the way Mr. Bianchi had taught her and tried again. "Dr. Tipp! Ollie!"

Her words came out stronger, but they were torn away by the wind and went unheard beyond the stage.

Carrie ran past her, leaping off the steps through the increasing rain. She yelled, "Doctor! We need a doctor!"

Another voice echoed hers. "Doctor to the stage!"

It went on, one voice after another.

A pair of black paws landed soundlessly, splattering the pink puddles of rain mixed with KC's blood. Oscar dropped his uniform from his teeth, his panther eyes boring into Laylea's, offering comfort and hope.

She grabbed the uniform and pressed over the wounds.

"Shock," she said, trying to control her own. "We need to keep her warm."

Oscar sang a rolling meow at her. He swiped KC's face with his rough tongue, then tucked his long, warm body alongside hers and purred.

Laylea felt the purr through KC's chest. Her muscles relaxed. Her mind cleared.

"Lee." Peter knelt at her side. "Can we help?"

Thad stood poised on Peter's arm, the front two of his eight legs twitching as if eager for action.

Laylea nodded. "We need to seal the wounds," she said.

The little spider flung himself to Peter's other arm, thread trailing behind as he began weaving.

Ollie used Thad's silk for bandages and anything was better than just trying to hold the blood in with her hands.

"We'll need to put it right on her skin," Peter said, concern heavy in his voice.

In order to open KC's jacket and uniform, Laylea would need to stop pressing on the wounds.

She looked around for help just in time to see Norman trip up the stairs and land on his knees. The silver medical sheers he brandished nearly stabbed Oscar.

He found his balance and held the scissors and a first aid kit out to Laylea, breathing through his nose violently, as if opening his mouth would only release sobs.

"You have to expose her chest, Norman." Laylea adjusted her hands to make room for him.

Norman cut, hands shaking. Sparks flashed nonstop from the stasis band, preventing him from shifting as he murmured through tight lips, "I've got you, KC, I'm here," over and over.

"Dizzy, I need you." Ms. Crow's voice startled Laylea. The librarian crawled to KC's head, dragging one leg behind her. She draped Laylea's broken collar over KC's neck, brushing the lizard with a finger as she caught Laylea's eyes for approval.

Laylea felt her heart well up with gratitude at everyone helping. KC had been betrayed by her blood, but her school family wouldn't abandon her.

Ms. Crow lowered her ear to KC's lips, then gave her a breath. KC's chest rose and fell beneath Laylea's hands.

The librarian shared another breath, then yelled out, "Witches, circle up!"

The command was repeated across the South Lawn, echoing in a round with, "Doctor to the stage!"

Between breaths, Ms. Crow chanted, "We've got you. We're here. Be here with us, too."

Laylea's hair whipped in her face. Icicles of rain bit her skin. She ignored it all, pressing on KC's chest for all she was worth despite the banshee cry of death searing the air.

The storm blew Dizzy into an awkward landing on her sister's shoulder. Water sprayed as she pointlessly shook the rain from her feathers.

The same gust tried to topple Dr. Tippleston, but Norman caught her. She took the scissors from his shaking hand, then handed his arm over to Ms. Crow. "Liz, can you remove this stasis band? We could use Norman's wolf warmth."

While Ms. Crow was distracted, Laylea took up her chant. "We've got you. We're here. Be here with us, too."

Ms. Crow wrapped her hands around the band. Dizzy croaked three times and the band sparked green.

Norman shifted instantly, leaping over KC to shove himself between her and Laylea. He tucked his nose against her neck, under Laylea's collar.

"Weave another layer, Thad." Dr. Tippleston said this with her eyes on her work as she cut through KC's uniform.

"Somebody get a tarp," Angel yelled, her words torn away by the wind as she struggled up the steps. "We need to block this rain."

She dropped a mylar blanket over KC's legs as she squeezed in beside Laylea, joining in for one round of the chant, in Spanish. Dr. Tipp joined on the next round, adding a melody in Chinese, Dizzy croaking along in rhythm.

Somewhere, beneath Dee's deafening keen, other voices rose, chanting nonsense until they picked up the words. Some sang in English, some in Spanish, some French and others in languages Laylea didn't know, all weaving around each other, building on the rhythm and strengthening the magic.

A branch, thick with white flowers, stretched overhead, cutting the heavy rain to a drizzle. Caliban grew more offshoots until the rain was just another rhythm adding to the spell.

"On the count of three," Dr. Tipp said. "Laylea will raise her hands. Angel, you peel back the fabric. Peter, you scoot in. I'll take the web and position it. Get ready."

Laylea pressed on KC's chest, chanted, and listened for the count while the doctors conferred on their next steps. She fixed a living, joyous KC in her mind, remembering her glee as they tracked Oscar through the halls, covered in glitter goo and holding each other up, laughing so hard she got the hiccups.

This was all she could do for her friend. She desperately wanted to stay there, to hold her hand or shift and shove Norman aside. But it was clear she'd just get in the doctors' way.

"Ready?" Dr. Tipp asked.

Laylea wriggled into a crouch before she nodded.

In the distance, Professor Wanja's voice sang out Ms. Crow's chant in Latin. Others began stomping or clapping the rhythm.

"One."

Peter, Angel, Tipp, and Laylea all prepared to move.

A hundred new voices joined in as the front doors to The Phoenix opened and patients spilled out.

"Two."

While outwardly chanting, Laylea inwardly cried, "Stay with me stay with me stay with me," and fought her desire to stay at KC's side.

Across the lawn witches took hands with true-humans and wyrdos and shifters. The growing chain of chanting humans wove through the overturned chairs, circled other pockets of wounded and healers, and climbed the steps onto the stage and over it.

"Three."

Diving deep to override her heart, Laylea shifted into a crab and scuttled backwards. Peter moved in while Tipp kneeled up to peel the web from his arms. Angel pulled back KC's shirts, starting the stab wounds bleeding fast. She wiped the blood away as Tipp positioned the web.

Laylea released the hard crab shell and rose to stand as a human, her eyes glued to Oscar's fat paw on KC's shoulder. It was the only bit she could see of her friends through the crush of bodies.

A warm hand wove into hers.

Riva squeezed and murmured, "We're gonna save her. Can't you feel it?"

She could. Hope filled the air with the words.

"We've got you. We're here. Be here with us, too."

The sparkle of magic lit up the darkness all along the chanting, stomping line of people and animals curved around pockets of the injured and caregivers.

Caliban's branches glittered as they reached in all directions, shielding the crowd from Dee's storm. Other branches trapped wolves away from the spellcasting. A wooden cocoon held Gerber off the ground, his body stiff and unmoving.

Ahanu helped Emerald limp to the stage, his wings spread from his human shoulder blades to steady them both. He took hold of Vaughn's hand where the werewolf sat on a barely-restrained Jonathan.

Emerald grabbed Laylea's free hand and began singing. Her crystal clear voice matched Dee's impossibly high keen. The rest of the choir followed her lead. They added harmonies.

The volume of the spell rose, filling the zoo. It overtook Dee's keening until Laylea couldn't hear the banshee at all.

Norman's piteous whining cut off suddenly as Oscar lifted his great, black, velvety head to stare at KC's face.

A warm breeze rose up, blowing the storm clouds out over the lake and letting the stars shine clear on the singing, chanting, battered community.

Out in the audience, healers helped blood-spattered guests rise and join in the spell. Griff sat up in Johnny's lap. He blinked, shifted, and squawked along with his chanting neighbors, spreading his wings to pull Johnny back against him when the man stumbled away. Mr. Bianchi struggled to his feet with an arm across Chloe's shoulders, blood sculpting his hair in spikes. He took Johnny's free hand as Chloe reached for Daniel's.

All across the South Lawn, the wounded stood and sang for KC.

Except for Dee. The banshee stood alone, silent, her face drained and despairing. Long, white hair lay limp against her shoulders. Laylea had never seen Dee at a loss before. There, alone in the middle of the crowd, she looked young and helpless and lost.

"Welcome back, KC." Dr. Tipp's voice grabbed at Laylea's hope. "No, don't move. You're gonna be okay."

Laylea choked on tears.

The doctor raised her voice so all could hear. "She's gonna be okay."

Too overwhelmed to speak, Laylea threw her head back and howled her joy. All around the South Lawn, gleeful voices rose to echo her.

49

"She's missing, Lee. And nobody is looking for her," Oscar growled.

"But you're bleeding," Laylea's voice cracked. She was too tired for this argument. And too hungry. "Everybody else healed some, but you didn't at all. There's something wrong—"

"It's too dark," Oscar declared. "My leopard will be able to sniff her out." He shifted and wriggled out of his coat, his altered uniform hanging awkwardly on his cat's fur. Limping away, he sniffed through the fallen chairs that hadn't yet been cleared from the South Lawn. As if he'd be able to smell anything past the blood on his own clothes.

Laylea gathered up his coat and knee brace and trailed after him, searching the Lawn for Jeannie or Dr. Tipp. They'd been working their way through the crowd, treating minor injuries and moving the seriously wounded into The Phoenix.

The magical spell that saved KC had filled the zoo with healing magic. Thanks to the brownies, nobody else had died, but there had been plenty on the brink. They'd all at least started healing.

Oscar's wounds were getting worse. In addition to the bleeding slashes from Gerber, spots of blood staining his shoulder showed that Oscar had torn open the P2 wounds on his human chest. Even shifting panther wasn't going to help. She tracked drag marks from his left rear paw as she followed him.

After KC was saved and taken into the Phoenix for further repair, Oscar had joined Mr. Bianchi and Ollie as they worked their way through the militia. Between the obedience spell that made the wolves take Mr. Bianchi's orders, Oscar's disruptive black cat magic, and Ollie's healing powers, they made quick work of unfreezing them and sending them off to be transported to several temporary holding facilities.

When Ollie turned to treat him, Oscar had run off. There were too many other people that needed further healing, so Ollie found Laylea. He thought she would be able to get Oscar to take care of himself.

But here they were, closer to dawn than dusk and Laylea couldn't even get him to talk to her.

She yawned and was nearly pummeled by a garbage bag.

Angelica deRio hurried by, said garbage bag slung over her shoulder. Mariella's black and orange wings flashed as she flitted ahead of her wife, leading her to a pile of blood-crusted napkins. She swirled around Uncle Johnny who had teamed up with the guy whose artificial leg had taken a bullet. Together, they huddled over Mariella's wheelchair, trying to fix it up. Beyond them, Big Mo and Jonathan had taken charge of collecting the chairs and separating them into stacks. Some needed repairs. Some could be cleaned and returned to storage. A bunch of kids were carrying the good chairs away while a bunch of adults catalogued the repairs needed.

Everybody was helping clean up the mess that Laylea had made. While she couldn't even get Oscar to a doctor.

Who knew what was on Gerber's claws? Even if they hadn't all been caught up in a massive healing spell, Oscar should not still be bleeding hours after he was slashed.

"Oscar!" she called, calling on her reserves to catch up to him. "Calliope wouldn't want you killing yourself to find her."

Oscar yowled at her and leapt away, bounding over uncollected seats and onto the stage.

Yeah, she thought, shoving his brace into a coat pocket as she trudged after him, *that was a low blow.* How would she feel if Griff were missing?

Not having powerful haunches or any remaining reserves, Laylea wove her way to the stage steps, past the pile of Linden bark that had been mounded right where Griffin had been crouching earlier, nervous about his magic act. Stripes of red decorated the path where blood had been swept aside along with the bark and the bullets.

Gerber Delcampo had fired through Cal's branches continuously until the moment his trigger finger stopped moving. It was a miracle, or maybe good karma, that he didn't kill any humans or animals before the venom paralyzed him. Or it may have simply been that he couldn't see a thing with Tessa's little black cat form clinging to his face. It was only thanks to her that Cal had been able to wrap the wolf up in her branches.

Against her strongest objections, Caliban had been ordered into The Phoenix so the doctors could treat her for shock, at least.

"Lee!" The stage shook as Bitters pounded on it to get her attention. He squeezed against the frame as folks carried patients by behind him.

Keeping one eye on Oscar digging through piles of chairs and instruments that had already been dug through several times, Laylea trudged over to the Enforcer. "Hi. Are you okay?"

"I am. Thanks for asking. Gerbrand was paralyzed. I know I didn't bite him. Was that you, by chance?"

"Maybe?" She shrugged as if it was no big deal. But her heart swelled at the possibility that she'd actually helped take him down. "He was trying to grab me again and some of the wolves in school are deathly afraid of spiders, so I guess I hoped that between that and just being small, I might get away."

"You could have been crushed."

She smirked at him. "Eight is a lot of legs, Bitters."

Bitters laughed. "If you ever want a lesson on how to control your venom dosage, you know where to find me."

Laylea blinked at him, not knowing what to say. With all the questions people had been asking, nobody had offered to help her learn how to be another animal.

Luckily, her stomach growled, preventing her from having to answer.

Bitters pulled a power bar from a pocket and held it out, laughing. "Here. I have to get back. The EBI and Great Coven—they're like supernatural enforcers or something— anyway, they want to confer with me about what to do next." He grimaced comically, completely missing the terror Laylea felt flash across her face.

Supernatural authorities would want to talk to her. Was that why Bitters had cornered her?

The stage wobbled. Laylea turned to see Oscar leaping off the back. She turned to follow him, a perfect excuse.

Bitters called after her. "Just wanted to let you know that Officer Garcia is doing well. He'd love to thank you."

"Oh, thank you," she mumbled through a mouthful of power bar. With everything that had happened, she'd nearly forgotten about Garcia. "I'll go see him later."

Before he could request her presence at an inquisition, she spun and dashed away. "Oscar, wait up!"

He did not.

She chased him down the path, hoping to tantalize him by yelling, "I know why they took Gerber away on a backboard."

He slowed a moment and looked back. But then his nostrils flared as his eyes landed on someone behind her. With a flick of his tail, he sprang onto the bridge crossing the Waterfowl Lagoon. He landed badly and a yelp escaped him before he continued on, limping past the Foreman Pavilion.

"Oh, yeah, he is meant to be a doctor," Angel Lopez exclaimed, putting a hand on Laylea's back and propelling her along. "They make the worst patients. Now, what's—"

Her armpadd squawked. "ETA?"

Angel released Laylea to tap it. "ETA thirty seconds if you stop asking."

It squawked again but nobody spoke.

"What's the problem?" Angel asked, striding across the bridge as if it weren't three o'clock in the morning.

Laylea blinked her eyes open. It was like the energy of keeping up with Angel made her eyes demand sleep. She couldn't sleep as long as Oscar needed her. "He's still bleeding," she said. "But he won't see a doctor."

Angel rubbed warmth into her arms. She'd abandoned her coat somewhere.

"Here," Laylea handed Oscar's coat to her.

"Thank you, Lee." As she pulled it on, she added, thoughtfully, "Sometimes, you have to treat the mind before you treat the body. What's on his mind?"

"He's searching for Calliope." Laylea threw her hands up in frustration. Angel wasn't worried about her daughter, so why was Oscar so bothered?

"Now that's easy," Angel beamed. All her cares seemed to fall away for an instant. "She's in the Foreman Pavilion."

Laylea stopped walking.

Angel kept going. She yelled over her shoulder, "I'll tell him if I see him."

Laylea ran back to the covered wooden pavilion they had just hustled past.

A few human kids huddled on a pile of blankets with Milly and Riva in one corner. Riva had wrapped her long soft arms around the neck of a boy with tear tracks streaking his face. Her heavy-lidded eyes brightened as she caught sight of Laylea. She slowly raised three claws at her, then dropped her furry head on the boy's shoulder. He leaned into the comforting sloth, his eyes closing. None of the kids was Calliope.

Joseph Lyman sat on the wooden floor on the far side of the pavilion, his back against a post, looking as peaceful as the young animals draped around him.

A quiet, demanding chirp drew her eyes to Griff, lying beyond Joseph with his beak on his mother's lap, He, too, was blanketed in a pack of dozing children.

His aunt Shauna's bullet had torn through his guts, throwing him backwards where he'd hit his head and been knocked unconscious. Norman's Uncle Johnny had applied pressure until the spell woke Griff up and he shifted to heal.

All but one of the wolves' successful gunshots had hit healing shifters. The one that hit a true-human stuck in the man's artificial leg.

Laylea looked around as she crouched by Griff. She didn't see Calliope anywhere.

When he bumped her hand with his beak, she scratched his head right where he liked it. His lion tail thwapped erratically on the wooden floor.

"He won't shift human." Inika patted his rump and sighed.

Laylea gestured at the baby animals and tiny humans lying boneless and trusting about him. "Would you?"

His mom grinned, then, as Laylea yawned, she said. "You should get some sleep."

"I know." Laylea grunted, swallowing another yawn. "Have you seen Calliope Lopez?"

"Calliope Lopez?" Joseph asked. "She's right here."

A tender smile wrinkled the man's face as he looked into the cup of his hand where a teardrop-shaped chrysalis hung from the top button of his coat. "The shock from Gerber's shield did it. Her parents were thrilled. They didn't know if she was ever going to pupate." He snorted. "I didn't even know that was a thing."

"We can only hope all the true-humans take it as well as Joseph here," Inika murmured.

"Well, I knew about werewolves," he said. "Quite a few of the Marshalls have worked at my company."

How many true-humans already had a clue about the supernatural world all around them? It was an interesting question. Based on how she backed Morioka's demand that Gerber be handed over to her custody, it seemed that Mayor Colbrook knew the police captain was more than she appeared to be. Maybe Laylea's revelation wasn't as world changing as everyone had thought it would be.

She couldn't think about the world. She needed to reassure Oscar and get him to a doctor.

"If you'll excuse me, I need to catch my friend." Laylea ruffled Griff's feathers one last time, then backed away. "Thanks for looking after everybody."

"Thank you," Joseph replied. "I'm glad my friends won't have to hide anymore. Unless they want to."

The words made her skin prickle with doubt.

Laylea considered them as she headed along the lagoon toward Café Brauer. Who hid because they wanted to? She was hiding because if she didn't, Walter would tear her apart to see how she worked. KC hid because her grandfather wanted to turn her into a broodmare for his wolf army. She didn't know why Mr. Bianchi had been hiding, but it was a good bet it had something to do with Grandpa Delcampo's unceasing need for power.

But none of them wanted to hide.

Just like the shifter community, or the witch community, or the wyrdos. All those people only lived in hiding because they were afraid of being hurt if they didn't.

Had revealing herself solved the danger?

Panther Oscar appeared in the doorway to the Brauer banquet hall. He picked his way tenderly across the lawn toward the fence, favoring his left rear paw.

"Oscar!" It took every last bit of her energy to call out to him.

When he spotted her, he straightened up and tried to lope.

She leaned against the fence, grateful he was loping toward her. Then she noticed that every time that rear paw came down, he shivered and his tail twitched violently.

"I found Calliope," she yelled. "She's pupating on Joseph Lyman's coat in the Foreman Pavilion. She's safe, so you can go see a doctor now."

Oscar rolled a growl deep in his chest. His tail lashed about, striking the fence.

"Stop it. You can't afford a broken tail. This is good news, you doofus."

The air shuddered around the black panther as his muzzle shortened, his body twisted, and he stood up.

"I want to see her." He winced, wrapping a hand around the fence for support.

"You don't trust me?" Laylea asked, astounded.

"I didn't demand to see Shala." His voice cracked. He sounded as tired as her but with a bonus edge of self-loathing.

She gawped at him. "When you were eight?"

"I didn't demand to see her body," he said, his eyes on the ground. "Nobody helped her."

"So you don't deserve help?" she asked, the question coming out a little less gently than she intended.

"No." He said it then pushed off the fence. "The Foreman?"

Without waiting for an answer, he limped off in that direction. Blood dripping from his uniform with every step.

Laylea watched him for a moment. She was never going to get him to see a doctor. She knew it like she had known earlier that she couldn't stop Gerber.

Succumbing to the desire that had been torturing her just as surely as her exhaustion and hunger she slipped into her canine fur, and ran through the zoo to The Phoenix.

50

The foyer of The Phoenix had been framed with the drywall sheets from the temporary wall on Halloween. Laylea trotted along the periphery, staring up at them and remembering the kids and their joy. She kept her other senses on alert, her ears twisting at every new voice with her mouth dropped open to activate the scent receptors on the roof of her mouth. There were too many legs wearing the blue school uniform for her to have a chance of seeing Shala. But she was sure Oscar's sister would show up there eventually.

So, she explored the drawings as she waited.

Behind her, shifters, wyrdos, and true-humans alike hurried about, everyone talking. She tried to focus on the sound of the voices and not their words. But she couldn't help but notice a distinct relief amongst the shifter adults. They were plenty concerned about the mess and the injured and how easily zoo security was overcome. They worried about how the world would respond to the dozens of videos that had uploaded to the net the instant the witches defeated Gerber's magical isolation of the zoo.

But they thought that they had defeated Grandpa.

"Mr. Samborsky!" Ali called, running into the foyer from deeper in the facility.

Laylea turned to see Brian Samborsky pushing a laundry cart. He looked more alive than he had earlier and certainly more alive than when Laylea had seen him sleeping. The scars she'd seen then stood out against his pale skin, raised and ugly.

"I'm Ali," Ali said, holding out a fist. "I'm friends with Brenda."

"Hi, Ali." His voice was deep and smooth. The tone was welcoming though his eyes were distrustful.

"You know she organized this whole thing, right?" Ali asked him. "Not the wolves, but everything else. And," Ali added quickly, "she's the reason so many of us were ready for the attack. She whipped us into shape."

"I heard it was a great success, until the wolves," he said evenly.

Ali's face scrunched. She rubbed at her arm as if her tattoos were glowing uncomfortably beneath her jacket. "You should be impressed. Sir." The sir came out like a reprimand.

Brenda's dad ignored it. "I am."

"You should tell her you're impressed. Sir."

"There's a lot going on," Mr. Samborsky said, pushing the cart away. "I have to deliver these linens."

"I don't know what your problem is, but she's done everything to grow the Double Deltas and get us ready for this fight."

"She should not have had to." He snapped, then turned his gaze into the cart with a sigh. "But it's over now and she can focus on her studies."

"It's over?" Ali squawked.

"The police arrested over two hundred wolves and Delcampo's top lieutenant."

"Gerber is seventeen years old and a moron. He's hardly Grandpa's secret weapon," Ali spat back, her face turning red. "This is just beginning."

Samborsky looked her in the eyes, his tone controlled again. "You're young," he said. "Of course it would look that way to you. But he saw that our community won't bow down to him. He'll back off."

Ali started to say, "What," but the word broke into a screech as she shifted, her uniform puddling on the floor. She hovered in place, flapping angrily and hitting a few of the busy people rushing to and fro before she soared up to the high ceiling and dove for the doorway out onto the South Lawn.

Mr. Samborsky bent creakily, like a man twice his age. He draped Ali's uniform over the side of his cart and continued on through the foyer, down a hallway, and out of sight.

Did he not hear about the videos on the net? In what universe did he imagine that Grandpa was going to see exactly who and where the true shifter was and not go after her? His plan was to create End to kill all the non-wolves. That wasn't the kind of person who backed off because of one lost battle.

Laylea raced through the sea of legs, trying to catch up to him, to wake him up to the danger.

But as she entered the hallway, Shala came out of a room and Laylea remembered why she was there.

With a flash of searing heat, Laylea shifted human. "Shala."

Shala brushed her aside, striding for the foyer. "Tell her I'm on my way."

Laylea hopped along beside her. "I don't know who you mean. I'm here cuz your brother needs you."

Shala scoffed and rolled her eyes. "My brother does not need me. He's got it all figured out."

Laylea squinted at her, baffled. "Oscar is bleeding and he won't get help because you didn't get help."

That stopped her. She popped one hip and propped a hand on it. "That's stupid. He thought I was dead."

"So go help him."

"He doesn't need me."

"I'm telling you that he does."

"And who are you, besides being the idiot who just started a war?"

All of her exhaustion caught up with Laylea with those words. She clenched her teeth against the anger and her fists against shifting. "I'm his best friend," she said. "And I'm the idiot who sacrificed a different friend's sanity to find you and the other sleepers."

She let that sit with Shala for a moment before saying, "Your brother, who loves you, is at the Foreman Pavilion. If he doesn't see a doctor really soon, he's probably going to bleed to death. I can't help him. You can."

She turned her back on Shala, planning to storm down the hallway. Her head spun and she put a hand out to steady herself on the wall.

Behind her, flapping wings turned into Dizzy. "Shala? Your mom is asking for you."

There was a long pause before Shala answered. "Yeah, I know. Can you point me to the Foreman Pavilion? And find Angel or Ollie?"

"No. He's not!" Jase voice carried to her from a nearby room. Her heart sped up.

Instead of running away, she inched closer to the room. The door was cracked open.

"Grandpa is gonna be madder than ever, Abuela." Jase's tone radiated disbelief.

Laylea peered through the crack to see an older woman looking up at Jase like he was a toddler. She didn't need to say anything to make it clear how little she thought of her grandson. In case he didn't catch her opinion of his opinion, she released a long sigh before saying, "Alpha Delcampo screwed up with this attack. He lost a lot of people. I promise you, he's learned his lesson."

Jase folded his arms and glared. "I'm not a little kid anymore. I told you that Denier was trying to kill non-wolves and that it was gonna get worse. It got worse. I told you the True was here and needed protection. But you didn't bother coming until your guy inside MSC told you we were being attacked. You could have prevented this."

"Lee, you look awful."

Laylea jumped. Her heart pounded. She'd been so focused on Jase, on the shock of finding out that he'd been trying to protect her, that she'd let Ned Biggerson sneak up on her.

She blinked at the big man and then quickly moved away from the door before Jase caught her eavesdropping. His grandmother, the Detroit Alpha, had a spy inside MSC. It gave her an idea.

"Lee?" Ned asked again.

She hurried farther down the hall and answered, just to stop him from saying her name again. “I’m kinda tired,” she admitted. “And hungry.”

“I’m sure we can find a bed.” Ned moved his knitting bag to his other shoulder and offered his arm. She took it gratefully.

“I’m looking for my friend, KC’s room,” she said.

“The Delcampo girl? This way.” He got them turned around and headed back toward the foyer. “Have you seen Junior?”

She thought about it and shook her head, a frown creasing her brow. She hadn’t seen Junior since she sent him to get help.

“I’m worried. He came to the bar and told us you needed help.”

They dodged out of the way as a cop hurried by with several sets of silver handcuffs.

“He went back into the closet to get more help, but he’s not here. Whoa.” Ned whistled through his teeth, making Laylea focus.

She followed his gaze to see a blur in black pushing through the foyer with barely a word of apology to anyone. Dee’s hair flared around her head, a messed up mix of straight and curly, white and ginger. Her eyes sparked with panic in a face so deathly pale, it was a surprise the banshee was standing.

Laylea stumbled away from Ned as Dee grabbed Jeannie Nellwin’s arms.

The doctor had acquired a set of paper scrubs which hung raggedly over her lab coat. Her hair was held back with a bandana and she had deep circles beneath her eyes.

Elbowing her way through the suddenly impassable crush of bodies, Laylea growled in frustration and found herself suddenly able to dodge through a sea of legs. Her puppy gut growled back at her but she pushed through the hunger and exhaustion. She stopped just close enough to hear.

“You said you saw his body,” Jeannie said, her fingers white where she gripped Dee’s forearms.

“I did. And I mourned. I only mourn for the dead. But then it stopped.” Dee grabbed a fistful of her hair. “Like tonight. Like KC. He died. And then he stopped being dead.”

Because he turned into a vampire, Laylea thought. She barked.

"Shh." Ned scooped her up and backed away. "Kyle needs to tell them himself."

But Kyle had lost his mind. She had no idea where he was or how to help him.

But she knew he needed help. Just like Oscar needed help and Shala had needed help. Just like they all needed help.

She wriggled in Ned's arms. He opened a door and stepped into a quiet hallway.

"KC is down there, last door on the right." He set her down and stood there until she padded away.

The floor was cold and the lights bright. Still she tripped a couple of times on nothing. She was so tired, even her dependable puppy legs weren't working.

Her brain seethed with worries. Brenda's dad and Jase's abuela were wrong. The only thing Grandpa was going to learn was that they knew what magic was, that Oscar really was a threat, and who the true shifter was. He was not going to back down. He was going to come after her.

Unless… she tripped again and rolled.

A quiet gasp came from the far side of a cart covered in medical equipment. She blinked her vision clear to see little Christopher sitting cross-legged just beyond it. Krystal lay with her head in his lap, her body stretched out, blocking a door.

He smiled at her. "You should get some sleep."

She whined exhausted agreement, eyeing Krystal with envy.

"Here." Christopher dug in a bag slung over one shoulder. He pulled out a burrito wrapped in a warm cloth. "Dr. Tipp said you'd be hungry."

Drool dripped on the pristine floor. From *her* muzzle.

He unwrapped the delectable burrito and fed it to her, bite by bite. If he hadn't, she might have tried to inhale the whole thing at once.

When she was done, Christopher wiped his hands on the cloth and pointed down the hall. "KC's in the last room on the right," he said. "We're watching her door, too."

Laylea looked up at the door behind Krystal with a question in her eyes.

Christopher whispered, "Caliban. Everyone wants to talk to her."

"Check it out," Dove hollered.

Laylea and Christopher both jumped. He yelped and slammed his hands over his mouth.

Dove raced down the hall with a manic energy that drained Laylea.

"Ned made me and Reg sweaters," she declared, spinning to show them her new cardigan. The zip in the middle went through a tiny ugly sweater that was being fought over by a pair of tigers with the Halloween wall in the background. It was a masterpiece.

Laylea offered a half-hearted "ahwoo" of admiration.

Dove leaned in, lowering her voice. "Get some sleep. Brenda's orders."

Christopher added, "We, at least, need to be ready for what comes next."

Laylea tilted her head at him and he explained, "The adults think we defeated Grandpa."

Laylea woke up a little at that. More than just Brenda's dad and Jase's abuela?

Dove rolled her eyes. "Yeah. They're all proud of themselves for stopping him, like they did anything."

A growl escaped Laylea.

"Thank goodness Bianchi knows better."

"And Ms. Lagat," Krystal added quietly.

Laylea howled a question and tilted her head.

"Yeah," Christopher told her, a twinkle in his eye as he hiked his sleeves to show her his bare wrists. "They were in charge of making sure we wore stasis bands."

"Bianchi's old school Double Delta," Dove said.

And a Delcampo, apparently. Even KC hadn't known.

Dove lowered her voice. "We're meeting tomorrow night, usual time, usual spot."

Laylea nodded. And yawned.

Christopher scooped her up and handed her to Dove. "Could you take her to KC's? I'm not sure she can make it on her own."

"Sure. Caliban okay?"

Christopher looked at the door behind Krystal. "She's sleeping. The docs agreed that's best."

Dove fist bumped him. She carried Laylea like a football down to the last door on the right. Inside, there were two single beds. KC lay unconscious on one, looking barely alive, Laylea's collar still wrapped around her neck. Someone had jerry-rigged the torn clasp with medical tape. Dove set Laylea on the empty bed and backed out, shutting the door quietly.

Laylea lay there for a moment, letting her eyes adjust and resting. When she felt ready, she took a running start and leapt the small gap to KC's bed.

KC mumbled something and scooted over a quarter centimeter.

Laylea tromped slowly up the thick blanket to KC's armpit, stepping carefully over tubes and cables. There, she circled once and fell down. Her brain did not give up as quickly as her body.

It wondered where was Junior? Where was Kyle? Hell, where was Toby? They were all missing and she had no idea how to find them.

Grandpa had attacked the school twice. They couldn't sit around and wait for him to do it again, definitely not now that he knew who she was. He'd just lost a lot of wolves. He'd probably welcome new recruits at MSC.

And over everything, her brain screamed that she should have stayed with Oscar.

The door cracked open. Light spilled in along with three people trying to shush each other.

Laylea opened one eye.

Vaughn Howe held the door open as Angel half carried Oscar in.

Her heart didn't leap so much as relax into a pile of goo, all of her muscles melting with relief.

Shala slipped in to help Angel arrange Oscar on the other bed. "I still don't see why he needs to be in this room," she complained in a weak approximation of a whisper.

"He'll worry about them, and they'll worry about him," Vaughn replied in a real whisper.

From the hallway, Dizzy called in, "They'll all sleep better."

"And they need to sleep," Ollie added from even farther away than Dizzy.

Angel's voice faded as she left the room. "It's the best medicine until we find out what was on Gerbrand's claws."

"Well, you could have waited till we got here to put him to sleep," Shala complained, adjusting a pillow under her brother's head.

"I'm not asleep," Oscar slurred.

Shala shot back. "Well, you should be."

He blew a pitiful raspberry at her.

Vaughn backed out of the room and Shala's figure blocked the light as she went to the door. Before it closed, she whispered, "I'm proud of you, baby brother."

Oscar sighed. The door closed.

With her friends close by, Laylea's brain released her from all the dangers still piling up around them. They'd defeated Gerber and survived with few casualties and no losses. And they'd depleted Grandpa's forces.

He'd need new fighters.

KC shivered.

Laylea mustered all her strength and stood up to grab the blanket in her teeth and pull it up over her friend's bare shoulders. Then she turned twice to the left, once right, and curled up in the crook of KC's neck, with her chin on her shoulder. From there she could see Oscar's chest rise and fall slowly, evenly.

With their help, she could perfect her wolf shape. Then she could go to MSC and fight Grandpa on his own turf. See how he liked it.

A smile spread her muzzle and with a sigh, she finally released into sleep.

AFTERWORD

Thank you for reading *Shifter School*. I hope you had fun. If you did, please go to Amazon or Goodreads or your fabulous blog and write a quick review. Reviews are really important to an indie author.

Do it now while the story is fresh in your mind!

Sign up at wyrdos.net to be the first to know all the latest on my books and audiobooks. I promise I won't inundate you with mail and I will not share your email with anyone. Just ask my sisters. I never share.

To learn more about Laylea's puppyhood, go get *WereHuman 1: The Witch's Daughter* now!

CHARACTERS

- **Adele Lagat** - *see Lagat, Adele*
- **Adrien Denier** - *see Denier, Adrien*
- **Ahanu** - student, thunderbird, Mer dorm
- **Ali** - student, hawk, Mer dorm
- **Amal** - brownie, co-owner of Brown's Resale, member of Team Wyrdos
- **Angel Lopez** - doctor, mother to Calliope, Coy, and Candy
- **Angelica deRio** - councilmember, wolf
- **Bailey Hillen** - grad student, witch, Laylea's brother, aka Bailey Woodford
- **Belle Suttrick** - student, Mer dorm, Miro's sister
- **Ben McBride** - former student, witch, warthog, trapped in Old School
- **Benniker** - zoo groundskeeper, wolf
- **Bertram Gorse** - *see Gorse, Bertram*
- **Bianchi, Enrico** - music teacher, wolf
- **Big Mo** - student, maned wolf, Centaur dorm, aka Maurice Braga
- **Bitters Brewster** - Council Enforcer, bouncer, highly poisonous spider, aka Veryl

- **Brenda Samborsky** - student, leader of LPSS Double Deltas, python, Mer dorm
- **Brian** - student, gorilla, Sphinx dorm
- **Brian Samborsky** - former PE and health teacher, sleeper, python
- **Britny** - student, goat
- **Caliban Meillissene** - dean of LPSS, linden shifter
- **Calliope Lopez** - Angel's eldest daughter
- **Candy Lopez** - Angel's youngest daughter
- **Carrie Marshall** - student, wolf, Mer dorm
- **Cate O'Leary** - witch, cow, infamous for the Great Chicago Fire
- **Chef Tod** - LPSS chef, Shetland pony
- **Chloe Serra** - student, moose, Sphinx dorm
- **Christopher** - student, paired Koi with his twin Krystal, Mer dorm
- **Clark Hillen** - former conditioned force soldier, pilot, Laylea's adopted father
- **Colbrook, Nancy** - mayor of Chicago
- **Conner Stone** - student, wolf, Mer dorm
- **Correnti, Toni** - shop teacher
- **Coy Lopez** - Angel's middle daughter, butterfly
- **Crow, Elizabeth** - librarian, counselor, Raven shifter, twin to Dizzy, aka Lizzy
- **Daniel** - student, elephant, Centaur dorm
- **David "Squirt" Safotu** - student, sea squirt, Mer dorm
- **Dee Morton** - homicide detective, banshee, member of Team Wyrdos
- **DeGee, Douglass** - contractor, lion, Griff's father
- **Delilah Crow** - *see Dizzy*
- **Denier, Adrien** - former Council Enforcer, wolf, KC's godfather
- **Diejuste** - voudon loa riding Jane Delphine, member of Team Wyrdos

- **Dizzy** - councilmember, witch, raven, invisible to most people
- **DJ Delcampo** - Daniel Joaquin, wolf, KC's brother
- **Dove Betts**- student, tiger, Mer dorm, twin to Reggie
- **Durrah, David** - former LPSS doctor, head of special testing
- **Dustin Huono** - student, wolf, Sphinx dorm
- **Emerald** - student, singer, selkie, Sphinx dorm
- **Elan Barrett** - sociology teacher, wolf
- **Fenn, Sidney** - school doctor, gorilla
- **Garcia, Jharrel** - police officer, 44 division, medium
- **Gerbrand Delcampo** - MSC militia lieutenant, wolf, KC's brother, aka Gerber
- **Gorse, Bertram** - former dean of LPSS, Lipizzaner, aka Albert Gorshkov
- **Grandpa Delcampo** - dean of Montana Shifter School, wolf, self-declared Alpha of the Americas, KC's great grandfather, aka Luis
- **Griffin DeGee** - student, gryphon, Sphinx dorm, aka Griff
- **Harper Pemberton** - student, rhesus monkey, Centaur dorm
- **Inika DeGee** - fashion designer, eagle, Griff's mother
- **Jase Batka** - student, wolf, Sphinx dorm, grandson of the Detroit Alpha
- **Jay Doe** - recovering Conditioned Force soldier, Laylea's "uncle"
- **Jeannie Nellwin** - doctor, Kyle's wife, KJ's mother
- **Jimmy Smith** - student, musician, wolf, Mer dorm
- **Johnny Gorman** - mechanic, Norman's uncle
- **Jonathan Umemoto** - student, wolf, Centaur dorm
- **Joseph Lyman** - CEO Lyman Corp, djinn
- **Junior Leo** - student, boogeyman, Mer dorm, member of Team Wyrdos
- **Kara** - student, Centaur dorm, dating Reggie
- **Kathleen Battles** - governor of Illinois, true-human

- **KC Dells** - student, wolf pretending to be a coyote, aka Karly Carlotta Delcampo
- **KJ Nellwin** - Jeannie and Kyle's kid
- **Krystal** - student, paired Koi with her twin Christopher, Mer dorm
- **Kyle Nellwin** - homicide detective, vampire, believed by some to be dead, Jeannie's husband
- **Lagat, Adele** - shifting teacher, pigeon
- **Lake Marshall** - Music Shoppe manager, councilmember, wolf, Carrie's uncle
- **Laylea Hillen** - student, dog, Mer dorm, member of Team Wyrdos, aka Lee Woodford
- **Leda** - student, egret, Centaur dorm
- **Lee Woodford** - see *Laylea Hillen*
- **Leticia Lopez** - aka Candy,
- **Lisa Sclero** - student, giraffe, Sphinx dorm
- **Lucio** - brownie, co-owner of Brown's Resale, member of Team Wyrdos
- **Luke, Oliver** - councilmember, leopard, Oscar's father
- **Madam Fan Hu** - Laylea and Bailey's landlady
- **Madame** - French teacher, spider
- **Malik Lopez** - pilot, butterfly, Angel's husband, Calliope's father
- **Mariella DeRio** - VR designer, firey-throated hummingbird, Angelica's wife
- **Marina Batka** - wolf, Jase's mother
- **McCobb, Randee** - teacher, PE & Health
- **Mendenkov, Rex** - former gym and health teacher, wolf
- **Merrilynne** - student, koi, Mer dorm
- **Milly** - dancer, student, mouse, Mer dorm
- **Milo** - Laylea's biological brother, dog
- **Miro Suttrick** - student, gynandromorphic butterfly, Centaur dorm
- **Morioka, Yaksha** - Captain of Chicago PD 44 division, demon, dragon, member of Team Wyrdos

- **Muldoon, Sigrid** - chemistry teacher, in love with Randee McCobb
- **Murph** - student, cheetah, Sphinx dorm until he transferred to MSC
- **Ned Biggerson** - knitter, The Office regular
- **Norman Gorman** - KC's special friend,
- **Old Lady Rucker** - Laylea's childhood neighbor, psychic, aka Letitia Rucker, aka OLR
- **Ollie Yublansky** - student, witch, stork, trapped in Old School, Sphinx dorm
- **Orin Morton** - co-owner of Brown's Resale, brownie, Dee's brother, member of Team Wyrdos
- **Oscar Luke** - student, leopard (black panther), Sphinx dorm
- **Pansy Linnehan** - student, trapped in Old School, phoenix
- **Patrick DelValle** - graduate, wolf, previous student alpha
- **Peter** - student, fox, Mer dorm
- **Quan DeGee** - student, lion, trapped in Old School, Sphinx dorm, many greats uncle to Griff
- **Raederie Rivers** - student, selkie, Sphinx dorm
- **Randee McCobb** - *see McCobb, Randee*
- **Reata** - wolf child
- **Reggie Betts** - student, tiger, Centaur dorm, twin to Dove, dating Kara
- **Rehyan Linnehan** - student, flamingo, Mer dorm
- **Rhea** - Laylea's biological mother, dog?
- **Riva** - student, sloth, Centaur dorm
- **Roxy** - disenhance lion in Lincoln Park Zoo
- **Sanna Luke** - artist, leopard (black panther), N addict, Oscar's mother
- **Seb** - bartender at The Office
- **Shala Luke** - former student, sleeper, leopard (black panther), Oscar's sister, aka Tishala
- **Shauna DeGee** - former councilmember, wolf, Griff's aunt
- **Sher Hillen** - doctor, witch, Laylea's mother, aka Katherine Coogan

- **Sierra** - former Denier intern beta, wolf
- **Sinesia Marshall** - former Chicago alpha, wolf, Carrie's great grand aunt
- **Siobhan Linnehan** - councilmember, grebe
- **Tara Rozella** - actor, Lake's Marshall's partner
- **Tessa Zedo** - student, domestic feline (black cat), Centaur dorm
- **Thad** - student, spider, Mer dorm
- **Theresa** - student, lion, Centaur dorm
- **Tippy** - 30lb terrier in Laylea's neighborhood
- **Toby** - bear in Lincoln Park Zoo
- **Vaughn Howe** - student, wolf, Sphinx dorm, restricted
- **Walter Bowman** - Consortium therianthologist, Laylea's biological father, true-human
- **Wanda Bargo** - LPSS administration, elephant
- **Wanja, Safiri** - shifting/geography/physics/ magic teacher, trapped in Old School, red colobus monkey
- **Woodford** - Laylea's brother, killed by the Consortium, true-dog
- **Yaksha Morioka** - see *Morioka, Yaksha*

ALSO BY GWENDOLYN DRUYOR

WYRDOS Urban Fantasy Series

WereHuman 1: The Witch's Daughter

WereHuman 2: The Warrior's Son

WereHuman 3: The Hunter's Heir

WereHuman 4: The Wizard's Mutt

Voices of Reason (AVAILABLE FREE TO NEWSLETTER SUBSCRIBERS)

Shifter School

Shifter Ghost

Shifter Witch

Free Wishes

Dee

Laylea

Junior

Doug vs. The Boogeyman(EXCLUSIVE TO MY NEWSLETTER)

MOBIOUS' QUEST Fantasy Series

Geoffrey's Queen

Hardt's Tale

First Edition, December 2025
ISBN 978-1-948421-33-1(ebook)| ISBN 978-1-948421-37-9(print) | ISBN 978-1-948421-36-2(audiobook)

Editing by Leslie Schipa

Published in the United States of America.

Wyrdos.net

www.ingramcontent.com/pod-product-compliance
Lightning Source LLC
Chambersburg PA
CBHW021434240626
47153CB00001B/143

* 9 7 8 1 9 4 8 4 2 1 3 7 9 *